PRAISE FOR SEISHI YOKOM

'Readers will delight in the blind turns, red herrings and dubious alibis... Ingenious and compelling'
ECONOMIST

'At once familiar and tantalisingly strange... It's an absolute pleasure to see his work translated at last in these beautifully produced English editions'
SUNDAY TIMES

'The perfect read for this time of year. Short and compelling, it will appeal to fans of Agatha Christie looking for a new case to break'
IRISH TIMES

'This is Golden Age crime at its best, complete with red herrings, blind alleys and twists and turns galore... A testament to the power of the simple murder mystery and its enduring appeal'
SPECTATOR

'A stellar whodunit set in 1940s Japan... The solution is a perfect match for the baffling puzzle. Fair-play fans will hope for more translations of this master storyteller'
PUBLISHERS WEEKLY, STARRED REVIEW

'With a reputation in Japan to rival Agatha Christie's, the master of ingenious plotting is finally on the case for anglophone readers'
GUARDIAN

'A delightfully entertaining locked room murder mystery... An ideal book to curl up with on a winter's night'
NB MAGAZINE

'Never anything less than fun from beginning to end... Truly engrossing'
BOOKS AND BAO

'A classic murder mystery... Comparisons with Holmes are justified, both in the character of Kindaichi and Yokomizo's approach to storytelling—mixing clues, red herrings and fascinating social insight before drawing back the curtain to reveal the truth'
JAPAN TIMES

'The perfect gift for any fan of classic crime fiction or locked room mysteries'
MRS PEABODY INVESTIGATES

SEISHI YOKOMIZO (1902–81) was one of Japan's most famous and best-loved mystery writers. He was born in Kobe and spent his childhood reading detective stories, before beginning to write stories of his own, the first of which was published in 1921. He went on to become an extremely prolific and popular author, best known for his Kosuke Kindaichi series, which ran to 77 books, many of which were adapted for stage and television in Japan. *The Honjin Murders*, *The Inugami Curse* and *Gokumon Island* are also available from Pushkin Vertigo.

BRYAN KARETNYK is a translator of Japanese and Russian literature. His recent translations for Pushkin Press include Gaito Gazdanov's *An Evening with Claire* and Ryūnosuke Akutagawa's *Murder in the Age of Enlightenment*.

THE VILLAGE OF EIGHT GRAVES

PUSHKIN
VERTIGO

Seishi Yokomizo

Translated from the Japanese by Bryan Karetnyk

Pushkin Press
71–75 Shelton Street
London wc2h 9jq

YATSUHAKAMURA

First published in Japan in 1971 by KADOKAWA CORPORATION, Tokyo.

English translation rights arranged with KADOKAWA CORPORATION,
Tokyo through JAPAN UNI AGENCY, INC., Tokyo.

First published by Pushkin Press in 2021

3 5 7 9 8 6 4 2

ISBN 13: 978-1-78227-745-3

Designed and typeset by Tetragon, London
Printed and bound in the United States of America

www.pushkinpress.com

THE
VILLAGE OF
EIGHT GRAVES

THE INHABITANTS OF EIGHT GRAVES

THE TAJIMI FAMILY ("THE HOUSE OF THE EAST")

Yozo	*the head of the family*
Koume and Kotake	*Yozo's aunts; twins*
Hisaya	*Yozo's elder son*
Haruyo	*Yozo's daughter*

THE NARRATOR'S MATERNAL FAMILY

Tsuruko	*Tatsuya's mother*
Ushimatsu IKAWA	*Tsuruko's father, Tatsuya's grandfather; a cattle-trader*

THE SATOMURA FAMILY

Shintaro	*Yozo's nephew; a former soldier*
Noriko	*Shintaro's sister*

THE NOMURA FAMILY ("THE HOUSE OF THE WEST")

Shokichi	*the head of the family*
Miyako MORI	*his sister-in-law; a widow*

CLERGY

Myoren	*a nun from the convent at Koicha*
Baiko	*the abbess of the Keisho-in monastery at Bankachi*
Choei	*a high priest from the Maroo-ji temple*
Eisen	*his curate*
Kozen	*a priest from the Renko-ji temple*

DOCTORS

Tsunemi KUNO	*a doctor related to the Tajimi family*
Shuhei ARAI	*a doctor; wartime evacuee*

PROLOGUE

The village of Eight Graves is perched amid the desolate mountains on the border of Tottori and Okayama prefectures. Naturally, arable land is scarce in these parts, and of what little there is, most is given over to a small handful of rice paddies dotted around, each measuring only ten or, at most, twenty *tsubo*, or about seven hundred square feet. The inhospitable climate makes for a meagre harvest, and no matter the calls to increase production, the rice paddies yield barely enough to feed the villagers. Nevertheless, owing to a wealth of other resources, the inhabitants there live in relative comfort.

Charcoal-making and cattle-rearing are the main industries in Eight Graves. The latter is a recent phenomenon, but the former has been the villagers' chief livelihood for generations. The mountains that envelop the village stretch all the way to Tottori and are blanketed in various species of oak—blue, sawtooth and jolcham. They grow in such abundance that the region has long been famed for its charcoal throughout the whole of Kansai.

In more recent times, however, it is cattle-rearing that has become the village's main source of revenue: the local breed, the *chiya-ushi*, serves just as well for working as it does for eating, and the cattle market at neighbouring Niimi attracts traders from far and wide.

Each household in the village is charged with raising five or six head of cattle: they aren't the property of the village farmers, but that of the landowners, who give the farmers the calves and sell them on when they are fully grown. The proceeds of the sale are then shared between the farmer and the landowner at a fixed rate. Thus, as in any agricultural village, the owners and the sharefarmers are pitted against one another: in such a modest settlement as this, there are stark differences in fortune.

In Eight Graves, there are two wealthy houses: the Tajimis and the Nomuras. Since the Tajimi family is situated in the east of the village, they are known as "The House of the East", while, by the same stroke of reasoning, the Nomura family is known as "The House of the West".

But a mystery remains: the origin of the village's name...

Inured to it across generations, those who have been born and laid their bones to rest there will scarcely have given a second thought to this bizarre name. But outsiders will wonder at hearing it for the first time. There must be a story there, they'll think. And indeed, a story there is—and a strange one. To tell it, we must go back some 380 years, all the way to the Age of Warring States...

On 6th July, in the year 1566, when the great daimyo Yoshihisa Amago capitulated to his enemy Motonari Mori and surrendered the Tsukiyama Castle, one of his young samurai refused to give himself up and fled the castle with seven faithful retainers. Legend has it that, in the hope of continuing their struggle another day, they saddled three horses with 3,000 *tael* of gold and, after enduring many hardships, fording rivers and crossing mountains, finally arrived at this very village.

To begin with, the villagers received the eight warriors hospitably enough. Put at ease by this reception and the villagers' simple ways, the warriors decided to stay in the village for a time, donning peasant clothes and even taking up charcoal-making.

Fortunately, the deep mountain terrain offered plenty of spots in which to take refuge, should the need ever arise. Because of limestone deposits throughout the area, there were caves, which also provided convenient hiding places. There were a great number of these caves and grottoes down in the valley, some so deep and labyrinthine that no one had dared to explore their furthest reaches. If ever you were pursued, you could easily hide yourself away there. Doubtless it was precisely this geography that led the eight warriors to decide to make the village their temporary abode.

Six months passed in peace and harmony, without any trouble between the villagers and the eight samurai. Meanwhile, however, Mori's men had redoubled their efforts, for the leader of the fugitives was famous even in the Amago clan, and who knew what terrible calamity might yet come to pass if he were left alive to fight another day. At last, their search for the eight men led them to these very mountains.

The villagers sheltering the fugitives gradually began to fear for their own lives. Not only that, but the glittering reward offered by Mori's men was also enough to make them rethink their hospitality. What tempted the villagers most, however, was the 3,000 *tael* of gold that had supposedly been carried on horseback. If only they could kill the fugitives, every last one of them, then no one else would ever know about the gold. Even if Mori's men did happen to know about it, even if they were looking for it, all the villagers had to do was insist that they hadn't ever heard about it, let alone seen anything of the kind.

There were many discussions about this, but eventually the day came when, having reached a consensus, the villagers took the eight samurai by surprise. It happened when the men were in a hut, burning wood to make charcoal. The villagers surrounded it and, in order to block the men's escape, set fire to dried grass on three sides. The youngest and strongest then burst into the hut, brandishing bamboo spears and hatchets ordinarily used for tree-cutting. The era had been plagued by conflict, you see, and had instilled the art of warfare even in the peasantry.

The samurai were caught off guard. They had trusted the villagers absolutely and this unprovoked attack came like a bolt from the blue. There were no weapons in that little hut, of course, so they had to defend themselves as best they could with billhooks and axes, but the odds were stacked against them and it was a losing battle. One fell, then another, and another… until at last the tragic moment came when all eight of them lay slain.

The villagers decapitated every one of the bodies and, with cries of triumph, set fire to the hut: but according to legend, those eight severed heads wore an expression of such tremendous reproach that it made anyone who saw them shudder in fear. The leader of the eight samurai above all retained the terrifying look he had worn as he lay there dying, hacked to pieces by the villagers and drowning in his own blood; with his last breath, he had cursed the village, vowing to visit his vengeance upon it for seven generations to come.

Although the heads secured for the villagers the promised bounty from the Mori clan, they were never able to find where the all-important 3,000 *tael* of gold had been hidden. They hunted for it high and low, in a frenzy, uprooting grass, boring through sheer rock, tearing up the valley, but never did they find so much as a speck of gold. Worse still, during their searches, a series of ominous events occurred: one man met his tragic end, trapped by a cave-in in the depths of a grotto; another, while drilling the rock face, caused a landslide and lost his footing, falling to the bottom of a ravine, leaving him lame for the rest of his days; and a third man, who was digging the earth at the roots of a tree, was horribly crushed under the weight of the trunk that suddenly collapsed on top of him.

Mysterious happenings such as these followed one after another, but what came next plunged the villagers into an abyss of terror.

Six months had passed since the massacre of the eight samurai. Who can say why, but that year there were a great many thunderstorms in the region, bringing with them terrible bolts of lightning: frightened, the villagers saw in this a sign of the eight warriors' curse. One day, the lightning struck a cedar in the garden of Shozaemon Tajimi, splitting the great tree in two with tremendous force, right down to its very roots. Now, the curious thing was that this Shozaemon Tajimi had been the ringleader of the attack on the warriors, and, since that day, he had been plagued by remorse and had begun to act strangely, tyrannizing his family and doing things that nobody in his right mind would do. Then the lightning struck the tree... He seized a sword lying nearby and struck dead several members of his own household. Then, running out into the street, one by one he felled every villager he came across, before finally taking refuge in the mountains, where he ended his life by self-decapitation.

All in all, there were more than a dozen wounded, but exactly seven had died by Shozaemon's hand. Counting Shozaemon himself, that made a grand total of eight deaths, which, rightly or wrongly, the villagers fearfully interpreted as another act of retribution from those eight warriors who had been murdered in cold blood.

In order to appease their fury, the villagers decided to disinter the bodies of the eight samurai, whom they had buried like dogs, and to reinter them with all due ceremony, erecting eight graves where they were venerated as divinities. Of course, it was this shrine in the hills behind the village that lent the place its current name.

Such is the legend of the village of Eight Graves, as it has been handed down since ancient times.

But people do say that history repeats itself—and not without reason. In more recent times, there was a terrible event that was reported widely in all newspapers and brought the name of this desolate mountain village to the attention of the entire country. That incident in particular serves as the prelude to the strange series of events that are about to unfold.

The incident in question took place in the 1920s, more than a quarter of a century ago…

At the time, the head of the House of the East—that is, the Tajimi family—was a thirty-six-year-old man called Yozo. Ever since Shozaemon, a hereditary madness had been passed down through the generations of the family, and Yozo had been afflicted with it from childhood. Examples of his cruel and violent temperament were plentiful. At the age of twenty he married a young girl by the name of Okisa, and together they had two children.

Having lost his parents at a young age, Yozo had been raised by his two aunts. When the incident took place, the Tajimi family comprised six members: in addition to Yozo and his wife, there was his fifteen-year-old son Hisaya, his eight-year-old daughter Haruyo, plus the two aforementioned aunts. The two aunts, twins and both old maids, had spent their lives, since the death of Yozo's parents, seeing to the affairs of the Tajimi family. While it is true that Yozo did have a younger sibling, this brother left the family early on in life to continue the line of succession in his mother's family, adopting the surname Satomura.

Two or three years before the incident took place, despite having a wife and children, Yozo suddenly developed an infatuation for the daughter of a local cattle-trader. The nineteen-year-old girl had just left school and was working at the village post office. Her name was Tsuruko. Yozo being, as I have already mentioned, a man of violent inclinations, the passion that he conceived for the girl was intense. One day, as she was heading home from work, he blocked her way and abducted her, taking her to his storehouse, where he violated her and held her captive, subjecting her to the unremitting torments of his crazed desires.

Of course, Tsuruko called for help with much crying and wailing. Astonished by what was happening, the two aunts and Yozo's wife tried to stop him, but their admonitions were stubbornly ignored. Tsuruko's parents were horrified when they eventually learnt what had happened. Hastening to their daughter's aid with tears in their eyes, they begged Yozo to let her go, but he refused out of hand. No matter how much they implored him, his only reply was a defiant glare, which seemed to threaten further violence.

In the end, the frightened individuals had no choice but to persuade Tsuruko to consent to being Yozo's mistress. Tsuruko was reluctant, but where might her refusal lead? After all, the key to the storehouse was in Yozo's possession, and he could come to satisfy his violent desires whenever he pleased.

Tsuruko mulled the situation over. If those were her options, wouldn't it be better to consent and become Yozo's mistress? That way, she would be allowed out of the storehouse. And if she was allowed out, then surely she could find another way to escape. She resigned herself to this course of action and asked her parents to inform Yozo of her decision.

Naturally, Yozo was overjoyed at the news. Tsuruko was immediately released from captivity and was provided with accommodation. Kimonos, hair ornaments, furniture and every magnificent object imaginable were bestowed on her. But that was not all: these luxuries had their price, and so, day and night, Yozo would steal into her house, lavishing caresses on her flesh.

These visits struck terror in Tsuruko. Rumour had it that there was such a crazed ferocity to Yozo's passion that no ordinary woman could have endured it. Unable to go on, Tsuruko tried to run away several times, but on each occasion Yozo would fly into a crazed fury. Terrified by his behaviour, the villagers would beg Tsuruko to go back, and in the end, with little alternative, she would return to Yozo grudgingly.

It was in this state of affairs that Tsuruko fell pregnant and gave birth to a boy. Delighted by this, Yozo named the boy Tatsuya. For a time, it was hoped that having a child would calm Tsuruko down, but it only intensified her attempts to escape, now with a baby in her arms. Not only had the birth failed to have the least effect on Yozo's unrelenting lust, but on the contrary: Yozo now fully believed that the birth gave him unreserved rights to the woman. He grew more and more arrogant, and his behaviour transgressed every boundary.

It was around then that Tsuruko's parents and the villagers began to realize that there was more to these events than met the eye, that her repeated attempts to escape were not just because she could no longer bear her life with Yozo. The fact was that she had long since promised herself to another. He was a young man by the name of Yoichi Kamei, and he taught at the village school. His respected position meant that the young couple could not meet openly, so they were forced to hide their love for one another. It was said that the couple would meet clandestinely in the secluded depths of grottoes. (Hailing from other parts, Kamei had developed a passion for the local geology, and he would often go on expeditions to explore the limestone caves.) The villagers were given to gossiping, and so, naturally, once a thing like this became known, there were those who began to speculate about Tatsuya's birth. "That child isn't Tajimi-san's, you know. He's the son of the teacher, Kamei…"

In such a small village, it was only a matter of time before the rumours reached Yozo's ears. His fury was like a raging fire. He was as mad in jealousy as he was cruel in love. He dragged Tsuruko by the hair, struck her, kicked her, beat her and, after stripping her naked, drenched her with iced water. Then he took Tatsuya, whom only moments ago he had cherished as the apple of his eye, and, seizing a pair of fire tongs from the brazier, branded his thighs, back and buttocks.

"He'll kill us both at this rate," thought Tsuruko. She was at breaking point. She grabbed the child and rushed out of the house.

For several days, she hid at her parents' house, during which time she learnt that Yozo's rage had only intensified. Terrified, she fled the village and hid with relatives in Himeji.

While he waited for Tsuruko to return, Yozo spent his days drinking. On previous occasions when Tsuruko had run away, her parents or representatives from the village had always brought her back with their apologies two or three days later. But this time, five days, then ten days passed without any sign of her reappearance. Gradually, his fury took on ever more diabolical dimensions. His two aunts and his wife were too frightened to go near him, and, for once, none of the villagers dared to act as a go-between. It was then that Yozo's madness finally exploded.

It happened one evening towards the end of April. Spring arrives late in the mountains, so the charcoal braziers were still in use. The villagers were suddenly roused from their slumber by a gunshot and screaming. A few moments later there came a

17

second shot, then a third. Cries, shouts, calls for help grew and grew. Those who rushed out to see what on earth was going on were met with a most peculiar sight.

They beheld a man dressed in an officer's tunic, with gaiters and straw sandals on his feet. He had tied a white bandana around his forehead, under which he had affixed two flashlights to look like horns. On his chest he wore a lamp—the sort that looks like a mirror and is used by those who visit a shrine in the middle of the night, at the hour of the Ox, to lay their curses. Over his tunic he wore a soldier's belt, which held a sword, and in his hands he was holding a hunting rifle. The villagers were stunned. They had still to recover their senses when the rifle went off again, shooting one of them dead where he stood.

The man with the gun was Yozo.

Dressed in this bizarre costume, he had, only a few moments before, killed his own wife with a single slash of his sword and, abandoning the body, rushed out into the street in his madness. He had not laid a finger on either of the aunts or his children, but now he was going about the village, slashing and shooting at random.

Details of the investigation later revealed that the owner of one house, having heard a knock at the door, was shot as soon as he opened it. In another house, where a sleeping newlywed couple lay, Yozo had prised open the rain shutters, slipped the rifle through the gap and shot the husband dead. Startled by the noise, the wife had run to the far wall and clasped her hands together, pleading for mercy: the rifle then discharged with another deafening bang. The sight of the young bride, her lifeless hands still clasped, brought tears to the eyes of the young policeman who rushed to the scene. It seemed all the more tragic that she had arrived in the village only a fortnight previously, after the wedding, and had no connection at all to Yozo.

Yozo terrorized the village like this throughout the night, and at dawn he fled into the mountains. The villagers had never known such a night of horror.

The next day, when hordes of policemen and journalists descended on the village after receiving urgent reports, they found the village bathed in blood, bloody corpses strewn everywhere. The groans of those at death's door issued from every other house. Some were crying out for help. It is impossible to say now how many were injured by Yozo, but as for the dead, there were thirty-two in all. It was a horror unmatched in the annals of crime in Japan.

In the end, it proved impossible to find the killer after he absconded, although it was not for want of trying. The police, together with firemen and a team of youths from the village, who had formed a sort of militia, combed every mountain peak and every valley, right down to the limestone caves. Their search carried on for several months, but ultimately they had to admit defeat, having failed to uncover Yozo's hideout. They did find evidence to suggest that he was still alive, however. There was the carcass of a cow that had been shot and from which the meat had been stripped in several places. (In this region, the cattle are kept in stables throughout the winter, but come spring, they are let out to pasture, where they roam free for days at a time, sometimes even venturing as far as the neighbouring prefecture. But once or twice a month, when they need salt, they come down from the mountains and return to their keepers.) Beside the carcass, traces of fire indicated that Yozo had lit gunpowder to cook the meat: it was obvious that in taking refuge in the mountains, far from having the slightest intention of ending his life, he had instead decided to go on living, come what may—a fact that plunged the villagers back into a state of terror.

Nobody ever did find out where Yozo had hidden himself. Common sense would suggest that he could not possibly have gone on living in the mountains for more than twenty years, but there were many in the village who nevertheless clung to the belief that he was still alive. There was something almost comical about such a notion, but then Yozo had sent thirty-two innocent victims to their death. Thirty-two… Each of the eight gods had demanded a sacrifice of four. It followed, therefore, that Yozo's death would be one too many. And that was not all: proponents of this theory would always be sure to add, "What has happened twice will come to pass a third time. It happened once with the Tajimis' ancestor Shozaemon; now it's happened a second time with Yozo. Sooner or later there will be another horrible and bloody affair just like this one."

In the village of Eight Graves, whenever children misbehave, their parents frighten them by telling them that a monster with flashlights for horns will come for them. Before their very eyes, there will appear an image that they have imagined so often before: a monster with a white bandana and two horns, a lamp on his chest, a sword in his belt and a hunting rifle in one hand. Instantly the tears dry. The nightmare has left its mark on each inhabitant.

But what about those villagers who were touched directly by Yozo's frenzy? What became of them? The curious thing about it was that those whom Yozo had killed and maimed had nothing to do with him or Tsuruko, whereas the people actually involved in the affair escaped, for the most part, unscathed.

For one thing, Kamei, the teacher so detested by Yozo, had that evening gone to play *go* with a monk in a neighbouring village, thus escaping the massacre. All the same, it was reported that, fearing perhaps what the villagers might think, he transferred to a school far away soon after the events of that night. Then there were Tsuruko's parents. As soon as they heard the commotion, they guessed at once how things would end and hid themselves under the straw in one of the cattle sheds, escaping without so much as a scratch. As for Tsuruko herself, she had, as we know, taken refuge with relatives in Himeji, and was thus spared the drama. Later, she was summoned by the police and had to return to the village, where she remained for some time, facing the deep resentment of the villagers.

"None of this would have happened if she had been obedient and submitted to Yozo," the families of the victims would say, brimming with hatred.

Hounded by these whispers and the fear of seeing Yozo alive again, Tsuruko wasted no time in leaving the village with her young child.

After that, she was never heard from again.

Twenty-six years went by, bringing us now to the post-war period.

The old legend proved right: the village was indeed to become the setting for yet another series of mysterious crimes. But unlike those first ones, these murders were not impulsive, but carried out with a strange and insidious logic and plunged the village back into a state of terrible fear.

These preliminaries have taken a long while to lay out, but the time has come to raise the curtain on this new drama. First, however, I should like to point out that what you, ladies and gentlemen, are about to read was written by a person directly involved in this affair, someone who played a most important role in it. How I happened to come by his manuscript has little bearing on this tale, though, so I shall dispense with any explanation…

CHAPTER 1

"MISSING PERSONS"

It must have been around eight months after I returned from the village of Eight Graves that I finally managed to regain a sense of composure.

Right now I am sitting in my study, atop a hill in a western suburb of Kobe, looking out at a picturesque view of the island of Awaji. Quietly drawing on a cigarette, once again living a peaceful life, I find myself struck by a curious feeling. As avid readers will know, the experience of terrifying events can turn the hair white, but at this very moment, even as I pick up the mirror lying on my desk, I cannot see all that many new white hairs. All the same, that strange feeling won't leave me: so dreadful were the events that I lived through, so numerous were the life-or-death moments... Thinking back on it all now, the cards seem to have been so completely stacked against me.

Not only is my life peaceful, but I also find myself now in a very fortunate position, even better than the one that I had before. Truly, I could never have imagined it, even in my wildest dreams. And it is all thanks to a man called Kosuke Kindaichi. Had it not been for that shaggy-headed, undistinguished-looking, mildly stuttering, strange little detective, my life would have met a swift end.

When at last the case was solved and Kosuke Kindaichi was preparing to leave Eight Graves, he said to me: "It's rare for someone to go through something as terrifying as you did. If I were you, I'd put it all down in writing—everything you've been through these past three months—so that you'll remember it your whole life."

"I've been thinking about that, too," I replied. "Perhaps it would be a good thing to record it for posterity while all the details are still fresh in my memory. That way, I'll even be able to give you your due. I can't see any other way of returning the great favour you've done me."

I decided to do as I promised as soon as possible. But the ordeal had been so overwhelming that my mind and body were exhausted. Added to that, I'm no writer, and I kept wavering, hesitant to put pen to paper. So it's only now that I'm finally making good on that promise.

Fortunately, my health did return to me in the end. Lately, I haven't been so troubled by those terrifying nightmares, and my physical health has improved greatly. As for my lack of faith in my writerly abilities, that still hasn't changed, but then this isn't a novel that I am writing. You see, I am merely trying to set down the unadorned truth of what I experienced. A report of the facts, as it were—a true story. Then again, perhaps the strangeness, the sheer horror of the story will compensate for any literary shortcomings.

The village of Eight Graves... Even the memory of it makes me shudder: what a horrible name, what a horrible place. And what a horrible, terrifying business it all was.

The village of Eight Graves... Until last year, my twenty-eighth year on this earth, I had never dreamt that there could be a village with such an abominable name, let alone that I could have had such a deep connection with it. I had some vague idea that I had been born in the prefecture of Okayama, but as for the county or the name of the village, I hadn't the foggiest. Nor did I want to know. For as long as I could remember, Kobe had been my home: that is where I was raised. I didn't have the least interest in the countryside, and, as far as she could, my mother avoided talking about her home town, claiming not to have a single relative left there.

Ah, my mother! Even now, I need only close my eyes to see every feature of her face with perfect clarity, just as it was before she died. As with any boy who loses his mother at the age of seven, I believed that no woman in the whole world was more beautiful than she. She was of short stature and petite in every way. If her face was small, then her eyes, her mouth and her nose were so little as to be almost doll-like. Her hands were as small as my own child's hands, and they were forever busy sewing whatever I had given her that needed mending. Always with a look of dejection about her, she rarely spoke or went out. But whenever she did open her mouth, that soft, gentle Okayama lilt of hers would be like sweet music to my ears. But even then, my youthful heart knew trouble: in the middle of the night, my ordinarily quiet mother was plagued by paroxysms of anguish. Sleeping peacefully one moment, she would suddenly leap out of bed and, with a tongue that seemed to spasm in terror, mutter rapidly and incoherently, until in the end she fell back onto the pillow, weeping bitterly. Such night terrors were a frequent occurrence. Awoken by her cries, my adoptive father and I would call out her name and shake her, but she would not always return to her senses. Then she would cry and cry, howling wretchedly, and only after she had exhausted herself with that would she at last cry herself to sleep like a child, in the arms of her husband. Throughout the night, my adoptive father would hold her like that, gently stroking her back...

Ah, but now I know the cause of all those terrors. My poor mother! Had I lived through a past as tragic as hers, I dare say that I, too, would have suffered those terrible afflictions. Thinking about it now, I cannot but feel a sense of gratitude towards my adoptive father. We clashed in later years, as a result of which I left home. Even now, I still regret that we never did have the chance to reconcile with one another.

My adoptive father was a man called Torazo Terada. He was the foreman of a shipyard in Kobe. Tall with a ruddy complexion, he was a whole fifteen years older than my mother. He cut a very imposing figure, but thinking back on him now, he was a fine and generous man. I have no idea how he met my mother, but he always took good care of her, and he doted on me. I learnt that he was not my real father only much later in life. He had even listed me as his son in his family register. That is why even now I still call myself Tatsuya Terada. Yet it always struck my younger self as odd that the family register recorded the year of my birth as 1923, whereas an amulet given to me by my mother was clearly inscribed with a different year: 1922. Hence, my real age is in fact twenty-nine, although I still consider myself to be twenty-eight.

As I have already mentioned, my mother died when I was seven. Her death marked a sudden end to my happiness, but that is by no means to imply that the years that followed were entirely miserable or unhappy. My father remarried the year after she died. My stepmother could not have been more different: she was a large, cheerful, talkative woman, and, like all such women, she had a pure and forthright nature. Moreover, since my father was a decent and generous man, he saw to it that my future was provided for, sending me first to school and then to a commercial college.

Yet, as so often happens with parents and children who are not of the same blood, there was something missing: to draw a culinary parallel, it was like a meal that looks delicious but, upon tasting, turns out to lack an all-important seasoning. Besides, my new mother had given birth to several children already, and so, while it cannot be said that I stood in her way, I suppose it was only natural that she was rather distant where I was concerned. It was for an entirely different reason, though, that I clashed with my adoptive father just after graduating from college. Still, I did leave home, and for a while I stayed with friends.

Not much changed after that. As with any able-bodied youth, I received my call-up papers when I turned twenty-one. Shortly after, I was sent to the islands in the south, where I spent many a difficult day. I was demobbed in 1946, and when I returned to Kobe, I was devastated to find that the whole city had been burned to the ground. I was all alone: I found that my step-father's house had been destroyed completely, and I had no idea where to find my stepfamily. I also heard that my stepfather had been killed by shrapnel during a bombing raid on the shipyard. To make matters worse, the commercial company where I had been employed before the war had gone bankrupt, and it was not at all clear when it would get back up and running.

I was at a total loss, but fortunately a kind friend from our schooldays came to my rescue. He had set up a new cosmetics company after the war and, although the prospects that it offered were not great, I had very little alternative, and so for almost two years, I was able to maintain a basic standard of living.

Were it not for the events that I am about to relate, doubtless my life would have continued in that impoverished, humdrum vein. But one day a spot of red was suddenly spilt on the grey of my life: I embarked on an adventure of dazzling mystery and stepped into a world of blood-chilling terror.

Here is how it all began.

It was on 25th May, in that unforgettable year. I arrived at work at nine o'clock and was immediately summoned by the manager.

"You weren't listening to the radio this morning by any chance, were you, Terada?" he asked, staring me right in the eye.

I shook my head.

"Well, your name is Tatsuya, isn't it? And your father's was Torazo, wasn't it?"

"That's right," I said, wondering what on earth my name and that of my adoptive father could have to do with this morning's radio broadcast.

"Well then, it must be you," he said. "There was somebody on the radio looking for you."

I was taken aback. In that morning's slot for missing persons, somebody had been seeking the whereabouts of one Tatsuya Terada, the eldest son of Torazo Terada, and asked anybody who knew him to send in his address, or, if Tatsuya himself were listening, to contact them in person.

"I took down the address. Here it is. Did you have any idea that somebody might be looking for you?"

He showed me his pocket diary, in which was written: *Suwa Legal Practice, 4th floor, Nitto Building, Kitanagasa-dori (District 3).*

A truly strange feeling struck me as I looked at the address. To all intents and purposes, I was an orphan. It was possible that my stepmother and her children could be alive somewhere, displaced by the war, but they were hardly likely to have engaged the services of the lawyer who was now searching for me on the wireless. Of course, had my adoptive father still been alive, he would no doubt have been moved by pity to try to find me, but he was long since dead. I had no idea, then, who this person could be. It was a strange and bewildering feeling.

"You should go, at any rate. If somebody's looking for you, you mustn't delay," said my manager on a note of encouragement.

He gave me the morning off, advising me to go there right away. I imagine that he, too, must have been curious, having had an unexpected hand in my fate.

Was I being deceived? Had I just become a character in some novel? Either way, just as my manager suggested, I headed straight for the address that he had given me. I arrived at Mr Suwa's office not without a feeling of apprehension in my chest. I must have spent at least half an hour with him.

"Well, well, there's no denying it. The radio really is a most effective device, is it not? I never imagined I would get a response so quickly."

Mr Suwa was a stout and agreeable old gentleman, which immediately set me at ease. I had often read in novels about unscrupulous lawyers, and so I was on my guard, uncertain that I wasn't being used as an instrument of some fraud.

After some questions about my adoptive father and my past, Mr Suwa asked me:

"But this Terada-san, was he your real father?"

"No. I was a child from my mother's previous marriage, you see. She died when I was seven years old."

"I see. And that has always been your understanding?"

"No. When I was young, I was under the impression that he was my real father. I learnt the truth only later, probably around the time that my mother died. I can't recall exactly when it was."

"And you don't happen to know the name of your real father?"

"I'm afraid not."

It was only then that I realized: the man looking for me could be my real father. All of a sudden, I could feel my chest pounding.

"Neither your late mother nor your adoptive father ever told you his name?"

"No, they never spoke of him."

"Your mother, of course, died when you were very young, but your adoptive father lived well into your adulthood. You don't find it strange that he said nothing about this? After all, he must have known the truth of the matter."

My adoptive father loved my mother deeply, and, thinking back on it now, I know that he cannot have been ignorant of the facts. I believe it was only the lack of opportunity that caused his silence. Had I not left home, had I not received my call-up, had he himself not perished, might he not have intended to tell me sooner or later?

When I said as much, Mr Suwa nodded.

"Yes, I dare say that is so… Returning to the present matter, and, please, do forgive me for seeming mistrustful, but you wouldn't happen to be carrying any documentation that might verify your identity, would you?"

After thinking for a moment, I extracted the little bag in which I always carried the amulet that my mother had given me and showed it to Mr Suwa.

"*Tatsuya. Born 6 September 1922*," he read aloud. "I see… But no family name given. You've been in the dark all this time. Ah, but what's this piece of paper here?"

Mr Suwa unfolded a sheet of *washi* paper on which a sort of map had been drawn with an ink brush. To tell the truth, I myself did not know what this map showed or why it was in my possession. The map was drawn in the shape of an irregular labyrinth and was marked with mysterious place names such as "Dragon's Jaw" and "Fox's Den". Some verses had been appended at the side of the map. They reminded me of pilgrim's songs, and it was clear that there had to be some connection between them and the map, for they contained the same words, "Dragon's Jaw" and "Fox's Den". There was a good reason that I had taken such great care of this puzzling sheet of paper, keeping it together with the amulet. Back when my mother was still alive, she would sometimes ask me to fetch it for her, and she would study it intently. Then her face, usually so subdued, would suddenly flush and the pupils of her eyes would glisten. It would inevitably end with her sighing deeply and saying:

"You see this map, darling? You must always keep it safe. Don't ever lose it. One day it may make you a very lucky person. So don't tear it up, don't throw it away. Most importantly, though, don't ever tell anyone about it…"

I had respected my mother's wishes and never let myself be parted from the map, but I was different then from the child that I had once been. In truth, after I reached adulthood, I had gradually stopped believing in the supposedly miraculous powers of this scrap of paper, but still, I hung on to it, since carrying it around was no real inconvenience. It was sooner from sheer inertia that I hadn't torn it up.

How wrong I was. That map would have such a tremendous influence on my fate. But I shall have occasion to reveal all that in due course.

Mr Suwa, however, showed no especial interest in the map and, since I offered nothing more on the subject, he carefully folded up the map and replaced it in the amulet.

"Well, there can hardly be any doubt, but just to make doubly sure, I do have one final request to make of you…"

I stared at him in perplexity.

"I wonder whether you wouldn't mind undressing. I would like to examine you…"

I blushed scarlet on hearing those words. That was the one thing I didn't want anybody to know. Ever since I was a child, there was nothing I loathed more than having to bare my body at the public baths, at school medical examinations, at the beach… This is because my back, buttocks and thighs are covered in scars—the cruel vestiges of having been burnt by fire tongs. I am not one to boast, but aside from these scars, my skin is pale and delicate, with an almost feminine beauty.

Against its purity, these purple marks stand out all the more hatefully, provoking a feeling of horror in all those who set eyes on them. Moreover, I didn't have the slightest idea how I came to have them. When I was young, I would occasionally ask my mother about them, but every time she would suddenly burst into to tears, sobbing violently, or, as I have already mentioned, succumb to the grip of terror. In the end, I stopped asking about them.

"Examine me? What can that possibly have to do with all this?…"

"You see, if you truly are the person I am looking for, there will be certain distinguishing marks on your body that cannot be falsified."

I steeled myself and took off my jacket. Then I removed my shirt, my vest and finally my trousers. Left standing only in my underpants, I felt embarrassed showing Mr Suwa my naked body. He made a thorough examination of me and at last heaved a sigh of relief:

"Thank you. I'm sorry to have put you through that. You may dress yourself again. I am satisfied that there is no reason to doubt your identity."

This is what he then told me:

"Somebody is indeed looking for you. I cannot yet reveal to you the name of this person, but it is someone who is a relation of yours. This individual wishes to know your whereabouts in order to adopt and provide for you. My client is extremely wealthy, and so you stand only to benefit. I'll make the necessary further arrangements and shall be in touch again in due course."

With that, the lawyer took down my address and place of employment. Thus ended my first interview with Mr Suwa.

Despite everything, I was left with the feeling that I had somehow been taken in. But when I returned to my office and gave my manager a summary of everything that had gone on, he stared back at me in amazement.

"Oh-ho! That's quite something," he exclaimed. "So you're the illegitimate son of some rich old man!"

He liked to talk, and so word quickly spread throughout the office. For a time, whenever I encountered my colleagues, I would have to endure their teasing on account of my presumed high birth.

That night I couldn't sleep. It wasn't from any sense of excitement at what awaited me, however. There may have been a measure of anticipation, but I was more unnerved than anything else. My poor mother, her dreadful terrors and those hateful scars on my body; none of this was the stuff of sweet slumber.

Somehow I just couldn't shake the premonition that something awful was about to happen…

A WARNING

Back then I knew nothing of Eight Graves, let alone the extraordinary legend associated with it. How then could I have ever suspected that I was bound to that place by fate?

And yet… I cannot deny that the sudden appearance of this stranger in my life filled me with a curious sense of apprehension. You, ladies and gentlemen, will no doubt think that this is just some literary turn of phrase, but that is not so.

As a rule, people do not care for extreme changes in circumstance. They sooner fear them than relish them. In a case such as mine where one cannot even imagine what the future holds, it is only to be expected. After all, is it too much to ask to be left in peace? And yet, far from fearing news from the lawyer, I looked forward to it, feeling dejected when the next day brought no word from him. Truly, it was a peculiar feeling, that combination of dread and anticipation. Like a caged animal, I paced back and forth for five days, ten days, but still no word came. With time, I realized, however, that Mr Suwa had not given up.

One day, when I returned from the office, the young wife of the friend with whom I was lodging said to me:

"Tatsuya, something odd happened today..."

"Odd, you say?"

"Yes, a strange man was here, asking all sorts of questions about you."

"About me?... All sorts of questions?... Ah, it must have been one of Mr Suwa's clerks."

"Yes, that's what I thought at first, but now I'm not so sure about that. He seemed like a country-type."

"Someone from the country..."

"Yes. He must have been... Oh, I can never really tell how old country people are. But he had on an Inverness coat with an upturned collar and a hat pulled down over his eyes. He was wearing dark glasses, too. I couldn't really see his face. He made such an uncanny impression..."

"What did he ask you?"

"Mainly about your character, your conduct... Do you drink? Do you ever have outbursts of violence, like a madman?..."

"Violence?... Like a madman?... What odd things to ask."

"Yes, I thought it was strange too."

"So what did you tell him?"

"Naturally, I vouched that you were nothing of the sort, that you're a very calm and considerate person. And so you are."

Her kind words notwithstanding, I still couldn't shake off that unpleasant feeling. I appreciated that the lawyer had to take all the necessary precautions, scrutinizing not only my identity but also my character and circumstances. It was only natural that he should enquire whether I drank or smoked, but these questions about whether I sometimes had violent outbursts like a madman just seemed bizarre. What on earth could he be trying to find out about me?

Two or three days later, the personnel manager at my office informed me that he had been subjected to a similar interrogation. His description of the man who had visited the office corresponded to that of the one who had showed up at the house. His questions had been the same too.

"Perhaps your father was an alcoholic, given to bouts of violence when he drank? He could be worried that he's passed the trait on to you. At any rate, I told him that you weren't at all like that, so you've nothing to worry about."

The personnel manager, who had already heard about my alleged illegitimacy, gave a little chuckle as he related all this, but I was in no mood to laugh. Dark clouds seemed to be gathering over me, leaving me with a profound sense of unease.

Imagine, ladies and gentlemen, that you had been told at the age of twenty-eight that the blood of a madman ran through your veins. What a shock it would be. Of course, nobody had told me this in so many words, but I couldn't help but think that the man making these enquiries was trying to make me aware of it. Not only that, but he seemed to want the whole world to know it too.

Growing ever more impatient and agitated, I almost had decided to pay Mr Suwa a visit and ask him to address any questions he might have directly to me. Perhaps, though, that would be too rash a course of action. In any case, it was just when I had managed to talk myself out of going to his office that I received that strange letter.

Sixteen days had passed since my visit to the Suwa Legal Practice. I had gulped down my breakfast and was getting

35

dressed for work as usual, when suddenly I heard my friend's wife calling to me from the front door.

"Tatsuya! There's a letter for you."

The very mention of a letter set my pulse racing. I immediately thought of Mr Suwa. Every day I had been waiting for news, and I had no friends or relations who might have written to me.

When I took the letter, I had a horrible premonition. The envelope was made of blotting paper, coarse and of very poor quality—hardly the sort of stationery used by a lawyer with an office on the fourth floor of the Nitto Building. What was more, the recipient's name and address had been scrawled in such a childish hand and so slowly that the ink had dripped all over the paper. When I turned the envelope over, I saw that the sender's name was missing. With heart pounding, I tore open the envelope and found a letter written in the same blotchy scrawl on cheap paper:

You must never set foot in the village of Eight Graves again. Nothing good will come of it. The gods here are angry. If ever you come back, there will be blood! Blood! The carnage that took place twenty-six years ago will repeat itself, and the village will once again become a sea of blood.

I must have fallen into a momentary daze. The voice of my friend's young wife seemed distant somehow, but eventually it brought me back to the real world. In a panic, I stuffed the letter back into its envelope and thrust it into my pocket.

"What's the matter, Tatsuya? It wasn't bad news, was it?"

"No, it's nothing… Only, why do you ask?"

"It's your face," she said, her eyes trained on me. "You're as white as a sheet."

That may well have been true. In fact, it must have been so: anyone in the world would have been shocked to receive such a peculiar letter. Trying desperately to maintain my sense of composure, I decided that my only option was to escape the woman's quizzical gaze, and so I left the house in a hurry.

Accustomed to solitude as I have been since childhood, I do not like asking for other people's opinions, nor do I rely on their sympathy. After the death of my mother, I was conscious of being all alone in the world, and it was so deeply ingrained in me that no matter what adversity I came up against, no matter what calamity befell me, never would I grumble or seek others' pity. It wasn't that I didn't trust others, but concern necessarily entails affection.

Ah, that pitiful, solitary nature of mine... On the face of it, it resembled strength, but how I was deceived, how those terrifying events would later prove those appearances wrong. Naturally, I didn't understand any of this back then. I only hope that readers will see why this letter affected me so.

The village of Eight Graves. I had encountered, at long last, this strange, sinister name... Eight Graves: the name alone was enough to strike fear into the reader, never mind the letter's threatening contents. *"The gods here are angry... The carnage that took place twenty-six years ago... the village will once again become a sea of blood..."*

What on earth did it all mean? What did the author of this letter really want? I was in the dark, plagued by questions to which I had no answers. And because I had no answers, I felt all the more troubled. The only thing I knew for sure was that there had to be some link between this letter and the search. Since Mr Suwa had found me, at least two people had begun to show an interest in me: the man making enquiries about me and the author of this note.

But no! A sudden realization stopped me dead in my tracks. Might it not be that these two men were one and the same person?

I retrieved the letter from my pocket. I tried to examine the postmark carefully, but the ink had blurred, leaving it illegible.

That morning I was all at sixes and sevens, so much so that I missed any number of trains. I finally made it to the office half an hour late. The moment I arrived, however, a clerk told me that the manager wanted to see me. I went straight to his office and found him in high spirits:

"Ah, Terada. I've been waiting for you. There was a call for you from Mr Suwa's office. He wants you to go there at once. It would seem that father and son are to meet at long last. If it turns out that you've found yourself a rich old man, you mustn't go forgetting us now. Ha-ha!… Hang on, what's the matter? You don't look at all well."

I no longer recall what I said to him. Whatever it was, it was likely just meaningless words. Leaving him and his quizzical face behind, I staggered out of the building like a somnambulist. Then at last I took my first step into that world of fear and horror.

THE FIRST VICTIM

I scarcely know how to describe the events that took place a short while after that. Had I a writer's talent, I might have made this scene the first climactic point of the story. But alas, I am no writer. And besides, however frightening the event may have been, it was over in the blink of an eye.

If I were faithfully to describe what I felt at the time, I would say that those vague sentiments I experienced were those of a man wondering at another man's death and at the fragility of life. Only as time marched on did I became overwhelmed by a sense of mounting dread…

When I arrived at Mr Suwa's office, I found another visitor waiting there already. The man had close-cropped salt-and-pepper hair and was wearing khaki-coloured clothes of what looked like an army cut. His tanned complexion and his gnarled fingers yellowed by nicotine immediately betrayed his country origins. Like my friend's wife, I too find it difficult to guess the age of country people, but I would have guessed that he was between sixty and seventy years of age. He was sitting awkwardly in an easy chair, but when he saw me, he started, half-rising and turning towards the lawyer. From that movement alone, I guessed that this man must be the person searching for me, or at very least have something to do with him.

"Come in, come in! I've been expecting you. Please, take a seat." Gracious as ever, Mr Suwa indicated the chair in front of the desk. "I'm afraid I've kept you waiting longer than I originally anticipated. I had wanted to let you know the good news earlier, but you know how slow the postal service is these days. In any event, I've finally received permission from my client. Shall we do the honours?"

The lawyer turned to the old man sitting in the easy chair.

"This is Ushimatsu Ikawa. He is your grandfather—that is to say, the father of your late mother. Ikawa-san, this is Tsuruko's son Tatsuya, whom I was just describing."

We both rose slightly from our seats and nodded to one another. We avoided looking each other directly in the eye. As first meetings go, it was rather underwhelming: the prose of reality is never as spectacular as the drama of the theatre.

"I hasten to point out, however, that Ikawa-san is not the person who has been looking for you."

Mr Suwa must have feared my disappointment at the impoverished appearance of my grandfather.

"Naturally," he quickly added, "Ikawa-san has been anxious to find you, too, but in this instance he is only the messenger. It is instead relatives of your father who have been trying to find you. Permit me to inform you of your true surname: it is Tajimi. Thus, you are in fact Tatsuya Tajimi."

Mr Suwa leafed through the notebook lying on his desk.

"Your father was the late Yozo Tajimi. In addition to you, he had two other children: a son, Hisaya, and a daughter, Haruyo. They are your older half-siblings. They have reached a certain age and are both a little frail. Both of them are unmarried... or rather, Haruyo was married in her youth, but has since separated."

My grandfather nodded along without saying a word. Since we had been introduced, he had sat there in silence, his eyes trained on the ground, but every now and then he would steal a glance at me. It was then that I noticed the tears welling in his eyes, and I couldn't help being moved by this.

"And so, since neither Hisaya nor Haruyo has any chance of being blessed with children, the venerable Tajimi line will die out. That is precisely what concerns your great-aunts, the twins Koume and Kotake. Naturally, they are both of a rare old age, but their excellent health has not prevented their taking care of the Tajimi family's affairs. After some careful deliberation, they decided to find you and name you as the heir... Those, more or less, are the facts of the matter."

My heart was pounding more and more. The feeling was indescribable. Was it joy, sadness?... No, it was nowhere near so clear-cut as that. I seemed to be overcome by a sense of mystifying bewilderment. And still, there were parts of what had only just been explained to me that I yet failed to grasp.

"That is about the sum of it, but your grandfather here can tell you more. Do you have any other questions for me for the time being?"

I took a deep breath and began with what was weighing on my mind most.

"My father… is he dead?"

"That would certainly seem to be the case."

"Seem?… What exactly do you mean by that?"

"Again, I believe your grandfather can provide you with all the necessary details. I'm afraid all I can say that he is believed to have died when you were two years old."

I was terribly disturbed by this revelation, but I didn't press the matter any further. I could hear it all from my grandfather later. I asked one more question.

"And my mother… just why did she run away with me?"

"It is only natural that you should ask… Certainly, there is a connection between that and the death of your father, but, all things being equal, I believe that is also a matter best left to your grandfather to explain. Is there anything else?"

His evasion of both my questions left me not a little perturbed, but my mind was already in such a terrible state of confusion.

"Yes, just one more thing. I turned twenty-eight this year, and until now, I never heard of these blood relatives. Why did they undertake to look for me only now? I understand what you have just told me for the most part, but there are still a few things that elude me. Besides the situation you've described, wasn't there a more immediate motivation?"

The two men quickly exchanged glances with one another, and then Mr Suwa fixed me in his gaze.

"You have a very incisive mind, Tatsuya-san. Who knows, the answer to that question may help you in this business, but, please, not a word about this to anyone."

The following is what Mr Suwa revealed to me after this preamble. My father, it seemed, had a younger brother called

41

Shuji, who left at an early age to carry on the line of succession on the maternal branch of the family. He even took their name: Satomura. Shuji had a son called Shintaro, who had set his sights on becoming a military man and had even risen to the rank of major in the army. During the war, he had made a name for himself at the General Staff Headquarters, but after the defeat he really went to seed and returned to the village, where in a state of depression, he had made a feeble attempt at farming. He was thirty-six or thirty-seven and without wife or child. Like all military men, however, he had a robust constitution. Naturally, if anything were to happen to Hisaya or Haruyo, it would be to him that the Tajimi fortune would fall…

"Whatever their reasons, your great-aunts have taken against this Shintaro. Or rather, it was his father, Shuji, now long deceased, whom they did not like. Quite aside from being the son of that man, Shintaro left the village at a very young age, returning only rarely, and has since become a perfect stranger to them. This sentiment is shared by Hisaya and Haruyo; rather than see their legacy pass into his hands, they have taken it upon themselves to find you… This, to be quite frank, is the Tajimi family's real motive. Now, since I have discharged my duties, I suppose you'll want to speak with your grandfather. I'll leave you two in private. Please, take your time."

My heart weighed heavily. There was at least one person who didn't want my return. As I thought about the strange letter I had received that morning, I felt as though I had suddenly come face to face with one part of the truth.

After Mr Suwa left, we sat together in silence for a long while. It wasn't at all like it is on the stage or in novels. Although we were blood relations, there was no outpouring of heartfelt emotion; instead, the fact of our being related made it only more awkward, as it meant we couldn't fall back on pleasantries. At least, that was how I interpreted my grandfather's long silence at the time. Unbeknownst to me, however, he was in fact experiencing such excruciating pains in his stomach that he couldn't talk.

Looking on as his forehead glistened with perspiration, I made up my mind to speak.

"Grandfather…"

He glanced at me, but with teeth clenched and lips trembling, he was unable to utter so much as a word.

"The village where I was born… Is it called Eight Graves?"

My grandfather gave a slight nod. An almost inaudible groan issued from his lips.

"There's something I'd like you to look at, Grandfather. I received a strange letter this very morning."

I took the envelope from my pocket and, extracting its contents, unfolded the letter for my grandfather to see. He reached out a hand to take it, but suddenly he collapsed.

"Grandfather, what's the matter?"

"Tatsuya… Water!… Water!…"

These were both his first and last words to me.

"Grandfather! What's the matter? Are you unwell?"

I thrust the letter back in my pocket and, as I was about to reach for the earthenware teapot standing on the desk, I noticed a trickle of blood run between my grandfather's lips. As he lay there almost paralysed, I instinctively called out for help.

A BEAUTIFUL MESSENGER

In the ten or so days that followed, I found myself in the midst of a bewildering and ferocious tempest. With the sole exception of the war, nothing in all my twenty-eight years had disturbed the greyness of routine, but now a drop of red had appeared, and in the twinkling of an eye, it began to spread, turning my whole life crimson.

At first, I assumed that my grandfather's death had been the result of some chronic illness, but the doctor who quickly appeared on the scene soon raised the alarm. He reported his suspicions to the police, causing a great commotion. The body was immediately transferred to the prefectural hospital, where the pathologist carried out a painstaking autopsy. The results established the cause of death to be acute poisoning, which immediately placed me in a tricky situation.

The police suspicions immediately fell on me, since I was the only person to have been with my grandfather in his final moments. Mr Suwa stated, during the course of the police investigation, that he hadn't noticed anything worrying as he spoke to my grandfather in the thirty minutes before my arrival; nor did he observe any noticeable change in my grandfather's health in the ten minutes after I arrived. If he had done, he would hardly have left us alone together. Yet the fact remained that shortly after Mr Suwa retired, my grandfather's agony began. I suppose it was only natural for people to suspect that I had drugged him somehow.

"You must be joking! Why on earth would he want to poison his own grandfather? And besides, he… that is, Tatsuya-san, had never met the man before. Why on earth would he do such an absurd thing, unless he were some kind of homicidal maniac?"

This was how Mr Suwa defended me, but as defences go, it was a pretty poor effort. Although it had not at all been his intention, his words were turned against me: the police took them to mean that if indeed I was a homicidal maniac, then I could well be the perpetrator of this crime. Moreover, it was through Mr Suwa that the police learnt the circumstances of my cursed birth—circumstances of which I was still unaware.

Filled with suspicion and scrutinizing my face all the while, the investigating officer asked me all manner of prying questions about the state of my physical and mental health. It was almost unbearable. Judging from the way in which he spoke, I believe he would have been satisfied, had I confessed that I experienced a ringing in my ears, or been plagued by strange hallucinations, or been a manic depressive, but to be perfectly honest, I have never suffered from anything of the kind. I am not exactly what you might call a gregarious type (my solitary ways have seen to that), but still I held myself to be a normal, ordinary sort of person.

The police seemed to doubt my explanations, however. For a second day, and a third, again and again I was subjected to questioning on my mental state. But then things suddenly changed. At the time I had no inkling why this might be, but later I learnt that the reason was as follows.

The poison used to kill my grandfather had burnt his tongue terribly, so it was clear that this was a kind that could not be taken by ordinary means. The pathologist himself had suspicions about this and during the autopsy he found traces of a gelatine solution in the victim's stomach. It was thus established that the culprit must have concealed the poison in a capsule pill taken by the old man and that a significant period of time would have had to pass for the capsule to dissolve in the victim's stomach. Since I was in the company of my grandfather for all of ten minutes, this revelation naturally placed me beyond suspicion.

That being the case, the police's suspicions now fell on Mr Suwa as my grandfather had spent the preceding night at Mr Suwa's residence. It also came to light that Mr Suwa himself was a native of Eight Graves. In addition to the Tajimis, there was another wealthy house; it was to this Nomura family that Mr Suwa belonged. Whenever any of the villagers had business in Kobe, Mr Suwa would put them up for the night. But Mr Suwa had no motive for poisoning the old man. So who was responsible for his murder?

The investigation stalled, but it was then that, in response to a telegram sent by Mr Suwa, somebody from the village arrived in Kobe to settle my grandfather's affairs and to take me back to Eight Graves. What this new arrival had to say dispelled all suspicions.

For years, it transpired, my grandfather had suffered from attacks of asthma, which were particularly acute whenever he was nervous or agitated. He always carried medication for this and, in preparing for a trip to meet his grandson for the first time, he would never have forgotten to take it with him. Everybody in the village knew that he took these pills, prescribed by the doctor especially. Was it not likely that the culprit had slipped a poisoned capsule in among them?…

On the basis of this new evidence, my grandfather's luggage was immediately searched, revealing a sweet tin containing three capsules. Their contents were analysed, but the results showed that they contained nothing untoward. Nevertheless, this suggested that he had mistaken the poison for his asthma medication, in which case the culprit was to be found not in Kobe, but further afield. As the case moved to Eight Graves, Mr Suwa and I thankfully found ourselves in the clear.

"You're a godsend, Miyako. I'm sure I'd have exonerated myself in the end, but, frankly speaking, those endless interrogations were becoming tiresome."

"Oh, they certainly put you through the mill, Suwa-san. But then, you're an old hand at this. As for poor Tatsuya-san here… What a terrible shock you must have had."

That evening, the last suspicions about us were laid to rest entirely. Mr Suwa wanted to celebrate, so he had invited me to

46

his house in Kobe's Kamitsutsui district, where I was introduced to a most unexpected visitor.

"This is Miyako Mori, our guardian angel. She came expressly from Eight Graves to solve the mystery of Ikawa-san's death. Miyako, this is the renowned Tatsuya Terada."

How to describe my astonishment? Between the sinister name of the place and old Ikawa's rustic appearance, I had every reason to think that this village was a world away from civilization. But the woman standing before me was exceptionally beautiful, even by city standards. Not only was she beautiful, but she was also charming, refined, urbane.

She must have been in her thirties. Her skin was white and as smooth as silk. Her face was long and classical without looking old-fashioned, her hair was tied up in a sort of chignon, revealing the nape of her neck in a very sensual way, and yet for some reason, the beauty and the elegance of the kimono that she had on that night set me on edge.

"Well, well, I dare say you're in shock, Tatsuya-san. In shock! But with such an exceptional woman by your side, you've nothing to fear in Eight Graves. I should also point out that this young lady lost her husband... You have before you a merry widow on the hunt for a new husband. You'd better get in line..."

Mr Suwa's good humour had not a little to do with the sake that he had consumed. I, on the other hand, was successively struck by chills and hot flushes.

"Come, come, Suwa-san, restrain yourself. Do forgive him, he'll say any old thing when he's had a drink."

"Have you known Suwa-san a long time?" I enquired.

"I should say. We're distant cousins. There aren't so many people who leave the village for the city, you see, so we get on quite well... I used to live in Tokyo, before we were bombed out."

"But, Miyako," Mr Suwa interrupted, "just how long are you going to spend in that cowtown? It's a crime to let a woman like you go to waste in a place like that."

"I keep telling you, I'll come back once the new house has been built. You really needn't worry; I've no intention of laying my bones to rest in a hole like that."

"I know, but aren't you kicking your heels a bit? How many years has it been? Since the end of the war... That must be four years now. How on earth do you manage it? It's almost as if there's something holding you there..."

"Don't talk rubbish... Anyway, I need to have a little talk with Tatsuya-san."

Having silenced Mr Suwa just like that, she turned to me with her beguiling smile.

"I've come to take you back, Tatsuya... You're aware of this, yes?"

"Y-yes..."

"It's such a pity about your grandfather. If I'd even suspected that such a thing might happen, I'd have come in his stead. People talk big in the country, but the moment they leave, they lose their nerve... Your great-aunts, Koume and Kotake, have charged me with the task of fetching you. My plan is to return in a couple of days, once I've settled Ikawa-san's affairs. You'll come with me, I hope..."

"Y-yes..."

Once again, I experienced a succession of chills and hot flushes.

Ah, that drop of red that had fallen upon the grey of my life... It was spreading and spreading and spreading without end.

CHAPTER 2

A SUSPICIOUS CHARACTER

At that first meeting, Ms Mori told me that she wanted to leave for the village of Eight Graves in a few days' time, but naturally, since she seldom left the country, she also had wanted to take advantage of this rare opportunity to go shopping, to visit friends in and around Kobe, and to see a show, which she had not done in a long while. In the end, one day gave way to the next, prolonging her visit, and it was not until the 25th of June that we at last departed for Eight Graves.

To think that I had first gone to Mr Suwa's office in response to the radio announcement on the 25th of May. Only a month had gone by, but what an incredible, bewildering month it had been. Before we left, I would pay almost daily visits to Mr Suwa's home, and Ms Mori would often telephone, asking me to accompany her to the shops or to the theatre.

I had very little experience with the opposite sex, so the novelty of all this brought me joy and not a little excitement. At the same time, however, that strange mix of unease, misgiving and fear, which had long since taken root, deepened with every passing day, bringing me to the point where I felt besieged by a feeling of intense despair.

Throughout all this, there was one vital thing that Mr Suwa and Ms Mori were reluctant to tell me, fearing that it would come as a terrible shock: that was the awful circumstances of my birth, which they kept from me until the day before our departure. I will not return to this subject here. Or rather, I cannot. What child can bear to take up a brush and evoke the terrible tragedy of his parents? My poor mother… Now I understand why she suffered so, why she sobbed so inconsolably at night. I also learnt the origin of those terrible scars that disfigured my body.

This knowledge felt like a lead weight pressing on my chest. But what horrified me most was the final revelation: the dreadful massacre of thirty-two villagers. Mr Suwa and Ms Mori related to me the details of this event as calmly and matter-of-factly as possible, trying not to frighten me, but still, the shock that it produced in me was unimaginable. How well I remember the moment when I first heard about it: my blood ran cold and my breath left me. I froze, dumbstruck, and then my whole body began to tremble uncontrollably.

"It's an unenviable role that I'm playing in telling you all this. Under any other circumstances, it would have been your grandfather, Ikawa-san, who would have told you, but in light of what's happened, Suwa-san and I both agree that it would be better if I did. I'm really very sorry. You must think it awfully cruel of me, but you'd have heard it all anyway once you reached the village… Please don't think ill of me."

As she tried to imbue her voice with a note of sympathy, Ms Mori fixed her gaze on my pitiful face.

"Not at all," I eventually managed to say. "On the contrary, I don't quite know how to thank you. I had to find out sooner or later. I can't tell you how much better it is to hear it from someone as kind as you. Only…"

"Yes?"

"What will the villagers think of me? If I go back to the village now, how will they react?"

Ms Mori looked at Mr Suwa.

"I wouldn't concern yourself with such questions, Tatsuya-san," the lawyer said calmly. "Worrying about what other people think will only give you a restless night's sleep…"

"Suwa-san is right. Besides, you haven't done anything wrong."

"I do understand, but still, I think I'd like to know. Forewarned is forearmed, so the saying goes."

They looked at each other once again.

"Perhaps you're right," Ms Mori said, nodding. "You ought to be prepared for it. Frankly speaking, the villagers are not all that well disposed towards you. Their feelings are unfounded, of course; after all, you aren't to blame for any of what went on... But when your parents or children have been killed, I suppose it's a natural reaction. It can't be helped, really. Everything takes ten times as long in the countryside: what takes one year to forget in the city takes ten years in that village. The memories stick, they take root—year after year, people stubbornly cling to them. Perhaps it's best that you understand this. The prospect of your return has set hares running..."

"So everybody in the village knows about my return?"

"Unlike in the city, it's impossible to keep anything a secret in the countryside. Word always gets out... And when it does, it spreads through the whole village like wildfire. But you mustn't pay too much attention to it. Besides, they'll gossip about anyone who comes from the city. You should hear the things they say about me now that I'm a widow. There'd be no end to my worries if I bothered myself about every last thing they said. I just try to take it all in my stride. No, don't go looking for a quiet life in the countryside."

"But Tatsuya-san's situation is rather different, Miyako," the lawyer cut in. "If it really is as bad as you make out, he'll need a fair amount of courage and determination."

Once again, I felt that lead weight in the pit of my stomach. However, despite my habitual reserve, I was overcome by an inexplicable surge of courage at the very last minute.

"No, thank you both for all the things that you've told me. As you say, Suwa-san, the trip will be an onerous one. But if I might ask one more thing, Miyako-san…"

"Yes?…"

"Really, I'm sorry to trouble you with all these questions, but…"

"Go on…"

"Even if I'm reviled by the whole village, is there anyone there who has particular cause to hate me? Cause, say, to want me not to come back, to stay as far away as possible?"

"What on earth makes you ask that? There's no cause to think that everyone in the village *hates* you. You mustn't exaggerate like that. If I gave you that impression, I'm really very sorry, but—"

"Ah, but there is. See for yourself. I received this letter not so long ago."

I produced the strange warning-letter that I had received that unforgettable morning, on the day when my grandfather was poisoned. As Mr Suwa and Ms Mori examined it, their eyes grew wide.

They looked at one another.

"There must be some connection between what's written here and my grandfather's death, don't you think? Doesn't this seem like a plot to keep me far away from the village, to prevent my return?"

Miyako paled, unable to respond to my question.

"I dare say," said Mr Suwa, frowning. "What do you make of this, Miyako?"

"Hmm…"

"What about Shintaro? You know him from your time in Tokyo, don't you? Do you think he could be capable of something like this?"

"Oh, please…"

Quick though she was to throw out this idea, the pallor of her cheeks and the faint tremor of her lips suggested otherwise.

"You mean my cousin?" I asked.

"Yes, the one who was in the army. Does this suggest anything to you, Miyako?"

"What on earth could it possibly suggest to me? I haven't the faintest idea… Anyway, the man's completely changed. He used to be full of fighting spirit, but these days he's like a doddering old man. He's hardly said a word to me since coming back to the village. And it's not just me. I doubt there's a single person in the village who's had a friendly chat with him. He's become such a recluse… So how should I know what he's thinking or feeling? But, no… I don't think he could be capable of such a terrible thing. The man I knew just couldn't…"

She was quick to defend Shintaro, but her words grew more and more confused, and this uncertainty was plain to see. There was something behind her words that seemed to refute them, but I just couldn't put my finger on it.

Did Shintaro Satomura have a strong motive for wanting to prevent my return to Eight Graves? This possibility, together with Ms Mori's display of confusion, only strengthened my deep sense of misgiving.

SETTING OUT

25th June. The day of our departure. The sky was leaden and threatening, typical for the rainy season. I was already dreading the trip, and the weather depressed me even more. To tell the truth, as we waited for the train at Sannomiya Station, I was in a rotten mood.

Mr Suwa had come to see us off at the station. He seemed strangely subdued.

"Tatsuya-san," he said, "you will look after yourself, won't you? I hate to cast a shadow over what should be a joyous departure, but for some reason I just can't shake the feeling that things aren't quite what they seem. We're missing something important, I'm certain of it. Your grandfather's death... that strange letter you received... that bizarre man going around, making enquiries about you... None of it bodes well."

I had asked Mr Suwa about the man who had showed up at my friend's house and at my work, but, sure enough, he was not one of the lawyer's clerks. To make matters worse, my description of him had given Mr Suwa quite a shock.

"The thing is, I did in fact engage somebody to look into you. But he was a darn sight better than this fellow. Hmm... It would seem that somebody else has taken an interest in you. And I dare say that person is to be found in Eight Graves. Do you have any ideas, Miyako?"

With an air of surprise, Miyako frowned and replied that she hadn't the faintest idea. She herself seemed to be quite troubled by this.

"People are strange creatures, are they not, Tatsuya-san," the lawyer continued. "Only a month ago, you and I were perfect strangers, yet now we could practically be family. And to think it was this strange visitor, this suspect in your grandfather's murder, who has brought us together. Strange though it may sound, I don't mind admitting to you that I've begun to feel rather like a father towards you. So if anything happens to you in the village, if you're ever in need of help, don't hesitate to contact me. I'll drop everything and come running."

I couldn't help being touched by his kind offer. It comforted me in no small measure as I made ready to embark on an uncertain future. Choked with emotion, all I could do was stand there in silence, my head bowed.

Miyako was the liveliest of the three of us that morning. Dressed casually for the journey in a bright-green raincoat that suited her very well, she looked like a budding flower against the overcast platform.

"What's that you're saying? That Tatsuya is in danger? Don't be silly. Nothing's going to happen to him. But if it did," she said, rolling her eyes mischievously, "don't forget that I'll be there. And I'm strong, too. Strong as any man. So you needn't worry. Come what may…"

"Quite," said the lawyer with a smirk. "I believe you are in safe hands, Tatsuya-san."

The hour of our departure had finally arrived. We said our goodbyes to Mr Suwa and boarded the train, leaving him behind. For all my fears and apprehensions, I felt a certain joy in setting out on this journey.

Each person has his own particular smell, be it powerful or subtle, alluring or repulsive. The smell doesn't always correspond to a person's physical appearance, however, though it is a part of their personality. In Ms Mori's case, hers was a faint, sensual aroma.

She enjoyed playing the older sister and liked to be of help to people. Although our acquaintance had been brief, in the days leading up to the journey, she had, from the very outset, assumed the role of guardian, advising me like an older sister and spoiling me with clothes and luggage for the trip.

"You needn't worry about it. All this was paid for with the money that your aunts gave me. First impressions are what matter most in the provinces. Being humble won't get you anywhere; they'll just take you for a fool. Whether it's the way you act or the clothes you wear, you've got to impress them. You've got to be confident."

I felt like a little boy, but strange though it was, I enjoyed it. The sense of excitement was thrilling, and I was intoxicated by the very smell of her.

The long journey gave me ample opportunity to find out more about Miyako's background. She was, I learnt, the sister-in-law of one Shokichi, the head of the wealthy Nomura family, having been married to his brother Tatsuo.

"What exactly did you husband do?" I asked.

"He ran a factory that manufactured electrical goods. I really haven't the faintest idea what kind, but he did very well for himself during the war. Made a killing, you might say…"

"And when did he die?"

"In '44, when the Pacific War was in its third year—just after Japan's fortunes began to turn. A cerebral haemorrhage—he always did drink too much."

"Still, he must have been quite young."

The question made her laugh aloud.

"He was a whole ten years older than me. People will still say that he died young, of course. Only, I'd never thought that it would be so sudden. It came as a terrible blow to me. Fortunately, there was someone at the factory—a real gentleman—who took care of all the arrangements for me. He was scrupulous when it came to transferring the money, so there was always food on the table…"

"And have you known this Shintaro fellow long?"

I posed the question in as off-hand a manner as I could, but her quick, piercing gaze immediately saw through me.

"Not so long, no… That is to say, I'd known *of* him for a while. We're from the same village, after all. I knew that he'd enlisted. But I only really got to know him after my husband got his claws into him. It was during the war, when the military controlled everything. My husband needed someone who could pull a few strings, so he would invite him over, go out drinking with him..."

"And you kept up that friendship after your husband died?"

Her eyes came to rest on me once again, and an enigmatic smile crossed her lips.

"Of course. In fact, we saw even more of each other than before. After my husband's death, I felt so alone; so it was good having someone to remind me of home. To be honest with you, though, I don't much care for military types. Then again, it was useful knowing someone attached to the General Staff Headquarters. You got to hear a lot of things..."

I learnt afterwards that when Japan's fortune had taken a turn for the worse, Miyako had gone about buying up diamonds and precious metals, the value of which was rumoured to be immense. But that is the kind of woman she was: her pluck and determination were second to none.

"I gather that Shintaro is still a bachelor," I said. "Does he still live in the Tajimi house?"

"It's true that he's a bachelor, but he doesn't live alone. He has his sister Noriko. She's..."

Miyako suddenly fell silent. Instinctively, I scrutinized her face, which seemed to flush with embarrassment.

"She's...?" I couldn't resist pressing her.

Miyako delicately cleared her throat.

"Forgive me. I shouldn't have said anything. But since I've started, I might as well finish. Noriko was born when... well, when your father went berserk in the village. It was the shock of it, you see... It caused her mother to go into labour prematurely. If I remember rightly, she was born at eight months. They thought she wouldn't live, but in a strange turn of events, the child survived while the mother died shortly afterwards. To look at her even now, you'd think she was just nineteen or twenty, although there's only a year's difference between the two of you. She lives with Shintaro in a house given to them by the family. They lead a simple, almost peasant's way of life."

Once again, my heart grew heavy. My father's evil deeds had left a long and lasting trail. There would be other victims, too, in the village, just like Noriko. I imagined the repercussions that my return to the village would have, and it sent a shiver down my spine.

THE KOICHA NUN

It had gone four o'clock when, several hours after changing trains at Okayama, we finally alighted at N——. We had spent the first part of the journey in relative comfort, travelling in second class; however, not only was there no second-class carriage on the local Hakubi-line service, but it was so crowded that we heaved a sigh of relief when we stepped off the train at last. Still, I couldn't suppress another groan when I learnt that in order to reach the village of Eight Graves, we'd have to travel another hour by bus, followed by a half-hour's walk.

Mercifully, the bus was practically empty, but it was there that I first encountered one of the residents of the village.

"Well, well, well… If it isn't the young mistress of the House of the West!"

The people in these parts had a habit of calling out in such booming voices, without any thought for the people around them. The man who had just sat down in front of Miyako must have been around fifty, heavy-set and with a rugged face, every bit like the old man who had recently died. I thought to myself that these physical characteristics must be common to the locals in this region.

"Ah, Kichizo! Where are you off to?"

"I had some affairs to see to in N——. I'm heading home now. Are you on your way back from Kobe? Poor old Ikawa… Such a dreadful business."

"I'd have thought you'd be pleased to have your old business rival out of the way."

"What a thing to say! You really mustn't joke like that."

"I'm not! I heard that you and Ikawa-san were having a spot of trouble recently over a client…"

I learnt afterwards that this Kichizo was a cattle-trader, just like my grandfather. There were only the two of them in the village. In places like that, traders and farmers are very loyal to one another, and as a rule they don't change their partnerships, but the sense of chaos and unrest that came after the war had reached even this remote mountain region, and the farmers had changed traders to their advantage, while the traders had, without any compunction, infringed on each other's territory. This was the "spot of trouble" to which Miyako alluded.

She seemed to have struck a nerve.

"If you'll forgive me for saying, I think that's in very poor taste, Miss," Kichizo said, his eyes darting about. "His death has caused me no end of troubles. The police really put me through the mill, and now the villagers keep looking at me strangely… Yes, we had a spot of trouble, but I'm not the only one who was at fault. He must have got tied up in some shady business, and then…"

"Calm down, nobody's accusing you of the old man's murder. Don't get yourself worked up… What has it been like in the village since I've been gone?"

"Well… The police keep summoning Dr Arai for questioning, the poor man."

"Ah, of course… Dr Arai was Ikawa-san's physician. But a doctor would hardly poison one of his own patients, surely? Wouldn't that be a little too obvious? And anyway, Dr Arai didn't have a grudge against him."

"Oh, no, he's being questioned as a witness… Somebody must have substituted Ikawa-san's medication. But, you know, Miss," Kichizo suddenly lowered his voice, "even if Dr Arai didn't kill him, the fact remains that the old man died after taking what he thought was the doctor's medicine. Someone has been spreading rumours that Dr Arai's pills can be lethal… They say he's lost a lot of patients lately."

"People can be so cruel… Who would go around saying things like that?"

"I shouldn't say it out loud, but I hear it was Dr Kuno."

"Well, I never…"

"Ever since Dr Arai was evacuated to the village, Dr Kuno's been a different man."

In any rural locale, it is the village doctor who sits at the top of the pecking order. As far as the farmers are concerned, nobody can hold a candle to him, not even the village mayor or the schoolmaster. In the past, some village doctors even began to conduct themselves with an inflated sense of self-regard because of this, allowing themselves to be particular about their patients, making night-calls only for the very wealthy, and so on. Not all of them, of course, but some; and nobody would dare to challenge the ones who did. Yet by the end of the war, throughout the length and breadth of Japan, the face of the country had changed. City doctors who had been bombed out had taken refuge in their home towns and, in order to acquire new patients, they had lavished care on the locals and impressed them with their city-learnt bedside manner. Although the villagers in general had a strong sense of loyalty, it was only natural that they should prefer this kindness and attention to being treated like fools. It was little wonder, then, that after the war there was a wave of people who switched from those lazy village doctors to the more industrious city ones. Wherever you went, these evacuee doctors had ousted the local ones, and seemingly Eight Graves was no exception.

The "spot of trouble" between the cattle-traders, the patient rivalry between the doctors… Disputes like these in such a small world as the village captivated my attention back then.

"Yes," he continued, "old Kuno went too far. But that's karma for you. When a village doctor loses his patients, it's a hopeless situation. If he lived in town, he could always moonlight, but not in a village. A proud man like that won't change his ways either. The rent has to be paid in cash, of course, but there was a time when some doctors would take rice in payment for medical bills. But now that rice is being sold on the black market, it's better to pay in cash. Nobody pays in rice now. And to make matters worse, he has all those children and can't afford to feed them. That's why Mrs Kuno's started growing potatoes, just like a peasant. What a humiliation for a doctor's wife…"

There seemed to be some bad blood between Kichizo and Dr Kuno. He was taking great pleasure in this downfall, but suddenly he lowered his voice again:

"The doctor's loathing for his rival is hardly anything new… It's obvious that he's the one who's been going around, spreading all these rumours behind Dr Arai's back. And if you ask me, I think he's the one who poisoned Ikawa-san…"

Miyako gasped.

"But even if he did hate Dr Arai, what possible reason could he have for poisoning an innocent old man like Ikawa-san?"

"To incriminate Dr Arai, of course! That would be more than enough reason. And besides, the old man isn't exactly innocent in all this. When Arai first arrived in the village, it was old Ikawa who was the first to let the old doctor go, and then he went round the whole village, telling everyone how much better Dr Arai's pills were. It's only natural that he'd loathe the man. Anyway, nobody but a doctor could get his hands on poison in a village like this."

"That's enough, Kichizo. You shouldn't go throwing around accusations like that when it's something so serious. Besides, this man is a relative of Dr Kuno's…"

For the first time, Kichizo deigned to look at me, and his eyes flashed with a hint of what was in fact profound astonishment.

"Ah-ha… Then this must be Tsuruko's…"

"Yes, this is his first trip to the village. He's bringing Ikawa-san's remains. I'll introduce you properly some other time."

All trace of levity suddenly vanished from Kichizo's face as he lapsed into silent contemplation. From time to time, he would look at me askance, but finally he leant into Miyako and said:

"You're taking him there? Is that really wise? They thought he'd never come to the village, no matter how much you tried to persuade him."

Those words chilled me for some reason. To hear them spoken as I was on the point of arriving in Eight Graves was hardly a gratifying welcome. He seemed to be about to go on but, when Miyako turned away in irritation, he stopped short and fell silent. Then, with an air of arrogance, he folded his arms and pursed his lips sullenly. Still, from time to time, I would catch a flash of hostility in his eyes as he peered at me. More and more, I had a terrible sinking feeling in my stomach.

We had almost arrived in the village. When the bus stopped, Kichizo was the first to alight, and he rushed off as fast as his legs would carry him. Miyako and I looked at one another. It was obvious: he wanted to make it back to the village before us, in order to inform them of our arrival.

"Suwa-san was right," said Miyako with a sigh. "You're going to need a lot of courage for this. Are you sure you're all right, Tatsuya?"

I must have looked daunted, but I nodded resolutely, feeling ready for whatever was to come.

In order to reach Eight Graves from the bus stop, we had to cross a mountain pass. The pass itself wasn't so very high, but the track was in such poor condition that the journey could be made only on bicycle or foot. Twenty minutes later, we had reached the pass. How well I remember the sombre feeling that enveloped me the very instant when I first looked down over the valley lying to the north.

The village of Eight Graves was situated at the bottom of a valley shaped like a basin. Mountains rose up on every side, and each one was cultivated up to a certain altitude. There were rice paddies the size of postage stamps and, strangely enough, some of them were fenced off. I learnt afterwards that the whole village, which made its living on cattle-rearing, was pasture for grazing. The cows roamed where they pleased, and the fences around the rice paddies were to protect them from the cows.

When I first laid eyes on the village, both the rainy season and the month of June were almost at an end. There was no rain that day, but there were low-hanging clouds in the sky, looming over the rough-finished houses at the bottom of the valley. The eerie atmosphere made me shudder.

"Do you see that enormous mansion at the foot of that mountain? That's your house. And do you see that lone cedar towering over it? That's the shrine of the eight graves. Until recently there were two of them, known as the twin cedars, but at the end of March there was a terrific thunderstorm that struck one of them down, splitting it right in two, all the way down to the roots. Ever since, the villagers have been terrified that another tragedy is about to occur."

Another chill ran irresistibly down my spine.

As we descended from the pass in silence, we could see a crowd of people gathered at the foot of the hill. They seemed to have come straight from the rice paddies. When I spotted Kichizo's figure among them, I bit my lip nervously. They were all clamouring over one another, but then one of them saw us and started shouting, causing all the others suddenly to fall silent and turn to look at us. In spite of their agitation, they stood rooted to the spot, all but a strange-looking woman who appeared from the crowd, glaring at us.

"Stay back! You mustn't come here! Go back!" she cried out in a shrill voice.

I stopped dead in my tracks, but Miyako took me by the arm.

"Ignore them," she said. "Let's go on. It's only the Koicha nun. She isn't all there, but she's harmless enough. She's nothing to worry about."

As we drew nearer, I could make out her nun's habit. But what an ugly woman she was! She must have been at least fifty, and a cleft lip revealed a set of enormous, uneven yellow teeth, which looked just like a horse's. We pressed on, but still she kept shouting, stamping her feet and gesticulating wildly with both arms.

"Turn back! Turn back! Do not set foot in the village! The gods are angry. If you come, the village will be bathed in blood once again! The gods demand eight sacrifices. Do you hear me? You must go back! Do you know why your grandfather is dead? He was the first sacrifice! Then there will be a second, a third, a fourth, a fifth… Until there are eight! Do you hear me?…"

Her shrill vociferations followed us as we passed through the village and across the river until we arrived at the gate of the Tajimi house. Like the Pied Piper, she led the whole crowd of villagers, each wearing the expressionless face of a patient in a mental asylum.

Such was my welcome at the village of Eight Graves.

TWO OLD LADIES

"You mustn't pay any attention to them. Country people speak before they think. But they're all a bunch of cowards at heart, so you've nothing to fear. So long as you don't let them see your nerves. Just be sure to keep your head held high."

It was entirely thanks to Miyako that I had managed to save face, but how would I have fared if I had been alone? Perhaps I would have run off in a daze. But the reality was that I had made it to the Tajimi house, albeit drenched from head to toe in perspiration.

"But who is this Koicha nun?" I asked. "Why is she hounding me like that?"

"She's another victim of the massacre. Her husband and child were killed... That's when she joined the convent at Koicha. But ever since that thunderstorm, when she saw the great cedar at the shrine split in two right before her eyes, she hasn't been quite right."

"So Koicha is a place then?"

"Yes, it's a little hamlet. It gets its name from the thick tea, or *koi-cha*, that the nuns used to serve visitors. The story goes that ever since then the nuns have always been known as Koicha nuns. That particular one is called Myoren, but nobody actually calls her that. Always 'the Koicha nun' or 'the old Koicha woman'... She's a madwoman, so it's best not to pay any attention to her."

What, I wondered, was the connection between the words spoken by the Koicha nun and the contents of the strange letter that I had received? For all its seeming madness, there was a certain logic to the letter, a logic of which I didn't believe this half-crazed woman was capable. Perhaps the author had taken inspiration from the nun's words and drawn on them in composing the letter. Whatever the link, I vowed to myself that I would get to the bottom of it eventually.

Looking at the house now for the first time, the place in which I had been born was far grander than I had imagined: as big as a rock, of heavy, solid build, surrounded by an earthen wall enclosing a thicket of imposing cedars that reached up to the heavens. No sooner had we passed through the gate than a young woman, whom I took to be a maid, appeared at the side entrance.

"Ah, Miyako-san! Welcome. What's all that racket going on outside?"

"Oh, it's nothing, Oshima. Pay no attention to it. Would you kindly go in and tell them that I've brought Tatsuya?"

"Tatsuya!..."

Her cheeks flushed, the maid looked at me wide-eyed before darting indoors.

"Please, this way," said Miyako.

From the spacious vestibule, I could feel a sense of coolness typical of old houses. I was so nervous that my heart was pounding. A few moments later, the maid reappeared, followed by a woman of thirty-five or -six with slightly frizzy hair and a wan, lifeless face.

"Well, well, if it isn't the young mistress of the House of the West. Please, come right this way."

She pronounced the words with an exaggerated, high-pitched tone that I would realize later was typical of the women in these parts. The tenor of her voice contrasted sharply with the sluggishness of her movements, which had more to do with her poor state of physical health than any lack of enthusiasm. Her heart was weak, her face swollen, and her eyes drained of colour.

"Ah, Haruyo, here he is. May I present the long-awaited arrival. Tatsuya, this is your sister Haruyo."

To all appearances, Miyako was quite familiar with the house: she had taken off her shoes and entered the vestibule immediately.

Nobody spoke in the vestibule. Haruyo even looked away in embarrassment. However, this first encounter with my half-sister ultimately left a favourable impression on me. She was no great beauty, but she was still a good-looking woman. What was more, she put my nerves at ease: she was gentle and kind-natured, clearly having been well brought up. I felt a sense of relief, as though a heavy burden had been lifted from my shoulders.

"So, what's your first impression?" Miyako asked Haruyo.

"He seems to have grown into a fine young man…"

Haruyo glanced at me briefly before returning her eyes to the floor, laughing and blushing like a young girl. She seemed to like me, and that too helped to put me at ease.

"Shall we go through?" Haruyo said. "They're expecting us."

We followed my half-sister down a long corridor. Grand though the house may have seemed from the outside, it was even larger when viewed inside: as we passed along this corridor almost a hundred feet in length, I felt as though I were inside a temple.

"Are your great-aunts waiting over in the annexe?"

"Yes, that's where they've asked for the introduction to take place."

At the end of the corridor, there were three steps leading up to two adjoining formal rooms, one modestly sized and the other larger, both covered in tatami mats. I learnt afterwards that the annexe was in fact an Edo-period addition to the house, built to receive feudal lords.

The larger of the two rooms had an alcove, in front of which sat the two heads of the Tajimi clan, Koume and Kotake, who had hastily thrown a *haori* bearing the family crest over their everyday kimonos. When I spotted those two figures from the corridor, I was struck by an uncanny feeling.

I have heard it said that twins can be born of the same egg or different ones, and, in the former case, that the resemblance is far more striking. Even in their old age, there could be no mistaking that my great-aunts were identical twins.

They must have been over eighty. Their snow-white hair was tied back neatly, and they both sat there slightly hunched over. They were so small that they looked as though they could fit in the palm of my hand, just like two little monkeys. When I say monkeys, I am naturally talking only about the physical size of them; their faces were not the ugly faces of monkeys. In fact, their faces bore the traces of former beauty. Despite their venerable age, they were fair-complexioned, and their tightly pursed lips—doubtless hiding bare gums—lent them an air of nobility. But still, their resemblance struck fear into all those who gazed on them. After all, it is neither rare nor strange to encounter twins among the young, but to see such a striking likeness between two octogenarians was not only extraordinary but also a little eerie. They even seemed to have gained in similarity over time: they had the same wrinkles, the same liver spots, the same mannerisms, the same smiles.

"Aunties," said Haruyo, bowing at the threshold. "Miyako-san, of the House of the West, has brought Tatsuya."

Was this how they did things in this house? I wondered. Haruyo's deference and courtesy to her great-aunts seemed almost excessive. Instinctively I bowed deeply, but Miyako remained standing with a grin on her face.

"Ah, yes... We thank you for your troubles, Miyako-san," mumbled one of the twins almost indistinctly. I had no idea which was which at the time, but I later understood that it was Koume.

"Please, step this way, Miyako-san. Thank you for all the trouble you've gone to," Kotake mumbled in turn, chewing her words.

"I'm sorry to have kept you waiting for such a long time..."

Paying little heed to traditional customs, Miyako entered the room and sat down informally, with her legs to one side.

"Come in, Tatsuya," she said. "These are your great-aunts. This is Madam Koume, and over there is Madam Kotake."

"You are mistaken, Miyako-san," said one of the old women. "It is I who am Koume, and this is Kotake."

"Oh, I do apologize. I'm forever getting it mixed up. Aunties, this is the long-awaited Tatsuya."

Silently, I knelt before my great-aunts, my head bowed.

"So, this is Tatsuya... Kotake..."

"Yes, sister?"

"Blood never lies, does it?... He's the living image of Tsuruko."

"Yes, sister... His eyes and mouth... Every bit like Tsuruko's when she was his age. Welcome home, Tatsuya."

I neither moved nor uttered a word.

"You were born in this house, in this very room in fact. Twenty-nine years have passed since then, and this room has remained exactly as it was. The sliding doors... the folding screen... the hanging scroll... the carved wooden transom... Isn't that right, sister?"

"Yes, sister," Kotake replied. "Twenty-nine years may be a long time, but how quickly they seem to have passed…"

The shadows of former days flitted across the eyes of the two old women. It was Miyako who broke the silence:

"How, if I might enquire, is Hisaya?"

"Ah, yes… Hisaya… He is unwell and has taken to bed. We'll save that introduction for tomorrow. He may not have long left…"

"Is he really in such a bad way?" asked Miyako.

"Dr Kuno keeps saying that he'll be fine, that he'll get better, but what would a quack like that know? I very much doubt that he'll see out the summer."

"What's the matter with him?" I asked, opening my mouth for the first time.

"He is consumptive. If that were not bad enough, Haruyo has poor kidneys, and she cannot have children. That is why she was returned to us by her husband's family. So you must take good care of yourself, Tatsuya. The fate of this house now rests on your shoulders."

"But there's no need to worry any more, sister. Now that this fine young man has come back to us, our fears for the succession are at an end. Fortune has truly smiled on us," Kotake said with a laugh.

"Yes, it's as you say, sister," replied Koume. "Truly, we can rest easy now."

The laughter of these two monkey-like women filled the twilit room and sent another shiver down my spine. The former softness in their voices was gone, having been replaced by something cruel and treacherous.

That is how I first set foot in the valleys of those legendary mountains and in this dwelling where the memories of those terrible tragedies were still fresh.

THE LEGEND OF THE FOLDING SCREEN

That night I couldn't sleep.

As with anybody of a nervous disposition, a change of bed always spells a restless night. After the long journey, my body was ready to collapse, but my nerves were on edge and my mind was racing. Thinking back on it now, it was only natural: only the day before, I had been sleeping in my friend's cramped little room, filled with all manner of furniture and disarray, whereas now I felt almost lost in the vast expanse of this spacious room. It was so big, in fact, that I didn't know where to put myself. I tossed and turned on the futon. The more I tried to sleep, the more alert and exasperated I grew, and the day's events paraded through my mind as in a magic lantern.

The parting at Sannomiya Station, Miyako in her beautiful travelling attire, the bus journey, Kichizo and his tales of the cattle-trader, the Koicha nun and the villagers, and the two simian figures of my great-aunts: these people and scenes came and went without order or coherence. But the one memory that stuck in my mind was the rather strange story told to me that night by my sister Haruyo.

Being of a certain age, Koume and Kotake had retired to their room after the introductions had been made. I then went to take a bath, but just as I stepped out into the corridor, my sister said to me:

"From tomorrow you'll be served your meals in the annexe, but this evening, since you're still our guest, you'll dine here in the main house. If Miyako-san would also care to join you..."

Later, she and the maid Oshima served us.

"Thank you for the kind invitation," said Miyako.

"You're very welcome. It's nothing special, but seeing as it's dinnertime… If it gets too late, we'll have one of the boys see you home."

"That's awfully kind. I'm sorry to put you to such trouble."

It was thus settled that Miyako would join us for dinner. I was grateful to have her by my side a little longer. Even once the meal was over, she was slow to leave, and the three of us passed the time in conversation. Naturally, it was Miyako who did most of the talking, chatting about all manner of inoffensive topics with that relaxed and informal air of hers. That was her way of buoying me up whenever my mood darkened, as it was wont to do; it also helped to ease the tensions between me and my sister. In spite of all her efforts, however, the conversation eventually ran dry, and it was then, during the sudden onrush of silence, that I availed myself of the opportunity to take a casual look around the room.

One of my great-aunts—was it Koume or Kotake?—had said something that had left a very strong impression on me. "*You were born in this house,*" she had said, "*in this very room. Twenty-nine years have passed since then, and this room has remained exactly as it was. The sliding doors… the folding screen… the hanging scroll… the carved wooden transom…*"

These, then, must have been the same things upon which my mother gazed every day. As I pondered this, a pang of nostalgia struck me in the chest, forcing me to see each of the objects in an entirely different light.

The large hanging scroll in the alcove depicted the bodhisattva Kannon, arrayed in white. I had only to think of my mother's distress to imagine the fervour with which she would have prayed before the goddess. The mother I knew was a great devotee of the Kannon: morning and night she would never forget to pray before a small statuette that she had placed in the alcove in our home.

There was a set of staggered shelves beside the alcove, and hanging on the wall beside them were two Noh masks with terrifying expressions: one depicting the female demon Hannya, and the other representing a *shojo*, one of those mythical red-faced, sake-drinking monkey creatures that live in the South Seas. It was as if demons and the Buddha coexisted in this room. And in fact the wooden transom, or *ranma*, bore the inscription: "With the hand of a demon and the heart of the Buddha". The sliding door was decorated with a landscape that mixed techniques drawn from Chinese and Japanese painting, but it was antique and had faded with age.

There was one other object that drew my attention: a six-panelled folding screen, which depicted three life-sized Chinese figures standing around a large earthenware pot. Seeing that I was lost in contemplation of the screen, Haruyo broke the silence.

"Ah, yes," she said, as though recalling something. "There have been strange goings-on with that screen lately…"

Though she had been sitting with us, Haruyo had hardly said a word until now, so this sudden revelation almost made me look at her twice.

"What kind of 'goings-on'?" asked Miyako, leaning in with interest.

"Oh, you'll probably laugh, but… well, it's been said that one of the figures actually broke out of the screen."

"Whatever do you mean?" said Miyako, agog.

My gaze passed from my sister's face back to the screen.

"But what actually does the screen depict?" she continued. "There must be some sort of story to it…"

"Yes, there is," Haruyo began, blushing. "I don't know it all that well, but it's apparently called the Three Sages screen. The three figures are Su Dongpo, Huang Luzhi and Foyin, the high priest of the temple at Jinshan. One day, Su Dongpo, together with his friend Huang Luzhi, paid a visit to the high priest, who was delighted by their presence and offered them a drink of bitter peach blossom. Each of the three men sipped the drink and grimaced. Dongpo was a Confucianist, Luzhi a Daoist, and Foyin, obviously, a Buddhist. Each of the three men grimaced in his own way, but the cause was the same for all of them. This is supposedly meant to symbolize that, while the origins of Confucianism, Daoism and Buddhism were different, their object is the same... At least, that's what I've been told."

"I've no doubt that's what the ancient Chinese did think. But what's all this about one of the figures breaking out of the screen?"

Clearly, Miyako was far more interested in this detail than in the legend depicted on the screen. And so was I, for that matter.

"Oh, it's a bit difficult to explain... I'm not sure what to make of it, but strange things really have been happening."

In that simple, trusting way of hers, she unfolded the following tale.

"We ordinarily keep the annexe locked, but just so that it doesn't get too humid in here, we air it twice a week. About two months ago, when Oshima and I came to open the rain shutters, I noticed something rather odd. It was as if somebody had been here shortly before us, but that time I didn't pay too much attention to it. A couple of days later, though, when we came to open the rain shutters, I had that same feeling again... The screen had been moved and the cupboard wasn't closed properly. And yet, the shutters were just as they ought to have been. I thought that my mind must be playing tricks on me, but still it bothered me... Without saying anything to Oshima, I purposely left the cupboard a fraction open and placed the folding screen at the very edge of the tatami mat. That way, if anyone were to break in, it would be obvious that the cupboard

74

and the folding screen had been moved. The very next day, I secretly came back to take a look…"

"And had anything been moved?"

"No. Everything was just as I had left it the previous day. I thought I must have imagined the whole thing. But then I went back a few days later…"

"And? What did you find?"

"The screen had been moved from the edge of the tatami and the cupboard had been closed."

"How on earth…"

Miyako and I looked at each other in astonishment.

"And had the rain shutters been touched?"

"That's just it: no, they hadn't. Before I opened them, I checked to make sure that the bolts were still in place. One by one, I checked them all, but there was no sign that any of them had been forced."

"Is it only possible to access the annexe from the garden?"

"The only other way is via the long corridor from the main house, but the door was closed on this side and locked on the other. There are only two keys: mine and another one that my great-aunts have."

"Could it have been someone in the family?"

"Impossible. My brother is bedridden and can't even walk, and my great-aunts are hardly likely to venture here… As for Oshima, what could she possibly want in the annexe?"

"That's bizarre."

"It certainly is," I said.

"Yes, it really is strange. It unnerved me terribly, but I didn't dare tell a soul about it. After much deliberation, I finally asked Heikichi, one of our woodcutters, to spend the night here."

(I learnt some time later that several cottages had been built on the grounds of this enormous mansion, especially

75

for servants and employees. They housed woodcutters, cattle-herders and the boatmen who once transported timber and charcoal downriver to the town of N——.)

"So, what happened then?"

"Well, Heikichi is fond of a drink, you see... So I convinced him to spend a few nights here in exchange for some sake. Nothing happened during the first few nights. However, after the fourth night, I came to check on him early in the morning, only to find he was gone. What's more, one of the rain shutters had been left open. Surprised by this, I went to look for Heikichi and found him asleep in his cabin with the blanket pulled up over his head. I woke him up and tried to question him..."

"And...?"

We stared at her expectantly. She was blushing slightly.

"Well... he said that right in the middle of the night a figure in the screen had come to life and broken out."

"Well, I never!"

Instinctively, our gaze was drawn back to the folding screen.

"Which one was it?"

"He said it was the Buddhist priest. I wonder whether that's really true, though. As I said, Heikichi does like a drink. He can't even get to sleep without it, and he isn't the type to stop at one either... In any case, I gleaned the following from his ramblings: before going to bed, he had remembered to extinguish the lamp, but in the dead of night, he was woken by a light coming from somewhere. He looked around and thought he saw someone standing in front of the screen. Startled, he called out, 'Who's there?' The figure, also seemingly startled, suddenly turned around, and, according to Heikichi, it was none other than the priest from the screen."

"He can't have been serious," said Miyako, leaning in. "So, what did this Heikichi do next?"

I watched Haruyo with bated breath.

"Well, he seemed serious enough. Apparently, the man was so startled that he turned away and vanished in an instant. Or more accurately, the light disappeared, after which Heikichi could no longer make anything out in the dark. At least, that's what he told me… But he also said he thought he could feel somebody brush past the side of his bed in the darkness. By that point, he'd sobered up, but he was still a nervous wreck. When he finally managed to summon up the courage to turn on the light and look at the screen, he saw all three men standing right where they ought to be. There was nothing out of the ordinary. That helped to steady his nerves a little, but then he suddenly thought to check the rain shutters: they were all shut tightly. He then checked the door to the hallway, but it was locked from the other side and wouldn't budge. Since there was no sign of anyone having been there, his fear grew once again. 'It could only have been the man in the screen,' he said. With that thought alone in his mind, terror seized him, and he tore open the rain shutters and fled."

"It's so strange."

"It certainly is."

Miyako and I exchanged a look of bewilderment.

"Yes, it's an odd story. But there was something else that Heikichi told me. He said that strange things had been happening in the nights before he saw the man in the screen come to life. He would apparently wake up in the middle of the night, unable to shake the feeling that somebody was watching him… Time and again, this feeling would terrify him. He was sure that it was the man in the screen. Of course, this was probably a delusion on his part, but it certainly does appear that somebody has been stealing into the annexe from time to time. And I have the proof to show it, too."

"What proof?" asked Miyako, overcome by curiosity and edging ever closer to Haruyo.

"After hearing Heikichi's story, I asked him to keep quiet about what he had seen. I returned to the annexe to take another look at it, and I found a strange scrap of paper that had been dropped behind the screen…"

"A scrap of paper?"

"I don't know what it is exactly, but the paper is old and shows a map marked with strange-sounding place names including 'Monkey's Seat' and 'Goblin's Nose'. And beside them, there are some lines of what looks like poetry."

I let out a faint cry. Miyako seemed to be similarly shocked by this revelation. She shot me a furtive glance before lowering her eyes to the floor. She must have known somehow that I had a similar piece of paper in my possession. I couldn't remember having told her about it, so I could only surmise that Mr Suwa must have been indiscreet after I showed it to him.

Haruyo noticed our reactions.

"Is something the matter?" she asked inquisitively, looking at each of us in turn.

Since it was obvious that Miyako knew, I couldn't hide it.

"The thing is… I too have a similar piece of paper. I don't know what it means either. It could be some kind of incantation for all I know, but I've had it ever since I was little. Only, mine doesn't mention a monkey's seat or goblin's nose…"

I was loath to take the piece of paper out in order to show them, so, deciding against it, I fell silent. Neither of them asked to see it, but it was Haruyo who realized that it must contain some hidden meaning.

"Well, that is strange. I've kept the piece of paper safe, so perhaps we should compare it with yours sometime."

Now Miyako and Haruyo fell silent. My sister had begun this

tale of adventure as a means of entertaining her guests, but in so doing she had involved me in it unwittingly, in front of an outsider. Haruyo seemed to regret her rashness. Not wishing to spend a moment longer debating the identity of the intruder, Miyako set off home in a hurry. It wasn't long before a futon had been unfolded in that very annexe, where I was to spend the night alone—all the while consumed by those terrible doubts and misgivings…

THE SECOND VICTIM

It was almost dawn by the time that I finally fell asleep. When I woke up, light was filtering through the shutters. My wristwatch, which was lying beside my pillow, told me that it was almost ten o'clock. I jumped out of bed.

The clamour of the city always wakes you early, no matter how late you go to sleep. Embarrassed at having slept so late on the very morning after my arrival, I hurriedly put away the futon and began opening the shutters one by one, when suddenly I heard footsteps coming from the main house.

"Good morning," Haruyo said. "Oh, don't worry about that. Oshima will do it."

"Good morning. I'm afraid I've slept in…"

"You must have been exhausted. And what with that bizarre story I told you last night… Did you sleep well?"

"Yes…"

"You don't look as though you did. Your eyes are all red. You really mustn't tell fibs. At least you didn't go running to check whether the door was bolted."

The previous night she had told me that she would leave the door in the corridor unbolted, so that if the need should arise, I could always get into the main house. She had a far more relaxed and straightforward way about her today, which pleased me.

I was taken to the main house, where Haruyo served me breakfast. Given the lateness of the hour, I was the only one there.

"Where are my great-aunts?" I asked.

"Like all elderly people, they get up very early. They're waiting for you."

"Oh, I am sorry."

"There's no need to apologize... This house is yours, after all, so make yourself at home. We're only simple country folk, but I do hope you'll stay with us.'"

Her words soothed my strangely forlorn heart. As I bowed silently, I saw her blush and lower her gaze. During the previous night's storytelling, I had expected her to take out the mysterious map, but in the end she must have decided against it as well. I didn't dare to mention it now. In any case, there was no rush: it seemed that I would be there for a long time yet.

After I had finished eating, Haruyo ventured tentatively:

"Shall we, then? They're expecting us... They'd like you to meet your brother this morning."

"Of course."

She had mentioned this already, so I was prepared for it, but once again in that same tone of voice, she said:

"Don't let your guard down when you meet him. He isn't a bad person, but being confined to bed for so long has made him a little erratic... And Shintaro will be there, too..."

I began to feel vaguely apprehensive.

"We're cousins, you see, but for some reason our great-aunts and our brother have taken against him. Shintaro's presence always puts Hisaya in a foul mood. But since you're here, we invited him expressly. He's come with his sister Noriko."

In other words, my great-aunts wanted to announce my return as soon as possible. Had their motive for this been pure affection, I might have been awfully grateful to them, but the suspicion that they had some ulterior motive for doing this weighed on me.

"Will anybody else be joining us?"

"Yes, Uncle Kuno will be there. He was Father's cousin, you see…"

"He's the doctor, isn't he?"

"Ah, you're very well informed. Miyako-san must have told you about him."

"No, actually. On the bus there was a cattle-trader by the name of Kichizo. He mentioned him…"

"Ah. Kichizo…" said Haruyo, frowning. "Yes, Oshima did mention yesterday that some of the villagers gave you a rather rude welcome. I'll be having words with them. Just be careful for the time being: they aren't a bad lot, but they can be rather pig-headed."

"Yes, I understand."

"Shall we?"

My brother Hisaya was resting in a sort of darkened mezzanine room at the back of the house. The room overlooked a garden in which dusky-white hydrangeas were in bloom. When Haruyo drew back the sliding door, I was immediately assailed by a terrible odour that made me recoil slightly. It reminded me of something: I had encountered that very same smell years ago, in a room where a friend was dying of pulmonary gangrene. It is said that tuberculosis can be managed with the correct course of treatment, but alas there is nothing that can be done for pulmonary gangrene. Just as my great-aunts had said, it seemed unlikely that he would see out the summer, but all the same, this verdict saddened me.

My brother was in unexpectedly fine spirits, however. As we entered the room, the prone figure raised his head and looked towards me. When our eyes met, it was as if a firework went off in those oily, gleaming eyes that invalids so often have. But only a moment later, with a mysterious smile on his lips, he laid his head back down on the pillow.

I knew that Hisaya was thirteen years my senior, which would make him forty, almost forty-one. To look at him, though, you would have thought him fifty. It must have been the illness. He was all skin and bone, and even his skin seemed dead. His prominent Adam's apple seemed to cast a grim, morbid shadow, but his face retained a certain vigour. A burst of fighting spirit seemed to be illuminating his final days. But what was the meaning of that enigmatic smile?

"We're sorry to have kept you waiting. Please, Tatsuya…"

"Come in, Tatsuya. We've all been very impatient to meet you."

Koume and Kotake were sitting side by side, as last night, looking like little monkeys. One of them indicated the spot by his bed next to her. Unable to tell which of them had spoken, I bowed and sat where she pointed.

"Hisaya, this is your brother Tatsuya. He's become a fine young man, don't you think?… Tatsuya, this is your older brother."

I bowed silently while Hisaya's eyes bore into me. At last, he spoke in a hoarse voice:

"A fine-looking man, indeed… Such looks are a rarity among Tajimi men."

His repellent laugh gave way to a violent fit of coughing, which filled the room with that same malodorous smell. The odour was one thing, but it was the words he had just spoken that prevented my raising my eyes to him. He went on cough-ing for a while, but finally stopped, after which he turned to address the other visitors.

"What do you say, Shintaro? Aren't you happy to see such a fine little brother return home? Now I can die in peace, know-ing that the inheritance is in such good hands. And you, Kuno, aren't you pleased?"

His sneering laughter brought on another coughing fit. One of the twins immediately placed a cup of water to his lips. He gulped the water down and pushed the cup away.

"Enough! That's enough, Auntie! Leave me alone."

Having rejected her attentions with a shake of the head, he then craned his neck towards me.

"Tatsuya, this is old man Kuno. He's a doctor. Lately there's been talk of a better doctor in the village, but if you ever fall ill, you must go and see Kuno. He's family. And the one sitting next to him is your cousin Shintaro. He returned to the village penniless, but, as they say, family is family... Anyhow, enough of that. You're here now. You'll have to make sure that the vil-lagers take to you. You know the saying: When in Rome...? But be on your guard: you mustn't let yourself be robbed of the Tajimi fortune."

He was overcome by another dreadful fit of coughing. The pitiful sight of him set me on edge, and once again, in the pit of my stomach, I felt something dark, as black as ink. Whatever his reasons, my brother did not attempt to hide his animosity towards Kuno and Shintaro. Why this hatred between blood relations? Slowly I began to understand the complexities of old family ties in the countryside, and the feeling it produced was dismal, wretched and indescribably depressing.

Whether because of all the excitement, my brother's cough-ing fit would not let up. It went on and on, so much that I wondered whether he wasn't going to choke. The sound he made as he tried to clear his throat between coughs cut right through me. In the humid heat of the rainy season, that foul odour continued to rise unbearably.

Nobody attempted to help him, however. Neither Koume nor Kotake so much as looked his way. They just sat there, having already abandoned all hope that he might live. It seemed so very heartless. Haruyo was sitting furthest away, her head bowed and her shoulders quivering. From her profile to the nape of her neck, she seemed to have been drained of all colour. Perhaps she too could not bear to look upon this pitiful spectacle.

Dr Kuno must have been in his sixties. He was slight and his eyes bulged, and he had a shock of wire-like ashen hair. From across the room his unblinking eyes were trained on the coughing figure of my brother. If looks could kill, his gaze would have done away with Hisaya in an instant. He had a long face with a proud nose, both of which suggested that he might once have been rather handsome, but old age had hardened his features, which no longer expressed anything but loathing and contempt.

From the moment I entered the room, my attention had been drawn to Shintaro, but no matter how I tried, I couldn't fathom what was going on in his mind. He must have been around the same age as Haruyo. He was a plump, pale giant of a man, with a shaved head and worn serge clothes, all of which conformed to his image as a soldier. He had grown a beard, which, as Miyako had said, aged him somewhat. He sat there with his arms folded, looking at nobody, seemingly indifferent to his surroundings. Was it due to disdain or a state of despondency? I wondered.

Immediately beside Shintaro was his sister Noriko. A single glance was enough to ascertain that she wasn't a good-looking woman. Man truly is mercenary: had she been pretty, I would likely have felt great sympathy for her and have blamed myself for the crimes of my father. But she wasn't, and so I felt nothing of the kind. Not only that, her plainness provoked in me a sense of reassurance somehow. With a vacant expression on her face, she was looking around the room. She was the very picture of innocence, but she didn't look at all dim-witted. She had a broad forehead and hollow cheeks, and, just as Miyako had said, I couldn't believe that there was only a year's difference in age between us. It was not that she looked really young, but rather that she lacked a certain maturity. Her manifest frailty hinted at her premature birth. She looked strangely at everybody in the room in turn, until her eyes finally came to rest on me. As she stared at me, her eyes seemed vacant, devoid of expression, save for a little naïve curiosity about this stranger in their midst.

My brother's coughing fit showed no signs of abating. His gasps for breath between each cough were rasping and cut straight through my bones. Nobody said a word. The atmosphere grew leaden, weighing on everyone in the room.

"Villains!" my brother suddenly cried out, waving his arms. "Villains! I'm lying here dying and not one of you is willing to lift a finger… Villai—"

He was overcome by yet another violent fit of coughing. Sweat was beading at his temples.

"Medicine… My medicine… Somebody… give it to me…"

Koume and Kotake looked at one another with slight nods. Then one of them opened a little box by Hisaya's pillow and extracted a sachet lying folded inside it, while the other sister put it in a cup of water.

"Here, take your medicine, Hisaya…"

At these words, my brother lifted his head from the pillow to which it had been glued and placed his lips to the cup. But suddenly a thought struck him, and he turned to face me.

"Take a good look, Tatsuya. This medicine is Uncle Kuno's. You'll see just how effective it is…"

To this very day, I cannot fathom what he meant by those words. Most likely, it was a simple reproach aimed at Dr Kuno, but in the event, it hit the mark a little too well.

He drank the medicine and rested his head a moment on the pillow. For a while, the coughing seemed to subside, and just his narrow shoulders twitched from exhaustion. But no sooner did he seem to be improving than my heart sank for suddenly his whole body began to convulse.

"Agh!… The pain… Wa—… Water!"

He slumped out of bed and with both hands gripped his throat. His grimaces of pain were excruciating to behold. In a flash, I saw the agonies of my grandfather once again, and a chill ran right through me.

"A-a… Aunties!… My b… brother…"

The two old women seemed paralysed by this display of extraordinary pain. One of them tried to give him some water, but he was no longer able to drink. His teeth simply chattered against the cup.

"Come now, Hisaya. Here's your water. Drink it…"

But he pushed the cup away, clutching at his throat once again. Then, with a terrible cry, he vomited blood onto the white pillowslip before slumping down, motionless.

KOSUKE KINDAICHI

I shudder to recall it even now. Like a dark mist, a terrible atmosphere seemed to descend at once over everything in that dimly lit rear room. I felt an approaching sense of danger, and my instinct was telling me to flee this place as quickly as possible.

You may well laugh at my cowardice, but this was not the first time that I had witnessed such a thing. First, my grandfather, then, my brother—one moment they were there, and the next they were in the terrifying throes of death. And what was more, hadn't they died in exactly the same manner?

Poisoning… It was only natural that the thought should cross my mind. And yet everyone else seemed unexpectedly calm. Dr Kuno gave him an injection, then a second, and a third, but in the end he just shook his head in resignation.

"He's gone. The excitement must have hastened his end."

I studied his face in astonishment. I couldn't understand the placidity of everybody else present. Yet there was a faint tremor in the doctor's voice as he spoke those words. He became flustered when he caught my eye and looked away. What was the meaning of all this? Did he know something that I didn't? I had a nagging suspicion that I was missing something…

In distinction from Dr Kuno, Shintaro's state of mind remained a mystery. He looked surprised when Hisaya had taken that sudden turn for the worse, but he managed to maintain his composure in the moments after his cousin's death. Noriko simply looked dazed.

I wanted to cry out, but the words caught in my throat.

"You're wrong, you're wrong!" I wanted to say. "This isn't a natural death. He's been poisoned, just like my grandfather!"

Only I didn't say those words: they stuck in my throat and in the end I had to swallow them. After all, my brother had been ill, and it was difficult to disagree with what the doctor had said. Everybody had expected it to happen sooner or later: nobody was shocked by it—neither the family nor the servants. Though annoyed by their silence, I kept my counsel, lest I cause any trouble. I lacked the courage to say that it was murder. Was that how people died of pulmonary gangrene? Had I not witnessed my grandfather's death with my own eyes, I am sure I would have taken Dr Kuno's words at face value…

It was decided that my brother's funeral would be held the following evening. It meant that there would be two funerals—the other being my grandfather's, whose ashes we had brought back so that the Ikawa family could hold a proper ceremony. My brother's sudden death prevented me from carrying this out, and so, hearing of this second misfortune, my maternal grandmother Asae along with her adoptive son Kaneyoshi and his wife, paid us a visit. Having no children of his own other than my mother, my grandfather Ikawa had adopted his nephew after her disappearance, naming him as his heir.

That day, I met Asae and Kaneyoshi for the very first time, but since they have no special part in this dreadful affair, I shall not dwell further on their account. I want only to record that a decision was taken on the spot to hold my grandfather's funeral at the same time as Hisaya's.

The twins, Koume and Kotake, said in turn:

"Ever since Tsuruko disappeared, this family has had practically no contact with the Ikawas, but since he went to Kobe on our family's business and met his terrible end there, it is only right that we should take care of the funeral arrangements. Tatsuya shall be the chief mourner for both families."

How quickly life can change in the blink of an eye! My dull, grey life had been turned upside down again in the course of a single day. I was overwhelmed by it all. One after another, various people came to offer their condolences. As chance would have it, this was how I got to know the villagers: as soon as they had finished with their sympathies, they all fixed their eyes on me searchingly.

Miyako came, too, accompanied by her brother-in-law, Shokichi Nomura. The Nomura family lived at the western end of the village and was supposedly in possession of a fortune comparable to that of the Tajimis. The head of the family, Shokichi, must have been around fifty. He had a calm disposition and a cool eloquence, fitting for his station, but even he could not hide the inquisitiveness that, despite his best efforts, flashed momentarily across his face when Miyako introduced us.

The double ceremony took place without incident and so this second day reached an end. My grandfather had been cremated for convenience's sake, although in these parts the custom is to bury the dead. The Tajimi family tomb stood behind the house, directly below the shrine of the eight warriors' graves. My brother's remains were interred in a new grave that had been dug there. I was the first to throw a handful of earth onto the coffin after it had been lowered. To this day, I remember perfectly the chill that ran through me then, as though I had let go of something precious.

We returned from the burial and began to welcome the villagers for the memorial service, but as we were doing so, Miyako came up to me.

"Tatsuya…" she said with an air of familiarity, "there's a man here who insists on meeting you, but I'm sure you've got your hands full…"

"What sort of a man?"

"I don't really know myself. He showed up at the main house just after we got back from Kobe. I think he's an old friend of my brother-in-law's… Said he happened to be passing through on some business or other. He's been staying with us ever since. His name is Kosuke Kindaichi."

Back then, I had never heard the name Kosuke Kindaichi. Miyako seemed not to have heard of him either.

"What does he want with me, I wonder?"

"I've no idea. He said he'd like a word with you… alone."

This troubled me deeply. I thought he might be a police inspector. If he was, I had no choice but to meet him.

"By all means. I'll wait for him in the room across the hall so that we won't be disturbed."

After a few minutes in that little room, a man entered, smiling. However, when I set eyes on him, I wondered whether it wasn't the wrong man. I had been expecting someone far more imposing.

"I'm sorry to trouble you. My name is Kosuke Kindaichi," he said, bowing.

I just stared at him, unable to take my eyes off the figure before me.

Kosuke Kindaichi… He must have been thirty-five or thirty-six. He was of slight build and had shaggy hair, and no matter the angle at which you looked at him, he seemed distinctly unimpressive. To make matters worse, he was wearing an old and threadbare serge *hakama*: at best, he looked like a village clerk or a primary school teacher. And to top it all off, he seemed to have a slight stutter.

"Ah, yes," I said, before introducing myself. "There was something you wanted to talk to me about?"

"Yes, I just have a few questions…"

He was still smiling, but his eyes were so penetrating that they sent a shiver down my spine.

"It's very rude of me to ask you outright like this, but are you aware of what's being said in the village?"

"Being said about what exactly?…"

"About your brother's death. There are wild rumours flying about."

My heart very nearly stopped. This was the first I had heard about these rumours, but, given what the Koicha nun had said to me only three days previously, it was not hard to imagine them and the scandal that my brother's death had provoked. To say nothing of the doubts that I myself harboured on the subject...

The colour left my face, betraying my immediate consternation. As he watched this, Kindaichi grinned.

"Just as I suspected. You yourself have had similar such doubts. But if that's so, then why haven't you voiced your suspicions?"

"Why should I have?" I managed to say at last. The back of my throat felt parched. "Why should I have said anything? After all, there was a doctor present, and he didn't notice a thing. What could a layman like me possibly have to say? How could I dare to argue?"

"Yes, that was only natural. But permit me to give you some advice: if you have even the slightest suspicion now, it will be in your best interest to express it frankly without worrying about what anybody else thinks. Otherwise, you may just find yourself in a difficult position."

"Whatever do you mean by that, Kindaichi-san?"

"Just imagine: the moment you return to the village, strange things begin to happen... From the very outset, the villagers have taken against you and these events only serve to engrain that animosity further. Of course, it's all pure superstition... But that's why it's all the more frightening. They're so stubborn in their beliefs that they can't be reasoned with. Besides, in both cases—your brother's and Ikawa-san's—they both dropped dead the moment they had anything to do with you. It's only to be expected that villagers will grow more and more suspicious. You have to be on your guard."

A dark anguish seized my heart, weighing it down like lead. I felt paralysed, as though I were bound hand and foot by an invisible black thread.

"If you'll forgive me," Kosuke Kindaichi continued, still smiling, "it can't be a very pleasant experience, listening to all this from a perfect stranger. But if you'll indulge my somewhat overbearing solicitude… In any case, your suspicions with regard to your brother's demise, tell me about them. I appreciate that it might be difficult for you to express your feelings about what happened, but do at least try to describe the circumstances of his death objectively."

It was indeed easier for me to tell it that way. Just as he asked, I recounted it all as best I could. Every now and then, he would interrupt me for clarifications, but finally, when I had finished telling the story, he asked:

"What would you say if you were to compare your brother's death to that of Ikawa-san? Doesn't it strike you that their circumstances are the same?"

I nodded grimly. Kosuke Kindaichi paused for a moment, but eventually he looked me in the eyes and said, "I very much doubt that this matter will end here, Tatsuya-san. At any rate, there's too much gossip in the village. And you yourself have your doubts. Sooner or later, the police could get involved…"

As he spoke, Kosuke Kindaichi looked at me enquiringly.

The events that followed proved him right. Three days later, a number of police officers descended on the village, arriving from the town of N—— and from the constabulary headquarters at Okayama. My brother's body was exhumed, and an autopsy was performed by the police pathologist Dr M—— with the assistance of Dr Arai. The results were announced two days later. There could be no doubt about it: the cause of my brother's death was poisoning. Moreover, the poison was of exactly the same kind that had been used to kill my grandfather.

Thus did the village of Eight Graves find itself drawn little by little into a dark and terrifying maelstrom.

AN INFERIORITY COMPLEX

I was feeling increasingly distressed, choked by a fire burning in the pit of my stomach. I knew that I had to act, but I was at a total loss where to begin... Perhaps the first thing to do was to think it all through rationally.

First, supposing that my grandfather and my brother had been murdered (although, frankly there was no longer any room for doubt on that front), what was the connection between those murders and my homecoming? Did the first take place to try to ward off my return, and the second because I had in fact returned? All this required careful consideration. Was this double murder connected to the flurry of events at the centre of which I found myself? Or was there perhaps some other motive, unconnected to me? Would these two murders have occurred, irrespective of whether I had been found, regardless of whether I returned? I had to think about this carefully.

I couldn't fathom the assassin's intent, their objective in carrying out these poisonings. It was a mystery not only to me, but to everyone else as well. What did they stand to gain by my grandfather's murder? Was it to prevent my return to the village that they had killed the messenger sent by my family? But that wouldn't necessarily have been enough to keep me away. And in the event, I did go back, thanks to Miyako.

When it came to Hisaya's death, I was completely in the dark. Sooner or later, he would have died of natural causes anyway. There had been scarcely any hope that he would see out the summer. The killer had foreshortened his life only by the slightest margin. And he had taken a considerable risk in doing so...

As it happened, no sooner had poisoning emerged as a possibility than the members of my family, along with Dr Kuno, came under harsh scrutiny. And it was the latter who was subjected to a most agonizing ordeal.

Even now I can clearly remember my brother's last moments. After being overcome by a violent coughing fit, he asked the twins, Koume and Kotake, for his medicine. One of them—although I couldn't tell which—then took a sachet from a box by his pillow. There was no sign at all that she had consciously selected the sachet; she had merely taken the first one that came to hand, or so it had seemed.

After suspicions were aroused by Hisaya's autopsy, the police immediately confiscated the rest of the sachets and sent them off for testing. Nothing out of the ordinary was found, however, meaning that, of the many sachets in the box, only one of them had been poisoned, and it had been purely by chance that Koume or Kotake—whichever one it was—had picked it out.

Apparently, Dr Kuno prepared these sachets for my brother once a week. Each one contained a mixture of guaiacol carbonate, charcoal and baking powder. It seems that even most rural doctors had given up dispensing this preparation, but it nevertheless seemed to give my brother peace of mind. He took it religiously three times a day, and if ever it ran out, he would dispatch a servant to fetch some more.

Therein lay the problem. To begin with, the doctor prepared the sachets weekly, but as he found this a tiresome and laborious process, and since there was no question of the drug losing its efficacy, he began instead to prepare it on a monthly basis, while continuing to deliver it weekly. It was for this reason that there was always a large stock of these sachets in the pharmacy, kept especially for my brother. Thus, the culprit could have substituted the medicine either at Hisaya's bedside or in Dr Kuno's pharmacy. This doubling of opportunity complicated the investigation, for in the first instance, the suspects were considerably limited, but in the latter, it was a rather different state of affairs. As with most invalids, my brother had an impossibly difficult temperament; in addition to Koume and Kotake, the only other person whom he allowed into the sick-room was Haruyo. Aside, of course, from Uncle Kuno, the family doctor. Hence, in the first instance, the killer would have to be found among this group of four; otherwise, things began to get complicated.

As so often happens in the countryside, Dr Kuno's running of the pharmacy was an altogether slapdash affair. Near enough anybody could come and go as he pleased. The layout was such that Dr Kuno's reception room was situated at the rear of the house, just behind his consulting room. Whenever he was busy examining a patient, he would lead customers through the pharmacy to wait in the back room, so even the slightest acquaintance with Dr Kuno was sufficient to afford the opportunity to make the substitution. The question, then, wasn't who had the opportunity, but rather who knew where to find the stock of my brother's medicine in the pharmacy. But the doctor was at a loss on this point. Though the doctor kept his formula a secret, he would make up almost a hundred of these sachets every month and would always be assisted in the very time-consuming task of dispensing them by a member of his family, including his children who still attended school. Was it not possible that any number of people could have heard about it? Obviously, if that was the case, nobody was going to admit to knowing anything. Countryside or not, it was unthinkable that anybody could have been so negligent in storing the medicine.

If we examine the murders of my grandfather and my brother side by side, it is clear that the culprit was in no great hurry. In both cases, nobody could have predicted when the victims would take the substituted pill or sachet, so one can only presume that he was content to know that they would be taken sooner or later. In other words, he had chosen a method involving the least risk in both cases. Was it sheer coincidence, then, that I happened to witness both of these two deaths?

By that reasoning, it was hard to believe that I should have found myself mixed up in this business. Ill luck had pitched me in the middle of a maelstrom, which tossed me about like some poor, abandoned boat. As I carried the burden of my father's iniquity, I could not help thinking that my involvement in all this was not in fact a coincidence, but some kind of terrible retribution. I had to be on my guard...

My sole ally in Eight Graves was Miyako. But she was a mere woman, and was herself looked upon with suspicion by the villagers, so it was doubtful that I could look to her for help. I had only myself to rely on. I had to fight. But fight whom? Who was this adversary of mine?

My first thought was the stranger who had sent me the letter. But to track down that person would be no easy task for a novice. Then there was the man making enquiries about my character. My friend's wife had said that she thought he might be from the countryside. It shouldn't be so difficult to find out whether he hailed from Eight Graves. In a village like this, it would be common knowledge if somebody had taken a trip to the city, even for a single night.

I asked Haruyo, with as much nonchalance as I could muster, whether anybody from the village had gone away on any trips lately. She herself was reclusive, but she replied that, with the exception of Ikawa-san and Miyako, nobody had left the village insofar as she knew. She added that, though she herself hardly went out, she would have been sure to hear from Oshima if anything out of the ordinary had happened—so few were the noteworthy events in the village.

Trying to appear even more nonchalant, I asked whether there was any chance that Shintaro might have gone anywhere lately. Haruyo seemed a little taken aback by the question but replied immediately that it was impossible. He couldn't have gone anywhere, she said, because Noriko was so frail that even the slightest overexertion exhausted her. That was why each day, unbeknownst to the twins or her brother, Haruyo sent Oshima to prepare meals and to help her with the laundry. So it was out of the question that Shintaro could go anywhere, even overnight, without the news reaching her. Finally, she asked me not to breathe a word of this to Koume or Kotake.

What she said surprised me. I had been under the impression that everybody in this family disliked Shintaro, but now I discovered that he had this secret help from Haruyo. It was a testament to my sister's kindness, which pleased me greatly, but, at the same time, I cannot deny that this feeling was somewhat overshadowed: such was my prejudice against Shintaro...

I tried to banish that baseless shadow at once and asked why everybody in the family, with the exception of her, hated Shintaro. At first, she insisted that this simply wasn't true, but in the end she relented under my persistent questioning.

"It's shameful, really. You've only just arrived, and you've spotted it already."

After a deep sigh, she continued:

"It isn't at all what it seems. It's only that Shintaro's father, Shuji, was far more balanced than our father, his older brother. He was a decent sort of man."

A look of heartfelt sorrow spread across my sister's face.

"It pains me terribly to have to say this, because it casts our late father and brother in a poor light, but since you ask... You have to understand, Tatsuya: in the countryside, nothing is as important as family. It's the eldest son who becomes head of the family, and, unless he's an imbecile or mad, there's nothing the younger brothers can do to change that. Just because the child is born two or three years later, it's impossible for him to replace his brother as head of the main family, no matter how brilliant his abilities. When there aren't any major differences in the brothers' faculties, there's hardly ever any problem. If the brothers are equally incapable, then you just have to resign yourself to it. But in the case of our father and Uncle Shuji, the difference was too great. Uncle Shuji was a fine man. He never brought shame on us. Our father, on the other hand… The source of the resentment lies with our great-aunts. The elder son, who was to become the head of the family, left much to be desired, whereas the younger brother, who could only begin a new branch of the family or succeed to another branch, was more than capable. Their resentment was compounded by the natural instinct to dote on an idiot child—so they began to shun Uncle Shuji. The sentiment only intensified when it came to Shintaro's generation."

Haruyo gently pinched the bridge of her nose.

"This whole family is hopeless," she said. "Whether it was my brother or me, neither of us amounted to much. No, no, don't say a word… I know what you're going to say. You'll try to defend me and say it isn't true. But I'm just dead wood…"

She smiled plaintively.

"Shintaro, on the other hand, is a fine man. He may have been living in a wretched condition ever since the war ended, but as far as his personal qualities go, there's no comparing him to Hisaya. That, too, provoked the resentment of our great-aunts. Hisaya was jealous of him. The Tajimi family is nothing but a bunch of weaklings and halfwits, so when anyone normal comes along, they're immediately intimidated. And that's just your average person, never mind someone of Shintaro's calibre. When you get down to it, the family's hatred is really just the jealousy that a mediocrity feels for an outstanding individual—it's a kind of inferiority complex."

Haruyo had a weak heart, and it was clear that she was exhausted and out of breath just telling me all this. Her face had paled, and dark shadows appeared under her eyes. It pained me to see her like this.

"But I'm happy," she said, forcing a smile. "Happy that you've come back. You're a decent man, a fine man even. I'm happy."

Her weary pupils flashed momentarily, and then, as her eyelids grew redder, she lowered her head.

CHAPTER 3

THE EIGHT GRAVES SHRINE

I was curious about this shrine, the source of all the ills in the village. I wouldn't solve the problems that must lie ahead of me just by visiting it, but I felt that I had to see it at least once. However, owing to my brother's death, the house was in disarray, and I had only to think back on the day of my arrival in the village to lose all desire to go out.

A full week had passed since my brother's death. A small memorial was to be held for him that evening, and Miyako had come early to lend a hand with the preparations. When I told her of my plan, she suggested going together.

"Why don't we go now?" she said. "I came here to help, but I can see that everything's already been arranged. And you're at a loose end yourself. The priest won't be here until this evening, so we've got a bit of time."

Both city types, we were unaware of the taboo on visiting shrines during a period of mourning. Had we known though, I doubt we would have paid much attention to it.

We told Haruyo of our plan. Though a little surprised, she assented right away with a nod of her head.

"By all means. Only, make sure you come back as quickly as you can. It won't be long before the guests start arriving."

"We won't be long," Miyako said. "It's practically next door."

We passed through the large tatami room and left by the back door. Immediately, we found ourselves at the foot of a steep hill, and after a short climb we came across a little reservoir perched on top of it. Fortunately, there were no houses in this area, so we didn't have to worry about bumping into anybody along the way.

After making our way around the reservoir, we came to a granite rock face about six feet high, atop which there was a stone staircase flanked by an old railing of blackened timber. At the foot of the stairs was a stone monument bearing the inscription: "Tajimi Family Cemetery". I had been here once before on the occasion of my brother's funeral. A steep, narrow path led off to the side of the cemetery. If you followed it, it would take you to a hill with a few scrawny red pines dotted among the little gravestones. This was where the inhabitants of Eight Graves had been laid to rest for eternity.

"By the way, is that man, that Kindaichi fellow, still hanging around?" I asked.

Miyako's brow suddenly clouded over.

"I think so."

"Who is he exactly? Is he with the police?"

"I'm not quite sure. I think he might be some kind of private detective."

"A private detective?" I repeated, surprised. "So, has he come to investigate the murder?"

"I doubt it… Besides, he arrived before the business with Hisaya had even occurred. And I hardly think my brother-in-law would hire a private detective to investigate an affair at the Tajimi house."

"Yes, that's true enough. But how is it that Nomura-san knows a private detective?"

"Haven't the foggiest… In any case, I shouldn't ascribe too much significance to his presence. I heard that he was investigating some case in the village of Onikobe and just stopped here to rest a little on his way back."

"Oh? So, there are people who trust a man who looks like that with cases?"

This slip of the tongue made Miyako laugh.

"That isn't very kind of you," she teased me. "You mustn't judge people by their appearances. He could be a famous detective for all you know."

Miyako's words proved right. Soon I would see for myself just how good this stuttering detective with shaggy hair and a dishevelled appearance really was.

We made our way up through the scattering of little graves and eventually came to a cutting in the hillside. As we passed through it, the sound of rushing water, which we had heard for some time, suddenly grew louder. Up ahead of us, there was a fast-flowing torrent rushing between the rocks. The width of the stream was impressive for somewhere this high in the mountains, and enormous boulders lay scattered wherever the eye turned.

"When we have the time, we should follow the river down one day," Miyako suggested. "There are so many caves and grottoes. It's a kind of scenery you won't find anywhere else."

However, instead of following the bank, we recommenced our ascent from the midpoint, walking parallel to the stream. After two or three hundred yards, we reached at last another stone staircase leading up to the Eight Graves shrine.

There were around fifty steps, and the climb was so steep that it made me short of breath. When I turned halfway to look back, I felt dizzy. The stairs led up to a flat clearing of around 200 *tsubo*, in the middle of which stood a shrine. The shrine itself was a modest, run-of-the-mill affair. We bowed respectfully and made our way around the back of it. There was no sign of anyone, not even a priest. Behind the shrine, there was another staircase of only ten steps, leading to another small plateau around a quarter the size of the previous one. There we found the eight burial mounds. The one in the centre towered over the remaining seven: it must have belonged to the great samurai, while the others were erected for the retainers. A memorial stone beside the shrine laid out the origins of these eight graves, but in a script so ancient that I could only vaguely guess at its meaning.

At the eastern end of the plateau, an enormous cedar reached skyward.

"That cedar is one of the twins," said Miyako. "The other one as I said was struck down by lightning last spring."

Led by Miyako's explanation, I turned towards the western end of the plateau, and my heart skipped a beat. Beside the remaining stump, around which a ritual rope had been placed, I saw the figure of an old woman crouching, her fingers working a string of prayer beads fervently. I could only see her back, but the silhouette looked like that of a nun. Could it be the Koicha nun? I wondered.

"We should go back," I whispered, pulling gently on Miyako's sleeve.

But with a shake of the head, Miyako replied: "It's all right. That isn't the Koicha nun. She's a nun from Bankachi. Her name is Baiko. She's a gentle soul, so you've nothing to worry about."

I found out afterwards that Bankachi was a corruption of Ubagaichi, a place name literally meaning "the town for old women". No doubt it must have had something to do with the legendary practice of abandoning old women in the mountains and leaving them there to die… It was in Bankachi that the Keisho-in monastery was located; Baiko was the abbess there.

The nun Baiko was applying herself fervently to prayer, but eventually she got up and saw us. For a brief moment she seemed perplexed by our appearance, but then she broke into a broad smile. Elegant and beautiful, Baiko was nothing at all like Myoren, the Koicha nun. Her fair-skinned, round face was as mild and gentle as the Kannon's. She wore a light-brown headscarf over her shaven head and had on a black travelling cloak. She must have been over sixty.

Still fingering her prayer beads, she walked over to us slowly.

"What devotion, Mother Abbess!" said Miyako.

"I have much on my mind, my child..."

A shadow crossed the abbess's brow as she took a long, hard look at me.

"The gentleman is of the House of the East?" she enquired.

"Yes," said Miyako. "This is Tatsuya-san. Tatsuya, this is Mother Baiko, from the Keisho-in monastery."

I bowed my head.

"How lucky I am to have run into you like this," said the abbess. "I was just about to make my way to the main house to help the priest from the Maroo-ji temple."

"We're much obliged," I said.

"How is he?" asked Miyako. "I heard that he'd been ill."

"There's no remedy for old age, as they say... That is why Eisen will be there in his stead today. I've been asked to lend a hand."

"Much obliged... Shall we make our way down together?"

When we came to the top of the stone staircase, Baiko hesitated and turned around.

"It's such a terrible pity..." she said.

"How do you mean, Mother Abbess?"

"I was thinking about the Kotake cedar," she replied, pointing to the tree that had been struck down by lightning.

"Come again?" I asked, startled. "You mean, that one was called 'Kotake'?"

"Yes," she replied. "And the other was called Koume. Twin cedars, you see. So, when twins were born to the House of the East, they were named after these two cedars." Her voice had darkened when she carried on. "To think, these trees must have been growing side by side for hundreds, maybe even thousands, of years, and then in a flash one of them is struck down forever… It fills me with such dread, as though it's a sign that something else terrible is going to happen."

Baiko, too, had her roots in the village: even she was unable to escape the legend of the eight graves. It left me feeling unsettled yet again.

A SENSELESS MURDER

When we arrived home, accompanied by Baiko, the priest had just turned up, and guests were arriving in dribs and drabs.

For generations, the Tajimi family had belonged to a Zen sect and worshipped at the Renko-ji temple in the village, but ever since his youth, my late brother Hisaya had practically worshipped a Shingon high priest called Choei from the Maroo-ji temple in the neighbouring village, and so the funeral and services were carried out by representatives of both temples.

Though perched just on the other side of the border, the Maroo-ji temple had strong ties to Eight Graves, with many worshippers coming from there. However, Choei, the high priest, was already eighty and bedridden, so most of the services were carried out instead by his curate Eisen, who had arrived at the temple after the war. The Keisho-in monastery at Bankachi was a branch of the Maroo-ji temple, so whenever they were short of hands, Baiko would offer her services.

In towns nowadays, temple services are often very simple affairs, but that is not the case in the countryside. Whenever anything happens in a family, regardless of whether it is joyous or sorrowful, money is no object. And so today, on the day of the memorial, the Tajimi family, which was said to be the wealthiest in the region, had invited dozens and dozens of guests.

The service began around two o'clock, but since it was conducted by representatives of both temples, it was getting on for five by the time it ended. The meal, which followed the service, was no small affair either.

The woodcutters, cattle-herders, boatmen and other household employees, together with the farmers, ate without ceremony on the dirt floor of a room near the kitchen. The family, on the other hand, along with the great and the good of the village, dined in the two tatami rooms, from which the partition had been removed. Each of the guests was to be served a feast of several courses on individual trays, but an even more elaborate *honzen* repast was to be set before the two priests.

All the instructions had been given by Koume and Kotake, but Haruyo, for whose health I feared, had been charged with seeing that they were carried out to the letter.

"Are you all right?" I asked her. "If you overexert yourself, you'll only pay for it later."

"I'm fine, thank you. You needn't worry. I'm being careful…"

In the kitchen, the two priests' meals had already been prepared and were lined up alongside almost twenty others. Haruyo looked pale and the life seemed to have drained from her eyes.

"But you don't look at all well," I said. "You ought to leave all that to Oshima and the others. Why don't you go and rest awhile in the annexe?"

"I can't. It won't be for much longer, though… Tatsuya, could you go and ask the guests to take their seats?"

"Yes. Of course."

I was about to go when Noriko stopped me.

"Tatsuya…" she said in a voice that trailed off, glancing at me before immediately lowering her eyes.

It was the first time that she had uttered so much as a word to me, let alone called me by my given name. My heart skipped a beat, but Noriko was so frail, like a flower trying to blossom in the shade, that I immediately laughed. Had she been more youthful, more feminine, more alluring, then maybe... Although, she had put on a touch of make-up that day.

"What is it, Noriko?"

"It's the abbess from the Keisho-in monastery... She'd like a word with you."

"Ah, thank you. Where is she?"

"This way..."

She led me to a room just beside the entrance, where Baiko was getting ready to leave.

"Are you leaving us already? I think we're just about to serve the meal..."

"Thank you, but I mustn't be late. I'm no longer a young woman, so I really must excuse myself."

"Tatsuya..." came Noriko's voice from behind me. "If the Mother Abbess would like, we could send somebody with her meal later."

I was impressed by this feminine presence of mind.

"Ah, yes, of course. We'll have your meal sent on for you, Mother Abbess."

"That's very kind of you."

Baiko made a slight bow of her shaved head, but then, after quickly looking round, she whispered in my ear.

"You must come and see me," she said. "I have something to tell you, something very important."

I was taken aback by this.

"You will come, won't you?" she asked, looking around once again. "It's imperative that you come. Alone. Without anyone. I wanted to tell you before, at the Eight Graves shrine, but the young lady from the House of the West was there… Please, don't forget. Only I and the high priest of the Maroo-ji temple know about this… Well, till tomorrow perhaps. I'll be expecting you."

She pulled away suddenly and once again stared right into my eyes, as though wishing to impart something. Then, bowing stiffly, she took her leave.

I was at a total loss. What, I wondered, was the meaning of these words that she had whispered to me? I just stood there, dumbfounded, rooted to the spot, looking dazed and confused. Eventually, I managed to pull myself together. I decided to ask her what she had meant by it all, but by the time that I went out into the vestibule, she was nowhere to be seen.

I suddenly realized that Noriko was standing behind me. "What was it that she wanted to tell you?" she asked, an odd hint of childlike curiosity floating in her eyes.

"Oh, er…" I replied, extracting a handkerchief from my pocket and mopping my brow. "I really haven't the faintest idea…"

I returned to the reception room to find that everybody had taken their seats. At the top of the room sat the priest Kozen from the Renko-ji temple and beside him the curate Eisen from the Maroo-ji temple. My place was to their left. To my left sat Koume and Kotake, followed by Haruyo, who had yet to take her place, then Shintaro and Noriko, and finally Dr Kuno with his wife and eldest son.

On the opposite side sat the village mayor, followed by the head of the House of the West, Shokichi Nomura, and his wife. Next came Miyako, and beside her was a gentleman of around forty-five, with a pale complexion and a fine moustache, to whom I had only just been introduced that very day—it was Dr Shuhei Arai. He told me that he had been evacuated from Osaka during the war, yet he had the crisp, pure accent of a

Tokyoite. He had an easy way about him, and it was only natural that Dr Kuno should have been eclipsed by him. Since he had been the one to carry out my brother's first autopsy, Koume and Kotake had insisted that he join us that day. After Dr Arai sat my maternal grandmother together with her adoptive son Kaneyoshi. The last two were unknown to me, or, rather, I had been introduced to them, but I had forgotten them since.

I passed the room and went straight to the kitchen, where I asked that Baiko's meal be taken to the monastery.

"What?" cried Haruyo. "Has the Mother Abbess gone already? What a pity. But we'll do as you suggest. Someone will take it to her later."

I turned to leave.

"Oh, Tatsuya…" Haruyo called after me. "I'm sorry to ask you, but would you mind carrying in one of the trays?"

"Of course not. Which one?"

"Do you see the two trays for the priests over there? Just carry one of them through and take your seat. I'll bring the other one."

"These ones? Which is which?"

"It doesn't matter. They're both the same."

We each took a tray.

"Oshima," said Haruyo. "If you could serve the others in order of precedence… I'll take my seat after I've carried this through."

"Yes, Miss," she replied.

Haruyo and I entered the reception room, carrying the trays together. I placed my tray in front of Kozen, the priest from the Renko-ji temple, while my sister placed hers in front of Eisen. Both priests bowed their heads in acknowledgement and turned up the sleeves of their vestments, preparing to eat.

Having served the most honoured guests, we took our seats, whereupon Oshima, assisted by some other maids, began to serve the rest of those present as Haruyo had asked her. After all the trays had been distributed, flasks of sake were brought in, and at last the meal could commence.

"I'm afraid it isn't much," I apologized, "but, please, do begin."

Bowing their heads slightly, Kozen and Eisen picked up the sake cups that were sitting in front of them.

This Kozen was a man in his early thirties, emaciated, and with a pair of very thick glasses that perched on his nose. In his case, it was very much the robes that made the monk, for otherwise one could be have been forgiven for thinking him a university student who had been held back several years. Eisen, on the other hand, though only a curate, looked well over fifty. His greying hair gave him an imposing appearance. He, too, was myopic and wore thick glasses, which made his eyes seem even narrower than they were. Down each of his cheeks there ran a deep crease that seemed to tell of the hardships of his past.

On occasions such as this, the conversation usually began with reminiscences of the deceased, but given the peculiarity of my brother's death, we avoided talking about him altogether, preferring instead to focus on Kozen. It so transpired that the priest was still a bachelor, so Nomura-san took it upon himself to find him a match. Hearing this, the young priest blushed as red as a lobster, and sweat began to bead on his forehead. It was so comical that Miyako even joined in the teasing. The priest looked ready to explode, which in turn made everybody present laugh.

It may well have been funny then, but only a moment later something terrible happened, something that made our blood run cold... Even now, to recall it makes my hand tremble as I write.

It seemed that neither Kozen nor Eisen cared all that much for sake. Having drunk that first offering, they turned their cups over and picked up their chopsticks. Many of the other guests followed suit, so Oshima was kept busy replenishing their bowls of rice.

It was then that a sharp cry made me look up.

"W-w-what's wrong? What's the matter with you?"

I saw Eisen trying to prop up Kozen from behind. Kozen had dropped his chopsticks and was leaning with one hand on the floor, while he clawed at his chest with the other.

"Argh... I ca—... I can't breathe!... W-w-water!"

Four or five people leapt to their feet at once and ran to the kitchen, while the others half-rose.

"Brother Kozen! What's the matter? Hang on!" voices called out.

The mayor came over and looked into the priest's eyes.

"I can't breathe!... M-m-my chest!... My chest!..."

Kozen clawed at the tatami mat with his fingernails, gripped by violent convulsions, the pain of which seemed almost inhuman. Then, with a terrible groan, he vomited blood over the tray.

Somebody screamed. The entire company got to their feet, and some even ran out of the room.

Such was the scene of the third murder.

AN AVERSION TO PICKLES

This nightmare of mine was far from over. This absurd, insane uproar, this farce of a murder, the meaning of which escaped me... Many more of these terrifying experiences still awaited me. Among them all, however, none chilled me as much as seeing Kozen's death throes.

The moment he saw Kozen vomit blood, Dr Arai leapt to his feet, but then he seemed to recollect himself.

"Dr Kuno, could you assist me?" he called out.

Even now, I cannot forget the look on Dr Kuno's face as I turned to look at him. He was still half-seated, leaning over his tray. His brow was drenched in perspiration, and his eyes were bulging. Clutching his cup, his right hand rested on his knee but trembled violently. Suddenly there was a sharp crack—he had been clenching the cup so tightly in his fist that he had crushed it.

Dr Arai's appeal for help seemed to bring Dr Kuno to his senses. He took out his handkerchief and mopped his brow, but only then did he realize that his palm was bleeding. Having hastily tied the handkerchief around the wound, he stood up and went over to help his colleague, his knees still shaking.

Dr Arai seemed puzzled by Dr Kuno's behaviour, but he promptly turned his attention to an examination of the priest.

"Could somebody get me my bag?" he asked. "It's by the entrance."

Miyako got up to fetch it. The doctor administered two injections, then a third, but finally he shook his head in resignation.

"It's no good. Nothing more can be done."

"What was the cause of death, Doctor?" asked Nomura, devastated by the news.

"I won't be able to say for sure until the post-mortem has been carried out, but it certainly looks the same as it was in Hisaya's case. What is your opinion, Dr Kuno?"

Dr Kuno just stared ahead vacantly, as though he hadn't heard Dr Arai's question.

Everybody was looking suspiciously at Dr Kuno, but right then somebody jabbed me in the back.

"It was him! It was him! He's the one who poisoned him!"

Startled, I spun around and saw, directly in front of me, Eisen, pointing his finger at me and with a savage look about him.

"You bastard! You're the one who poisoned him! You bastard! First, you killed your own grandfather. Then, you killed your brother. And just now you tried to kill me, but instead you killed him by accident!"

A worm-like vein on Eisen's forehead looked as though it was ready to explode, and behind his thick glasses his eyes were completely bloodshot. An icy chill passed through the room.

Somebody came running up behind me and pushed me aside, putting herself between me and Eisen. It was Haruyo.

"Can you even hear yourself?!" Her voice was trembling with indignation. "What possible reason could Tatsuya have to want to kill you? You've only just met him! He doesn't have anything to do with you!"

Eisen looked stunned, as if only just returning to his senses. He looked around. Everybody's attention was focused on him. This seemed to shock him even more, and in confusion he mopped his brow with the sleeve of his robe.

"I... I... I'm sorry... I didn't mean..."

"You didn't mean what, exactly? Hmm? We're waiting. Why should Tatsuya want to poison you? Why should he want to kill you, eh?"

Breathing heavily, Haruyo took another step closer to Eisen.

"I... I didn't mean anything by it," he said, losing more and more of his composure. "It was just the fright of seeing something so awful, it made me lose my head for a moment... I don't know what came over me... Please, I beg you, forget what I said..."

"No matter how frightened you were, you can't go around saying such things! So once again, I'm asking you to explain clearly: what did you mean by that?..."

"Calm down, Haruyo, it's all right," I said. "You mustn't work yourself up like that. It'll do you no good."

"But he's gone too far..."

Haruyo hid her face behind her sleeve and began to weep, her shoulders convulsing with her sobs.

But why, really, had Eisen said such an outrageous thing? Even if he did lose his head, he was hardly likely to blurt out something that wasn't already a possibility in his mind. As soon as he realized that Kozen had been poisoned, he must have suspected that he was the intended victim. But why?...

"First, you killed your own grandfather. Then, you killed your brother. And just now you tried to kill me..."

Those were his words. Why had Eisen said this? Why would I have set my sights on Eisen after my grandfather and brother? I didn't know. It was a mystery to me. I couldn't understand any of it.

Whatever his reasons, Kozen's poisoning stirred up yet another maelstrom of terror in the village. It was only natural, for before the victims—that is, my grandfather and my brother—were members of the Tajimi family. But now there was a victim whose only connection to the House of the East was that he had served at the family temple. It was difficult enough to grasp at the meaning of those first two murders, but this third one surpassed all reason. Could the killer be some maniac who was content to poison his victims at random?

Having been alerted to the situation immediately, the village constable came running to the scene of the crime. He was followed later that evening by a deluge of officers from the town of N——, led by Detective Inspector Isokawa, a veteran of Okayama constabulary's Criminal Investigation Bureau. When the investigation into the strange death of my brother was launched, he chose N—— as his base of operations and had been making daily trips to the village ever since. His arrival was thus by no means unexpected, but what was strange was the presence of that stuttering Kosuke Kindaichi as well. What surprised me even more was that this Kindaichi fellow seemed to enjoy considerable respect among the officers. Even Inspector Isokawa spoke to him with marked deference.

Their investigation found that the poison responsible for Kozen's death had been mixed into a dish of pickles. With regard to the opportunity, it was established that, with the exception of the soup, the priests' food, along with the twenty or so other meals, had been assembled in the kitchen and left there while the sutra was being recited in the reception room. During that time, there were constant comings and goings in the kitchen, as maids and serving boys came to fetch water and cups. Thus, practically anyone could have found an opportunity to mix the poison into the priest's food. One mystery remained, however: how could the culprit know which tray was meant for Kozen? It was obvious enough which two trays were meant for the priests, so the culprit could rest assured that he wasn't going to poison himself by accident, but even the Buddha himself couldn't have guessed which of those two trays would make its way to Kozen.

It was purely by chance that I had picked up the tray with the poisoned dish, while my sister had taken the other one. It was also purely by chance that I had been standing on my sister's right as we entered the room, which is why it was I who set down the tray with the poisoned dish before Kozen. Neither my will nor that of my sister played any part in it. Thus, if I had picked up the other tray, or if I happened to have found myself standing on my sister's left, then Eisen would have become the killer's third victim.

Did it not matter, then, which priest took the poison? But what a senseless murder that would be…

It all seemed mad. It all seemed deranged. Yet the criminal's execution was so exceedingly brilliant that, clearly, he could be neither a halfwit nor insane. If this business seemed mad to us, was it only because we could not figure out his plan? Were the three successive murders just three points on the circumference of a bloody circle that the murderer was drawing? And was it not possible that we would fail to grasp the meaning of these killings until the circle was completed?

That evening, we were subjected a curious experiment at the scene of the crime, which is to say in the large tatami room. Apparently, it was conducted at the instigation of Kosuke Kindaichi. We were all asked to resume our seats, just as we had been sitting during the meal. Fortunately, Dr Arai had had the presence of mind to forbid anyone from touching anything at the scene. The only thing that had been moved was the body, which had been taken away for the post-mortem examination; all the trays remained exactly as they had been left. And so we each sat down in front of our own.

"Take a good look," Kosuke Kindaichi ordered us. "You need to be sure that you're in front of the tray you had earlier. Check this carefully."

We all did as he asked, paying particular attention to the amounts of food left on each of our small plates. We were all able to confirm that everything seemed just it should be. Kosuke Kindaichi then went around, checking each bowl of pickles one by one and making notes in his notebook.

"I see… Hmm… Interesting…"

He was checking to see who had eaten the pickles and who had not. He must have made the following deduction: given the obvious distinction between the ordinary meals and those prepared for the priests, the culprit could be reasonably sure that he would not be served the poisoned dish. However, knowing that dishes are often swapped from tray to tray and that food is sometimes moved from one dish to another so as to even out the portions, he would still have to be on his guard. Anybody

116

could have swapped the dishes or moved the food from one bowl to another after the culprit had added the poison; thus it was unlikely that the criminal would have touched the pickles on his tray...

It was only much later that Kosuke Kindaichi revealed to me the results of his investigation. The only person who had not touched the pickles was me!

I never did like pickles...

EISEN'S TRIP

I felt utterly exhausted. I was too tired even to think. It was all too much for me.

A man's ability to withstand strain and tension has its limits, naturally. When that limit is crossed, the thread holding the weight of that strain snaps, while the sack containing all that tension bursts open. When that happens, they say you're burnt out. Well, that night I was well and truly burnt out.

It was decided that Kozen's post-mortem examination would be carried out on site, so the body was moved to another room. On Inspector Isokawa's instruction, a telegram was sent to the constabulary headquarters for the pathologist Dr M—— again.

After the formalities had been concluded, we were inter-rogated one by one late into the evening. In the previous two cases, it was impossible to know where or how the poisoning had taken place, but this time it was clear. The killer had been under our very roof and had taken advantage of the pandemonium in the kitchen to add the poison. In other words, the person who had murdered my grandfather, my brother and now the priest was in fact somebody close to me. The very thought of it sent a chill down my spine.

The interrogation was as gruelling as it was unrelenting. It was I who was subjected to the fiercest questioning by the police. This series of unfortunate incidents had clouded the minds of even the most level-headed officers, in whose eyes I had already become a kind of monster: a maniac who killed, without reason, anyone in his path… Unable to imagine another culprit, they had found in me their prime suspect.

After all, I had such a notorious father. The violent blood that ran in his veins also ran in mine. Rather than fuelling a blazing fire, had it not perhaps this time manifested itself in the cool composure of a maniacal poisoner?…

My birth was entwined with a terrible, bloody tragedy. Was this dark star pushing me to commit those same heinous crimes?…

Another disadvantage was my status as an outsider. To the villagers, I had the incomprehensibility of a perfect stranger. That is why nobody could defend me with any real conviction. Perhaps even my sister had considered the possibility of my guilt. The thought made my pain all the more intolerable.

If this was true of my sister, then it was only natural that the suspicious eyes of the police would fall on me. I was subjected to barrages of questions from all sides. Sometimes oblique, sometimes direct, they came at me with a ferocity that was unrelenting, so much so that I was drained both mentally and physically.

In the days of Edo, they devised a torture in the form of sleep deprivation. For days on end, the prisoner would be kept awake, until he reached a state of such utter exhaustion that he could be made to confess to absolutely anything. That evening, of course, the police's methods did not quite stretch to that, but they did, nevertheless, place me under such strain and duress that I felt as though I were a prisoner being tortured.

Maybe I was a monster without realizing it. Maybe I did have some dark alter ego lurking inside me, and this other me was committing all manner of horrors without my knowing it… Yes, even ridiculous things like that did cross my mind. I was on the verge of saying: "Yes, it's true. I did it. It was all me. Here is my confession. Now will you all please leave me in peace?"

It was none other than Kosuke Kindaichi who rescued me from these thoughts, however.

"Come, come, Inspector. Whoever the culprit is, you aren't going to solve the case overnight. After all, there's no clear motive. In the cases of both Ikawa-san and Hisaya, the motive seemed to be clear at first, but the more you think about it, the more you have to admit that it isn't clear at all. As for Kozen… well, the motive is nowhere to be found. What can the murderer have in mind? Until we establish a motive, we can't just go around making rash accusations."

This Kosuke Kindaichi seemed to have a curiously powerful effect on Inspector Isokawa: his words alone saved me from the onslaught of any further interrogation.

"Yes, you're quite right," said the inspector with a bitter laugh. "This case is truly fiendish. What took place twenty-six years ago was unprecedented in its atrocity, but at least the case itself was clear-cut. This one, on the other hand, may be a more modest affair, but it's far more challenging than the last… Damn it! Can they really be giving us this much trouble after two generations?"

It had already gone eleven by the time the police officers left, leaving two detectives behind to keep watch over Kozen's body. The post-mortem was due to be carried out in the house the very next day, once the pathologist Dr M——had arrived.

Shortly after the police left, the guests, who had been detained for questioning, sneaked away, leaving the enormous house in an atmosphere of abject desolation, like a beach after the ebb of the tide.

I no longer had the strength to do anything. I was overcome by a feeling of sadness. Drained of energy, I collapsed in the middle of the tatami room, in all its disarray, and, despite myself, tears flowed one after another…

Nobody spoke a word to me. I could hear the clatter of dishes being washed in the kitchen, but no voices. No doubt Oshima and the rest of the maids would be talking about the day's tragedy, but they must have been whispering on my account. If that was so, their suspicions about me must have taken root. Even the restrained clatter of dishes seemed to imply this.

Oh, how alone I was! Nobody took my side or said a kind word to me. As I was overcome by this wretched feeling of loneliness, somebody suddenly took my shoulders and, as though having read my mind, said: "Don't worry, I'll always be on your side."

It was my sister Haruyo.

She hugged me tightly.

"It doesn't matter what others say. I'll always be on your side. Never forget that. I believe you. More than that: I know it. I know you could never be capable of something like that…"

Never has the compassion of another touched me so. Instinctively, I placed my head in her lap, just like a child.

"Oh, Haruyo… What should I do? Maybe I was wrong to come back here. If that's the case, I can always go back to Kobe. Tell me what to do, Haruyo."

"Don't talk nonsense," she said, stroking my back gently. "You mustn't even think about returning to Kobe. You're family. What could possibly be wrong with your being here? This is your home. This is where you belong."

"But, Haruyo, what if my being here has been the cause of all these terrible deaths? Then I shouldn't stay here another minute. Tell me, Haruyo, who's doing this? And what does it all have to do with me?"

"Tatsuya," she replied, her voice quavering, "you mustn't think such silly things. How could you possibly have anything to do with all this horrible business? Isn't that much clear from what happened to Hisaya? When could you have had the opportunity to substitute the sachets? You'd only just arrived…"

"But… but that isn't what the police think. They seem to think I have some knack for black magic."

"That's only because everybody is so on edge right now. Once they've calmed down, they'll come to see that it's all a misunderstanding. You really mustn't despair, Tatsuya…"

"Oh, Haruyo!…"

I tried to speak, but my voice caught in my throat and no sound came from my mouth. For a while, we sat there in silence.

"Oh, yes, that's it," my sister said, as though suddenly remembering something. "The other day you asked me something odd."

"I did?"

"Yes, you asked me whether anybody had left the village recently… What exactly did you mean by that?"

Her tone suggested that something had occurred to her. I looked her up and down. Her face was puffy with exhaustion, but she had a certain glint in her eyes.

Without omitting any details, I told her how a man had been going around Kobe, making all sorts of enquiries about me and my character. I then added that this stranger had no connection whatsoever with Mr Suwa, who had been entrusted with the task of finding me, and that he appeared to have come from somewhere in the countryside.

My sister's eyes widened in astonishment, and she asked me when exactly this had happened. I managed to work out the date, counting the fingers on my hands. My sister did likewise and sighed heavily.

"Just as I thought," she said, leaning in. "The days match exactly… When you came to me, Tatsuya, you asked whether anyone *from this village* had gone away. That's why it didn't even occur to me. But there was somebody who went away then, somebody not of this village but with close links to it."

"Who? Who was it, Haruyo?"

"It was Brother Eisen, from the Maroo-ji temple."

I looked at my sister in amazement. I felt as though I had been hit over the head.

"Is that true, Haruyo?" I asked, my voice trembling.

"Absolutely. There's no doubt about it. He said some truly bizarre things to you earlier, so I went for him. It was then that I remembered. At the beginning of last month, he went off somewhere, supposedly to some temple or other, for five or six days."

A shiver ran through me. I was so agitated that I felt as though my teeth were chattering.

"What kind of a man is Brother Eisen?" I asked. "Does he have any ties to our family?"

"None at all. He turned up at the Maroo-ji temple shortly after the war. They say that he was in charge of a mission out in Manchuria before that. He seems to be an old friend of Father Choei, but ever since he fell ill, Brother Eisen has been carrying out his role. I've no idea what his background is, though."

If the man who had showed up in Kobe was indeed Eisen, then what could he possibly have wanted? Why was he so interested in me?

"Could it be that Brother Eisen knows something about these murders? Judging by what he said today…"

"He must do," said Haruyo plainly. "Otherwise, he wouldn't have said such terrible things… He apologized for it afterwards, claiming that he had lost his head, but whether he lost his head or not, he'd hardly be likely to blurt something out that he hadn't been already thinking. Do you remember what he said?"

How could I ever forget? Shuddering at the very memory of it, I merely nodded without saying a word.

"Wasn't there anything in what he said that particularly struck you? Of course, he must be under some misapprehension. But there must be a reason for that misapprehension."

Nothing leapt to mind. I was reminded once again of my isolation in that village, and I hung my head in despair.

Just then, Oshima came in.

"Excuse me, sir…" she said, bowing at the door. "The mistresses have asked to see you."

"Thank you, Oshima," said Haruyo. "Tell them we'll be right there."

But just as Haruyo was about to get up, Oshima stopped her.

"You needn't trouble yourself, Miss… They've asked to see the master alone…"

Haruyo and I looked at each other in bewilderment.

POISONED TEA

It had been a week since I arrived in this house, but never yet had I found myself alone with my great-aunts. Whenever I met them, it was always in the presence of Haruyo or somebody else.

Now all of a sudden—and what's more, late in the evening, after such a terrible occurrence—they had expressed a desire to see me without my sister. A sense of unease assailed me. I had no particular cause to refuse, however, so I got to my feet and followed Oshima. With an anxious look, my sister watched me go.

123

The twins occupied the rearmost part of the main building—that is, two rooms measuring eight and six tatami mats, found at the far end of the hundred-foot-long corridor that led to the annexe. They both slept in the larger of the rooms, their pillows snugly placed side by side.

When I followed Oshima into the room, I found Koume and Kotake quietly sipping tea without showing any signs of turning in for the night. As always, I was unable to identify which was which. As they turned to look at me, their mouths drew into broad smiles, like a pair of drawstring purses.

"Ah, Tatsuya... Thank you for coming to see us. Come, sit down here."

"You may go, Oshima. We won't be needing you again tonight."

These strange, monkey-like figures spoke like this in turn. I took a seat where one of them had indicated, while Oshima silently withdrew, bowing her head.

"Is there something I can do for you, Aunties?" I asked, looking from one twin to the other.

"Oh, my child, you mustn't stand on ceremony. This is your house, after all. You should make yourself more at home. Isn't that right, Kotake?"

"Quite right, Koume. There's nothing to be afraid of, Tatsuya. Now that Hisaya is dead, you are the rightful master of this house, and you should act accordingly."

When people live to such a venerable age, even the most unsettling events must be like water off a duck's back. In any event, neither Koume nor Kotake acted as though there had been any drama at all that day. This only unsettled me all the more. I could feel the skin crawl on the soles of my feet.

"Well then, what can I do for you?" I repeated the question.

"Ah, well, you see... There was nothing in particular. Only you must be exhausted, so we wanted to offer you some tea."

"That's right. Your nerves must be frayed after all these dreadful events. But we have a fine tea for you. Would you mind doing the honours, Koume?"

"Right away."

Koume artfully mixed the thick green tea in a cup and served it to me. Attempting in vain to fathom their intentions, I kept looking from one old woman to the other in perplexity.

"What's the matter? Koume has prepared the tea for you especially. Won't you even try it?" Kotake urged me.

Having no reason to object, I placed the cup to my lips. Startled, I looked at them again.

A strange, bitter taste lingered on my tongue... As I watched, I saw Koume and Kotake exchange a look that seemed pregnant with meaning. A shiver ran down my spine and I broke out in a cold sweat.

The maniac behind these poisonings... Could it be these two old women?

"Why the strange face, Tatsuya? Don't you like it? Come on, drink it up..."

"Yes, come on..."

"Oh-ho-ho, what a strange child you are... Why do you look so anxious? It isn't as though it's poisoned... Come now, drink it up in a single draught."

Would the poisoner be so ingenuous? These two old women with their drawstring-purse mouths seemed cheerful enough. But still, how anxiously they stared at my hands as I held that cup.

"What are you waiting for? Come now, drink up and get to bed. It's already late."

"Yes, you must be exhausted after everything today. Just drink up the tea and you'll have a good night's sleep. Nothing beats a good night's sleep."

I found myself in a corner. I couldn't spit out the bitter-tasting tea, but what would have been the point of that anyway? I had already swallowed some of it. What did it matter now? Seized by a kind of desperate courage, I drained the cup in a single gulp. I was in the grip of an indefinable mix of thrill, terror and despair, my hand trembling like a leaf...

"There, he drank it."

"Yes, there's a good boy."

Koume and Kotake looked at one another. They seemed to be enjoying this, smiling and hunching their shoulders like little girls.

Another shiver ran down my spine. I looked down, as though trying to see what was happening inside my body. Wasn't my stomach about to twist in agony? Wasn't a trickle of blood about to well up in my chest?...

"Excellent... You may go now, Tatsuya."

"Koume is right. You must return to the annexe and rest now. Go, get some sleep."

"Yes, get some sleep."

I bowed to them and got to my feet unsteadily. I was so dizzy that the whole room seemed to be spinning. Haruyo was waiting for me anxiously in the corridor.

"What did they want to see you about?" she asked me.

"Nothing. They offered me a cup of tea."

"Tea?"

She frowned, looking suspicious, and only then did she notice my face.

"What's the matter with you, Tatsuya? You look so pale. And you're sweating terribly..."

"I'm fine, really. I'm just a little tired. I'll be right as rain after a good night's sleep. Good night, Haruyo."

I brushed aside the hand that my sister offered me and

126

staggered my way to the annexe. There, I found that Oshima had already prepared my bed. I felt unsteady, as though I were drunk on bad sake. After changing into my nightclothes, I turned off the light and stretched out under the duvet.

When I was a child, I was taken to see a play in which a samurai was forced to drink what he knew to be poisoned sake. He then spent three years locked in the keep of a castle, watching himself as his health declined until at last the light of his life was extinguished... That was exactly how I felt that evening. I tried to focus, alert to any changes going on inside my body, and as I did, I sank into a state of profound despair. There, in the darkness, I closed my eyes, and a multitude of dismal and bloody scenes unfolded before me.

But nothing untoward happened. Or rather, before any pains had time to manifest themselves, my overwrought nerves, unable to endure any more strain, yielded. Before I knew it, I was sound asleep. And when, in the dead of night, I suddenly awoke, alert to some unknown presence, I had no idea what hour it was.

A MYSTERIOUS RITE

Ever since I was young, I have had a peculiar idiosyncrasy. Perhaps it would be more fitting to call it a "condition". It happens whenever I am extremely tired, or if I have to sit an exam and my nerves are frayed. At night, I'll go to bed and start to drift off, but then I'll wake up with a start. Only I won't really wake up. I'll be half-conscious, while my muscles will remain perfectly asleep.

Only somebody who has experienced this can appreciate the true terror and distress that it causes. My mind will be awake. I'll have a vague awareness of what is going on around me. Yet my body will be completely immobilized, so much that I won't be able to move anything. If I try to speak, I'll find that my tongue is frozen, and I'll be incapable of making so much as a sound. In short, I'll be in a state of perfect paralysis.

That is how I found myself when suddenly I awoke that night. There was a strange presence with me in the room, however. It was another person: I could sense something in the air, a feeling of somebody holding their breath. Even before that, I could clearly discern, though my closed eyelids, a strange glimmer of light coming from somewhere in the darkness. And yet, despite it all, there was absolutely nothing that I could do. Every muscle in my body was totally unresponsive.

My fear brought me out in a sweat that scalded me like boiling water. I wanted to speak, to cry out, but, as always, my tongue was frozen and no words came. I tried to move my limbs and sit up, but my body refused to move, as though it were trapped beneath the duvet. Even my eyelids seemed to be glued shut and would not open. Anybody watching me would have thought that I was dead.

This is probably what reassured my visitor, who stealthily crept up to me. Then, after some hesitation, the figure finally reached the side of my bed and peered down at my face from above. At least, I had a feeling that someone was looking down on me.

For a few moments, the stranger sat by my bedside without stirring, just watching me with bated breath. Gradually the breathing grew stronger. I felt a warm breath caress my face. It was then that something bizarre occurred. A drop of warm liquid fell on my cheek.

A tear!

Startled by this realization, I took a deep breath. My visitor, too, must have been surprised, for the figure immediately drew back in panic and watched for any other reaction on my part. By now reassured, the stranger again moved closer, but suddenly drew back again for some reason. After a few moments of stillness, the stranger, still breathing heavily, got to their feet.

It was then that my paralysis began to wear off. The heaviness in my eyelids, against which I had been struggling frantically, lightened.

I opened my eyes, and all of a sudden my whole body was overcome by a terror that electrified me. Somebody was standing in front of the folding screen with the three sages. The figure was facing away from me, so all I could see was the back, but it looked just as though the priest Foyin had stepped out of the screen and come to life.

I suddenly remembered the story that Haruyo had told me only the other day—that the woodcutter Heikichi had spent the night in this room, and that he too had seen a figure emerge from the screen...

I opened my eyes wide in order to try and see who this figure was. But the vague glimmer that had lit the room suddenly disappeared, and the mysterious silhouette vanished into the darkness, as though sucked back into the screen.

It took my every last ounce of strength to overcome that accursed torpor. All I could do was to breathe as deeply as possible, hoping that the effect of it would wake me up. I had found that this was occasionally successful in shaking off the paralysis. However, before my efforts could have any effect, I had to hold my breath once again, for I could hear somebody coming along the long corridor...

Soft, catlike footsteps, the gentle rustle of a kimono... The sound passed through the connecting door and moved towards the veranda. It stopped just outside my room, on the other side of the sliding door, and waited there, motionless, for a few moments.

I closed my eyes and held my breath again. My heart was pounding and the sweat was streaming down my forehead.

One moment, a moment more…

When at last the sliding door opened, a dim light entered the room, followed by a figure. But that figure was not alone: there were two of them. I opened my eyes ever so slightly and looked towards the door. An odd sensation assailed me.

It was Koume and Kotake. One of them was carrying an antique lantern. Amid the darkness, its dim light revealed their vague silhouettes.

They were both dressed in matching black kimonos and had quartz prayer beads around their wrists. Even more curious was that they were both leaning on walking sticks.

Trying to move as quietly as possible, they stole up to my bedside and, raising the lantern, leant over me. Needless to say, I quickly closed my eyes.

"He's sound asleep," one of them whispered.

"The medicine worked," the other replied with a chuckle.

"Look, Kotake… He's drenched in sweat…"

"He must have been exhausted… He's breathing heavily…"

"Poor thing… And the way they hounded him…"

"He looks all right now, though… I doubt he'll wake up anytime soon."

"You're right. Let's go down to the shrine. Today is the anniversary, after all. Even if it's not the right month…"

"Yes indeed, Koume."

"Shall we, Kotake?"

"Yes, let's."

Shuffling their feet and bearing the lantern aloft, Koume and Kotake made their way out to the veranda and quietly closed the sliding door behind them.

Finally, I awoke and sat bolt upright in bed.

Was it all a dream?... No, this had been no dream. Koume and Kotake were making their way around the veranda and heading in the direction of the lavatory. As they went, the light from the lantern cast the shadows of the two old women on the sliding door.

Behind the large tatami room in which I was sleeping was a smaller room with a wooden floor. I suppose you would call it a storage room. It was crammed with all sorts of old furniture, including wicker baskets, wooden trunks, a large chest of the kind used to store suits of armour and even an antique palanquin, which a previous owner must have used on his travels. This seemed to be the room that the twins had entered.

I took a deep breath.

I have, I believe, already mentioned that there were two masks hanging on the wall beside the alcove in my room—one depicting a demon, the other a sea spirit. Well... as soon as the old women went into the storage room, a faint light appeared in the demon's eyes. The light flickered just like a candle, growing now brighter, now fainter. For a few moments, I just stared at the light in a daze, until at last it dawned on me what was going on.

I realized that there must have been a small hole in the wall behind the demon mask, which was allowing the light from the lantern carried by one of the twins to filter through. Was this, then, not also the source of that strange glimmer that I had noticed when I woke up earlier on? In other words, wasn't the glimmer caused by a light in the storage room shining through the demon's eyes? And if that light had suddenly disappeared, was it not because whoever had stolen into my room had also escaped into the storage room?

I could feel my heart beating wildly in my chest, clamouring like an alarm bell. I leapt out of bed and crept over to the shelves. That was when I heard the click of a lid being closed

131

in the other room. Suddenly, the flickering in the demon's eyes died away, and the room appeared to be empty.

I experienced an indescribably thrilling sensation.

It was not poison that the twins had given me, but a sleeping draught. They hadn't wanted anybody to see them entering that strange room, so they had tried to ensure that I would be asleep. What, though, could they possibly be doing in that room in the dead of night?

I turned on my lamp warily, before slipping out and entering the storage room on the other side of the alcove. It was dark there, but, just as I expected, there was a beam of electric light coming through the section of wall directly behind the staggered shelves.

"Aunties!… Are you there?…" I called out in a low whisper.

Naturally, I expected no reply. But I wanted to try, nonetheless. Sure enough, no answer came. I resolved to flip the light switch in the storage room. But there was no sign of Koume or Kotake. Apart from the door through which I had entered and the cedar side door leading to the lavatory, there was no way in or out of this room. There was a small window in the northern wall, but it was fitted with bars and the aperture was firmly shut. What was more, the window was bolted from the inside.

I felt another thrill run through my entire body.

There must be a secret passage leading off from this storage room. There could be no doubt about it. The presence of a secret passage provided the only rational explanation for both Haruyo's misgivings about the tatami room as well as the intruder who had frightened the woodcutter Heikichi.

So that was it! Heikichi had claimed that he felt as though he were being watched constantly when he spent that night in the tatami room, so the intruder must have entered the storage room via the secret passage and spied on him through the eyes of the mask before entering the tatami room.

I approached the wall from which the light was coming. I removed a little mirror that was hanging there, and, sure enough, I found behind it two round peepholes. When I placed my eyes to them, I could see the entire tatami room.

Why would somebody have wanted to install a peephole? The thought flashed across my mind, but before I had time to consider the answer, my eyes were drawn back to the storage room. I had to find the location of the secret passage. In addition to the three antique dressers with black-iron casing lining the wall, there were five or six wicker baskets and, standing on a plinth in one corner, a black-lacquer armoury chest. The wicker palanquin was hanging from the ceiling. What drew my eye most, however, was not the pieces furniture, but a large oblong chest standing right in the middle of the room. I immediately associated it with the clicking noise that I had heard earlier. Its lock was broken and just dangled there unfastened.

I lifted the lid. It contained two or three silk bedsheets. Just as I was about to pick them up, however, I heard the clatter of feet beneath me.

I held my breath. The sound was getting nearer. Were Koume and Kotake coming back?

I hastily turned out the light, returned to the room next door and turned out the lamp, too. Just as I was slipping into bed, I heard the sound of the lid being opened in the other room. Then a faint light appeared again in the eyes of the demon mask.

A few moments later, the twins entered my room. I closed my eyes quickly. Bearing the lantern aloft, they peered into my face.

"Look, he's sound asleep, exactly as we left him… How could you think there was a light in the storage room? It must have been your imagination, Kotake."

"Yes, you're right. I don't know what I was thinking. It must have been that fright earlier…"

"You've been talking all sorts of nonsense tonight. Who on earth would be in the passage? Other than *him*…"

"No, I'm certain of it… When the light went out and we were lost in the dark, somebody definitely brushed past me."

"Oh, don't start with that again… Anyway, we should go. Otherwise, Tatsuya might wake up. We can discuss it elsewhere."

Leaning on their canes, the twins made their way down the corridor and back to the main house.

The whole scene had seemed otherworldly to me.

CHAPTER 4

THE FOURTH VICTIM

I was drowning in a sea of tasks that needed to be done and problems that needed to be solved.

First, I had to examine the secret passage. I also had to find out why Koume and Kotake had to use this passage in the dead of night, unseen by prying eyes. Then, there was the matter of who else had used the passage to enter my room and what they had wanted there. Not only that, but I would have to do all this by myself, clandestinely, because even Haruyo seemed to be unaware that this hidden passage existed.

That night, however, not only was I far too exhausted, but also because of the sleeping draught given to me by Koume and Kotake, I lacked the energy to do anything or even to think. Shortly after the twins left to return to the main house, I fell into a deep sleep, dead to the world.

When I awoke the following morning, my head was still heavy. Evidently, the sleeping draught had taken effect only in the small hours. My thoughts were clouded, my limbs weak, and my whole body felt languid. The prospect of the police's return that day only served to darken my mood further. Drowsiness was no excuse to wallow idly, however. There were pressing matters that could not be put off. That morning, I had to pay a visit to Baiko.

The mother abbess, it seemed, knew something of great significance to do with my situation. I had no idea whether this information would help me to solve these poisonings, but right then it seemed to be my only hope. Once the police arrived, I wouldn't be able to leave, so I decided to go straight after breakfast.

I had just got out of bed when Haruyo arrived. She must have been worried after the strange invitation that I had received from my great-aunts the previous night. She seemed relieved to see me.

"Oh, have you just woken up? How are you feeling?"

"I'm fine, thank you. I'm sorry to have worried you last night."

"I'm just glad you're all right, although you still look a little peaky. Try not to fret too much."

"Thank you. I'm sure I'll get used to everything in time."

I decided not to tell her, for the time being, what I had seen the previous night. Given her frail health, I didn't want to add to her troubles.

"I don't know why, but our great-aunts are sleeping late this morning. We needn't wait to have breakfast with them."

While the two of us ate, I asked my sister about Bankachi. My question seemed to surprise her, and she asked in turn why, all of a sudden, I was interested in that place. I gave her a brief account of my conversation with the abbess the previous day.

"Baiko...?" she said, her eyes wide with surprise. "What on earth could she have to tell you?"

"I haven't the faintest idea, but under the circumstances, I'd like to find out whatever it is that she knows about me. In any case, I'd like to leave before the police arrive, otherwise it might be difficult to slip away."

"Yes... Yes, of course... Only it's odd, isn't it?... What could the mother abbess possibly know?"

Deep concern reverberated in her voice. I asked Haruyo what sort of a person this nun was. She told me that she didn't know why Baiko had decided to take holy orders but explained that she had come from a respectable family in the village and had been a nun for as long as she had known her. Even Choei, the high priest of the Maroo-ji temple, demonstrated a deep faith in her and always spoke very highly of her. Consequently, unlike the Koicha nun, Myoren, who had become a nun through sheer opportunism, Baiko was respected throughout the whole village.

"But I wonder what she could possibly have to tell you…"

My sister's tone betrayed a flicker of apprehension. She seemed reluctant to let me go. However, discreet in all things, she did not dare to detain me any further.

Ah, if only she hadn't let me go, I would not now have to relive that horror…

It was around nine o'clock when I finally set out. While the so-called House of the East was located, as well you may imagine, in the east of the village, the Keisho-in monastery was situated in Bankachi, just past the village's westernmost extremity. It was a distance of a mile or so, but since I wanted to avoid meeting anyone as much as possible, I decided to take a detour through the hills.

By now, it was the 3rd of July, and the rainy season showed no signs of letting up; however, the weather was exceptionally fine that day. The birds were chirping merrily in the trees, the green fields stretched out underfoot, and in the rice paddies the verdant seedlings rustled. Here and there, cattle lay sprawled out on the path.

After about half an hour walking, I came to a large mansion. It was the House of the West, the one belonging to the Nomura family. It couldn't hold a candle to the Tajimi house, but it had a large storehouse and a long line of stables, making it stand out from all the other buildings around. It was in one of these annexes that Miyako lived with an elderly maid from her days in Tokyo. From that point on, the path descended into the village, skirting the rear of the Nomura house.

As I passed the grounds, immersed in thoughts of not wanting to meet Miyako, a shrill voice suddenly stopped me in my tracks.

"Hey, you! Where do you think you're going?!"

A figure sprang from an alley, blocking my path. It was the Koicha nun. Startled by her appearance, my legs froze on the spot. She was hunched over, carrying something on her back, but as soon as she saw me, she straightened up triumphantly.

"Go back! Go back! You mustn't take so much as a step out of the House of the East! Wherever you go, a rain of blood is sure to fall. Who is it that you're off to kill this time, eh?"

When I saw those yellow, crooked teeth sticking out of her hideous cleft lip, I couldn't suppress the cold rage welling inside me. I looked her straight in the eye with all the anger that I could muster. I was about to walk on, but, teetering there with her heavy burden, she blocked my way, moving right and left, like a bully picking on a small child.

"No! You won't pass! Don't take another step! Go back! Return to the House of the East, then pack your things and leave this village at once!"

Thanks to the stress and a lack of sleep, I was not in my right mind that day. Unable to control my exasperation, I pushed the nun aside with brute force. This single gesture was enough to send her flying into the wall of the Nomura house. As she slumped onto the ground, the bundle she was carrying made a curious noise.

The nun was astonished. Her cleft lip began to tremble and suddenly she burst into tears.

"Murderer!… Help!… He's trying to kill me!… Quick! Somebody! Help me!…"

Five or six young lads, cattle-herders no doubt, came running to her aid from the back door of the Nomura house. When they saw me, their eyes widened. I didn't dare say a word to their looks of mute reproach.

"Don't just stand there," she shouted. "Grab him! Take him to the police! He just tried to murder me! Ah, it hurts, it hurts!... He just tried to kill me!"

The boys silently encircled me. Had I said so much as a word, I am certain they would have leapt on me. A cold sweat was streaming under my arms. I didn't believe myself to be so cowardly, but it was impossible to reason with these people, and it could never have ended well. Nothing is more frightening in this world than ignorance and stupidity.

I tried to speak, but my tongue froze and no words came out. They took another step towards me, while the nun just kept wailing, spouting all kinds of nonsense. I was in a tricky position, but someone suddenly came rushing out the back door of the Nomura house.

It was Miyako.

With a single glance, she must have understood what was happening. She rushed to my side in order to protect me.

"What's going on here? What do you want with him?"

One of the young men mumbled something, but I couldn't catch his meaning.

Miyako didn't seem to understand either and turned to face me.

"What's going on, Tatsuya?"

I explained as succinctly as I could.

"Just as I thought," she said, frowning and turning back to the youths standing there. "It's the Koicha nun who's at fault here, not Tatsuya. Got it? Now get back to work!"

They all looked at one another and, with a shrug of resignation, went back inside the grounds of the Nomura house. Some of them even stuck out their tongues. The nun, seeing that her allies were gone, got up and fled, crying like a child all the while…

"You gave me quite a fright," Miyako said with a smile of relief. "I wondered what on earth you could have done! Where are you off to, anyway?"

I quickly explained to her about Baiko.

"Oh!" she exclaimed, frowning again. "I wonder what she could possibly have to tell you."

She paused in thought for a moment before adding:

"Well then, I'll accompany you to the monastery. No, no, don't worry. I'll wait for you outside… But I should go with you, just in case something else happens along the way."

Naturally, I was grateful to have her by my side.

The Keisho-in monastery was about a hundred yards from the Nomura house. The name "monastery" seems too grand a word for what it was: a hermitage would sooner describe it. Behind a brushwood hedge stood an ordinary little straw-thatched dwelling. Around five yards from the gate, there was a raised sliding door leading into the building. Two rooms led off the veranda immediately to the left of the entrance. The rain shutters were open, but the sliding doors, which seemed to have been fitted with new paper only recently, were closed, giving an impression of tidiness. A single maple stood in the immaculate front garden.

It struck me as odd that there was a light switched on behind one of the sliding doors. It was a sunny day, and the house didn't appear to be all that dark. Puzzled, I opened the front door and announced myself, but no answer came. I called out a second time, then a third, before stepping into the vestibule. Then I stopped dead in my tracks, as though a bucket of icy water had been thrown over my head.

The internal door was ajar, and as I crossed the dirt floor of the vestibule, I could see into a small tatami room. The mother abbess was lying face down in the middle of the room. The tatami mats were flecked with dark specks, and, by the nun's side, the tray that had been delivered from the Tajimi house lay upturned.

My knees buckled. I felt my throat run dry and my eyes cloud over.

"Wherever you go, a rain of blood is sure to fall…"

The Koicha nun's words came back to me like a bolt of lightning.

She was right. It was just as she said. Here was yet another murder… As I reappeared through the gate, Miyako came up to me.

"What's the matter? Has something happened? You're as white as a sheet."

"She's dead…"

That was all I could say. As she looked at me, her eyes grew wide in amazement. Suddenly she turned on her heel and ran through the gate into the house. I followed after her.

The nun was well and truly dead. The traces of blood on the tatami mats suggested that cause of death was the same as that of my grandfather, my brother and also Kozen. A dark speck of dried blood clung to Baiko's lips.

Miyako and I exchanged a look of dumbfounded shock. It was then that I noticed a scrap of paper that had fallen beside the overturned tray. I picked it up automatically.

The scrap had been torn from a pocket diary, and on it, written with a thick fountain pen, was the following:

TWIN CEDARS:	*Koume*
	Kotake
CATTLE TRADERS:	*Ushimatsu Ikawa*
	Kichizo Kataoka

LANDOWNERS:	Hisaya Tajimi (House of the East)
	Shokichi Nomura (House of the West)
PRIESTS:	Choei (Maroo-ji temple)
	Kozen (Renko-ji temple)
NUNS:	Myoren (Koicha nun)
	Baiko (Bankachi nun)

Of these names, Kotake, Ushimatsu Ikawa, Hisaya Tajimi, Kozen and Baiko had been crossed out in red ink.

A TERRIBLE LOT

"B-b-but... This m-m-must be..."

He was stuttering terribly.

"Th-th-this must be our m-m-motive..."

I don't know whether it was surprise, joy or excitement that made that strange little detective scratch that dishevelled head of his, but whatever it was, it sent a little cloud of dandruff flying like scattered particles of mica.

"Damn it!" Inspector Isokawa roared.

The two men sunk into an icy silence as they examined the scrap of paper. Kosuke Kindaichi kept scratching at his head and tapping his foot compulsively, while the inspector stared wide-eyed at the writing on the scrap of paper.

Watching the two of them, I felt confused, as if I had drunk some bad sake. My head was spinning, my eyes were twitching, and I felt as though I were about to throw up at any moment. A languorous sense of fatigue spread throughout my entire body, and I would have had no compunction about collapsing there and then.

Truly, what I would have given only to run away and disappear then.

All this took place only a short while after Miyako and I had discovered Baiko's body and that strange piece of paper that had fallen beside it. I was in such a terrible state of shock that I couldn't even react to what was going on. Miyako, however, had more presence of mind, possibly because she was not directly implicated, and immediately called for help and sent for the police.

Fortunately, Inspector Isokawa and a few other officers who were investigating the case had spent the night at the local police station. As soon as they heard the news, they came rushing to the scene of the crime. Seeing as they had to pass by the Nomura residence along the way, Kosuke Kindaichi had come with them.

After telling them what had happened, Miyako immediately showed them the scrap of paper that we had found beside the body. Both the inspector and Kosuke Kindaichi froze in astonishment when they saw it.

It was an understandable reaction. What could it all possibly mean? Apart from the two cedar trees, each of the names that had been crossed out in red ink belonged to one of the recent victims. Was the killer looking for pairs of people who shared the same job, circumstances or status in the village and murdering one of them? But why would anybody do that?

On the face of it, however, that is what this list implied. The first entry to be crossed out was the Kotake cedar, which had not been felled by human hands but by a bolt of lightning. Not only had the villagers seen in this an ill-fated omen, but it was the very event that seemed to have set this terrible chain of events in motion.

Perhaps the culprit was hopelessly superstitious and had believed that the lightning spelled great misfortune for the village, and so, in order to placate the gods of Eight Graves, he sought to offer up eight sacrifices, beginning with the felled cedar. Perhaps the fact that the cedar had been one of a pair had encouraged him to seek out other pairs in the village and to try to kill one from each.

What an idea! Can you imagine a more outlandish scheme? Can you imagine a more insane murderer? The shock of it filled me with such indescribable horror that, when the initial shock finally passed, I found myself in a state of stupor...

"Ahem..."

Kosuke Kindaichi cleared his throat. It had taken him a long time before he was ready to speak. I was in such a daze then that his words seemed to echo from afar.

"Thanks to this list," said Kosuke Kindaichi, "I think I've finally solved the mystery of Brother Kozen's death. I had been racking my brains, trying to work out how the culprit could have known to whom the poisoned tray would be served. Nothing could have been simpler than poisoning one of the trays, but there was only a fifty-fifty chance that it would be set down in front of Brother Kozen. Of course, that's assuming that Tatsuya isn't the murderer... But let us stick to that hypothesis for the moment. How could the killer have been satisfied with those odds? The more I thought about it, the more I was forced to draw the following conclusion: namely, that the murderer's intended victim was not necessarily limited to Brother Kozen. Could it not just as well have been Brother Eisen?... It's such a ridiculous notion, not to care whether the victim is A or B, that it seemed almost unimaginable... The thought has been nagging me since last night. But now, having seen this piece of paper, I see that it is likely just such a case. The killer simply didn't care whether he killed Brother Kozen or Father Choei. But since Choei is ill, his lot fell to Eisen. And the result was that Kozen drew the short straw. What a terrible, grotesque and senseless crime… Nevertheless, this is the key to Brother Kozen's murder."

I had hit upon the same theory the previous night. Just like Kosuke Kindaichi, I too had been plagued by these same thoughts and doubts. But if this shed light on the mystery of Kozen's death, then we were still no closer to solving the string of other murders. Worse than that: it all seemed even murkier than before.

"Well… yes… quite…" said the inspector, clearing his throat in turn. "Do you mean to say, Kindaichi-san, that the deaths of old Ikawa and Hisaya, and now that of Mother Baiko, were simply down to luck of the draw? In other words, that it could just as easily have been Kataoka-san instead of old Ikawa, Nomura-san instead of Hisaya and the Koicha nun instead of the mother abbess?"

Kosuke Kindaichi paused for a moment, before nodding ominously.

"That is correct, Inspector. It may very well be just as you say. However… There may also be another explanation."

"Another explanation…?"

"Judging by this piece of paper, these crimes may well be the work of a madman, prey to all manner of superstitions. And yet…"

"And yet?… And yet what?…"

"And yet, on the other hand, I can't help thinking that it all seems much too clever. They're too subtle to be the crimes of some crazed maniac. I can't help wondering whether there might not be another motive…"

"Undoubtedly possible," the inspector ventured. "So you believe that the murderer wanted to make these crimes look as though they had been committed by some superstitious lunatic in order to hide the real motive?"

"That's it exactly. Even in a village as superstitious as Eight Graves, these crimes are too outlandish."

"So what, then, is the real motive?"

Kosuke Kindaichi carefully re-examined the piece of paper before shaking his head.

"I just don't know. This list alone isn't enough for me to draw any conclusions. Then again…" For the first time, he turned to us. "Miyako-san?"

"Yes?" Miyako replied. She looked tense, which was only natural, but still she tried to force a smile. "Can I help at all?"

"It's about the writing on the paper… Could you take another look at it for me? Do you have any idea whose handwriting this might be?"

The page had been torn from a small pocket diary. Usually, in this type of diary, each page contained four days, but this page looked as though the top third had been cut off using a pair of scissors. The remaining two-thirds bore the dates 24th and 25th April.

The ten names were written across the page, beginning on the 25th, so it was just possible that the missing third contained even more cursed names.

"It looks like a man's handwriting," Miyako said.

"Yes, that's what I thought, too," Kosuke Kindaichi replied. "Is there anyone in the village with handwriting like this?"

"Well…" she said, tilting her head in an alluring manner. "I'm not sure… I'm afraid I'm not very familiar with other people's handwriting."

"What about you, Tatsuya?"

Naturally, I shook my head right away.

"I see… In that case, we'll have to circulate it."

Kosuke Kindaichi was about to hand the piece of paper over to the inspector, but suddenly he had a change of heart.

"Ah, yes," he said. "We still have to check the dates. Inspector, would you happen to have your diary with you? Would you mind checking it for me? What day is 25th April?"

The date in the inspector's diary corresponded exactly with that on the torn-off piece of paper. Kosuke Kindaichi grinned.

"So then, this piece of paper has been torn out of a diary for this year. It's a pity that there's nothing written on the back. And we still don't know who the diary belongs to. But we'll find all that out soon enough… Ah! Here comes Dr Kuno."

THE LIGHT-FINGERED NUN

But why did Dr Kuno look so worried?

He made his way through the small crowd of onlookers to the hermitage garden, where he left his bicycle and, carrying his doctor's bag under one arm, staggered towards us like a drunkard. I had known him by then for all of eight days, but already he seemed to have aged in that short time. He had sunken cheeks and dark bags under his eyes, and his eyes shone with a restless, oily glint.

"I'm sorry I'm late," he muttered almost inaudibly, as he removed his shoes and stepped into the hermitage. "I had to make a house call in the neighbouring village…"

"On the contrary, it's we who must apologize for taking up your valuable time. I'm afraid there's been another incident…"

"Just like the others?" he asked in a trembling voice. "In that case, forgive me, but I'm not sure I'll be able to help you… Last time, I made a mistake and… Is Dr Arai not available?"

"I believe that Dr Arai has already left to make arrangements in town for Brother Kozen's autopsy. In any case, Dr M——is due to arrive soon. They sent a telegram to him yesterday evening

147

on account of the priest. We're intending to ask him to carry out the autopsy on this latest victim, too, but we'd be grateful if you could take a look first…"

Dr Kuno's reluctance was manifest. He had, of course, been referring to his fatal misdiagnosis of my brother, for which he felt terribly ashamed. It was understandable, therefore, that he should want to avoid any involvement in this case if at all possible. But still, that didn't explain why he looked so worried.

When he sat down beside Baiko, he was shaking as though he were suffering from malaria.

"What's the matter, Doctor, are you feeling unwell?" Kosuke Kindaichi asked.

"No… I'm fine, really… I'm just a little tired. It's probably overwork."

"That's no good. They do say that doctors are their own worst patients, you know… Well, what's your expert opinion?"

"There can be no doubt about it," Dr Kuno said, after briskly examining the body. "It's the same as with Brother Kozen and Hisaya. But still, you should wait for Dr M——to confirm this…"

"And when would you place the time of death, Doctor?"

"Well…" said the doctor, grimacing. "I would say between fourteen and sixteen hours ago. It's 11 o'clock now, so that would put it somewhere between 7 and 9 o'clock yesterday evening. But really, you'd better have Dr M——confirm all this. This kind of thing isn't my speciality…"

Dr Kuno packed up his doctor's bag and closed it.

"Well, if you'll excuse me," he said, getting to his feet.

"Ah, just a moment, Doctor," Kosuke Kindaichi called out. "If you wouldn't mind waiting, there's one other thing I'd like to show you. Have you ever seen this handwriting before?"

Kosuke Kindaichi was showing him the page that had been torn out of the diary. Never in all my life shall I forget the look that appeared on Dr Kuno's face then. His thin body shuddered, as though an electric current had passed through it. His eyes bulged and his jaw trembled violently.

"So, you do recognize it, Doctor? The writing, I mean…"

Kosuke Kindaichi's question seemed to startle the doctor, who looked up suddenly.

"No! No, I'm afraid I don't!" he snapped.

He quickly recovered his senses, however.

"Sorry, I was just a little taken aback by the content of the note, that's all," he explained, staring at Miyako and me in turn. "I've no idea who wrote this. Whoever it is, they must be a fool or insane. I don't know. I don't know anything. Not a thing, do you hear me!"

Under Miyako's inquisitive gaze, his trembling voice fell silent before rising once again.

"I don't know anything," he said. "I really don't know a thing about any of this."

With that, he stormed out of the hermitage, leaving Kosuke Kindaichi and the inspector stunned. Then, plying the pedals like a drunkard, he teetered off on his bicycle.

We all looked at each other in shock. Finally, Inspector Isokawa broke the silence with a chuckle.

"His mistake from the other day seems to have put him on edge. But nobody has suggested that he knows anything."

Kosuke Kindaichi paused for a moment before turning to the inspector.

"No, Inspector. Dr Kuno's reaction was rather suggestive. At least, to me it was," he said, looking at the scrap of paper. "I believe I can hazard a guess at least at one of the pairs of names on the missing part of the paper."

"Well…?" said the inspector, raising his eyebrows. "Who then?"

"Dr Tsunemi Kuno and Dr Shuhei Arai. I believe we will find those two names under the heading 'Doctors'."

Miyako and I looked at each other in amazement. Her beautiful face had lost that morning's freshness and now seemed strangely bleak.

"In any case, it was a great stroke of luck finding this piece of paper. It's possible, of course, that the killer left it there intentionally, or that a third party placed it there to some other end. Either way, it sheds light on the criminal's motive, or at least what we are meant to believe is his motive. Inspector, please keep this piece of paper safe. Since Miyako and Tatsuya are relative newcomers to the area, they aren't able to identify the handwriting, but this is a small village: somebody will surely recognize it sooner or later."

The matter of the strange note was left at that, and our attentions now turned to the cause of Baiko's death. Once again, I found myself at the sharp end of the inspector's questions.

It was plain to see from the general scene what had caused the nun's death. Clearly, she had been eating the meal sent to her from the Tajimi house and had ingested the deadly poison. According to Dr Kuno, her death had probably occurred at some point between 7 and 9 o'clock the previous evening. The timing fit perfectly with the delivery of the tray.

"Who was it that arranged for the tray's delivery?"

Once again, the inspector cut me to the quick.

"Ah, well, you see... It was me..." I replied. "Since Baiko was leaving before the meal, I asked my sister to have hers sent on."

Kosuke Kindaichi looked at me in surprise. The inspector stared at me, grimacing.

"That was exceptionally considerate of you. Not many men would have thought to do that..."

Ah, so once again I was a suspect!

"Actually, it was wasn't my idea… It was Noriko who suggested it."

"Who is Noriko?"

"She's the sister of Satomura-san, from another branch of the Tajimi family," Miyako explained.

"I see. And then you passed the idea on to your sister, is that right? Where?"

"It was in the kitchen," I said. "There were an awful lot of people there. And, as you know, the kitchen is right beside the tatami room, so anyone paying attention could well have overheard me."

"And so what did she do, your sister?…"

"She asked Oshima to make the necessary arrangements, and then we both took a tray each and carried them into the main room."

"So, none of the guests would have had the chance to get near the tray intended for Baiko, since the meal was about to begin?"

"Hmm…" I paused for a moment before answering. "I don't know when the tray left the house, but if it was after all the commotion… You see, half of the guests fled the scene when Brother Kozen died…"

"All right," said the inspector, clicking his tongue. "We'll look into that and try to establish exactly when the tray left the house. Are you able to tell me who fled the scene?"

"Let me see, now…" I had trouble remembering precisely. "I was in such a state of shock that all I can remember is the sound of footsteps running out of the room."

"You yourself didn't run, though?"

"No. Far from it. I felt as though my feet had been nailed to the floor. And anyway, I had the place of honour, so everybody would have seen me run if I had done."

"I remember that clearly," Miyako said, throwing me a lifeline. "From the time when the meal started until the police arrived, Tatsuya didn't leave the room once."

"Ah, yes," said Kosuke Kindaichi, as though remembering all of a sudden. "You were also present at the dinner, Miyako-san. What about you? Are you able to remember who left the room?"

"Hmm… Well, I seem to recall that all the women ran out at once. And when Brother Kozen took ill, there were others who ran to fetch water… But I couldn't say in all certainty who left and who stayed in the room."

"Very well. We'll return to the kitchen at the Tajimi house and carry on the investigation there. For now, though, if we could return to the events of this morning… Tatsuya, you say the mother abbess asked you to visit her because there was something she wanted to tell you. Do you have any idea what it was?"

"I'm afraid not," I replied immediately.

This was the only answer I could give, for I too had been plagued by that very question. There was only one way to find the answer: to pay a visit to Choei, the high priest at the Maroo-ji temple. Had Baiko not told me, *"Only I and the high priest of the Maroo-ji temple know about this…"*? For some reason, I was reluctant to share this with the inspector. Instead, I preferred to pay the priest a visit by myself.

Full of suspicion, the inspector tried to read my face.

"All the same, it's curious, isn't it? Every one of them was killed just before some crucial moment. What could the nun possibly have to tell you?… Anyhow, it seems that once again, my dear Tatsuya, you are closely tied to the victim. Wherever you go, murder is sure to follow…"

I didn't need the inspector to point this out to me. I myself was only too well aware of it, and it weighed on me terribly.

"Indeed, these are unfortunate coincidences, I must admit. Earlier on, the Koicha nun said much the same to me."

"The Koicha nun?" came a voice suddenly from the next room. It was one of the detectives who had accompanied the inspector. "You met the Koicha nun earlier today?"

"Yes, it was on my way here… I bumped into her by the back door of the House of the West."

"Which direction was she coming from? From here, perhaps?…"

"Now that I think about it, she was, yes…"

"Hold on, Kawase, what's all this about the Koicha nun?" the inspector asked.

"It's just that there are several dusty footprints leading from the dirt floor of the kitchen out onto the veranda, Inspector. Somebody wearing straw sandals must have come in without taking them off. The mother abbess was very neat and tidy, and in all likelihood she would have cleaned them up if she'd noticed them. So I'd say they must have been left here after she died…"

The detective's words grabbed my attention. Whoever left these footprints had passed from the kitchen into the room in which we were standing and then gone out onto the veranda. There were several white marks between the tray and Baiko's head. They weren't very obvious on the tatami mats, but they were plain to see on the dirt floor. The imprints were flat and as small as a child's. I immediately thought of the Koicha nun in her dusty straw sandals.

"Hmm. That would imply that the Koicha nun was here before Tatsuya and Miyako. But if she was here, then why didn't she raise the alarm?"

"Perhaps she was up to her usual tricks…"

"Meaning…?" the inspector asked.

Detective Kawase smirked.

"She's a kleptomaniac, that one. Doesn't steal much, but whenever there's nobody around, she helps herself to anything that comes to hand. She steals money from the temple offertory box and the rice from offerings at the graves. Since it's only small things and the like, the villagers turn a blind eye to it. But she's been known to go about in broad daylight, wearing clothes she's stolen when they were hung out to dry. That caused some uproar, I can tell you! The mother abbess took pity on her and tried to help her, but the Koicha nun repaid her only by stealing from her. All she had to do was ask, and the mother abbess would have given it to her. But the Koicha nun preferred to steal. It's not the object per se that these people are interested in, so much as the theft itself…"

Kosuke Kindaichi was listening to what the detective had to say with great interest.

"In that case, is there any evidence that the Koicha nun stole something from here today?"

"I believe so. If you'll kindly step into the kitchen… It's in complete disarray. She's even gone rummaging through the pickling jars. Seeing her lying there, she must have decided that the mother abbess didn't need it any longer. Was she carrying anything when you saw her, Tatsuya?"

"Well," I said, glancing at Miyako, "as a matter of fact, she was. She was carrying a large bundle on her back."

"That's right," Miyako said. "And she was carrying something in her hand as well."

"B-b-but you say this h-h-happened right b-b-before you arrived here?" Kosuke Kindaichi stammered, scratching at the bird's nest on top of his head.

Back then, I just couldn't understand why this strange detective had suddenly become so excited. However, it later transpired that the Koicha nun's kleptomania and the theft that she had committed just before we arrived at the hermitage were of great significance to this series of murders.

AN ADVENTURE IN THE SECRET PASSAGE

As I put pen to paper in order to write this account, what troubles me most is that, though this is a kind of detective story, it is impossible for me to write it from the detective's perspective. In any ordinary detective novel, the story is told by the detective himself; that way, it is possible to show the reader how the investigation progresses and what the detective uncovers, possible to hint at a culprit or the solution to the murder. In this case, however, I was not always by the detective's side. In fact, those times when I did find myself at his side were sooner the exception. That being so, the fact of the matter is that I cannot show you the progress of the police investigation and what they had discovered. Since it would be a disservice to the reader who is trying to solve this mystery, however, I shall provide all the necessary details, even if in reality I found them out only much later. Another thing that makes this account different from any ordinary detective story is that not only must I recount incidents that have already taken place, but I must also investigate my own part in them and the suspicions surrounding me.

I decided to seek out the hidden passage later that night. Although it had absolutely nothing to do with Baiko's mysterious death, it did present me with another adventure altogether. I shall get to that in good time, however. For now, let me explain what Kosuke Kindaichi and the inspector discovered later that same day. I found this out only much later, but for the benefit of the reader, I shall recount it all now.

First, there was the tray that was delivered to Baiko. They discovered that it left the Tajimi house shortly after all the commotion surrounding Kozen's death and that it was taken to her by a young cattle-herder called Jinzo. According to him, it was Oshima who had asked him to take the tray to Baiko. Jinzo said that when he went into the kitchen, there was only one tray left. By that point, the dining area was already in an uproar, but Jinzo was too drunk on the sake that had been offered to the guests to realize that something was amiss, and so, carrying the tray, he had staggered out the back door. If he had known what was going on in the room, he would have been sure to tell Baiko, and if she had heard this, then perhaps she would have avoided touching the food. But it was after Jinzo left that the other servants learnt of Kozen's murder, meaning that the killer had only narrowly avoided missing his mark. Baiko had been unlucky.

As for the opportunity to poison the food, well, the killer had any number of chances. I have mentioned already that when Kozen began to vomit blood, the guests all shot to their feet and some even fled the room. Since everybody was preoccupied by what was going on with Kozen, it would have been perfectly feasible to slip out of the room unnoticed. What was more, when Oshima and the other helpers in the kitchen heard the commotion, they all came rushing into the dining area, leaving the kitchen empty and the tray unattended for a period of time. When Jinzo had entered the kitchen, he found nobody else there.

To put it plainly, after Kozen was poisoned, both the dining area and the kitchen were in such chaos that the killer had any number of opportunities to take advantage of the situation. This line of inquiry did not help us much, but at least we could conclude that the majority of guests could have committed the crime.

*

Setting all that aside for now, the time has come for me to describe my adventure that night.

That evening, at dinner, my sister Haruyo was particularly talkative. Naturally, she had already heard what had happened to Baiko, but she seemed unusually intrigued by the fact that Miyako and I had been the ones who found the body. With astonishing persistence on her part, she plied me with all kinds of questions, such as why I happened to be with Miyako and whether I had run into her on the way.

"Miyako's an intelligent woman," she added after all that. "She's smarter than most men. That overwhelming intelligence of hers frightens me. You'll think that this is just the jealousy of a provincial woman, and perhaps you'll be right… But still, I can't help feeling a little afraid of her. Just look at how she treated Shintaro."

She seemed to hesitate, but then forced herself to carry on.

"They say she really took advantage of him, you know. Before the end of the war, when Shintaro was doing quite well for himself at the General Staff Headquarters, Miyako did everything she could to lead him on, and he let himself get caught up in it all. After her husband's death, he was forever calling on her at her home. Rumours of their impending marriage even made it all the way back here. But what happened? The war took a turn for the worse. Shintaro found himself out on his ear, and Miyako no longer had any use for him. Though they both live in the same village now, they hardly speak a word to one another. And they were once so close! Even if that's all gone now, you'd think the fact that they both lived in Tokyo would count for something. To say nothing of the fact that they used to see so much of one another and were even rumoured to be on the verge of getting married. But now they're so cold to one another, like perfect strangers. Intelligent woman that she is,

Miyako used the inheritance from her late husband to buy up great quantities of diamonds during the war, so that, however bad the inflation, her wealth would be protected. Shintaro, on the other hand, was like a lost soul with no future. Perhaps it was only to be expected that Miyako would grow weary of him after that. But still, she's much too calculating for my liking. In fact, rumour has it that it was none other than Shintaro who secretly advised her to buy up all those diamonds…"

I couldn't understand what had made my sister so talkative that night. Less still could I understand why she, who was ordinarily so kind and good-natured, had suddenly taken it into her head to slander Miyako like this. I just stared at her in astonishment. She must have noticed the look on my face, for very quickly she blushed crimson and held her tongue. She fidgeted nervously for a moment, seeming rather ashamed of herself, before lifting her gaze and looking to me for forgiveness.

"I'm talking all sorts of rubbish tonight… It's wrong to talk behind someone's back like that. You must think terribly ill of me, Tatsuya."

"No," I tried to console her in the gentlest voice I could muster. "I've no reason to take offence just because you've said a few things about Miyako."

She seemed to perk up a little when I said this.

"I'm relieved to hear that… Still, you never can judge a book by its cover. In any case, you and I ought to make sure that we take care of one another."

Haruyo looked as though she would have liked to carry on talking, but I excused myself shortly after that, saying that I was tired. I marked a certain sadness in her eyes as I left.

Tired though I was, I had in fact the reason already alluded to for wanting to get back to my room: I intended to explore the secret passage.

When I returned to my room, I found the rain shutters closed and the bed already made up, but I hardly even glanced at it as I made my way through to the storage room behind. There, I opened the lid of the large chest that I had noticed the previous night. Just like before, there were a couple of silk bedsheets lying at the bottom of the chest. I pushed them aside, and my hand came to rest upon a stiff lever. I tried moving it back and forth, then I gave it a sharp jolt.

The bottom of the chest suddenly opened, revealing what looked like a black pit below. The sight of it took my breath away.

I was right. There was indeed a secret passage. It had allowed somebody to sneak into the annexe, and the twins had used it on the night of their mysterious pilgrimage.

Ah, that strange pilgrimage… What on earth could they have been praying to down there in the dead of night? My heart was pounding. My forehead was streaming with sweat.

I returned to my room again to check that everything was as it should be, then I turned out the light and went back to the storage room. According to my watch, it was a little after 9 o'clock.

I lit a candle that I had found earlier and turned out the light in the storage room. By the dim glow of the candle, I examined the interior of the secret passage. There was a broad stone staircase leading down from the chest. From my position at the top, I began to make my way below.

I looked around again and spotted another lever on the underside of the chest. I tried pulling it, and suddenly the bottom of the chest clicked softly shut. I was now locked in the secret passage. Seized by a sudden fear, I pulled at the lever again and watched as the bottom of the chest sprang open again. Reassured by this, I pushed the lever once more to close it. Now, if anybody were to open the lid of the chest, they would be none the wiser about what lay beneath. Holding the candle in one hand, I made my way carefully down the worn steps.

What was I going to do now? I asked myself. I didn't know. To begin with, I had no inkling that this secret passage was in any way connected with the recent series of murders. All I imagined then was that it might have to do with some Tajimi family secret. Nothing more than that. But still, it was worth the risk. In order to break the cloud of suspicion hanging over me, I would have to uncover all the secrets of this family.

The stairs seemed to go on and on, but they were not especially steep. Two old women like Koume and Kotake could manage them easily, I was sure, with the aid of their walking sticks.

When I finally reached the bottom, I found myself in a gallery. As I shone the candle all around me, I realized that I was in a kind of limestone cave, but the cave didn't seem to have been formed naturally. The flickering light of the candle illuminated streaks of greying limewash on the walls. Here and there, almost perfect stalactites hung from the roof. Somebody must have hollowed it out artificially, but over time, because of the situation and the damp, it had come to look like a real stalactite cave.

As I stood there in that extraordinary cave, I could feel my heart pounding. Somehow I managed to pluck up the courage to continue through a tunnel leading off it. It was then that I noticed this tunnel was not a dead end and that there had to be another exit somewhere. The incessant flickering of the candle told me that there was a draught, and if there was a draught, then there had to be a way out into the open air.

How long had I been walking? The darkness and my inexperience made it difficult to guess. Suddenly, I found myself at the bottom of a broad staircase. As with the previous one, it too had been cut from the natural rock. They must have led back up to the surface. Truth to tell, I was a little disappointed to have reached the end of the tunnel so soon.

In any case, I had no choice: there was nowhere else to go. Holding the candle in my right hand and clinging to the wall with my left, I mounted the staircase, but after taking only my first step, I stopped dead in my tracks. The wall on which I was leaning seemed to be giving way. Startled, I examined it by the light of the candle, but I couldn't see anything out of the ordinary. It was just another wall covered in streaks of limewash.

I tried leaning on the wall again. I pushed and pushed, but the rock hardly moved. I took another close look at the wall and this time I noticed some kind of dark cloth that was dangling by my feet. Naturally, I picked it up. What I saw made me gasp. It was the sleeve of either Koume's or Kotake's cloak. It must have got caught under the rock.

I felt a thrill run through me. Had Koume and Kotake moved this rock the previous night? Surely, if they had managed to move it, then I should be able to as well.

I decided to take another look, and it wasn't long before I had figured out the trick. There was a long vertical crack running through the rock face. When I held the candle in front of it, the flame flickered violently, indicating that there must be a cavity on the other side of it. Moving the candle down the crack, I saw that there was, separate from the rest of the wall, an arch-shaped rock, big enough to allow a fully grown adult to crawl through the space on all fours.

As I looked around at the bottom of the stairs, I spotted three or four miniature stalagmites beside the arch-shaped rock— only one of them wasn't in fact a stalagmite, but rather an iron lever. Needless to say, I immediately pulled on it.

Just as I thought. As I pulled the lever, the arch-shaped rock opened away from me, revealing a passage just big enough for someone to fit through. It was pitch dark on the other side.

I took a deep breath and, after making sure that the rock would say where it was after I let go of the lever, I crawled into the hole. There was another lever that had been made to look like a stalagmite on the other side. After checking that I could use this lever to open and close the rock, I set about exploring this new cave.

Unlike the man-made tunnel from which I had just come, this limestone cave had been formed naturally. Stalactites covered the vault of this cave. It was smaller than the previous one, too, so I had to take care not to bump my head.

I will return to describe the scenery of that cave in more detail later, but for now I must press on with the story. I had little time to stop and admire anything then, anyhow.

Why had Koume and Kotake ventured into such a dangerous place? What could they have been praying to in the depths of this cave? My mind was plagued by all kinds of suspicions.

At any rate, I soon reached a point where the passage forked. What to do? Which of the paths had my great-aunts taken?… I tried looking at the ground, but the rock floor and pools of water meant that no footsteps remained.

I took a chance and opted for the path leading off to the right. Soon enough I noticed the flame of the candle begin to gutter. At the same time, I could hear the sound of rushing water. There had to be an exit somewhere nearby.

I quickened my step. Soon enough, a way back into the open gaped wide before me, but it was blocked by a waterfall with a drop of around six feet on one side. A sharp gust of wind extinguished the candle.

I must have taken the wrong path. Obviously, Koume and Kotake had taken the path to the left, otherwise they would both have been soaked to the skin.

I was just about to turn back in order to explore the path that I had seen leading off to the left, when suddenly I had a change of heart. It was getting late, and I decided to leave it until the following evening. And anyway, I was more interested to find out exactly where in the village this waterfall was located.

Having made up my mind, I passed through the curtain of water. However, the moment I jumped through, somebody let out a cry and leapt aside. It was a woman's voice.

In my surprise, I took a few steps back to try and make out who this stranger was. In the starlight, I could just about see the silhouette of a woman.

"Oh, it's you, Tatsuya!" the voice said, with a note of relief.

The figure was already clinging to me. It was Noriko.

NORIKO'S LOVE

"Is that you, Noriko? You startled me."

Despite the initial shock, I was in fact relieved to see that it was her. She was so naïve that it would be easy to pull the wool over her eyes.

"You startled me as well," she said with a laugh. "Jumping out and surprising someone like that... What a thing to do!"

She peered at the waterfall, full of curiosity.

"But what are you doing, hiding in a place like this? Is there something in there?" she asked.

She seemed to think that I'd been looking round the cave out of sheer curiosity. She certainly didn't show any sign of knowing about the secret passage. Naturally, that suited me just fine, so I went along with it.

"I just wanted to take a look. There's nothing there. Just a damp limestone cave."

"Oh, is that all?"

She gave up staring at the cave and returned her gaze to me, her eyes glittering.

"But what are you doing here at this hour? Was there something that brought you here especially?" she asked.

"No, nothing really. I couldn't sleep, so I thought it would be a good idea to get some fresh evening air. I just happened to wind up here."

"Oh," she said, hanging her head in disappointment. Almost immediately, though, she looked up again and said cheerfully, "Well, I'm glad to have bumped into you anyway."

I couldn't imagine where all this was leading. Bewildered, I beheld her profile in the pale starlight.

"And why's that, Noriko?"

"Oh, no particular reason… Would you like to stop at mine on your way back? Only, there's nobody there and I feel ever so lonely…"

"Shintaro isn't at home then?"

"No."

"But where has he gone?"

"I really don't know… Lately, he's been going out every night. Whenever I ask where he goes, he just clams up and won't tell me."

"Tell me, Noriko…"

"Yes?"

"Why did you come here tonight?"

"Why did I come here?…"

She opened her eyes wide and stared at me, before lowering them again and kicking at the ground with her left foot.

"I was just so lonely… I couldn't bear it any longer. I had all these thoughts in my head, and for some reason I just felt very sad… I couldn't stay alone in the house another minute, so I came out for a walk."

"Where do you live?"

"Just down there. Do you see it?"

We were standing on a narrow path only two or three feet wide, halfway up a steep hill. The precipice behind us and the slope in front were carpeted by a thick bamboo grove. Through the bamboo, we could just make out, near the bottom of the hill, a little thatched roof and the upper parts of some brightly lit sliding doors.

"Won't you come in for a while? I can't stand being alone…"

She grabbed my fingers and refused to let go. I was absolutely bewildered. Despite her insistence, I had no desire to go to her house. Having said that, I couldn't go back through the cave. In the event, I had little choice but to escort Noriko away from that place.

"I'm not sure I'd feel comfortable going into your house… Why don't we find somewhere nearby to sit down and rest awhile?"

"But why wouldn't you feel comfortable?"

"Well, what if Shintaro were to come back and find me there?"

"So what if he did?…"

She was staring at me again with those ingenuous eyes of hers. She seemed not to care what others might say or think. Or rather, it wasn't that she didn't care, but simply that she didn't even understand. She had the naivety of a newborn baby.

She didn't insist too much and, after following the path down through the bamboo grove, we eventually came to a gently sloping meadow, where we decided to stop. The grass was damp with the evening dew, but Noriko just sat down without seeming to mind. I followed suit.

The spot where we found ourselves was perched on the edge of a ravine that enfolded the village of Eight Graves. All the way down the valley, terraces of rice paddies and fields were staggered stepwise, with little thatched farmers' cottages dotted among them. Their inhabitants seemed to have the habit of sleeping with the windows open and the lamps on. In each house, the sliding doors were bathed in a light whose reflections multiplied beautifully on the water of the rice paddies where the planting had just finished. The sky was speckled with stars, and the Milky Way seemed to leave a trail of silver smoke in the sky.

Spellbound by the beauty, Noriko stared up at the starry sky for a while before finally turning to me.

"Tatsuya," she whispered softly.

"Yes?"

"It's just... I was thinking about you earlier."

I looked at her in surprise. She didn't seem particularly embarrassed and carried on in that same innocent-seeming way.

"You know, I couldn't bear the loneliness any longer. I felt as if I were all alone in the world, and in the end, I began to cry. I just couldn't hold the tears back. It's so silly of me. I can't understand why I felt like that, but then... But then I suddenly thought of you. I thought of that first time we met and... Well, I don't know why, but I suddenly felt this pain in my chest, as if it were being squeezed tightly... And that only made me cry even more. It was the last straw... So, like I said, I went out for a walk. I was wandering around like a madwoman and that's when I bumped into you. You gave me the fright of my life! I could feel my heart pounding. But at the same time, I was so happy, Tatsuya... Maybe the gods heard my prayer and took pity on me."

What was this, if not a declaration of love? Did she really love me? It was all so sudden that I was bewildered and at a loss for words. I looked at her again, but she didn't seem to be in the least embarrassed. She had the innocence of a character from Hans Christian Andersen or the Brothers Grimm. There was nothing provocative about her: on the contrary, she was just naïve and forthright.

But what could I possibly say to that? When I looked in my heart, I didn't find the slightest bit of love for Noriko. After all, are love and passion not the result of mutual understanding? I hardly knew her.

What was I supposed to say to her? It was against my nature to console her with sweet nothings. And it would have been an unforgivable crime to deceive such an artless young woman. I had no choice but to remain silent. But Noriko didn't seem to expect an answer from me either. She seemed satisfied, having said her piece. Perhaps she imagined that she was loved in return. That possibility worried me even more. I had to stay as far away from that dangerous topic of conversation as I could.

"Noriko," I said at last.

"Yes?"

"Before you were evacuated here, you lived with your brother in Tokyo, didn't you?"

"That's right. Why do you ask?"

"Did Miyako visit you often?"

"Miyako? Sometimes... But usually it was Shintaro who visited her."

"I heard that they had been planning to get married."

"Yes, there were rumours about that. Maybe they did want to get married. I don't know. Maybe if the war had ended differently."

"Does Miyako still visit?"

"No, hardly ever these days. She came a couple of times in the beginning, but my brother kept running away from her."

"Running away? Why was that?"

"I'm not sure, really. I suppose it could be because she's rich now, whereas he's poor. Despite appearances, my brother is a very proud man. He can't stand people taking pity on him."

Noriko answered my questions without a moment's hesitation. She must have wondered why I was asking all these questions. I felt a little guilty, but I was determined nonetheless to get to the bottom of this.

"What do you think? If Shintaro were willing, would Miyako still want to marry him?"

"Hmm…" Noriko tilted her head to one side, considering the question. Her neck was long and graceful, like a swan's; it even had a certain sensual quality to it.

"I don't know," she finally answered. "I'm not clever enough to read other people's hearts. And besides, Miyako is one of those people with such a dark and complex nature…"

I looked at her in astonishment. Earlier that day, for the very first time, I had learnt that my sister Haruyo wasn't too well disposed towards Miyako, and now I had found that Noriko was apparently of the same opinion. *"You never can judge a book by its cover,"* Haruyo had said. Now Noriko seemed to be saying the very same thing. In my sister's case, there was certainly an element of jealousy, but I doubted that Noriko, in her naivety, harboured such feelings. If that was how Miyako was seen by these two other women, could it be that they were right? And there I was, thinking that she was just spirited and independent…

SHINTARO'S FACE

How long did we spend sitting there? I wonder. Unfortunately, I had forgotten my watch, so I had no idea what time it was. But we stayed there a long while, in any case. Noriko just wouldn't let me go. We didn't have much to talk about, but she seemed content just to sit by my side and share her reminiscences. They were as pure and artless as children's fairy tales, but strangely enough, as I listened, I noticed that my strained, frayed nerves began to relax.

It was the first time that I had experienced this feeling since my arrival in the village. Until that point, I had always seemed to unnerve the villagers and rub them up the wrong way, so this was an unexpected moment of respite. As I listened to Noriko's unbroken monologue, somewhere in the distance a grandfather clock broke the surrounding silence. It struck midnight.

Surprised by the lateness of the hour, I got to my feet.

"It's already gone twelve," I said. "It's late. I should be getting home."

"Yes, you're right…"

Even Noriko couldn't argue with that, but still she seemed reluctant to go.

"My brother won't be back yet," she said.

"Where does he go, though, I wonder. And every night, at that…"

"I don't know. He used to like playing *go*, but since we came back to the village, he's had no one to play with. He doesn't know many people, you see."

Noriko spoke of her brother's nocturnal outings without the slightest hint of concern or worry. Still, it troubled me. Where on earth could Shintaro be going every night?

"When does he usually come home?"

"I'm not really sure. It's always after I've gone to bed."

"And when do you normally go to sleep?"

"At 9 or 10 o'clock most days. Tonight's an exception, of course, but I'm glad I stayed up. I wouldn't have run into you otherwise. Tell me, Tatsuya, will you come again tomorrow night?"

She asked as though it were the most natural thing in the world. Disarmed by her ingenuousness, I couldn't refuse.

"I could do. But not if it rains."

"No, of course not…"

"But promise me something in return, Noriko. Please, under no circumstances tell Shintaro that you met me here tonight."

"But why not?" she asked, rolling her eyes.

"Because I'm asking you not to," I said. "You mustn't tell him about tonight, or about tomorrow night for that matter. Otherwise, I won't come."

My ultimatum seemed to have its effect.

"All right, I won't tell another soul. But in return, will you promise to come every night?"

Truly, women are born diplomats. For all her naivety, Noriko had got what she wanted from me.

"Yes, I'll come," I said, with a wry smile of resignation.

"You promise?"

"I promise. You ought to hurry back before Shintaro gets home."

She nodded obediently.

"You're right. Goodbye then, Tatsuya."

"Goodbye."

Noriko took five or six steps down the hill before turning back.

"Good night," she said.

"Good night, Noriko."

She began making her way down again, but for some reason she kept looking up at the top of the hill. Suddenly she stopped and cried out.

"What is it?" I asked, startled.

I turned to look towards the top of the hill.

Some two hundred feet higher up, where the top of the ravine narrowed, there was a little cottage separated from the rest of the hamlet. There was a light on behind the closed sliding doors. The moment I turned around, I saw a black shadow sneak past those sliding doors. Though the figure was gone in a flash, I could have sworn that I had seen a man wearing Western clothes and a flat cap. Then, before I even had time to think, the light went out and the sliding doors were plunged into darkness.

Noriko gasped in astonishment and ran back towards me.

"What was that?" she asked.

"What was what?"

"That shadow. You must have seen it. It looked like a man wearing a cap."

"Yes, but what's so strange about that?"

"Don't you think it's odd? In a convent? At this time of night?"

I turned once again to look at the convent. With only the starlight in the sky, it was silent and pitch dark.

"So is this Koicha then, Noriko?"

"Yes. And that's where Myoren lives. It's so strange. Why would a man be visiting her at this hour? And why would she turn out the light?"

"Why wouldn't she turn out the light?"

"Myoren always sleeps with the light on. She says she can't get to sleep any other way."

I had a terrible feeling about this.

"Wasn't the Koicha nun summoned by the police today?"

"Yes, but when she returned, she was boasting that she hadn't said a word to them. It never does to make her angry. She'll never tell you what she knows if you provoke her. But I wonder what's going on up there. Why did she turn out the light? And why was that man there?"

Suddenly, an indecent thought crossed my mind, making me blush. Indeed, there's no accounting for taste. It was not beyond the realm of possibility that the Koicha nun, too, could have her suitors. But I could never have said all this to Noriko.

"Oh, it's nothing," I said. "She must have had a visitor, that's all."

"But it's so strange. Why would she turn out the light if she had visitors?"

"I'm sure she's fine… But you really must be getting home. If you dawdle any longer, it'll be one o'clock by the time you're back."

"You're right. Well, good night then, Tatsuya."

"Good night."

Noriko ran straight down the slope, looking round several times. I waited until she had completely disappeared from sight before taking the path back through the bamboo grove. It was then that I heard hurried footsteps coming towards me. I stopped in my tracks.

Somebody was coming down the hill.

I looked up, but the path was too tortuous to allow me to see whose footsteps they were. This person was definitely coming my way, however. Not only that, but he was making his way cautiously, as though he were afraid of being seen. I quickly hid myself in the undergrowth of the bamboo grove, so that I could watch without fear of being seen.

Little by little, the steps drew nearer, but with each passing step, the slower they became. Evidently, he was on the lookout.

My heart was pounding, my mouth was dry, and my throat felt tight.

Finally, the steps drew right up beside me. A shadow stretched across the path, soon followed by the man himself. For a moment I thought my heart was going to stop beating.

It was Shintaro. He was wearing a flat cap and overalls and had a *tenugui* towel tied around his waist and putties around his ankles. What was more, he was carrying a pickaxe under his arm. All this would have been enough to shock anyone, but then there was his face…

His eyes were bulging, so much so that they looked ready to burst out of their sockets at any moment. While his pupils glittered with a strange fever, his lips were twisted and trembling, and beads of perspiration gleamed from his forehead down to his nose.

In the presence of others, we so rarely show what we feel deep down. But when we think that no one is looking, it often escapes us in spite of ourselves. Shintaro was no exception. He didn't look desperate so much as grim and aggressive.

My heart seemed to stop in fright. I very nearly cried out. Had I done so, the sharp point of that pickaxe would surely have swung down on the crown of my head.

I managed to stop myself in the nick of time however, so Shintaro didn't realize I was there. Tiptoeing as he went, he walked right past me, disappearing completely into the bamboo grove.

Only much later did I leave my hiding place. My knees were trembling, and I felt dizzy.

I waited until I had recovered a little before returning to the cave behind the waterfall and making my way back to my room safely and without any further incident. Needless to say, sleep did not come easily to me that night.

THE DISAPPEARANCE OF DR KUNO

After such a restless night, I slept late the following morning. When I finally woke, there was a ray of bright morning sunlight filtering through the rain shutters. I looked at my watch, which I had laid at my bedside: it was 9 o'clock.

I jumped up, packed away the futon and opened the shutters. Having heard all the clattering, Haruyo came rushing over from the main house.

"Good morning," I said. "I seem to have slept in again."

My sister bowed but said nothing and just stared at my face. Intrigued, I looked back at her in turn. She seemed tense for some reason and was looking at me enquiringly.

"Good morning," she said at last in a hoarse voice. "There's something that I need to tell you, Tatsuya."

There was something unusually formal about her tone.

Something must have happened, I thought. She looked so deeply suspicious that a sense of ink-black foreboding rose up inside me.

"Well, what is it?" I asked, not without trepidation.

Her eyes were fixed on me.

"There was another murder last night," she whispered. "The Koicha nun, Myoren, has been killed."

Fearing that somebody might overhear, she had whispered this as quietly as possible, but her words seemed to explode on my eardrums. My limbs began to tremble. I looked at her, dumbfounded. She took a couple of steps back, as though frightened by my reaction, but still she kept staring at me without blinking.

"The police came here first thing this morning," she said. "They asked me whether you'd gone out last night. Naturally, I told them that you'd gone to bed early and couldn't have gone out, but... Oh, Tatsuya, tell me that you really were here last night!"

"Of course I was. Where else would I have been? Remember I was so tired that I went to bed early..."

She stared at me with her eyes wide open and full of fear. Her lips began to quiver.

What was the matter with her? What was she afraid of? Why was she looking at me with that glint of fear in her eyes? Suddenly it dawned on me: what if Haruyo had visited the annexe while I was in the caves last night? She would have seen that I wasn't there and then this morning, when she found out that the Koicha nun had been murdered, the seed of doubt would have been planted in her mind. I had lied to her either way. Doubtless that had only added fuel to her suspicions.

Oh, what a mess! Of all nights... Why did there have to be a murder on the very first night that I sneaked out of the annexe? And to think, I had been right there, only a stone's throw from the scene of the crime.

Haruyo was on my side. If I had confided in her about the events of the previous night, she would certainly have understood. But what then? She was too honest a person to tell an outright lie. And even if she did, the look on her face would give it away immediately. She would always end up telling the truth, regardless. It pained me to make her suffer like this, but for the moment I had to keep it a secret. Besides, I didn't want anybody else to know about the secret passage.

"Haruyo," I said, breaking the silence eventually. "Was the Koicha nun poisoned like the rest of them?"

"No," she answered, her voice shaking. "It wasn't poisoning this time. Apparently, she was strangled."

"When do they think it happened?"

"They're saying that it was last night at around midnight."

Once again, a wave of dark foreboding rose up from the pit of my stomach. The shadow that Noriko and I had seen the previous night must have been the killer. Perhaps we had witnessed at first hand the very moment that the murder took place...

I was in a state of profound shock. Was the shadow cast on the sliding door not that of a man wearing a cap? And had I not seen Shintaro come down the hill wearing a cap only moments later?

The human mind is a curious thing. Since the previous night, I had been troubled by Shintaro's strange behaviour and that indescribably grim visage of his. I had even seen it in my dreams. But I had simply imagined that he went out on his nocturnal outings with an altogether more lascivious aim in mind. And yet, until then, I hadn't made the connection between Shintaro and the shadow on the sliding door. Why was that? Perhaps it was because of the pickaxe that I had seen him carrying. A pickaxe and a nun... It seemed incredible that those two things could have anything to do with one another. Wasn't that why I had kept Shintaro and the shadow separate in my mind?

"What are you thinking, Tatsuya?"

"Oh, nothing really."

"Tatsuya..." she insisted, her voice suddenly growing softer. "You can tell me anything, you know. I'm on your side. Even if the entire world were to suspect you, I'd still trust you. You mustn't ever forget that."

"Thank you, Haruyo."

Such kindness made my heart ache. I had already decided to keep the events of the previous night a secret for now, but I couldn't help feeling that I would be exposed sooner or later, and then suspicions about me would really start mounting. Would she still believe me then? I wondered.

Shortly after that, we left the annexe to go and have breakfast. Koume and Kotake had already finished theirs and retired to their rooms, but my sister had waited for me. Or perhaps she had just lacked any appetite.

She served me, and I ate in silence. Suddenly, as if the thought had only just crossed her mind, she turned to me.

"By the way," she said, setting her chopsticks down on her bowl and staring at me, "there was another strange thing that happened this morning."

"Another strange thing?"

"Dr Kuno has disappeared."

I looked at Haruyo in surprise.

"Dr Kuno has…"

"Yes, disappeared. Do you remember that strange note that was found beside the mother abbess's body yesterday? Well, it turns out that it was written by Dr Kuno."

"Well, I never…"

"I don't know the details, but that's what the police seem to have concluded. They went to his house early this morning, but he was gone. His family couldn't say when he had left either. The police turned the house over and found a note under his bed. It said that he had to hide for a while but that he was absolutely innocent and they weren't to worry."

I was strangely troubled by this. I had long suspected Dr Kuno, but never had I imagined that he would give up just like that. It was almost a disappointment.

"When did he up sticks?" I asked.

"Nobody knows. Apparently, he said he wasn't feeling well last night and went to bed early. His wife hasn't seen hide nor hair of him since. When the police arrived this morning, she thought he was still in his room. She went to wake him up but found the bed lying empty. It caused quite a ruckus."

"Did the bed look as though it had been slept in?"

"Apparently not. Which suggests that he must have left shortly after going to his room. Oh, yes, and they're saying that he took all the money that was in the house with him."

"When did he go to his room?"

"Around half past nine."

If he left immediately, he would have had plenty of time to go and strangle the Koicha nun.

"Listen, Haruyo," I said, setting down my chopsticks and leaning towards her. "Do you really imagine that Dr Kuno could be capable of committing all these mysterious murders?"

"To be honest, no," she said with a sigh. "He's always been fond of detective novels, but…"

"Detective novels?" I repeated, a little taken aback.

"Yes, his wife's forever complaining about it. She says it's ridiculous for a man to be so engrossed by them at his age. I don't really know much about these novels, but I imagine they must have murders and all sorts in them. That said, it doesn't mean that Dr Kuno is acting them out, of course."

Like my sister, I myself was not too familiar with detective fiction. But of the few novels I had read, I never once imagined that their authors or readers would include such wicked people. Come to think of it, though, did these events not have a hint of the detective novel about them?

My thoughts were in compete disarray. I just couldn't make any sense of it.

That afternoon, Kosuke Kindaichi paid us an unexpected visit. The prospect of another interrogation made my heart sink, but, surprisingly enough, the detective was all smiles.

"No need to be alarmed," he said with a chuckle. "I've just dropped by to see how you're doing, that's all."

"Oh," I said, little reassured.

Fortunately, Haruyo came to my rescue.

"Have you found Dr Kuno yet?" she asked.

"Not yet. Inspector Isokawa headed straight to town, but I'm afraid I don't know whether his investigations have resulted in any leads."

Kosuke Kindaichi seemed strangely unperturbed by Dr Kuno's disappearance.

"Kindaichi-san…" I said. "It's about that piece of paper we found beside the mother abbess's body. Are you really sure that it was written by Dr Kuno?"

"Oh, yes, without a shadow of a doubt. The page had been torn out of a pocket diary that Dr Kuno's bank distributed to all its customers as an end-of-year gift. There are only three households in the village that received one: the Nomuras, the Kunos and yours. We had the handwriting examined and established conclusively that it belongs to Dr Kuno."

"Is that why Dr Kuno has run away?"

"It would certainly seem that way."

"So then, Dr Kuno is the murderer?"

"Ah, yes, the murderer… They do say that flight itself is a form of proof, so you could be forgiven for thinking so. But here we have a number of inconsistencies."

"Inconsistencies?"

"Yes… You'll be aware that the Koicha nun was murdered last night?"

I looked fearfully at Kosuke Kindaichi, but he didn't appear to have any ulterior motive.

"A most curious case," he continued, "but let's leave that to one side for the moment. The nun was killed at around midnight. For a whole host of reasons, we can be sure about the timing. But here comes the interesting part: there is evidence to suggest that Dr Kuno took the 10.50 up-train last night."

My eyes opened wide in amazement.

"So Dr Kuno has a perfect alibi, then?"

"Precisely. Even if he decided to get off at the next station, there was no connecting train for him to take in the opposite direction. And he could never have made it back on foot by midnight. So we can say that, insofar as last night's events are concerned, Dr Kuno is in the clear. The same, I should think, applies to the other murders as well."

"Then why has he run away?"

Kosuke Kindaichi smiled.

"I doubt he could very well stay in the village after writing that absurd note... It was well worth his running away."

"Could it be, then, that last night's murder has nothing to do with the others? After all, didn't the note suggest that the killer's plan was to murder only one of each pair? But the mother abbess was already dead. Isn't it odd that the Koicha nun was killed as well, in that case?"

The question had been troubling me all morning.

"Ah," said Kosuke Kindaichi. "You've spotted the problem as well. You're absolutely right. But all the same, the Koicha nun's murder is a continuation of these recent events. I'm sure of it. Only, I doubt that it was in the murderer's original plan. Something unexpected must have happened to seal the Koicha nun's fate. But what could that something be? The murderer made a mistake, you see. Oh, yes, the murderer certainly made his first mistake when he killed the mother abbess. Do you see my meaning, Tatsuya? You're well placed to understand it. But then, perhaps it's only natural if you don't..."

Kosuke Kindaichi looked at me and sighed, before quietly taking his leave.

Why had he really come? I wondered.

SOMEBODY FROM LONG AGO...

That evening, I ventured back into the caves through the secret passage.

To go back so soon was certainly a risk after the events of the previous night. I also feared that Haruyo might become aware of my little expeditions. However, I simply couldn't resist the urge to return. What's more, I had promised Noriko that I would meet her, and I wanted to satisfy myself that she hadn't told anyone about our last meeting.

I retraced my steps through the storage room and once again, candle in hand, made my way down the stairs cut away from the natural rock. This time, however, at the bottom of the stairs beneath the large chest, I hesitated for so long in indecision that I made myself late.

Eventually, I made my way through the dark tunnel. I was less anxious this time, having made the trip once before. I passed through the hidden passage without incident, but when I reached the fork, I stopped dead in my tracks. In the tunnel leading to the right—that is, towards Koicha—I saw some flashes of light. I immediately blew out my candle and froze there in the dark.

There was a sharp bend in the right-hand tunnel a short distance after the fork. That was where the flashes of light were coming from. The light seemed to lick the walls of the tunnel before disappearing again. After two or three flashes, I realized that somebody around the corner was trying to light a match.

I felt as though I had been knocked over by a cold wave. My heart skipped a beat and then started beating fiercely. My whole body came out in a fierce sweat.

There was somebody else in the tunnel. I thought back to the night before last: somebody had crept into my room—was it that same somebody who had given Koume and Kotake a fright in this very spot… Had the stranger come back?

There was another faint flash of light. Only this time it didn't disappear; it instantly flared up and then the light changed colour. It dawned on me: this person lit a candle. The light flickered on the walls for a moment before finally settling down. Whoever it was must have a lantern. Now the light began to draw nearer. I quickly hid myself in the other tunnel leading off to the left. My heart was pounding, but come to think of it, this was the perfect opportunity to find out the identity of the intruder who had been breaking into the annexe. Swaying, the light from the lantern slowly advanced towards the bend in the tunnel. Pressing my back to the wall, I waited impatiently for the figure to appear.

At last the lantern turned the corner, and I could now see its yellow light streaming right in front of me. The sound of footsteps was getting closer and closer. I held my breath, waiting for the figure to appear at the fork in the tunnel. Then finally I saw… I was so stunned that you could have knocked me down with a feather.

"Noriko…?"

It was indeed her. She jumped when she heard my voice, but as soon as she recognized me by the light of the lantern, she called out my name and threw her arms around me.

"Noriko!" I said, still reeling from the shock. "What on earth are you doing here?"

I couldn't believe my eyes, but Noriko seemed unaccountably calm.

"I was looking for you. I'd been waiting for so long that I'd begun to wonder if you weren't coming."

"Did you already know there was a tunnel here?" I asked in an accusatory tone, forgetting myself.

"I'd no idea! I was waiting for you in the same spot as last night. I waited for so long, but you never showed up. Then it occurred to me that you might be hiding in the cave, so I came to take a look. It goes on and on, doesn't it? Well, I thought you might be in here, so I ran back to the house to fetch the lantern."

I was amazed by her daring.

"But weren't you afraid?" I asked.

"A little, yes. But the thought that you might be here took that fear away. I'm so glad I did, now that I've found you."

She was completely ingenuous. At the same time, it pained me to know that her feelings for me were so profound. In any case, there was no time to lose: I had to get on with the business in hand.

"Noriko…" I began.

"Yes?"

"I hope you haven't told anyone about last night."

"I haven't told a soul."

"What about this evening?"

"I haven't told anyone about this either."

"Not even Shintaro?"

"Not him."

"How has Shintaro been today, anyway?"

"He's spent the whole day in bed. He said he had a headache. But it's strange, you know. He's just the same as you."

"Meaning?"

"He told me not to tell anyone that he was out late last night. I think it's odd. Why is it that all men like to lie?"

My heart was pounding.

"Noriko, have you heard that the Koicha nun was murdered last night?"

"Yes, I heard about it this morning. It gave me quite a shock. Do you think that the person who killed Myoren was the same man whose shadow we saw on the sliding door last night?"

"Has Shintaro said anything to you about it?"

"Shintaro? No… Why do you ask?"

She looked at me, puzzled by my question.

All of a sudden, I heard a cry behind me, followed by the sound of footsteps running deeper into the cave. Startled by the noise, Noriko and I froze momentarily, but then, recovering, I took the lantern from her hand and set off in pursuit of the stranger.

"Tatsuya!" Noriko cried out.

"Wait for me there, Noriko."

"No, I'm coming with you."

There was an immediate sharp bend in the tunnel leading off the left, too. It must have been because of this feature that the fugitive hadn't noticed our presence until the very last moment.

Guided by the sound of the footsteps, we ventured further into the cave, but the tunnel had as many twists and turns as a sheep's innards. The sound of footsteps and the faint reflection of the lamp that this person was carrying were not enough—we just couldn't keep up.

How far had we gone? We could no longer hear the footsteps or see the glow of the lamp. At a loss, we paused in the middle of the tunnel.

"It's no use," Noriko said.

"Yes, he's got away."

"But who was it?"

"I've no idea."

"The cave seems endless, doesn't it?"

"I know… But there must be a way out somewhere."

"Shall we see what's up ahead?"

"Are you feeling brave enough?"

"Yes, with you by my side."

"All right, then, let's keep going."

We had given up on catching the mysterious figure, but now I had something else in mind. Moreover, it was what I had set out to do in the first place. I was determined to find whatever it was that Koume and Kotake had been praying to.

Lit by the lantern, we had been advancing carefully for around five minutes, when all of a sudden the tunnel widened. Surprised by this, I raised the lantern high to take a good look around. That was when it happened. Noriko let out a cry and clung to my waist.

"What is it, Noriko?"

"L-l-look, Tatsuya... There's somebody over there!"

"What?!"

In disbelief, I shone the lamp where Noriko was pointing. What I saw there chilled me to the bone.

About three feet above the ground, a part of the wall had been hollowed out as an alcove. Enshrined there, atop a stone sarcophagus, was a samurai, sitting resplendent in a suit of armour. At first, I thought the armour might be decorative. But, no: although I couldn't make out the face behind the visor, there was definitely somebody sitting there under all that armour. And, without flinching, that somebody was staring back at us...

CHAPTER 5

UNDER THE ARMOUR

For a moment, I was speechless. My tongue was paralysed, and no words would come out of my mouth. Shameful though it is to admit it, my knees were shaking and my whole body had gone as stiff as a wire.

Then again, nobody could laugh at my cowardice. Anyone would have been just as petrified at meeting such a strange sight in a pitch-dark cave like that. Ah, but how frightening he was in his silence and immobility, just staring out at us through his visor.

"W-w-who's there?" I asked, clearing my throat.

No reply came. He didn't even move. A curiously serene indifference, as if he were removed from the rhythms of the world, seemed to envelop his body.

I looked at Noriko.

"Tatsuya…" she whispered in my ear. "Maybe it's a mannequin? Or a wooden idol?"

The same thought had crossed my mind, but I was unconvinced. The line of the body lacked the solidity of a wooden idol. No, there was something distinctly human about it. At any rate, I was fairly sure that he wasn't alive, which reassured me somewhat.

"Stay here, Noriko. I'm going to take a closer look."

"Are you sure, Tatsuya?"

"Yes, don't worry."

Leaving Noriko's side, I went over to the alcove, lantern in hand, and climbed up. A shiver ran down my spine as I imagined the samurai reaching out to grab me. However, he remained imperturbable, seated majestically on top of his sarcophagus. I brought the lantern closer.

Mingling with the smell of the burning candle, an odour of mould and damp stung my nostrils. It was emanating from the armour itself. Although I was no connoisseur of antiques, I felt quite certain that this was the armour and helmet of a high-ranking samurai. In any case, they looked very old indeed: the threads had begun to fray, and the breastplate and the tassets had half-rotted away.

As I held the lantern higher, I tried to see what was under the helmet. As I peered in, my whole body was suddenly seized by indescribable terror that made my hair stand on end.

It was neither a mannequin, nor a wooden idol, but a man. He wasn't alive, of course, but how terrifying this cadaver was. His skin was a strange, dull colour—neither grey, nor brown, nor terracotta—yet it looked polished. It had the look of soap about it.

The dead man looked as though he had been somewhere between thirty and forty years of age when he died. He had the same flat nose and high cheekbones that were characteristic of the locals. His eyes were close set, his forehead narrow, and his jaw tapered to a point, imbuing him with a stern and sinister look. His eyes were wide open, but they had lost their lustre—dry now, they looked as though they were made of clay.

He was so terrifying that I felt a cold sweat trickle down my body. My teeth were chattering, and I felt as though I was going to be sick at any moment. Hadn't I seen that face somewhere before?

But who was he? Where had I seen him? Before I could remember, Noriko came running over, alarmed by my behaviour.

"Tatsuya! Tatsuya! What is it? Is there something under the armour?"

Her voice returned me to my senses.

"Don't come any closer, Noriko. Keep your distance."

"But, Tatsuya!…"

"It's all right, I'm coming down."

As soon as I jumped down from the alcove, Noriko assailed me with questions.

"What's going on, Tatsuya? You're sweating terribly…"

"It's all right. I'm fine."

My mind was elsewhere. Who could this dead man be? In front of the sarcophagus, there were vases, an incense holder and other things. This had to be the place where Koume and Kotake came to offer their prayers. The figure must have had some connection to those elderly twins. But what could that possibly be?

"Tatsuya," Noriko said, clinging to me with an anxious look on her face. "Did you really see something under the armour? It's not a mannequin?"

"No, but maybe you can help me… Were there any men in the village between the ages of thirty and forty who died recently?"

"Why would you ask me that?" she said, her eyes frantic. "You know just as well as I do who in the village has died recently. The only ones aged between thirty and forty were the priest and your brother."

"My brother Hisaya…"

It was like an electric shock. Suddenly, an idea flashed in my mind.

Did the face not resemble that of my late brother? Those same close-set eyes, that same narrow forehead, that same tapering chin, that same look of reproach…

And yet… and yet… Was it at all possible? After all, Hisaya had been laid to rest in the Tajimi family tomb. Yes, he had been exhumed for the second autopsy, but after that was over, he had been placed back in his coffin and reinterred. Was it not I who had thrown that first handful of earth on top of the coffin? Had I not seen the coffin buried in the ground with my own eyes? Although the gravestone had not yet been erected, my brother was undoubtedly lying under six feet of earth.

Still, the dead man's resemblance to my brother was uncanny. There had been no other recent deaths in the Tajimi family. Could somebody have exhumed my brother's body and installed him in a place like this? It was strange, though. It had been a full nine days since my brother died, and yet there were no visible signs of decomposition.

Deeply perplexed, I just stood there, frozen to the spot, when suddenly a woman's voice called out behind me:

"Who is it?... Is somebody there?..."

Noriko and I both jumped and turned around. There was somebody coming towards us, carrying a lantern.

"Is somebody there?..." the voice repeated.

As the lantern drew nearer, Noriko again clung to me in fright.

"Who's there?..." the voice called out a third time.

The advancing stranger raised their lantern higher. The voice was echoing through the cave so much that it was strangely distorted. But then I realized for the first time who it was.

"Is that you, Haruyo?" I cried out. "It's me, Tatsuya!"

"Tatsuya! I thought it was you. But who's that with you?"

"It's Noriko."

"Noriko?" my sister repeated, her voice cracking with surprise. She quickly ran over to us.

"Ah, so it is. Noriko. Just as you said."

She cast a suspicious look at both of us, before turning around again and taking in her surroundings.

"But what on earth are you doing here?"

"All in good time, Haruyo, but what are you doing here yourself?"

"I…"

"Have you known about these caves for a long time?"

"Not at all. This is my first time down here. It's so eerie," she said, looking around and shuddering. "But I had heard about them. When I was little, I heard that there was a secret passage leading from the house. But Koume and Kotake told me that it had been walled up long ago…"

"So you only discovered it this evening?"

Haruyo bristled at my inquisitive tone, but in the end she looked me in the eye and said gravely:

"Tatsuya… Last night, I came to find you in the annexe, but you weren't there. And the doors were all bolted from the inside. I just couldn't understand it. I waited so long for you by the annexe, but you never came back. In the end, I just gave up and went back to the main house, but this morning you were there! I couldn't believe it. But you wouldn't say anything, and I didn't dare ask you what had happened. I was so worried that I decided to come again this evening, but once again you were nowhere to be seen and everything was bolted from the inside. That was when I remembered hearing about the secret passage. I said to myself, it must be somewhere in the annexe… So I started looking for it, and that's when I spotted this. It was caught under the lid of the large chest in the storage room."

She extracted a handkerchief from her pocket.

"This is yours, isn't it? So, I lifted the lid and saw drops of wax on the bedding there. It took a bit of effort, but in the end the bottom of the chest shuddered open. And here I am…"

Haruyo gave us another suspicious look before carrying on.

"But you, Tatsuya… How did you find out about the secret passage? Who told you about it?"

I no longer had any reason to keep it from my sister, but I hesitated to reveal how I had found out in front of Noriko.

"I'll explain once we're back home," I said. "But first, I need you to tell me who that is, Haruyo."

I shone Noriko's lantern over towards the alcove. It was only then that Haruyo noticed the thing. She cried out in surprise and recoiled, but immediately she pulled herself together and took a couple of steps forward.

"But how is it possible?" she whispered with a gasp. "Who on earth could have brought this down here?"

"You mean, you recognize it?" I asked.

"Yes… I saw it once a long time ago. Tatsuya, you remember that little building just behind the annexe? You asked me the other day if it was a Buddhist shrine. Well, it isn't actually Buddhist at all; it's Shinto. Officially, it's dedicated to the god of the harvest, but in reality…"

My sister hesitated.

"You must have heard the story already. A long, long time ago, the villagers here killed one of Yoshihisa Amago's generals. It's to him that the shrine is dedicated. This armour belonged to the general. It's a relic. It was placed on that sarcophagus and erected in the shrine, but around fifteen or sixteen years ago, it suddenly vanished. At the time, it was thought to be the work of a thief, albeit a rather peculiar one… But it's odd, isn't it? Who could have brought it down here, I wonder."

Now we understood where the armour came from, but the real question remained: who was the man beneath it?

"That's all clear enough, Haruyo, but take a closer look… Look under the helmet. There's actually somebody there, isn't there. Who is he?"

My words seemed to give her a jolt. She turned to look at me and gave a feeble laugh.

"Don't, Tatsuya, you mustn't try to frighten me. You know I have a weak heart."

"I'm not joking, Haruyo. See for yourself. There really is somebody there. I just climbed up on the sarcophagus to take a look with my own eyes."

Haruyo looked up in dread at the warrior. From his plinth, the armoured body was casting a dismal look down on us. Haruyo took a deep breath. Then, holding the lantern aloft, she moved towards the figure, as though being drawn by him.

Noriko and I looked on, holding hands, our palms sweating.

Clinging to the walls of the alcove, Haruyo peered under the helmet. Suddenly, she began to tremble violently. She looked at me frantically.

"Can you help me get a little further up, Tatsuya?"

Her forehead was pale and covered with sweat. I helped her right up into the alcove. She examined the face beneath the helmet with a look of terror and curiosity. Then her breathing quickened. She had recognized the man...

I was watching my sister with bated breath, when Noriko suddenly pulled on my sleeve.

"What is it, Noriko?" I asked.

"There's something written here, Tatsuya."

She was pointing to a spot on the wall about six inches above the sarcophagus where Haruyo was standing. And indeed, there was a stone with some horizontal writing engraved on it. I brought the lantern closer to read the inscription. What I read there made me gasp.

"The Monkey's Seat..."

Where had I heard those words before?... Of course! I had heard them the very night that I arrived at the Tajimi house. Haruyo had been telling me about the intruder in the annexe, and she said that he had dropped a sort of map bearing that very name. I had a similar map. Could it be that these were maps of this underground labyrinth? Once again, I found myself bemused by a riddle that had just presented itself.

Suddenly, I heard a scream coming from above. I looked up and saw Haruyo stagger back.

"Be careful!" I shouted, spreading my arms just in time to catch her.

"Oh, Tatsuya, Tatsuya... What on earth's happening? Have I gone mad? Or am I dreaming?"

"Pull yourself together, Haruyo. What's the matter? Do you recognize the man? Who is he? Who is that man?"

"It's Father..."

"What?"

"It's our father... the man who twenty-six years ago ran off into the mountains and was never heard of again."

She was clinging to me and crying as though she had lost her mind.

I was in a state of shock. It was as if someone had driven a red-hot poker right through my head. Noriko stood dumbfounded by my side.

THREE GOLD COINS

For someone like Haruyo, who had a weak heart, that evening's fearsome discovery must have come as a terrible shock. After begging Noriko not to breathe a word of this to anyone, we parted ways, leaving her at the fork in the tunnel and making our way back to the annexe via the chest. In the bright light of the room, Haruyo looked alarmingly pale.

"You have to pull yourself together, Haruyo. Maybe you should rest a little... You don't look at all well."

"I'm fine, thank you. It's only natural that someone with a bad heart should be a bit of a coward. It just gave me such a shock, that's all."

"But are you sure that it was Father?"

"I'm absolutely certain, Tatsuya. At first, I couldn't believe my eyes, so I had to check again and again... I was eight when Father ran away into the mountains. But I can still remember his features perfectly. I can see him clearly whenever I close my eyes..."

Tears glistened in her eyes. Despite all the horror he had unleashed, he was seemingly still her dear father. I felt my heart clench.

"Don't you think it's strange, though, Haruyo? When Father ran away, he was thirty-six, wasn't he? The body doesn't show the passage of time at all."

"You're right. He must have died in those caves soon after he ran away. That would explain why no trace of him was ever found."

"But it's been more than twenty years since then. How can it be that his body has remained intact all that time, without decomposing?"

"I've no idea. I'm too ignorant to understand these things. But you know, Tatsuya, there are so many mysteries in the world. There are mummies and the like..."

"You're right, of course, but that was no mummy. Although it's true I've never seen one in real life."

"But tell me, Tatsuya," she said, leaning closer to me. "How did you come to know about the secret passage? When did you realize it was there?"

I gave her a brief account of what had happened the night before last. She was taken aback by my story.

"What!" she cried. "Koume and Kotake?"

194

"Yes," I said. "Koume and Kotake… Judging by what they said, they must make the trip to the caves every month, on the day of his death."

"In that case, they must have known for a long time that Father's body was down there."

"It seems that way, yes. Besides, who else would have dressed him in the armour and installed him there in the alcove?"

Haruyo's face darkened. She buried her chin in the collar of her kimono and lost herself for a few moments in silent contemplation. Suddenly, her head shot up. A grimace contorted her face, and there was a strange glint in her eyes.

"What is it, Haruyo? Has something just occurred to you?"

"I'm frightened, Tatsuya. I'm frightened… But it must be, I'm sure of it."

"What is, Haruyo? What are you talking about?"

"Listen, Tatsuya," she said in a high-pitched voice. "It's been so long since this memory last wrenched my heart. But lately… what with all these deaths, all these terrible poisonings… Ever since they began, I haven't been able to put it out of my mind."

She shuddered.

"Since it's you, Tatsuya, I can tell you," she continued, "but please, don't breathe a word of this to anyone."

With these preliminaries over, she began to unfold the following tale…

It happened twenty-six years ago, which is to say a little after the massacre took place. Haruyo was eight and, ever since she had witnessed the killing of her mother, she had suffered from violent nocturnal terrors. Every night at around midnight, she would have these blazing fits of tears. Eventually, Koume and Kotake took pity on the girl and allowed her to sleep between them.

195

"Only, sometimes they would disappear in the middle of the night," she said. "Once I made a terrible scene, crying and wailing as I looked for them all through the house. After that, they never left me alone. Instead, they would take turns disappearing, so that only one of them would be gone at any given time. Whenever I asked where the other one was, I always got the same answer: that she had gone to the toilet and would be right back. I was too young to question this, of course, so I'd usually just fall asleep again. But one night I overheard them talking, whispering the most dreadful things…"

That night, Haruyo had gone to sleep as usual between Koume and Kotake, but in the dead of the night she woke to hear lowered voices. Realizing that her great-aunts were trying not to be overheard, she pretended to be asleep while she eavesdropped on their conversation. It was the word "poison" that first made her prick up her ears. She caught snatches of sentences: "It can't go on like this any more… if he's caught, it'll be the death penalty… he's not going to die anytime soon, at this rate… if he escapes, it'll be a disaster." Lastly, she heard one of them say, "But what if we were to poison his food?"

"The things that are engrained in you in childhood last a lifetime," Haruyo said. "Even now you can't imagine the terror that grips me whenever I think back on that conversation."

Her shoulders convulsed once again, and gently she wiped her tears with the back of her sleeve. Her tale had begun to affect me, too, and an icy chill ran down my legs.

"You mean to say that, for a little while after the massacre, Koume and Kotake gave Father shelter down in those caves?"

"That does seem to be the only explanation, now that I think about it. They must have brought him his meals down there."

"Yes, and they wound up poisoning him…"

196

"Tatsuya… Even if it did happen, you mustn't think ill of them. They were acting in the interests of the family, the village, maybe even Father himself. He was their favourite, after all, the golden child. But to poison him… I can't even begin to fathom it."

Tragedy seemed to stalk this family at every turn. The very thought of it made me shudder.

It seemed likely that my sister's hypothesis was correct. Koume and Kotake must have secretly led Father to his death for the sake of the family and village, even for his own sake, considering what might have happened to him if he were ever caught. Looking at it that way, it could even be seen as an act of mercy. Still, though, I was plagued by unspeakably dark thoughts.

"Don't worry, Haruyo, I understand. I won't breathe a word of this to anyone. I'll make sure that Noriko doesn't, either. You should try to put all this out of your mind."

"You're right. It all happened so long ago… But I can't help worrying: what if all these recent poisonings are somehow connected?"

"Haruyo," I said, looking her in surprise, "are you implying that Koume and Kotake…"

"No, no, it isn't possible. But when I think back on Hisaya's death…"

If they had killed the father, then could they not also have killed the son? There was certainly a logic to Haruyo's suspicion. It stood to reason. Besides, did these old women, having reached that venerable age, not have something inhuman about them, something unchecked by common sense? That is what my sister feared.

"You mustn't think such nonsense, Haruyo. You're getting carried away with yourself. But now tell me about the secret passage. Why does the house have one?"

"Well, I don't know the details, but the story goes that among our ancestors there was a very beautiful girl who was in service at the feudal lord's castle. She came to his attention, but, owing to obscure circumstances, she had to leave the castle. The feudal lord couldn't forget her, though, and from time to time he would visit her secretly at this house. That's why the annexe was built, so I suppose the secret passage must have been dug out around the same time, in case of emergency. But Tatsuya…"

"Yes?"

"You really mustn't go down there. I don't want anything bad to happen to you."

"All right, I won't go down there any more."

I said this to calm my sister's fears, although I didn't have the least intention of stopping.

Whenever one question was answered, another would immediately rear its head. The mystery of Koume and Kotake's nocturnal wanderings had been solved, but several new mysteries had presented themselves. How had the body remained so intact, and what was the meaning of the Monkey's Seat? Why, moreover, had I been given this map of an underground labyrinth? Before she died, my mother had told me that it would bring me good fortune. But how could that bizarre map and those poems possibly result in that?

In the end, I had squandered my chance to broach the subject with Haruyo. After that evening, she was confined to bed with a high fever, so for the moment my questions would have to wait.

Haruyo's fever must have been brought on by the shock that she had received in the underground cave. In her delirium, she would occasionally rave about the armour and her father. I kept a vigil by her bedside day and night, not only because I was afraid that she might reveal our secret, but also because, of all the family, she was the one to whom I was closest. And in any event, she would always send Oshima to find me if ever I left her side for too long.

Koume and Kotake shared my concern and would appear at Haruyo's bedside from time to time. Having heard about my sister's illness, Shintaro and Noriko also dropped by to check in on the patient. I availed myself of the opportunity to tell Noriko that, under the circumstances, I wouldn't be able to meet her for some time. She nodded meekly in understanding. Before she left, she promised not to tell anybody about the other night and asked me to reassure Haruyo of this. Miyako and Mrs Kuno also paid a visit, during which the latter, her face wan and drained of life, informed us that the whereabouts of her husband were still unknown.

Throughout each of these visits, I worried what Haruyo might let slip in her delirium, so I stayed by her bedside constantly in order to smooth anything over if ever the need arose. In this way, I kept watch over my sister for a whole week, and then ten days, completely forgetting about everything else that was going on. Besides, there were no developments, and I had not seen Kosuke Kindaichi for some time.

The time passed in the twinkling of an eye. Dr Arai had even gone so far as to say, "Well, with a weak heart like hers, a fever like this could..." But one day, Haruyo's fever abated and her delirium passed, and now he assured us of her speedy recovery. Finally, I could heave a sigh of relief.

"I'm sorry to have put you to so much trouble," Haruyo said, thanking me. "You must be exhausted. I'm fine now, so you'll be able to sleep in the annexe again."

For the first time in many days, I returned to the annexe, but despite my exhaustion, I didn't feel like sleeping. I wanted to use this long-awaited opportunity to slip back into the underground passage.

For some time now, I had been trying to solve the mystery of the well-preserved corpse. Fortunately, there was an encyclopaedia in the Tajimi house, which I scoured until I found what I believed to be an explanation for what I had seen. In order to ascertain whether or not I was right, I needed to sneak back into the tunnel.

Luckily, that night I managed to find my way to the samurai without any mishap or running into anybody. I clambered up into the alcove to examine the corpse once again, and grew ever more certain that I had solved the riddle.

You see, the body had turned to mortuary wax. According to the encyclopaedia, when a body is buried somewhere humid, the fats in the body are broken down into fatty acids. That fatty acid combines with the calcium and magnesium content of the water in the body and environment to produce insoluble calcium palmitate and magnesium palmitate. In other words, the body is transformed into soap, while preserving its original appearance. The process is called saponification. Of course, not just anybody could be turned into soap in this way: it happened only to subjects with the right quantities of fat, and in burial places where the humidity had a high enough content of magnesium and calcium.

The composition of my father's body and the location of his burial must have met the conditions perfectly. That way, after all these years, his body had turned to wax, while retaining his old features. How this process must have frightened Koume and Kotake! A body that would not decompose must have struck them with a mysterious sense of menace. Imagine, seeing that the body of a man who had committed the most extraordinary crimes during his life was the object of such a miracle in death. Their terror must have been incredible. If they had clothed him in armour and placed him on this pedestal, then they must have considered him a god.

I was satisfied with this verification of my hypothesis, but a nagging curiosity lingered on. I carefully moved my father's body aside and lifted the lid of the stone sarcophagus beneath him. When I think back on it now, this sudden action had such a tremendous effect on the course of my fate.

Inside, I found an old hunting rifle and a Japanese sword. There were also two broken flashlights and a lamp. Were these not relics of that terrifying night that was still the source of the villagers' nightmares? A shiver ran through me. I was about to close the lid, when suddenly something caught my eye. At first I couldn't really make it out, so I shone the beam of my lantern on it. The light made it glitter. I reached into the bottom of the sarcophagus and picked it up. It was oval-shaped and made of metal, measuring around six inches by four. It felt heavy in my palm. On one side there were markings like a grain of wood, while the other side was rough. For a moment I just stared at it, but soon enough I was jolted out of this stupor.

Was this not an old gold coin of the kind known as *oban*?

All of a sudden, I noticed that my teeth were chattering and my whole body was shaking. I reached my trembling hand once again into the bottom of the sarcophagus.

There were three of these coins.

MORE POISONED TEA

As I returned to the annexe, I felt as though I were in the grip of a fever. I immediately drank down a pitcher of water, so parched was my throat after all that excitement.

Now I saw for the very first time why my mother had taken such care in giving me this map and telling me to keep it safe. Only now did I understand why she had told me that the legends and stories and rumours about this village should not be treated as sheer make-believe.

Was it not said that those eight samurai who had fled the massacre of the Amago clan, only to be murdered here by the villagers' ancestors, had also brought with them 3,000 *tael* of gold on horseback? It was said that the villagers then had any number of reasons for killing those samurai, but was one of them not their lust for gold? And was it not also said that the gold had never been found?…

Could the gold, then, be hidden in this underground labyrinth? My father, who had taken refuge in that very place after fleeing to the mountains twenty-six years ago, must have stumbled upon the hiding place as he roamed about that maze. When Koume and Kotake poisoned him, he must have had barely enough time to pick up those pieces of gold. The twins hadn't even bothered to wonder how he had come by such wealth, and so, in their ignorance, they had simply decided to hide away the coins with the rest of his belongings in the sarcophagus.

Yes, that must have been it. There could be no mistake. What other fitting explanation could there be for these three gold *oban*?

I had heard that it was not until the late sixteenth century, under the daimyo Nobunaga Oda, that coins were first minted to be equal in weight and value. Before then, ingots of gold were simply beaten with a mallet before being cut and weighed. Unlike the minted coins, these ones bore no official seal or inscription written in black ink. Didn't the coins that I saw earlier bear a marked resemblance to these more ancient ones? The Amago clan had been decimated in 1566, and for years afterwards as the warlords divided up the country, anarchy had reigned in the making of currency.

After the defeat, the eight samurai must have loaded up their horses with as much gold as they could carry, hoping to bide their time until a counterattack could be launched. It was possible that the 3,000 was an exaggerated figure. It could well be that as the story was handed down from generation to generation, the number was settled upon for convenience's sake. But that didn't matter. What mattered was these fugitive samurai had taken whatever money they could, great or small, and hidden it somewhere where it still lay undisturbed. Was this not proved by the evidence of the three gold *oban* inside the sarcophagus?

I quivered in excitement and fear. I took out the amulet that I always kept on my person and, with a trembling hand, extracted the map that been drawn with brush and ink on *washi* paper. It showed a plan of a complex labyrinth, on which three points with strange-sounding names had been marked: the Dragon's Jaw, the Fox's Den and the Devil's Abyss. Beside each of them was a poem.

> *Whosoever ventures upon the Trove of the Buddha's Treasure*
> *Shall know the dread of the Dragon's Jaw.*

> *Do not lose your way in the hundred and eight tunnels of the Fox's Den*
> *For they are darker than shadows in the night.*

> *Do not draw the pure waters of the Devil's Abyss*
> *Even if thirst should consume your body.*

There could no longer be any doubt. Until then, I had glanced over these lines without paying them much attention, but now, reading them carefully, it became apparent to me that these words were describing a route to the hidden treasure. Those strange names—Drago... 'w, Fox's Den and Devil's Abyss—must have been important landmarks along the way, tricky spots where your life would be in peril if you got lost.

I had no idea how my mother had come by this map, nor did I have any idea who had written these poems or when. But that didn't matter to me. It was enough to know that this was a guide to finding the 3,000 pieces of gold.

In my excitement, I set about examining the map, but the closer I looked the more discouraged I grew. The map was far from perfect. In some places the lines were blurred, while in others they came to an abrupt end. Those must have been regions that the author of this map had not had the time to explore. What troubled me most, though, was that none of the markings corresponded to places or tunnels that I recognized. It was then that I realized the significance of the map in my sister's possession. She had already said that there was a location on hers called the Monkey's Seat. Then it hit me... We each had two parts of the same map. Hers was the beginning and mine was the continuation. But if that were so, then why was the location of the treasure not marked on mine? Could there be a third map?

For the rest of the night I couldn't sleep. It wasn't a question of greed, however. Even if I did find the gold, there was no guarantee that I was legally entitled to keep it. Still, with all its romantic associations the discovery had sent me into a state of wild euphoria. Is hidden treasure not a symbol of eternal longing? Do we not still love to devour *Treasure Island* and *King Solomon's Mines*?

The following day I longed to ask Haruyo about the map but didn't dare to do so. This was probably a mark of my ambition. Had I known that her map revealed only more of the labyrinth and not the location of the treasure itself, I would have had less compunction about asking her. But that would have meant taking advantage of her ignorance for my own benefit. The prospect of a guilty conscience gave me pause for thought. And yet, I didn't want to confide in her either. Treasure-hunting is a solitary pursuit; it's the secrecy that makes it enjoyable. In the end, I skipped the chance to raise the subject with Haruyo.

If memory serves, Kosuke Kindaichi came to visit us for the first time in a long while that same day. After enquiring about my sister's health, he revealed to me a most curious thing.

"I come bearing news," he said. "Do you recall what I said to you when I was last here? That the Koicha nun was murdered around midnight, but that Dr Kuno had taken the 10.50 train to N——, thus giving him a watertight alibi? Well, it turns out that there has been some mistake."

"A mistake?"

"That evening, it was not Dr Kuno who boarded the 10.50 train, but somebody else entirely. The stationmaster was mistaken. Such things do happen from time to time, although they can be something of a bother."

Kindaichi scratched at his dishevelled head of hair before continuing.

"But if Dr Kuno didn't take the 10.50 train that night, then what does that mean for our investigation? The 10.50 train for N—— was the last train to leave the station that night in either direction, and the police began their search before the first train the next morning. One thing is therefore certain: wherever Dr Kuno went, he didn't take the train."

"But if he didn't take the train," I said, frowning, "then where could he have gone? It's been more than ten days already…"

"It is my opinion that he must have fled into the mountains on foot. After all, twenty-six years ago, after the massacre, that's exactly what the killer did, is it not? And he was never found. Perhaps the same has happened again…"

Kindaichi must have noticed the altered look on my face.

"Are you all right?" he asked. "You don't look well… Ah, of course. My apologies. I forget that the events of twenty-six years ago are a taboo subject in these parts. Forgive me. In any case, I really must be going."

With these words, Kindaichi wandered off again. I was still none the wiser why he had come.

That evening, Koume and Kotake invited me for another cup of tea.

"You've been such a help these past few days, Tatsuya. It's thanks to you that Haruyo has regained her strength. We're in your debt."

"Yes, Koume is right. I don't know what we'd have done if it weren't for you. You can't ask for that level of dedication even from the servants."

Curled up as usual, like little monkeys, the twins chewed their words. On edge and at a loss for what to say, I merely bowed.

"You mustn't be so tense. Relax a little. If you don't, then you'll make us feel tense as well. Tonight, we wanted to show you our gratitude, and Kotake suggested offering you some tea."

The very mention of tea made me flinch. I looked at them, but they both just stared back blankly.

"We know it isn't much, being served by two old women like us," Koume said with a chuckle, "but it's the thought that counts, is it not? Come now, be a good sport."

Kotake began whisking the thick tea with care.

"By the way, Tatsuya, about Haruyo's illness…" Koume said, as though the thought had suddenly struck her. "What do you think brought it on?"

"Brought it on?"

"Yes," said Koume, moving closer. "She never was a strong child. She was always having to rest. But she's never been so ill, never had such a high temperature... What do you think caused it?"

"Yes, indeed," Kotake chimed in. "Dr Arai asked whether she had been anxious or had some kind of shock lately. We couldn't think of anything, so we wondered whether you might know something. Has she had a shock of some kind?"

"I can't think of anything in particular. But ever since Hisaya's funeral, she's had to worry about one thing after another. Maybe that was what caused her illness."

"That must be it. What other explanation could there be? Isn't that right, Kotake?"

"Yes, quite right. She said so many fantastic things when she was delirious, though. She was talking about a tunnel and a suit of armour... She even called out, 'Father!... Father!...' What could she have meant, Tatsuya?"

Kotake stopped whisking the tea and looked me in the eye. With her bleary eyes, Koume also gave me a searching look. I could feel hot perspiration running under my arms.

This was why they had invited me: they wanted to find out what Haruyo had meant in her delirious ravings. But, no—in truth, they must have known already. That was what worried them. And so, what they really wanted to find out was how much I knew.

I said nothing.

"Haruyo is Haruyo, and Tatsuya is Tatsuya." Koume laughed with an air of nonchalance. "Why should Tatsuya know what Haruyo meant by any of that? Isn't that right, Tatsuya? Go ahead, Kotake, serve Tatsuya his tea."

"Right away... Please, Tatsuya. I hope it's to your liking."

I remained silent, looking from one to the other. They both feigned innocence as they watched me and the cup in front of me. I found myself in the grip of some unspeakable fear. I remembered the story that Haruyo had told me, how twenty-six years ago, doubtless with that same look of innocence, the twins had discussed poisoning my father. I couldn't help thinking that those two old women were grotesque, inhuman monsters.

"What's the matter, Tatsuya? Kotake has been good enough to make you some tea. You'd better drink it up before it gets cold."

I was cornered. I took the cup in my trembling hand and placed it to my lips, my teeth chattering against the rim. Closing my eyes and praying to the gods, I drank it down in one gulp. The tea had that same bitter tang that it had the other night.

"Ah, there's a good boy. He drank it all up! You should go back to your room and rest now, Tatsuya."

As I staggered to my feet, the old women looked at one another, smiling like a pair of Cheshire cats.

A MONSTER IN THE CAVES

Having said all that, this was the second time that Koume and Kotake had invited me for a cup of tea, so I knew what their intentions were and was less apprehensive than I had been on the previous occasion.

Haruyo's ravings about the secret passage must have raised their suspicions. Because of their venerable age, they may have appeared senile at times, but they actually had all their wits about them. They must have wanted to sneak into the underground caves to find out just how much Haruyo knew about their secret. So, to prevent me from waking up, they had slipped me another sleeping draught.

Their wish was my command. Besides, after so much worry and excitement, I was exhausted. It would do me a world of good to have a sound night's sleep. By all means, then. As far as I was concerned, they could take as long as they liked down there.

After returning to the annexe, I turned out the light and slipped into the bed that Oshima had prepared. I was so on edge that the sleeping pill had little effect, however. Despite myself, my eyes and ears were on the alert, waiting for the moment when the twins would appear. This must have slowed the action of the sedative.

I must have spent a good hour like that, tossing and turning in my bed. Then at last I heard the sound of soft footsteps coming along the long corridor. Carrying a lantern again, Koume and Kotake crept into my room. I quickly pretended to be in a deep slumber.

Bearing the lantern aloft, they peered over me.

"There, I told you. He's sound asleep. You worry too much, Kotake."

"You're right. Only, he pulled that face when he drank the tea. I was worried that he might have realized... He looks all right for now."

"He's fine. He doesn't look as though he'll wake before we return."

"Let's go then, Koume."

"Very well."

The twins crept out of my room and, once again, their shadows were cast on the sliding door as they made their way round to the storage room. After I heard the chest lid open and then shut again, pitch darkness and perfect silence returned. There was not a soul around.

"What now?" I wondered aloud as I lay there in the bed. Should I wait for them to come back or should I go after them?

After some hesitation, I decided that I had no choice but to wait for them. After all, I knew where they were going. They were heading for the Monkey's Seat in order to check on the wax corpse. There was no point in following them.

Secure in this belief, I lay there in bed, waiting for them to return. Thinking back on it now, though, it was that very decision that led to the terrible event that ensued. If only I had decided to go after them, then that awful tragedy might never have taken place.

No amount of regret can change the facts, however. Who could have known then that such a cruel fate was lurking just around the corner? In any case, what happened happened, and I hope that the gods will forgive my negligence.

After they had been gone a while, I relaxed a little, and the sleeping draught began to take effect: a wave of drowsiness overcame me, and a few moments later I was asleep. Because of this, I have no idea when exactly the drama took place.

I was woken forcefully by one of the twins. As ever, I couldn't tell whether it was Koume or Kotake, but the alarmed look on her face roused me from my slumber instantly.

"What is it, Auntie?"

I bolted up in bed and stared at my great-aunt's face, which was contorted by fear. She had turned on the lamp before waking me, so the whole room was bathed in light. With that simian face of hers, she was trying vainly to articulate something, but no words would come out. I saw that her kimono was covered in mud and that it was torn in places.

Clearly, there had been some accident. I had a sinking feeling in the pit of my stomach.

"Auntie! Auntie! What's happened? Where is your sister?"

"Oh! Koume... Koume..."

"Yes, where is Koume?"

"She's been carried away… Oh, Tatsuya, Tatsuya… The body has come back to life… It was terrifying, Tatsuya… The body came back to life and started moving… You must go quickly! Help Koume! Otherwise, she'll be dragged into the cave and killed! Quickly, Tatsuya, you must hurry! Save Koume!"

I looked at her in shock. She was crying like a child. I put my hands on her shoulders and shook her violently.

"Auntie! Auntie! What on earth are you talking about? I don't understand what you're trying to tell me. Calm down and tell me again."

Far from calming down, she only grew more distraught. I didn't know what to do with her. Often, when women of that age get agitated, they lose all control, like a child of five or six. She kept sobbing and wailing and speaking too rapidly for me to understand anything. The more I heard, though, the more her meaning became clear to me.

The twins had made their way down to the Monkey's Seat via the secret passage in order to check on the wax corpse, which had been worrying them. Something strange seemed to have happened there. According to Kotake, the armour-clad samurai had suddenly risen up and turned towards them, ready to pounce.

It was impossible that this wax corpse had come back to life of course, so Kotake must surely have suffered some optical illusion. What seemed more likely was that somebody had been hiding there. Perhaps somebody had been lurking near the Monkey's Seat when Koume and Kotake appeared. In a tricky spot, the intruder must have quickly hidden himself in the alcove, crouching behind the samurai. Perhaps, in the dim light of the lantern, his movements would have given the impression that the samurai was alive.

Thus far, there had been nothing particularly odd about her story. I myself knew that somebody had been skulking about in

211

the caves. That this stranger had attacked Koume and Kotake was something else entirely, however. It was even more astonishing that the person had seemingly abducted Koume.

"Auntie, Auntie," I said, dressing as quickly as I could. "Are you saying that somebody has dragged Koume off into the depths of the caves?"

"Yes! Who would exaggerate at a time like this? I can still hear her voice now, pleading for help… Go now, Tatsuya. Quickly. Rescue her!"

"What did the man look like, Auntie?"

"I've no idea… As soon as he rushed at us, we dropped the lantern and everything around was plunged into darkness."

Kotake began to sob like a child once again. It was then that Haruyo, having heard all this commotion, came running in. When she saw what was going on, her pallid face froze.

"What is it, Auntie? Tatsuya? What's happened?"

"Oh, Haruyo, Haruyo!" cried Kotake, tears glistening in her eyes.

She broke down again, so I gave my sister a summary of what had happened.

"I'll go down to the Monkey's Seat and check," I said. "Is there a lantern that I can borrow?"

"I'll go with you, Tatsuya…"

"No, Haruyo, you have to stay here. You're still not fully recovered. You mustn't exert yourself."

"But…"

"No buts, Haruyo. I need you to stay here and look after Kotake. But first, fetch me a lamp quickly!"

With a look of resignation, she went back into the main house and returned carrying a lantern.

"Are you sure you'll be all right?" she asked.

"I'll be fine. Don't worry. I won't be long."

"Be careful down there."

I left Kotake and my crestfallen sister behind and, carrying the lantern in one hand, made my way underground though the chest.

By now, I was so used to the tunnels that I didn't need to worry about getting lost down there, and so, after slipping through the rock, I took the left path at the fork.

I had almost made it as far as the Monkey's Seat, when suddenly I stopped in my tracks and hid the light behind my hand. There was a faint light coming from up ahead.

There was somebody there! I took out a couple of matches, just in case the need should arise, then I hurriedly extinguished the lantern.

Fortunately, whoever was there didn't seem to have noticed the light coming from my direction. The faint light from their lamp continued to flicker on the wall where the tunnel curved away. Being careful not to make any noise, I groped my way towards the bend.

From there, I could see the cave directly ahead of me. Somebody was standing there with a lamp, looking up at the Monkey's Seat.

Pressing my back to the wall, I took four or five steps sideways, like a crab, edging my way closer to the intruder. I was only a few steps away, when a cry of surprise escaped my lips.

"Noriko!"

She gasped and turned around. It really was her. Lifting her lamp higher, she tried to see who was there in the darkness.

"Tatsuya? Tatsuya, is that you? Where are you?"

I stepped out of the darkness and grabbed her by the shoulders. A surge of violent emotion leapt inside me, and I could feel my body burning.

"Noriko, what on earth are you doing here?"

"I came to find you," she said, clinging to me. "I waited here last night, and the night before that, all in the hope of seeing you. If only you knew how much I've missed you."

Ah, the power of all-consuming passion! In the simple hope of meeting me, she was willing to brave darkness and never-ending caves... Her innocence truly made my heart clench.

"You did? I'm sorry, I've been so busy these last few days that I just couldn't slip away."

"It's all right. I understand. Your sister is sick, so I can't expect too much. Besides, I got to see you tonight, and nothing could make me happier."

I was so moved that I took her in my arms. Delighted by this, she yielded to my firm embrace. Our hearts were beating in unison.

I stroked her hair for a short while, but I soon pulled myself together, realizing that this was no time for caresses.

"Noriko," I asked, gently releasing my hands from her shoulders.

"Yes?"

"When did you get here? Did anything out of the ordinary happen while you were waiting here?"

My question seemed to bring her back to reality with a jolt. A look of terror flashed in her eyes.

"Well, yes, there was something odd, actually. It happened when I reached the fork in the tunnel. I heard a terrible cry come from here. I was so stunned that I just stood there, frozen. Then somebody rushed past me. Somebody small, like a monkey... The figure ran off, stumbling, in the direction of your house."

It must have been Kotake.

"So, what did you do then?" I asked, breathless.

"I didn't do anything," she replied. "I was so stunned that I couldn't move. But then I heard more screaming from here.

I thought I heard a cry for help. I was terrified, but I quietly inched my way towards where the shouts were coming from."

Once again, I was in awe of her fearlessness.

"What happened after you heard those screams?"

"As I came closer, the screams got further and further away, until in the end I couldn't hear them any more. Whoever it was must have ventured far into the depths of the caves."

There could be little doubt that it was Koume who had protested so loudly as she was being dragged off into the unfathomable black depths of the caves.

THE MISSING GOLD

I relit the lantern and, together with Noriko, set about examining the area around the Monkey's Seat once again.

Just as I suspected: there were footprints on the wet ground, leading off into the depths of the caves. Clearly, these marks must have been left by Koume and her captor.

Whoever her captor was, Koume must have been like a sparrow in the talons of an eagle, or a young rabbit in the jaws of some wild beast. My blood ran cold as I imagined her struggling, with desperate howls, against this cruel demon who was abducting her.

"Noriko! Noriko, are you certain that the cries you heard led off into the depths of the caves?"

"Yes, it was such a desperate voice. I can still hear it even now."

Noriko shuddered at the memory. I held up the lantern to try to illuminate the depths of the cave. We had not ventured past this chamber until now, but it was clear that the intricate underground labyrinth extended much further.

"Shall we see what's that way?" Noriko asked.

"Are you feeling brave enough?"

"Yes," she said, smiling broadly. "With you by my side."

She was still delicate and frail, a baby born before term. Yet, frail though her body was, it was home to an uncommonly bold and bright spirit. Perhaps it had to do with the trust that she placed in me. Nothing seems frightening when you have your beloved by your side. Or, rather, she had convinced herself that, with me there, the danger would all but vanish.

"OK, let's go," I said. "But first I'd like to take another look at the Monkey's Seat."

I was intrigued by what Kotake had told me. *The body came back to life and started moving,* she had said. I had to see for myself what had gone on. I went over to the Monkey's Seat and lifted the lantern higher to illuminate the alcove.

It was just as I thought. The eerie samurai was still seated on top of his stone sarcophagus, staring out at us under his helmet with his waxen gaze. Only his position seemed slightly different from the last time that I had seen him. Had somebody perhaps moved him to lift the lid of the sarcophagus?

A thought suddenly struck me: there ought to be three gold coins inside, the three that I had found but put back. I wondered whether they were still there.

"Hang on, Noriko… I'm going to climb up into the alcove."

I clambered up and moved the samurai to one side, then I lifted the lid of the sarcophagus to take a look.

It was empty! Somebody had stolen the three gold coins… I despaired, furious with myself. Why hadn't I taken the gold when I had had the opportunity? Why had I left it there for someone else to find?

Each them must have weighed over 40 *monme*. Even if they were only 80 per cent pure gold, then that would be at least 32 *monme*. The price of one *monme* of gold alone was then around 2,000 yen, so each coin must have been worth at least 64,000 yen. In other words, I'd lost almost 200,000 yen! An entire fortune, gone! Unable to control my frustration, I began to grind my teeth.

It wasn't just the financial loss that infuriated me, however. Those three coins were in fact the strongest proof yet that a vast treasure was hidden somewhere in the caves. Had the person who stole those three coins realized that as well? If they had, then it was only reasonable to assume that they would go hunting for the rest. In that case, did I not now have a formidable rival in my hunt for the treasure?

Why, oh, why, hadn't I hidden the coins in a safe spot?

"What's wrong, Tatsuya? What can you see inside?"

Noriko's voice brought me back to reality.

"Nothing... there's nothing here."

I wiped the beads of sweat from my brow, before closing the lid and replacing the samurai on top of the sarcophagus.

I jumped down.

"Tell me what's wrong, Tatsuya. You're as white as a sheet."

I couldn't hide my disappointment. It was as if those coins had been snatched right out of my hand.

"Oh, it's nothing. I'm fine," I said, trying to buoy myself. "The assailant must have hidden himself behind the samurai. The twins wouldn't have suspected a thing. He must have pounced on them as they were praying and abducted Koume, dragging her off into the depths of the caves."

"How awful!" exclaimed Noriko, agog. "So the cry I heard earlier must have been Koume's."

"Precisely. And the figure who went running past you was Kotake."

"I see," said Noriko, growing more and more amazed. "But what were they doing here in the first place?"

"Well, there could be a number of explanations…"

"And who do you suppose the person who abducted Koume was? And what does he want, dragging her off into the caves like that?"

It was just as I'd feared. Somebody in the village of Eight Graves was carrying out some senseless, hare-brained scheme. He was going about systematically killing one of each pair in the village. And, of all the possible pairs, weren't the twins the most ideal target? And to think: the impetus for all this madness was that bolt of lightning that had struck down one of the twin cedars. It had been only a matter of time before one of the twins, who shared their names with those trees, would fall victim to this insanity.

I had gooseflesh. I was horrified at the idea that this poor, defenceless old woman was now in the clutches of a murderer. Whoever the killer was, his task now would be easier than tearing an old rag to shreds.

"Come on, Tatsuya, there's no time to lose! If he does have Koume, then we can't just abandon her. We have to go and find her."

Are all women possessed of such courage when the need presents itself? Noriko was far braver than I. With her encouragement, I steeled myself for what lay ahead.

"All right," I said. "Let's go."

No sooner had I said this than we were faced with a problem. Apart from the path by which I had come, there were three others leading off from the cave. Which one should we choose? We examined the marks on the ground, but Koume's tracks just vanished. Perhaps the abductor had carried her off on his back into the depths of the cave. With a woman so old and small as Koume, it wouldn't have required much effort.

"We haven't a clue where to go," Noriko said.

"We haven't indeed."

"Since they're all the same, let's just pick one at random."

She was full of courage, but I felt more circumspect.

"We can't. We've no idea what could be lying in wait down those tunnels."

"I suppose you're right."

We were looking at each other, hesitating, when suddenly there came a sound of hurried footsteps. We jumped in fright. As we turned around, we could see a light coming towards us.

"Is… Is that you, Tatsuya?"

It was Haruyo. I was so relieved to hear her voice.

"Haruyo! What are you doing here? It's dangerous in your condition…"

"I'm fine. I was worried about you. And there was something I had to give you…"

"What is it?"

"Here…"

She rushed towards me and only then did she notice Noriko's presence.

"Oh!" she exclaimed. "Noriko! I didn't see you there."

"Yes, we met by chance down here. What is it you wanted to give me?"

It would have taken too long to explain what Noriko was doing here, and, since I was so little inclined to try, I attempted to sidestep the question, instead urging Haruyo to speak.

"Here, I told you about it before," she began. "It's the map that I found in the annexe. I realized earlier—it has place names like the 'Monkey's Seat'. So I wondered whether it could be a map of these underground tunnels, and I rushed here to give it to you."

My heart jumped for joy. I had been itching to get my hands on this map, but I hadn't had the heart to deceive my sister in order to acquire it. Now it was she who was bringing it to me voluntarily. I couldn't believe my luck, but I did my best to hide my true emotions.

"Thank you," I said flatly. "It looks as if Koume was kidnapped and carried off down one of these tunnels, but we don't know which one."

"Take a look," Haruyo replied, indicating the map. "It must have been the middle one. The other two are dead ends."

I examined the map by the light of the lanterns, and indeed, of the three paths leading away from the chamber, the two on either side were dead ends. Only the middle path led somewhere, twisting and turning into the depths of the caves.

I wanted to study the map in more detail, but there was no time for that then.

"Thank you, Haruyo. We'll try the middle path. But you should go back to the house now."

"Yes, but... What about Noriko?"

"Noriko wants to come with me."

"Well, if Noriko's going, then I'll come with you."

There was a nervousness in her voice. I stared at my sister; she looked strangely tense.

"But, Haruyo, what about Kotake?"

"I gave her a sedative before coming here. She's fast asleep. In any case, I'm coming with you."

She seemed exasperated and pressed on into the tunnel. Surprised by this uncharacteristically bold move of hers, Noriko and I exchanged glances.

Why this sudden anger? I wondered. What were we going to discover at the end of the tunnel?

CHAPTER 6

HARUYO'S FURY

A long, long time ago, I read a detective novel that took place in a series of limestone caves.

I don't intend to retell the story or how it ended, but, suffice it to say, it was about the murder of a man in one of those caves. That isn't the point, however. I was so struck by the romantic descriptions of those caves that I longed to see their beauties with my own eyes one day.

I no longer have the book, and only vague memories of it are lodged in the recesses of my mind, but there are a few passages in particular that I recall: "Not far from the entrance to the cave, the limestone ceiling hung so low that it was impossible to walk standing upright. I had to duck low as I went. But gradually the ceiling grew higher and higher, and I reached a gallery where the walls were encrusted with fluorite crystals, which glittered brilliantly, like a hundred thousand jewels in the darkness…" Then there were descriptions of great chambers created by nature: "The ceilings were almost a hundred feet high, with hundreds, perhaps thousands of stalactites hanging from them. And in the middle of the hall there was an enormous, sparkling, pearlescent stalactite, hanging down like a vast chandelier. The walls all around were covered with incredible patterns and arabesques, created by nature to draw the eye. It felt like standing in a majestic, exquisite palace that had been preserved from antiquity…"

Only then, as we searched in those limestone caves, did I realize what a vast gulf there is between fiction and reality. The cave into which Noriko and I had followed my sister looked every bit the natural limestone cave. Countless stalactites hung low from the ceiling, and all around the walls were covered with patterns and arabesques. But these ones did not glitter. They had their own strange beauty, but they were nowhere near as romantic as described in the book. The floor, the walls, the ceiling—everything was damp and dripping, and every now and then a drop would land on the back of my neck. The humid air was leaden and stale, and it produced an extremely unpleasant sensation on the skin. More to the point, try as I might, I saw no fluorite crystals glittering brilliantly like jewels.

We walked through this eerie, never-ending cave blindly, with a sense of boundless apprehension. The lanterns lit only a few yards around us, but beyond that everything was plunged into an ominous black. The intense feeling of unease gradually suffocated me, and several times I wanted to turn back.

Are women more courageous than men in situations like this? Whereas I hesitated, Haruyo and Noriko carried on silently through the caves, showing no sign of fear—Haruyo up ahead, Noriko by my side. None of us spoke a word.

The tunnel seemed to have an endless number of offshoots, and we often came to points where the tunnel divided in two. At each fork, Haruyo would check the map by the light of her lantern, before setting off again at a determined pace. She didn't consult with us even once…

Ever since I had arrived in that village, my survival had depended on the trust I placed in my sister. Never before had she shown any displeasure with me. She had always been calm and affectionate towards me, and I had always felt at ease with her. What, then, had happened to her that night? Why, all of a sudden, was she being so standoffish? What had I done wrong? Had I done something to offend her?

We came upon yet another fork in the tunnel. Once again Haruyo consulted the map, and once again she charged on without even turning to look at us.

I could bear it no longer. I caught up with her and, placing my hand on her shoulder, stopped her in her tracks.

"Haruyo! Haruyo, just wait a minute. Why won't you talk to me? What are you so angry about?"

In the light of the lanterns, her face looked pale, waxen and harsh. Drops of perspiration were beading on her forehead.

"I… I…" she said, panting desperately, "I'm not angry with anyone."

"But you are, Haruyo. You're angry with me. I'm sorry if I've done something to upset you, but just tell me what I've done wrong. Whatever it is, I'll make up for it, I promise. This sulking will only drive me to despair."

She stared at me without uttering a word. Then her face suddenly creased, like a child ready to burst into tears.

"Oh, Tatsuya…" she said, clinging to my chest and choking with tears.

"Wha… What's the matter, Haruyo?"

I was taken aback. Noriko looked shocked, her eyes wide open.

"I'm sorry, Tatsuya. I'm sorry. I didn't mean to be angry. It's my fault, really. You haven't done anything wrong. It's all my fault. I'm sorry. Forgive me, please."

Still clinging to me, Haruyo continued to sob. As she pressed her face to my chest, I could feel her tears seeping through the fabric of my pyjamas, scorching my skin.

I was at a total loss. What could explain this sudden change in Haruyo's behaviour? My first instinct was to console her, but I didn't know how. I took her hand and stroked her head. All I could do was to wait for the crying to stop. Noriko, too, seemed utterly confused and at a loss for words as she too watched helplessly.

It took some time, but in the end Haruyo managed to calm herself down. I stroked her shoulder in silence.

"You must be absolutely exhausted, Haruyo," I eventually said. "That's why you're getting upset over nothing. Let's go back, so you can have a good rest."

"I'm sorry," she said.

She finally pulled away from me and looked shamefaced as she wiped away her tears.

"Really, it's all been too much for me this evening," she said. "I've been getting worked up over nothing. And now I've been crying… I'm sorry you had to see all that, Noriko. It must have given you a fright."

"I was more worried than anything else. Maybe you haven't quite recovered yet."

"Noriko's right," I said. "It must be exhaustion. You've hardly made it out of bed lately. And it can't be good for your health being in a damp place like this. We should go back."

"Thank you. But we can't go home yet. Not until we find Koume."

She was absolutely right. We couldn't just abandon that poor old woman, who was as frail as a baby sparrow. Yet at the same time, I was loath to ask Haruyo to make her own way back.

"Fine," I said. "Why don't you just rest here for a while. That way, you'll regain your strength."

"All right then," she said without any further protest.

"Noriko, can you find somewhere that we can rest awhile?"

"Yes, I'll go and look now."

Taking a lantern with her, Noriko went to inspect the surrounding area. Soon enough, her voice cried out:

"Tatsuya! I've found somewhere. It's dry enough to sit… Haruyo, over here!"

Noriko had found a cavity in the wall. There was a group of stalagmites that had fused together to form a sort of bench that was at an ideal height for sitting. It almost looked like an outsized porcelain pillow. The three of us sat down beside one another. Haruyo looked exhausted and was breathing heavily.

"Are you all right, Haruyo? You mustn't force yourself…"

"It's fine. It'll pass in a minute or two."

As she massaged her brow, she looked around at the scenery revealed by the lanterns.

"Ah, this must be the Goblin's Nose," she said.

"Why do you say that?"

"Look over there," she said, shining a light towards the opposite wall. "Do you see that rock sticking out? It looks just like a goblin's nose."

We had reached a point where the tunnel suddenly widened out into a gallery, and, just as she said, there was a rocky prominence that jutted out from a cavity on the opposite wall, just like a goblin's long nose. What was more, fissures in the rock face formed a sort of relief that looked almost like a *tengu* mask.

"You're absolutely right," I said. "Now that you mention it, that part of the wall does look just like a goblin mask."

"Then we're definitely at the Goblin's Nose. Just look, it's marked on the map as well," she said, extracting the map from her pocket and showing me where we were.

Aside from the Goblin's Nose, the map also showed the locations of the Monkey's Seat and the Echoes' Crossing. What's more, just like mine, her map contained three poems.

Upon the road that forks like a leaf of hemp
The first milestone is the Monkey's Seat.

Rest awhile by the Goblin's Nose
And lend your ear to the Echoes' Crossing.

Take care upon reaching the Echoes' Crossing
For its path separates the living from the dead.

"In that case," I said, "the Monkey's Seat is the first landmark in this underground labyrinth."

"It must be," said Haruyo. "And the Goblin's Nose is the second. So the Echoes' Crossing must be somewhere nearby."

"But what does it mean?" Noriko said. "'Lend your ear to the Echoes' Crossing'?"

"I don't know. But since it says to rest awhile and to lend our ears, it must mean that we'll eventually hear something if we just sit here and listen."

As I was speaking, Haruyo raised her hand to silence us.

"Shh!... Do you hear that? What's that sound?"

Noriko and I held our breath.

"Can you hear something?" I whispered.

"Yes... I thought I heard a strange voice... There it is again!"

Instinctively, she placed her hand over her mouth. I too could hear it distinctly. A sort of high-pitched howl echoed from the depths of the caves. A moment later, the cry came again, and again, and again. This was followed by the sound of hurried footsteps, which reverberated so much that it seemed as though an entire army was on the move.

"Someone's coming!"

"Haruyo, Noriko! The lanterns, quickly! Put them out!"

Having extinguished the lights, the three of us sat there in total darkness.

The rush of footsteps subsided, but it was clear that somebody was heading our way from the depths of the cave. I could hear the faltering steps drawing nearer and nearer.

Of course! These were not the cries and footsteps of multiple people. Just as the name suggested, there must be a spot somewhere in this complex labyrinth with extraordinary acoustics. It must have been enough even for a single sound to reverberate from wall to wall, multiplying indefinitely, so that it could be heard from far away.

The sounds that we heard must have been those of a single man coming towards us, for otherwise we would have heard more than one voice.

The man seemed to trip over something and stumble. The sound echoed through the damp air, fading away gradually.

"It's an echo, isn't it?" asked Noriko, who had only just realized.

"Yes, an echo," I replied.

"Shh! Be quiet! He's getting closer..." whispered Haruyo.

He must have passed the Echoes' Crossing, for all we could hear now was isolated, muffled, regular footsteps drawing nearer. We held our breath when we saw a beam of flickering light appear in the distance. The stranger must be carrying a flash-light. We instinctively pressed our backs to the wall.

The swaying light of the torch drew nearer and nearer. Twenty paces... Fifteen paces... Ten paces... Five... At last, the figure passed by right in front of us.

Fortunately, he didn't notice our presence. As he passed before our eyes, however, we did recognize him.

Dressed in his dark-grey robes, it was Brother Eisen, from the Maroo-ji temple.

THE DEVIL'S ABYSS

That night we had to abandon our search for Koume and return dejected, having failed to find her.

The underground labyrinth was so extensive that it seemed

227

to be almost without end. Moreover, Haruyo's condition kept worsening, so we just couldn't risk going on any further.

It was the sight of Eisen that caused the sudden deterioration in Haruyo's health, however. In her current state, she had to avoid too much agitation or excitement at all costs. Eisen's appearance had come as a great shock not only to her, but to Noriko and me as well. And what a fearsome sight he was! Eyes bulging, nostrils flaring, jaws clenched... What was the meaning of such a terrific, indescribably fierce appearance? When I saw that face pass a few inches away from me, I felt terrified, as though an icy blade were threatening to pierce my heart. Immediately afterwards, I remembered having seen such a look once before. But where?

I didn't have to think for long to find the answer. Yes, it was the night of the Koicha nun's murder. Shintaro's face as he came stomping down the hill, armed with a pickaxe! Did they have something in common: Shintaro's look of savagery that night and now Eisen's heinous expression? Thinking about it, Shintaro must have had some connection to the murder of the Koicha nun. But what about Eisen?... What had he done? What had he seen in the depths of these caves?

In any case, Eisen's sudden appearance had completely overwhelmed Haruyo. The three of us waited until he had gone, and once we could no longer see his shadow or hear his footsteps, we relit the lanterns. Haruyo looked dreadful. She was terribly pale, as though every last drop of blood had been drained from her body. Her forehead was drenched in a cold sweat, her breathing was laboured, and she looked as though she was about to pass out.

We exchanged a few words about Eisen's strange behaviour, but Haruyo seemed unwilling to talk about it or to listen. She simply bowed her head and placed one hand to her heart.

"We have to go back," exclaimed Noriko, unable to bear it any longer. "If we don't, Haruyo's going to collapse. We've no choice: we'll just have to come back and continue the search tomorrow."

Haruyo made no further protest. Supporting her on either side, we made our way back to the first fork, where Noriko took her leave of us. Haruyo and I then made our way back to the annexe.

I didn't sleep a wink for what remained of the night. I was worried about Haruyo, and even more so about Koume. I had no intention of returning to the caves for a second time that night, but could I abandon the search just like that? I didn't know what to do. Of course, I would go back the following morning, but what was I going to find there? Would it be Koume's cold, lifeless body?…

Everything was going to come out into the open. The secret of the cave, Koume's and Kotake's iniquity… Although it couldn't be helped, I wondered what consequences these revelations would have for me. I was supposed to have spent my nights sleeping peacefully in the annexe. What on earth would the villagers and the inspector think when they learnt that I had been able to roam wherever I pleased, thanks to the secret passage? After all, I was already a prime suspect.

To escape my dark thoughts, I focused all my attention on Eisen. What connection could he possibly have to this string of murders? Then I remembered that only the other day he had subjected me to those slanderous accusations. And what of his mysterious journey? He had left the village at exactly the same time as that stranger had turned up in Kobe, making all kinds of enquiries about me. Just what was Eisen trying to achieve?

At that point, something occurred to me, which made me sit bolt upright in my bed. My eyes were drawn to the folding screen that depicted the three Chinese sages. I stared at the priest Foyin. Hadn't the woodcutter Heikichi claimed to have seen the priest come out of the screen one night as he slept in the annex? Just the other night, I too had had a similar hallucination. Could it have been Eisen?

I remembered the dark-grey robes that he had been wearing. Dressed like that, he could easily have been taken for a character from the folding screen. And if anybody could disguise himself in such a costume, surely it was Eisen. Yes, the person stealing into the annexe from time to time via the secret passage must have been this priest from the Maroo-ji temple. I replayed all the events from the very beginning and remembered a distinct hint of incense: every last one of them seemed to obey a particularly Buddhist sense of fatalism, with deeds echoing down through generations and determining not only our destinies but those of our descendants. And what was Eisen if not a bonze?…

Could he really be the murderer? Nothing could have been more certain in my mind.

The whole night I tossed and turned, tormented by these thoughts and hoping for my great-aunt's safe return. When dawn eventually broke, however, there was still no sign of Koume. I was at a loss. I didn't know what to do. I decided to talk it over with Haruyo, but when I entered her room, I realized immediately that she was in no fit state to help me. Her face was pale, and she could barely open her eyes. By her side, Kotake was sound asleep, snoring like a man, still under the effects of the sleeping draught.

"You must do as you see fit," Haruyo said. "I can't even think clearly, let alone do anything."

"All right. But in that case, I'm going straight to the police."

At the very mention of the police, her eyes suddenly opened. Then came a nod of resignation.

"Perhaps it's for the best. Actually, it's the only way. But I feel such a sense of pity for my great-aunts…"

She turned to Kotake, who was still asleep. Tears misted in her eyes like dewdrops.

"I won't be long. Maybe they'll send a whole army of policemen. In the meantime, try to think of what we're going to tell Kotake."

"I will, don't worry. Thank you for everything, Tatsuya."

At the police station, Inspector Isokawa had only just got up, but my story had the effect of a bomb going off. His eyes widened in disbelief. His first instinct was to subject me to an interrogation, but then, thinking better of it, he dispatched a subordinate to go and fetch Kosuke Kindaichi. Shortly afterwards, the detective arrived from the House of the West, no doubt having just been woken up. He was accompanied by Miyako.

I cannot begin to describe how happy I was to see Miyako's face just then, as I was about to submit to an interrogation in which I was surrounded by enemies. Anything I had to say would only arouse the suspicion of the inspector and Kosuke Kindaichi. How agonizing it was to be on the receiving end of such suspicious looks! I had come prepared for this, of course, but still, it was comforting to know that I had at least one ally at my side.

Inspector Isokawa made me repeat my story for Kosuke Kindaichi. Every now and then, the inspector would interrupt, asking for clarification on details that escaped him the first time around.

Kosuke Kindaichi grew more and more excited. He kept scratching his head all the while. When I had finished with my story, however, he calmed down and stared at me. A long time seemed to pass like that before he eventually sighed and said:

"Tatsuya, the very first time we met, I gave you some advice, didn't I? I told you: if you see anything strange, if you have the least suspicion about anything, tell us... I warned you that in the delicate position you were already in, things could easily go from bad to worse..."

"I know. I'm sorry," I said, hanging my head. "I let my curiosity get the better of me. And I wanted to solve the mystery on my own, without any help."

"That was a very dangerous thing to do. It's that kind of reckless behaviour that could cost you your life. Where do you propose to start with all this, Inspector?"

"Where, indeed... Let's start with the caves, in any case. Koume has been abducted and we can't abandon her."

"And what about Brother Eisen?"

"Hmm... We'll have to question him as well. Are you certain that it was him you saw in the caves? I hope you aren't saying this just to implicate him..."

"No, of course not! It wasn't just me who saw him. My sister was there and so was Nori—"

I bit my lip. The inspector, Kosuke Kindaichi and Miyako were all staring at me, full of suspicion.

"You were saying?" the inspector asked with a wry smile.

"...and so was Noriko. She's... she's Shintaro Satomura's younger sister."

"That much, I know. But what was she doing there? You haven't even mentioned her until now. You made it sound as though it was only you and your sister in the caves..."

"Ah, well..." I said, stumbling over my words. "Seeing as she's only a young girl, I didn't want her to get mixed up in all this."

"I see," said the inspector with another wry smile. "You can see my dilemma, Tatsuya. How are we to know the extent to which you're telling us the truth? Either way, you'll be forced to spit it all out sooner or later. Now that we know that, thanks to this secret passage, you've been free to roam as you please, we'll have to review your alibis—in particular, the one for the night of the Koicha nun's murder. Only we'll have to leave that for another time. We can't delay the search for Koume any longer."

Inspector Isokawa made all the necessary arrangements and ordered one of his officers to arrest Eisen. We then set off for the House of the East with Kosuke Kindaichi and Miyako Mori in tow.

Along the way, Miyako took my hand.

"Don't worry, Tatsuya. No matter what people say, I believe you. You mustn't let yourself be bothered by what the inspector or anyone in the village says."

"Thank you, Miyako. I won't…"

"That's the spirit! By the way, I heard that Haruyo has fallen ill again."

"Yes, it was the terrible shock that did it for her. I hate to think what will happen if the inspector takes it into his head to question her while she's in this condition…"

"Don't worry, I'll ask the inspector to postpone her questioning for as long as he can. I feel so sorry for Haruyo. And with that weak heart of hers, too…"

Miyako's presence was a real source of comfort to me. Until then, Haruyo had been the one person on whom I could depend, but now that she had taken ill again, not only could I not count on her for help, but the situation was reversed: it was she who needed me to take care of her. I was awfully grateful to have someone as lively and quick-witted as Miyako by my side.

At last, our party arrived at the House of the East. The servants must have suspected Koume's disappearance already: they were all gathered in front of the house, anxiously discussing the events of last night. When they saw the police arrive en masse, they looked at each other meaningfully.

Fortunately, the inspector did decide to leave Haruyo's questioning until later, preferring to go down into the caves directly. I asked Miyako to take care of everything while I led Inspector Isokawa, Kosuke Kindaichi and two other officers over to the annexe. A short while later, we were making our way down into the caves via the chest.

Not without a considerable degree of curiosity, Kosuke Kindaichi scrutinized the mechanism of the chest and the secret passage itself, but he made no comment. Carrying a flashlight, I went ahead of the inspector, leading the procession. Behind him, the other three followed in silence.

After passing through the hidden door, we soon came to the first fork. I was about to head towards the Monkey's Seat, when Inspector Isokawa stopped me.

"Where does that tunnel lead to?" he asked.

This was the question that I had been dreading, but now I had nowhere to hide.

"It leads to Koicha," I replied.

"What?" said the inspector, agog. "Have you ever taken the path before?"

"Yes, only once…"

"And when was that?"

"On the night of Myoren's murder…"

"Damn it, Tatsuya!…" the inspector began, but he was immediately interrupted by Kosuke Kindaichi.

"Come, Inspector, we'll deal with that later. Right now, we have to search these caves as quickly as possible."

With that, we pressed on in silence.

When at last we reached the Monkey's Seat, I shone the light on the waxen corpse and briefly explained the phenomenon. Seeing the corpse and hearing my story, the inspector, Kosuke Kindaichi and the two officers were in a state of shock. However, once again, Kosuke Kindaichi proposed to leave this for later and to carry on with the search without any further delay.

A short while later, we arrived at the Goblin's Nose. There, I briefly recounted the events of the previous night. Now the time had come to move on towards the Echoes' Crossing.

Everything until the Goblin's Nose was familiar, but it was terra incognita for me after that point. I went one step at a time, watching where I placed my feet. We soon realized that we had reached the Echoes' Crossing, because our every step, our every cough or the slightest noise we made echoed with extraordinary reverberations. I couldn't help thinking that a lone scream would produce a spectacular effect. If only I had known then what tragic scene was shortly about to unfold…

Soon after we made our way past the Echoes' Crossing, I cried out and stopped dead in my tracks.

"Wh-what is it?" Kosuke Kindaichi asked, running up to me. "Have you seen something?"

"Kindaichi-san! Look… look down there!"

I immediately switched off my flashlight.

Far below us, we could see flickering lights. What was going on? Kosuke Kindaichi, the inspector and the two officers hurried to switch off their flashlights as well.

We could see a fabulous luminescence, like fireflies darting around in the depths of the opaque darkness.

"What is that?"

"What could it be?"

For a moment, we held our breath as we scrutinized the pale glow. We switched our flashlights back on and looked around. We then realized that we were standing on the edge of an underground precipice. Surprised, I tried to peer down to the bottom. What I saw was an inky, blackish water that looked viscous and stagnant.

The Devil's Abyss! Yes, this must surely be the Devil's Abyss. *"Do not draw the pure waters of the Devil's Abyss, even if thirst should consume your body…"* Without even realizing it, I had crossed the boundary of my sister's map and found myself in territory of my own. Thus, the Fox's Den and the Dragon's Jaw had to be somewhere nearby.

That was when it happened, however.

Kosuke Kindaichi, who had, like me, been leaning down to peer into the Devil's Abyss with his own flashlight, suddenly called out:

"There's something in the water down there!"

He jumped up and began shining his flashlight all around.

"There's a way down over here! Quickly!"

He made his way down the precipice and we all followed behind him.

I was stumbling, because my knees were shaking. I noticed then that the glittering light we had seen was coming from a moss that covered the rock face. It must be some kind of phosphorescent moss.

We quickly reached the water's edge. In the darkness, the pool of water had seemed a long way away from us, but in truth the surface was only twenty feet from the top of the precipice. Kosuke Kindaichi, who had arrived there before the rest of us, was examining the inky water's surface.

"Over there!" he said. "There's a body floating over there."

We all turned and shone our flashlights in the same direction. At the focal point of our five beams of light, we recognized a small monkey-like body floating on its back.

There was no longer any doubt: it was Koume.

CRISIS POINT

It should go without saying that, after the discovery of Koume's body, my situation became more difficult. Naturally, I couldn't have had the least motive to kill her, but the villagers, having only my word for it, thought otherwise.

Besides what did motive matter? In this string of murders that began with my grandfather, what possible motive could one imagine? Murder without motive, murder without meaning, murder with neither rhyme nor reason… This was the work of either a madman or an imbecile. Nevertheless, the villagers were content to lay their suspicions squarely on me; for, after all, did the blood of a violent and cold-blooded killer with thirty-two victims to his name not run through my veins?

There is no doubt in my mind that had another likely suspect not presented himself, I would surely have been arrested and locked up.

And this was a far likelier suspect than I…

Once we had carried Koume's body to the top of the precipice, the two officers departed—one to summon Dr Arai, the other to fetch lanterns and hurricane lamps to provide some proper lighting. A short while later, the Devil's Abyss was lit up as it had never been since the dawn of time, and both the post-mortem and a thorough search of the area were able to get under way.

I can still remember the scene even now. The Devil's Abyss was larger than I had imagined. We found ourselves standing at the very edge of an island in the middle of a rock pool. To our left, the walls towered up to a ceiling more than two storeys high. A narrow path had been cut into the rock, making it possible to reach the opposite bank around a hundred feet away.

The water stretched off to the right. Armed with his flashlight, Kosuke Kindaichi followed the bank in that direction. He returned after a while and reported that the further you went, the more the ceiling lowered, and that after about 300 yards, it plunged down beneath the water.

It didn't take long for Dr Arai to carry out the examination. Koume had been strangled before her body was thrown from the precipice into the Devil's Abyss. Given how old and shrunken she was, the assailant, whoever he was, would have found dispatching her as easy as twisting a child's arm.

For their part, Inspector Isokawa and his two officers made a thorough search of the crime scene. One of the men found an important piece of evidence.

"Inspector," he said. "I found this at the bottom of the precipice…"

It was a dark-grey chequered cap. I gasped the moment I laid eyes on it. The inspector turned to me.

"Do you recognize this cap?"

"Well… er…"

While I hesitated, Kosuke Kindaichi came over and took the cap from the inspector's hand to examine it.

"Ah, this hat belongs to Dr Kuno. Is that not correct, Tatsuya?"

"Yes, I think so. I was just wondering about that…"

"Oh, but it most certainly is. Dr Arai, would you care to take a look?"

Dr Arai mumbled something noncommittal, but it was clear from the expression on his face that he concurred with the detective.

The doctor and I looked at one another.

"So, does this mean that Dr Kuno is hiding somewhere in these caves?" the inspector asked.

"He must be," Kosuke Kindaichi replied. "That is why, Inspector, I kept stressing how vital it was that we search the caves as quickly as possible. But, ah… What do we have here?"

Kosuke Kindaichi had spotted something in the lining of the cap. It was a strip of paper. He brought it into the light and let out a whistle.

"What is it, Kindaichi-san? Have you found something?"

"See for yourself, Inspector. It's a continuation of the list that Tatsuya found by the body of the mother abbess…"

He proceeded to show it to me. There was no doubt about it: it was a thin strip cut out of that same pocket diary—same paper, same pen.

TWINS: *Koume*
              Kotake

Kotake's name was crossed out in red ink.

"Hmm…" the inspector sighed. "The writing certainly looks like Dr Kuno's, doesn't it, Kindaichi-san?"

"It does indeed."

"Then what are we to make of it? Tatsuya has confirmed that it was Koume who was killed, but here we have Kotake's name crossed out."

"Yes, I thought that was odd, too. But the twins look so alike so it's possible that the killer mistook Koume for Kotake. Or perhaps there was no mistake at all, and the killer simply didn't care which one he killed…"

"I see… So do you suppose that Dr Kuno is still hiding somewhere in the caves?"

"I do. That's why, Inspector, it's vital that you conduct an extensive search as quickly as possible."

"Well, if you think that's the best course of action... But these caves are vast. Can we really be sure that Dr Kuno is somewhere here?"

"I guarantee it, Inspector. Dr Kuno has to be here. It's the only place he can be."

The detective's words were so assured that I stared at him despite myself.

They wasted no time in removing Koume's body. It will come as no surprise that afterwards I was immediately questioned by the inspector.

"This time, Tatsuya," Kosuke Kindaichi said with a chuckle, "there's no getting away from it. You'll have to tell us the whole truth and nothing but the truth. If you hold anything back, you'll only make it worse for yourself."

I took his advice and answered as truthfully as I could. But there were two things that I didn't disclose: the first was that I had seen Shintaro on the night of the Koicha nun's murder; the second was the mystery of those three gold coins that had disappeared. The first omission was to protect Noriko: the latter, myself...

I couldn't tell whether Kosuke Kindaichi was aware of this, but he didn't follow up with any other questions, and the interview ended there. Fortunately, I wasn't taken to the police station but simply requested not to leave the village.

Haruyo's questioning followed mine, but, thanks to the intervention of Dr Arai, it was a very brief affair.

I had escaped the shame of being arrested, but it's hard to say whether I was lucky or not: these latest deaths provoked a new wave of enmity towards me in the village, and only more unpleasantness awaited me.

Once the inspector and his team had gone, a feeling of loneliness came over me. There were only three of us left in this enormous house: Kotake, Haruyo and me. But now Kotake was only a shadow of her former self. It is often said that when one twin dies, the other soon follows. That was not the case here, however. Though alive in body, Kotake's spirit had died at the moment of Koume's passing, dementing her and plunging her into a second infancy.

While Kotake had fallen into this pitiful state, Haruyo's health continued to worsen. I couldn't look to her for company. Worse still, she was in such a bad way that I no longer dared even to ask for her help. As such, I was forced to take care of all the arrangements for Koume's funeral myself. What troubled me most, however, was that despite all the commotion, nobody came to the house to offer their condolences. Word of Koume's death had certainly spread throughout the village, so why had nobody come? I felt a tremendous sense of anxiety, which was only intensified by the behaviour of the servants. Not only did the villagers not come, but the servants began avoiding me. They would come whenever they were summoned, of course, and they would carry out whatever I asked of them, but, that being done, they would always try to get away as soon as possible. It weighed on me more and more, eventually crushing me like a lead weight.

I found myself wishing that Miyako had been there, but she had returned home while I was down in the caves and I hadn't seen her since. I felt as though I had been abandoned by everyone, even by her. But just when I thought I couldn't bear the loneliness any longer, Noriko and Shintaro turned up.

"Sorry that it's taken us so long to come," Shintaro apologized. "It must have been hard for you by yourself."

He was in such uncharacteristically high spirits, smiling with all his teeth. I had never seen him so animated before. The Shintaro I had seen before always wore a scowl and had a look of despondency about him. What could he be so happy about today? I wondered. He offered his condolences to Haruyo and comforted Kotake—all with the greatest tact.

"We're sorry we're late," said Noriko. "We wanted to come earlier, but we were detained by the police…"

The inspector and his officers must have headed straight to Noriko's house after leaving the Tajimi residence.

"They were asking all sorts of questions," she added.

"What did you tell them?" I asked.

"Well, I had no choice but to tell them everything. Shouldn't I have done?"

"Of course you should, but does that mean your brother knows everything now, too?"

"Yes."

"And what did he have to say?"

"He didn't really say anything…"

"He wasn't angry then?"

"Why would he be angry?" she asked in astonishment. "On the contrary, he's quietly delighted…"

Delighted? Was that why he looked so happy today? If that was the case, then I had even more to worry about…

Noriko was in love with me. Because of her innocence, her innate sense of optimism, she had no doubts about being loved in return, for the simple reason that she herself was in love. But did I love her? Naturally, I had grown to like her more and more in recent times. Strangely enough, she even seemed to have grown more beautiful. But was that really the case? Or was it that love is truly blind?… I wondered. But, no, it couldn't be—for even Haruyo and Oshima had remarked how lovely Noriko had become lately.

"It's astonishing, really," I had heard Oshima say. "Frankly speaking, I never imagined that the young mistress would grow so pretty."

Thinking about it now, it must have been love itself that sped up Noriko's development. Through the surge of emotions conferred on her by love, this former child had suddenly acquired the freshness of real youth and gained a beauty all of her own.

Still, I couldn't believe that I actually loved Noriko, and Shintaro's premature hopes troubled me.

"What are you thinking, Tatsuya?" Noriko asked.

"Oh, nothing really..."

"I heard a rumour that the whole village is going on a manhunt in the caves."

"I can well imagine."

"It'll be a pity if they do... It means I won't be able to see you."

Despite it all, she still wanted to meet me in the caves. The strength of her emotions made me uneasy.

"Tatsuya...?" she asked after a moment.

"Yes?"

"Did you tell the police about last night? About Brother Eisen, I mean..."

"Yes, I told them everything."

"That must be why they took him to the police station today. The villagers are awfully angry with you."

"Why's that?" I asked, my heart pounding.

"They think you're lying just to incriminate him. Be careful, Tatsuya. The people in the village will believe almost anything."

"I'll be on my guard, don't worry."

Once again, I felt that lead weight in the pit of my stomach. I would have to face the villagers sooner or later. Yet back then, I could never have imagined the storm that awaited me...

The little village of Eight Graves was on the verge of a tragedy, in which I found myself at the very centre.

MY MOTHER'S LOVE LETTERS

That very day, at the request of Inspector Isokawa, the village youth organized themselves into groups to scour the caves. The search revealed that the tunnels branched out in all directions beneath the village and beyond. It was the perfect hiding place. Given the magnitude of the task, there was no way that the search would be completed for at least two or three days.

While all this was ongoing, I busied myself with the arrangements for Koume's funeral. In the afternoon, a few people came to offer their condolences. In order to avoid showing my face, I asked Shintaro and Noriko to see to these guests, who, having done their duty, were always quick to leave again.

Eisen arrived towards evening. I knew that he had been taken to the police station earlier that day, so I wondered what tale he could have spun them. He looked sullen and wore a sour expression, but he still performed the service.

The burial itself took place the following day. Compared to that of my brother Hisaya, this one was a rushed and sad affair, strangely devoid of any serenity. The only thing that compensated for it was the opportunity to talk to my cousin Shintaro.

Until that day, the very mention of his name reminded me only of the fierce expression that I had seen on him the night of Myoren's murder. Talking to him face to face, however, I could see that he was far from the aggressive man I believed him to be. He wasn't at all the villainous type, but rather surprisingly straightforward and simple. So much so, in fact, that he still hadn't recovered from the shock of the country's defeat in the war. How could I have got him so wrong?

But in that case, who had sent me the strange warning? I found myself back at square one again, and the mysteries were only piling up.

Kosuke Kindaichi turned up unannounced the day after the burial.

"You must be exhausted after yesterday," he said. "I've been so busy these past few days that I'm worn out myself."

"I hear you've been searching in the caves," I said. "Have you found Dr Kuno yet?"

"Not yet, I'm afraid."

"Are you really sure that he's hiding there?"

"But of course! Why do you ask?"

"It's just that it's already been a fortnight since he disappeared. How could he survive down there for two whole weeks?"

"Perhaps somebody is bringing him food."

"You think so? Even with all this going on?"

"Of that, I cannot be certain. But in any case, Dr Kuno is undoubtedly hiding somewhere in the caves. The hat we found just the other day proves it. He was wearing it when he left."

"Ah, yes," I said, puzzled. "All the same, it's curious, though, isn't it, that he's able to hide himself so well."

"Curious or not, he's somewhere in those caves. That much, I am certain. If not, I'll be in trouble—after all, it's my neck that's on the line."

"Why do you say that?"

"Well," said Kosuke Kindaichi, grimacing, "the search has been going on for three days now, and we still haven't found any trace of him. Some people are starting to grumble. Then again, they are working for free, so it's only natural. But if we don't find Dr Kuno, they'll likely string me up…"

He gave a feeble shrug.

"What do you intend to do?" I asked sympathetically.

"What can I do?! We just have to carry on with the search. Tomorrow we'll comb it from top to bottom. My hypothesis is that we'll find him somewhere on the opposite bank of the Devil's Abyss, but the villagers are too afraid to venture over there. I think I'll try it tomorrow. What do you say, Tatsuya? Care to join me?"

I looked at the detective in astonishment. He didn't show any sign of having an ulterior motive, which reassured me somewhat.

"Yes, of course. I'd be glad to. But tell me, Kindaichi-san, there's one thing I don't understand. What was Dr Kuno doing? What was he up to? What were all those scribblings in his diary?"

"Ah, so that's what you've been wondering. Well, clearly he had his reasons for writing it all down. Yes, and there's a curious story about that diary, too…" Kosuke Kindaichi gave a wry smile. "Last spring, the good doctor fell victim to theft. While he was visiting a patient, he happened to leave his doctor's bag on his bicycle and when he returned, he found that it was gone. According to his wife, he always kept his pocket diary in that bag. He was apparently distraught, and his family wondered how the simple theft of a doctor's bag could have left him in such a state."

"I see… And the doctor's bag was never returned to him?"

"No, but it turned up in the strangest of places only recently…" Kindaichi chuckled. "You'll recall, of course, that we searched the Koicha nun's hermitage after she was murdered? Well, we found a heap of stolen goods there, but nothing of real value. A clay teapot without a spout, a ladle without a handle, and all kinds of rubbish. Among it all, we found Dr Kuno's doctor's bag."

"Then Myoren was the thief?"

"Quite so. You'll be aware, of course, that she was a kleptomaniac. Dr Kuno must have fallen victim to this mania of hers."

"And the diary…?"

"It wasn't there. Either she must have lost it, or else Mrs Kuno made a mistake and it was never there in the first place… What a pity that the Koicha nun was murdered."

With a look of desolation, Kosuke Kindaichi fell silent.

Changing the subject, I enquired about Eisen. I wanted to know what explanation he had given for being in the caves that night.

"It's all very simple," Kindaichi replied with a smile. "The Maroo-ji temple is situated to the far west of the village, but to reach Koicha at the eastern end, you have to traverse hills and valleys. If you take the underground passage, it takes half the time. So whenever Eisen's obligations call him to Koicha, he goes there via the caves."

"I see… And do the tunnels go as far as Bankachi?"

"Yes. I was surprised myself when Brother Eisen showed me. It really is a vast network of caves."

"But how could he know all this? After all, he's only been at the Maroo-ji temple a very short time."

"It was apparently the high priest who showed him the caves. He told me that Father Choei himself uses them whenever he wants to make his way back to the temple without running the risk of bumping into anybody."

I didn't believe a word of it. It was possible, of course, that Eisen had taken the underground passage to reach Koicha and that he had strayed into the labyrinth. But from there to ending up in my room…? Besides, Kosuke Kindaichi didn't appear to take Eisen's explanation at face value either. I took the following ironic comment as proof of this:

"All the same, it's curious. The locals don't take much notice of these caves, yet every outsider seems drawn to them somehow… Both you and Brother Eisen…" Kosuke Kindaichi laughed but immediately regained his composure. "By the way, how is Miyako-san getting on?"

This question was something of a sore point, for I had begun to worry about Miyako's sudden change in attitude towards me. Over the past few days, she had begun acting almost like a perfect stranger. When we were burying my brother Hisaya, she had helped us as if she were a member of the family, but now she only showed her face out of a sense of obligation. As soon as her duties were done, she would run from us as though from the plague. Gone were the smiles and kind words whenever we met.

I couldn't understand the reasons for her metamorphosis. Miyako had been my one true ally in this village where I was surrounded by enemies. This sudden coldness had left me feeling forlorn, so when Kosuke Kindaichi asked after her, the question very nearly brought me to tears.

He didn't appear to have any ulterior motive in enquiring, however, and soon afterwards he left just as breezily as he had arrived.

"Give my regards to Miyako whenever you see her," said Kosuke Kindaichi.

It was that evening that I discovered the letters.

No matter how I tried that night, I couldn't sleep. Thoughts of Kosuke Kindaichi, Miyako, Shintaro, Noriko, even Eisen kept racing through my mind. As I tossed and turned in bed, a strange idea possessed me.

As always, the folding screen was standing by my bedside, and I couldn't help imagining that there was somebody standing behind it. It was an absurd idea, but it obsessed me nevertheless. I was unable to put it out of my mind. Finally, I got up, turned on the lamp and looked behind the screen. Naturally, there was nobody there. But on the other hand, I did spot something odd.

Since the lamp was on the other side of the screen, the light produced a kind of magic-lantern effect through the lining. There were handwritten letters pasted all over one of the panels, and in places the text was legible.

Intrigued by this, I began to read, and I soon realized that this was a correspondence between two young lovers. Even more intrigued now, I tried to find the names of the sender and the addressee. Imagine my amazement when I managed to decipher the two names: Tsuruko and Yoichi.

Yes, these must have been the letters that my mother had exchanged with her lover Yoichi Kamei. My poor mother! She had loved a young boy but found herself in the clutches of some monster. Her only consolation had been to paste her love letters to the back of a folding screen. On the nights when my father stayed away, she no doubt did as I was doing then: she lit the lamp and, with tears in her eyes, reread them with the light shining through the screen.

I sat behind the screen, reading my dear mother's handwriting through a veil of tears. It was then that I noticed that not all of these letters dated from the period before she arrived in this house. She must have continued to write to her lover even after falling prey to that monster of a father. Their letters were filled with such tremendous sorrow.

My mother lamented:

What a pitiful fate that I must allow my body to be defiled by this demon. How wretched I am…

She remembered the past:

I cannot help thinking back to that day when I first gave myself to you by the Dragon's Jaw…

So the rumours in the village were true: my mother had been carrying on an affair with the young schoolteacher before she submitted to my father's violence.

She relived the joys she had known back then:

Even in that terrifying darkness, the bed of rock was my paradise...

Then she rued her lot:

...but, abandoned by fate, I have known only fleeting happiness...

She confessed further that ever since that day of infamy, her life *"had been like a strange dream..."* I felt as though with my own eyes, I had seen her shock at this sudden change in fate.

That night I didn't sleep a wink.

IN THE FOX'S DEN

The following morning, after a sleepless night, I was heavy-headed and still drowsy when Kosuke Kindaichi and Inspector Isokawa turned up.

"Sorry we're late," said the detective with a smile. "I hope we didn't keep you waiting."

I was a little surprised to see them, but then I remembered Kosuke Kindaichi's invitation to assist in the hunt for Dr Kuno.

"Well, shall we?" said Kosuke Kindaichi.

"Are you coming with us?" asked the inspector.

"Are you sure you want me to come with you?" I asked in return. "Won't I be in your way?"

"On the contrary, you'll be a great help. You seem to know the caves better than any of us," said the detective.

I wondered what exactly he meant by that, but he just carried on smiling innocently. The inspector stood there in silence, as though having ceded his authority to the detective.

"Very well," I said. "In that case, I'll be glad to go with you. Will you give me a few minutes to get ready?"

"Just a moment." Kosuke Kindaichi stopped me. "Inspector, there was something you wanted to ask Tatsuya…?"

"Ah, yes. It's about that letter you received in Kobe, the one warning you not to come back to Eight Graves…"

"What about it?"

"Do you still have it? If you do, I'd like to take a look at it."

I looked at them both in silence. For some reason, I felt alarmed.

"Has there been some development?" I asked.

"There has, but we'll get to that presently," said Kosuke Kindaichi. "But if you could show the letter to the inspector…"

I immediately fetched the threatening letter from the desk. The detective and the inspector examined it carefully, and then they both nodded.

"It's the same hand," said the detective.

Inspector Isokawa agreed.

"What's all this about?" I asked, succumbing to anxiety. "Have you found a new clue about the letter?"

"Not quite," replied the inspector. "Rather, the police in N—— received a strange letter yesterday. It reminded me of the one that you received: same style of writing, same kind of paper…"

"And?" I asked impatiently. "The two letters are alike?"

I wondered whether we were about to unmask the identity of that strange letter's author.

"I think it's safe to say that they were written by the same individual. Of course, the contents of the letters differ, but when it comes to the handwriting, the paper, the way the ink bleeds…"

"There's definitely something interesting in the way the ink bleeds," Kosuke Kindaichi cut in. "Whoever wrote this letter chose the kind of paper specifically so that the ink would bleed. It makes graphological examination very difficult."

"But what does this new letter say?" I asked. "Does it mention me?"

"I'm afraid it does," the detective replied, staring at me with what looked like pity. "The author makes an accusation against you. In terms just as strong as in the other letter, the author claims that you are the murderer and asks why you haven't been arrested and put to death."

I felt a weight in my chest.

"And you don't know who sent it?" I asked.

"No, but it must be somebody from the village. The envelope is postmarked from Eight Graves."

"So somebody in the village is trying to frame me..."

Kosuke Kindaichi nodded.

"But does the letter offer any proof that I'm behind all these murders?"

"Rest assured, it contains nothing of the sort. The author simply keeps repeating that Tatsuya Tajimi is the murderer. But that's what's so curious, you see. Whoever sent these letters is far from stupid. At the very least, they know how to conceal their handwriting and that it was necessary to do so. But anybody so intelligent must also know that simply claiming that Tatsuya Tajimi is the murderer isn't enough to make the police act. There's no evidence. So what is this person hoping to achieve? What is the intended result? I can't understand it, and that's what troubles me."

"So the intention isn't to have me arrested? You think it's something else?"

"I'm of that opinion, yes. Otherwise sending the letter would

252

be not only pointless but also risky. Clearly, the author hopes to gain something by running that risk. But what?"

I felt an icy chill run through my heart.

Before long, we found ourselves in the limestone caves.

This time, I had chosen to lead the inspector and Kosuke Kindaichi to the caves not through the chest in the annexe, but through the shrine in the back garden. Haruyo had told me about this shrine before. "Though it may look Buddhist, it's actually Shinto," she had explained. "To all appearances, it's dedicated to Inari, the god of rice and harvests, but the truth is that it's always been dedicated to a great samurai from the Amago clan, who was killed by the villagers centuries ago. The armour was his. It's said to be a sort of relic." As the reader knows, the samurai's armour was now clothing the wax corpse at the Monkey's Seat.

It turned out that this little shrine served as yet another entrance to the secret passage. In other words, anybody who entered through the chest in the annexe would also be able to escape through the shrine in the garden. When you entered through it, a staircase led you down into the passage, and at the foot of the stairs was the moving rock. If you carried on past the rock, you would eventually wind up at stairs leading back up to the annexe.

That day, however, we moved the rock and proceeded on to the fork, then past the Monkey's Seat, and from the Goblin's Nose on to the Echoes' Crossing. It was just the three of us. With the aid of miners' lamps, we made our way through the dark subterranean passages in silence. I didn't much feel like talking; I couldn't put what Kosuke Kindaichi had told me about this new letter out of my head. His words were like a dark mist hanging over me.

All of a sudden, I noticed something odd: there wasn't another living soul in the caves.

"Why is nobody searching for Dr Kuno today?" I asked.

"The village youths are on strike," Kosuke Kindaichi said.

"On strike?"

"Yes… They're saying that there's no point in continuing with the search, that Dr Kuno can't be here, since they would have found him by now after three days of searching. So today the refused to come."

"So the search has been for nothing?"

"Why do you say that?"

"Won't it all be for nothing unless you find Dr Kuno?"

"That may be so. But still, the search has narrowed our field of investigation."

"How so?"

"Because we no longer have to look in those places that have already been searched."

I looked at him in astonishment. I even wondered whether he was in his right mind.

"But Dr Kuno has legs, Kindaichi-san… What if he's moved in the time that they've been searching for him?"

A look of surprise appeared on Kosuke Kindaichi's face. He smacked his forehead, as if the idea had only just occurred to him.

"You're quite right," he said. "That is also a possibility. Why didn't I think of that?"

Then he laughed. The inspector carried on walking in silence, holding his miner's lamp in one hand. Neither of them was giving anything away. I felt more alone than ever.

Soon we arrived at the Devil's Abyss.

Kosuke Kindaichi had set the objective of reaching the opposite bank. It just so happened that getting there was also my own objective: somewhere beyond the Devil's Abyss lay the Fox's Den and the Dragon's Jaw. By all accounts, the treasure wouldn't be far from this final landmark.

As I stood there on the bank of the Devil's Abyss, looking towards the far shore that was shrouded in darkness, I felt an irresistible chill run down my spine. Over there, my fate awaited me—or rather, not just my fate, but the path left to me as a child by my mother. It was only natural, then, that as I stood on the brink of that fate, there should be some trepidation in my heart.

Kosuke Kindaichi also appeared to need some courage before he could cross over to the other side of the abyss.

"Shall we, Inspector?"

"If we dare… It would seem that nobody in recent times has make the journey across."

"There's nothing to fear. What do you say, Tatsuya?"

"I'm ready," I said resolutely.

"Marvellous! Then it's decided. After you, Inspector."

As I have already said, to our right lay a dead end, but to our left there was a stone wall that towered straight up as though it had been hewn from the rock. In the middle of this wall there was a path so narrow that you could barely scrape through it. Worse still, sand and dust constantly rained down from the wall, so it was a truly perilous crossing.

Having fixed his miner's lamp to his belt, Kosuke Kindaichi pressed himself against the wall and began moving sideways, like a crab. I followed suit, and so did the inspector a moment later.

Clinging to the rock as we went, we advanced inch by inch. Every now and then a rock would crumble beneath our feet and the debris would plunge down into the abyss, hitting the water with a splash. My heart skipped a beat every time that happened. Naturally, the waters of the Devil's Abyss could not have been all that deep, but the problem was not their depth:

indeed, who could have endured the prospect of tumbling into that ink-black water?

The most unsettling aspect of all this, however, was the phosphorescent moss. These dancing lights that glittered all around made it impossible to gauge the distance that still had to be traversed. One moment, it would appear as though the lights were nearby, and the very next they would recede into the distance. If you looked at them inadvertently, you could feel your whole body being drawn towards them. I nearly lost my balance several times because of this.

We were all silent. None of us dared to speak. As we crawled like lizards through the darkness, I could hear the detective's heavy breathing in front of me and that of the inspector behind me.

We had made it to the midway point. Suddenly, Kosuke Kindaichi cried out. I heard the sound of something falling, and his lamplight went out, leaving us nearly in darkness. For a moment, I thought that the detective had lost his step and gone plunging into the abyss below. I felt my blood run cold.

"Kindaichi-san! Kindaichi-san, are you all right?" I shouted into the pitch dark ahead.

"Kosuke! Kosuke!" The inspector's voice came from behind me.

I sensed something move in front of me. I heard the crackling of a match being lit, and then Kosuke Kindaichi's face appeared in the light of his lamp. To my surprise, the face was level with my knees.

"What a fright that gave me!" Kindaichi said. "I really thought I was going to fall into the water. Watch your step here. There's a big step down."

Peering into the darkness, he continued:

"We're nearly there, Inspector, Tatsuya. Just a little more and the path begins to widen."

256

Encouraged by these words, I quickened my pace. I negotiated the drop of about three feet in turn, after which the path widened slightly. Of course, you still had to hold on to the wall, but it was no longer necessary to go sideways.

We soon reached the opposite bank and found ourselves faced with the mouths of five tunnels, each of differing size. Seeing this, Kosuke Kindaichi groaned. Without delay, he began with the one on the far right but returned almost immediately.

"This one's a dead end," he shouted.

He tried the next one but again reappeared very quickly.

"This one seems deeper. Inspector, could you give me the ropes?"

We had brought two ropes with us. Kosuke Kindaichi placed one of them over his left arm and, unrolling the other, handed one end to the inspector.

"Whatever you do, don't let go. My life depends on this rope. Tatsuya, come with me."

I followed Kosuke Kindaichi, but after a hundred yards we reached a dead end.

"Damn! Another waste of time…"

Using the rope to find our way back, we returned to our starting point.

"Another dead end?" the inspector asked.

"Yes… Perhaps we'll be luckier with this third one."

Leaving the inspector behind once again, we made our way into the third tunnel, but we soon realized that it, too, led nowhere.

After these three failures, we tried the fourth tunnel, where we soon discovered that it branched out into countless others. Kindaichi instructed me to wait for him at the first fork, holding the rope. He then unrolled the second rope that he had been carrying and gave one end of it to me.

"Stay here," he said. "Whatever you do, don't let go of either rope. If I pull on the one connecting us, you will pull on the one connecting you and the inspector in turn. He'll know to come and find you. As soon as he arrives, tie the end of the rope that I'm holding to a rock, then you can both come and find me. You just have to follow the rope."

In short, the inspector's rope acted as the trunk path, while mine served for the branches. All a person had to do was repeat this strategy scrupulously in order not to get lost in this maze of tunnels, no matter how complex it might be.

Holding his end of the rope, Kosuke Kindaichi set off into one of the tunnels but returned shortly afterwards.

"It's amazing," he said. "This tunnel branches out into another three smaller tunnels. Luckily, they don't seem to go very far."

Still holding the rope that connected us to the inspector, we proceeded into the tunnel and soon arrived at this second group of offshoots. As before, Kosuke Kindaichi gave me the end of his rope and set off into the tunnels.

I had placed my lamp at my feet and held the ropes in either hand. Before long, I heard soft footsteps coming from the main tunnel. I shuddered. Yes, I was sure of it. Somebody was heading my way.

I quickly extinguished the lamp, plunging myself into darkness. I was on my guard. I could see a faint glow coming towards me, and it looked just like the light from one of our miner's lamps. My heart was pounding. I would have run if I could, but that was out of the question. With this rope, I was holding Kosuke Kindaichi's life in my hands.

As I stood there in the darkness, breath held and on guard, I stared at the approaching light. When the light was only a few feet away, I could just distinguish the features of a dark face, lit from below. When I recognized those features, I thought my heart was about to explode.

"Kindaichi-san!"

No sooner had I called out his name than I regretted this rash decision, for the shock made the detective literally jump.

"Wh-wh… Who's there?…" he asked.

"It's me! It's me, Tatsuya. Wait, I'll relight the lamp."

Kosuke Kindaichi seemed unable to believe his eyes.

"Tatsuya! But how did you get here?…"

"I've haven't moved an inch. I've been standing in this same spot all along. The tunnel you took must have led you in a full circle. You gave me quite a fright. I didn't know it was you, so I turned out the light. I'm sorry to have startled you like that."

"A case in point!" he said. "There was a fork in the tunnel a while back. That's why it's vital to have a rope. All the time I thought I was walking away, but without knowing it, I was really making my way back to the start."

Despite this latest failure, Kosuke Kindaichi refused to give up. He wouldn't rest until he had painstakingly explored all of the remaining tunnels.

Without a doubt, this must have been the Fox's Den. *Do not lose your way in the hundred and eight tunnels of the Fox's Den…* The number was surely a rhetorical flourish, but to us, they seemed innumerable. Nonetheless, Kosuke Kindaichi was determined to search them all, one by one.

I was growing tired of the search, but in the end I didn't have long to wait. After the detective had ventured into the umpteenth tunnel, I suddenly felt a tug on the rope.

I was about to dash off into the tunnel, when I remembered his instructions. I pulled on the inspector's rope and tied the two ends to a nearby stalactite. It was then that the inspector came running.

"What's happened?" he asked.

"I don't know. He must have found something in this tunnel."

Following the detective's rope, we made our way into the tunnel. After about 300 yards, we spotted the light. The tunnel seemed to come to a dead end. Kosuke Kindaichi was crouching in front of his lamp, his eyes fixed on the ground.

"Kindaichi-san! Kindaichi-san, have you found something?"

As soon as he heard the inspector's voice, Kosuke Kindaichi stood up and dusted himself down. He beckoned us over and pointed to the ground silently. In the lamplight, his face looked curiously tense. We ran towards him but stopped dead in our tracks.

At his feet, there was a mound of earth from which the torso of a man wearing Western clothes was exposed. The corpse's face had decomposed, and the stench was suffocating.

"He wasn't buried properly, hence the terrible smell," Kosuke Kindaichi told us. "In fact, it was the smell that led me here."

"But who is it?" I asked, jaws clenched in terror.

Inspector Isokawa was holding his breath, staring at this dreadful sight.

"It isn't easy to be certain, given the advanced state of decomposition. But I'd hazard a guess that it's Dr Kuno."

The detective turned to the inspector and handed him a silver cigarette case.

"I found it on the body of the corpse," he said. "Open it. I think you'll find it interesting."

What the inspector found inside was not cigarettes but a small slip of paper on which was written:

DOCTORS: *Tsunemi Kuno*
                                                    Shuhei Arai

The first name had been crossed out in red ink. But to make matters worse, the handwriting itself was none other than Dr Kuno's.

Had the doctor put an end to his own life? I wondered.

AN OLD PHOTO

Kosuke Kindaichi must have known already that Dr Kuno had been dead for a long while. Why else would he have insisted on continuing with the search, even when the youths had failed to discover anything after three days of looking.

Thinking back on it now, I feel a sense of shame. I thought I had been clever enough to corner him with my argument, but the truth of the matter was that he had known everything all along. He had managed to deduce that Dr Kuno was already dead and that his body was lying somewhere in the depths of the caves. It changed the way I looked at him. Could that stuttering man with the shaggy hair be a genius in disguise?

In any case, the discovery of Dr Kuno's body forced a sharp reappraisal of the case. After all, Dr Kuno had been the prime suspect. For reasons that were as yet unclear, he was the one who had made that scandalous list of names in his pocket diary. What's more, he had absconded as soon as the fact was uncovered. It was hard to see a likelier suspect... But now all that had been turned on its head.

All anybody had to do was look at Dr Kuno's decaying corpse to know that he had been dead for some time. It was obvious even to my untrained eye. In fact, the post-mortem examination later revealed that Dr Kuno had been dead for a fortnight or so. This meant that he had died shortly after his disappearance, and by the time that Koume was killed, he must have been dead for ten days. This fact alone was enough to exonerate him and to prove that he was, on the contrary, yet another victim of the killer responsible for all these other deaths.

As for the cause of death, it was established, once more, to have been poison. The same poison that had claimed so many victims, starting with my grandfather, had been used to kill Dr Kuno. But how had the poison been administered? The discovery of some bamboo wrapping beside the body provided the solution. Inside the wrapping there were two hardened rice balls, both of which had been poisoned. But who could have given this food to Dr Kuno?

Dr Kuno's wife testified that his flight had been so sudden and unexpected that nobody could have prepared any food for him to take. Furthermore, he was so unskilled with these things that there was no way that he could have prepared them for himself. Even assuming, at a stretch, that he had tried to prepare them at home, somebody would surely have noticed.

After insisting on all of this, Mrs Kuno blushed to add that her family, large as it was, always worried about not having enough food to put on the table. In recent years, they had lacked the money even to cook white rice, let alone to make rice balls.

Clearly, somebody had brought him this parcel of food after he absconded.

How awful it must have been for him, shivering away in that little cave… Who could say how it had come to this? At any rate, he must have found himself in dire circumstances. Was it then that some stranger found him and, feigning kindness, offered him these balls of rice? Unaware of the danger, he must have wolfed them down. One, two, three, four, five…

Then it would have been the same old story. Excruciating pain, groaning, vomiting blood, paralysis of the limbs… All the while, the criminal's snake-like eyes watching over him as his strength left him and he breathed his last.

I shuddered just thinking about it. How many more would have to die? When would this bloody chain of events finally end? If only to return to my old, dull, grey life. I could bear this no longer...

But it wasn't that easy, of course. I couldn't escape this insanity. And besides, something even more terrible was lurking just around the corner.

For one thing, Dr Kuno's murder made my position all the more precarious. Until now, suspicion of him had been the only thing to relieve the pressure on me. But now, that pressure valve was completely gone. All the suspicions that had previously been laid on Dr Kuno were now transformed into an even deeper sense of sympathy for him, while all the hatred was now directed towards me.

One day, my sister came to see me, looking deathly pale.

"You need to be careful, Tatsuya," she said. "Somebody has written something about you and stuck it up in front of the village hall."

"Something about me?..." I asked warily.

"Yes. They're saying that all these recent murders are your doing. They must have put it up last night."

I could feel my stomach clench, and a wave of anger washed over me irresistibly.

"What does this person want from me?"

"Nothing, it seems. All it says is that you're the criminal. As proof, they submit that all these murders took place only after your arrival in the village. It says that so long as you're in the village, there'll be no end to the bloodshed... That's the gist of it, anyway."

It was a painful sight to behold: the effort of making this revelation had left Haruyo breathless. She wasn't especially courageous at the best of times, and now I worried that this latest series of misfortunes had made her heart even weaker. I was so touched that I tried to feign an air of nonchalance, but this time it was all too much. Instinctively, I moved towards her.

"Who could have done this, Haruyo? Who is blaming me for all this? The inspector told me that they also received a letter like that. Somebody in the village must truly hate me. They're doing whatever they can to force me out of the village. Who on earth could it be? Why do they hate me so much?"

"I just don't know… But you have to be careful, Tatsuya. I think it's unlikely, but you never know what might happen: the villagers are so obtuse…"

Even then, Haruyo must have sensed the threat looming over me in the village. She looked truly distressed, but it was I who failed to appreciate the gravity of the situation.

"I promise I'll be careful. But I'm beside myself with rage… Who could hate me so much that they would do this? And why?"

Though I wasn't usually given to weeping, this time I couldn't hold back my tears. Haruyo placed her hand on my shoulder gently.

"It's only natural," she said. "But don't take it to heart. It's all a misunderstanding, and sooner or later it'll be cleared up. But until then, you'll just have to be patient. Whatever you do, don't lose your head, and don't do anything rash."

What she feared most was that I would get tired of all this and leave. For my departure would have caused all manner of troubles. Kotake had lost her mind and lapsed into a second infancy, and Haruyo's heart was so weak that even the slightest effort would make her breathless. But it wasn't for these practical reasons that she wanted me to stay. It was because she loved me. She loved me so much that she didn't want to let me go even for a single minute. I understood how she felt: or at least I thought I did. Thinking back on it now, I am forced to admit that what I understood was only a fraction of the reality...

Be that as it may, somebody was working hard to entrap me. The police hadn't yet come to arrest me, however. In fact, I'd seen neither hide nor hair of the police since the discovery of Dr Kuno's body: Inspector Isokawa and Kosuke Kindaichi had simply vanished. The villagers hadn't gone so far as to take direct action, and no new crimes followed. And Miyako, too, seemed to have disappeared—we no longer saw her.

Later on, I realized that this period of relative calm was like the slow flow of a gentle stream just before it goes crashing down a waterfall. Blissfully ignorant of the torments that lay ahead of me, I relished this temporary sense of peace. Now was not the time to go hunting for the treasure, so I decided to use this brief period of respite to sort through my mother's love letters.

With Haruyo's permission, I engaged a craftsman from the town of N——to come and dismantle the folding screen and to carefully remove the love letters that my mother had exchanged with Yoichi Kamei. I didn't want the screen to leave the house, let alone have those letters seen by prying eyes. I asked the craftsman to come every day at noon, so that we could set to work together in the annexe.

Nothing then gave me more pleasure than this work. Ever since my arrival in the village, the only good thing to have happened was the discovery of these letters, which brought me great comfort. As is the case for all those who lose their mother in childhood, I missed mine terribly, despite my age.

To begin with, Haruyo would often visit the annexe to observe our work, if her health permitted. But she was so moved by reading my mother's letters that she stopped coming back, for fear that her heart might break.

Every night I sorted through the letters that we had rescued from the folding screen. Reading them gave me the most intense pleasure, even though not a single one of them failed to mention her terrible misfortunes...

> *The tortures I endure day and night wear me out, both in body and in soul...*

There were tearstains on the following line:

> *If I do not obey him, he drags me out, pulling me by the hair...*

In the following terms, she lamented my father's molestations:

> *Under the pretext of comforting me, he takes me in his arms and undresses me and licks me all over. There is no word strong enough to express the disgust I feel for him, the loathing, the horror...*

Or again:

> *Sometimes he will take his leave of me, enjoining me to relax. I lie down and read. Or else I write letters. But when he comes back, he knows exactly what I have read and to whom I have been writing. It terrifies me. His obsession is such that, even in his absence, I feel his soul cling to mine without ever leaving me for a single moment. It distresses and upsets me all the more when I think about it...*

Did my father have a gift for telepathy? How could he know my mother's every move, even when he was away from her? How could he have guessed all these things one after another? In such circumstances, nothing could have been more natural than my mother's terror. But then I suddenly remembered the Noh mask hanging in the alcove and the hole in the wall behind it.

Of course, of course! My father had only pretended to leave the house, whereas in reality he must have taken the secret passage into the storage room and observed my mother clandestinely through the peephole. Then he would return and tell her all the things that she had done in his absence. It must have thrilled him to provoke such terror in her. It was a trick worthy of a sadist. He must have tormented that fragile woman right to the bitter end, just to satisfy his lust.

My poor mother! Never to know a moment's peace in all those years... But how ingenious of her to hide all her thoughts in this folding screen. Even my suspicious father would never have been able to read them through the screen. And all she had to do was light the screen from behind in order to read those old love letters whenever she wanted.

I shared my mother's suffering with such intensity of emotion that night after night my pillow would be damp with tears. Still, I was glad to have learnt her secret. I wondered even whether I had not been guided in all this by my mother's spirit. Little did I realize then, however, that the screen held an even greater secret—one that was about to turn my life upside down.

It happened on the day that the craftsman was due to finish his work. Just as he was putting everything back together again, he turned and said to me:

"Sir, there's something strange stuck here. Shall I remove it?"

"Something strange?"

"It looks like a piece of card. Only, it hasn't been glued down, but placed in an envelope. It's the envelope that's stuck to the screen. What would you like me to do with it?"

I had spotted it before: when I had placed the lamp on the other side, I had noticed a rectangular object pasted to the top-left corner of one of the panels. It was about the size of a postcard. I hadn't noticed that the piece of card had been placed in an envelope, however. I was intrigued. Could it contain something very important?

"Take it off," I instructed the craftsman.

The envelope was made from a very fine quality paper. It was securely sealed, but as soon as I touched it, I knew that it contained something on a hard piece of card.

That evening I waited for the craftsman to leave before opening the envelope. With trembling fingers, I extracted its contents. I stared in astonishment.

It was a photograph of me. But when had it been taken? I didn't have the slightest memory of it. It couldn't have been taken that long ago, however, because I didn't seem to have changed all that much. It was a photo from the waist up. I was posing for the camera and smiling. It looked like a portrait taken in a photographer's studio, but I, for one, couldn't remember having it taken at all.

I was at a complete loss. My mind was in a state of confusion. But little by little it dawned on me. Though the sitter was the spitting image of me, he was not in fact me. The resemblance was so striking, though, that even I had been fooled. The eyes, the mouth, the cheeks were all the same, but it was not me. Besides, there was the age of the photograph itself: it looked too old to have been taken only a year or two ago.

My hand still trembling, I turned the photograph over. The words seemed to dance before my eyes:

Yoichi Kamei (27)
Autumn 1921

A SHOWER OF STONES

It was incredible. My mother's lover and I were like two peas in a pod, alike in every way. Was there ever more tangible proof of adultery? So, I was not the son of Yozo Tajimi. I was the child of my mother and her lover Yoichi Kamei.

Nothing could have come as a greater shock to me. I thought I was going mad. Yet if the discovery brought me joy and immense relief, it also, I must admit, brought bitter disappointment.

If I was not the child of Yozo Tajimi, then the crazed blood of this family did not flow in my veins: while this fact alone delighted me, it also meant that the considerable fortune of the Tajimi family had slipped through my fingers.

Shameful though it is to admit, I cannot deny that this fortune exerted a considerable influence over me. I had even grown to covet it secretly. One of the cattle-herders had told me that the Tajimi family drove 120 cattle to pasture. The price of a single cow at market back then was 100,000 yen. Such sums made me dizzy. And the cattle didn't make up even a tenth of the entire legacy.

"The Tajimis' wealth is incalculable," one of the servants had told me. So my desire to acquire it was only natural. But now, all of a sudden, the fortune had lost all its meaning for me. I had lost every last right to it. What disappointment, what despair! I felt as though I had been thrown into an abyss of darkness, but then a thought struck me: had Koume and Kotake not realized this already? My sister, of course, had been too young when the massacre took place, but surely the twins must have met Kamei? If they had seen him even once, they could not fail to have recognized his likeness in me, for our resemblance was glaring.

Just then, a terrible memory suddenly surfaced in my mind. It was the scene of my brother Hisaya's death, which had happened to be our first and last meeting. As soon as he saw me, a mysterious smile crossed his lips. What was it that he had said? *"A fine-looking man, indeed... Such looks are a rarity among Tajimi men."*

That mysterious smile, that poisonous laugh—they had troubled me long after his death, but now their meaning was perfectly clear to me. He had known at once that I was no Tajimi, that I was the son of Yoichi Kamei. But why, then, had he not exposed me as a false heir? It went without saying: he didn't want Shintaro to succeed him.

Even now, I shudder to think of Hisaya's terrible obsession. It all stemmed from his hatred of Shintaro. He had been ready to give the family's entire fortune over to a perfect stranger just to spite him. It had nothing at all to do with being kind to me. To him, I was nothing more than a puppet, a wooden marionette whose role was to dance and humiliate Shintaro. Alongside bitter disappointment, I now felt fierce anger.

That night I couldn't sleep. I cursed my father, my mother, my brother and the fate that had led me to this village. How could I possibly return to Kobe now without losing face? I couldn't very well tell my colleagues who had seen me off and wished me luck that it had all been a mistake.

That feeling of anguish kept me awake throughout the night. But in this world, it is never so clear-cut what is happiness and what misfortune. That night, it was my insomnia that preserved me from grave danger.

It must have been at around midnight that I was jolted out of my semi-slumber by the cry of voices coming from outside: it was the villagers. They were so loud that they seemed to shake the very earth. Their cries echoed amid the nocturnal stillness.

No sooner had I realized what was going on than I heard a banging on the roof tiles and on the rain shutters. They were pelting the annexe with stones. I got up and dressed in a hurry. Their battle cries redoubled in violence.

The situation was serious. I crept over to the shutters, my knees trembling, and peered outside. Through the slats I could see a red glow above the low walls. They were carrying flaming torches. The voices rose again, and another deluge of stones came crashing down on the roof and the shutters. I didn't know what was happening: all I knew for sure was that an angry mob was trying to storm the Tajimi house.

To find out what was going on, I ran down the long corridor to the main house, where I crashed into Haruyo in her nightgown.

"What's happening, Haruyo?" I asked.

"Oh, Tatsuya! You must run… Run now!" she cried.

I saw that she was carrying a pair of my shoes.

"You have to go, Tatsuya! Quickly! It's you they've come for!"

"Me!?" I asked, stunned.

"They're saying they're going to tie you up and throw you into the river! Quickly! You must go, I'm begging you!"

Haruyo took me by the hand and dragged me back to the annexe. Fear sent a shiver down my spine, but at the same time I was overcome by a feeling of uncontrollable rage.

"What do they want with me, Haruyo? Why do they want to throw me into the river? I'm not going to run away from them. I won't do that. I'm going to go out and reason with them."

"You can't! It's no good. These aren't reasonable people, Tatsuya! They're a baying mob."

"But, Haruyo, it's outrageous! If I flee now, it will be like admitting my guilt."

"There isn't time! There's no alternative. Sometimes you have to admit defeat in order to be victorious later. Go now, and bide your time!"

The cries and jeers of the crowed began to echo from inside the main house. All the colour drained from Haruyo's face, and my whole body froze.

"I've bolted the door in the corridor, but it won't be long before they break it down. Quickly now!"

"But, Haruyo!…"

"Time's running out, Tatsuya!" My sister's voice suddenly harshened. "Don't you understand what I'm telling you? Don't you understand how much I care for you? Run! Do you hear me? Run, now!…"

I had no alternative. Besides, the sound of stones pelting the roof and the shutters was an urgent reminder of the danger that I was in.

"Where should I go?"

"Your only chance is to make your way down into the caves. If you go down there, nobody will dare venture past the Devil's Abyss. Meanwhile, I'll try to buy you some time and calm the villagers down. If it carries on like this for too long, I'll bring some food down for you. But tonight you must do exactly as I tell you…"

She looked terrible. Her breathing was laboured, and she had to pause for breath every few words. I couldn't allow myself to put her through any more of this.

"All right, Haruyo. I'll do as you say."

I took my watch and ran to the storage room. It was half-past midnight. Fortunately, the miner's lamp and flashlights that we had been using recently were still there. I grabbed them and, just as I was opening the lid of the chest, Haruyo appeared with my coat.

"So that you don't catch a cold," she said.

"Thank you, Haruyo… I should go."

"Be careful."

Tears were welling in her eyes. I could feel myself starting to cry as I slipped as quickly as I could into the chest.

Cruel fate had chased me into a labyrinth of darkness.

THROUGH THE SHADOWS

I did not know then the terrible danger that awaited me.

As I descended into the underground tunnels through the chest, I could hear the footsteps and insults of my assailants overhead. They must have already broken into the annexe. Judging by the uproar, there was a considerable number of them. Their cries and shouts brought my whole body out in a cold sweat. I was right to follow Haruyo's advice, I thought.

I turned off the miner's lamp and groped my way through the dark tunnel. Fortunately, I was by now well acquainted with the place, so it wasn't difficult for me to find my bearings, even in the shadows.

It wasn't long before I found myself at the foot of the second stone staircase, which led up to the shrine at the back of the garden. No doubt whoever built this passage long ago had intended to link the shrine to the storage room. That must have been how he happened upon the caves in the first place and struck upon the idea of extending them.

I felt along the wall, trying to find the door, when suddenly I saw a light up above, coming from the top of the staircase.

"Hey! There's a tunnel down here!"

"Be careful, it's treacherous!"

"Should we go down there? I have a bad feeling about this…"

The voices echoed in the narrow tunnel, reverberating like a cracked bell.

In a daze, I pulled the lever. Never had the rock seemed so slow to open. As footsteps drew nearer and nearer, the passage opened with what seemed like extreme reluctance. If it hadn't opened in time, I would have had no choice but to turn back towards the first staircase leading up to the storage room, but already I could hear footsteps and angry voices coming from that direction too.

For a moment I froze in a state of excruciating terror, but luckily the rock opened just enough for me to squeeze through and pull the lever on the other side to close it behind me. I was just in the nick of time. Even before the rock had fully closed, I could hear footsteps on the other side.

"Hey, look! That rock's moving!"

"Damn it! The bastard must have fled through there!"

"How do we move the rock?"

"Wait, wait! Let me take a look."

Leaving these voices behind, I crawled through the dark tunnel.

Only then did I appreciate the scale of the plan hatched by the villagers. Evidently, they had entered the caves through every available passage. I had to reach the fork as quickly as possible; otherwise, the ones who had taken the tunnel from Koicha would block my way.

As I found out afterwards, the villagers had indeed done as I feared: all entrances to the caves were guarded. As soon as I ventured down into the caves, word was sent to those guarding the Koicha entrance to close in on me. Luckily for me, however, it was night, and the news didn't travel as quickly as they had hoped. What was more, the villagers were not used to the tunnels and had to move slowly. With all these advantages, I was able to reach the fork with a solid lead.

I was not out of harm's way yet. My pursuers were increasing in number, and their cries, like a hundred claps of thunder, made the air in the tunnels tremble. Still dazed, I took the passage that led from the Monkey's Seat to the Goblin's Nose.

The Echoes' Crossing lay a little past the Goblin's Nose, and from there it wasn't far to the Devil's Abyss. Once I'd crossed that, I'd be safe. The villagers would be afraid to go any further. But even if they did, there was always the Fox's Den, and it would be nigh-on impossible for them to find me there. They would have to search every last nook and cranny.

Spurred on by these thoughts, I reached the Goblin's Nose. Suddenly, I froze. I could hear a frenzy of voices coming from the Echoes' Crossing, which still lay ahead. The reverberations were like a raging storm that was drawing ever nearer to me.

Of course! I had forgotten. It was there that I had run into Eisen. Had he not said that there was another tunnel leading to Bankachi? They must be coming from that direction too. I was cornered! I could hear the roar of voices multiplying behind me, while up ahead footsteps were drawing closer.

I switched on my flashlight and looked around. It was then that I noticed the large rocky prominence that formed the Goblin's Nose overhead. I immediately clambered up to perch on top of it. Fortunately, there was a hollow where I could curl up and hide. No sooner had I done this and dowsed my light than the flames of torches appeared at the corner of the Echoes' Crossing, followed by hasty footsteps.

"I don't understand it… If he ran this way, we would have bumped into him. Could we have missed him without real- izing it?"

"Don't be an idiot! The tunnel isn't wide enough for that…"

"True… Then he must still be on his way."

"The fool hasn't dared to light his lamp. He must be run- ning blindly in the dark. It'll take some time before he gets here."

"Hmm… Tetsu's right. We'll just have to wait for him."

Judging by their voices, there must have been three of them, all standing right below the Goblin's Nose. They intended to set a trap for me.

I was on tenterhooks. What if the others were to catch up? They would search every last inch of this place, and besides, the Goblin's Nose would be the first place they looked.

Their voices carried up to me.

"It really does look like a goblin's nose, doesn't it?"

"You're right. It's strange to think that nature made all of this. Though they say that somebody carved the mouth and eyes from the rock…"

"What about up there? Above the nose? Could he be hiding up there?…"

I felt as if a noose were tightening around my neck. Fortunately, however, the eldest of them replied:

"Don't be so stupid, Shinsuke! Just look!" He raised his torch higher, making the shadows dance on the roof of the cave. "If anybody was up there, we'd be able to see him."

I breathed a sigh of relief, thanking my lucky stars for the cavity above the Goblin's Nose.

The three of them sat down and chatted while they smoked. My ears pricked up when they began talking about this evening's manhunt.

"Is that really what you're saying, Tetsu? You don't give a damn that after twenty-six years the same thing is happening in the village again?"

The voice sounded familiar. With fear and trepidation, I peered down from the Goblin's Nose. The three of them were sitting exactly where we had been hiding when we saw Eisen. It was the cattle-trader Kichizo, whom I had met on the bus when I arrived in the village.

The figure beside him mumbled an answer that I didn't catch. Kichizo raised his voice.

"How old were you then, Tetsu? Three?... No wonder you can't remember how terrible it was! I was twenty-three back then. I'd only been married for two months. We were still getting to know one another; it was still our honeymoon... She was six years younger than me. Only seventeen! I know they say we always rose-tint the past, but really, she was such a beautiful girl. Some even said she was too good for me. And you, Tetsu..."

Kichizo was incensed.

"That night he shot her. There was no bad blood or anything. He just killed her like a fly. It makes my blood boil just thinking about it..."

Kichizo's voice echoed ominously in the cave. I shivered, as though an icy wind had blown over me.

"Of course," replied Tetsu. "Of course that's how you're going to feel if you lose somebody like that. But really, what's the use making all this fuss and going after this other guy now? Shouldn't we leave it to the police?"

At these words, Kichizo only laughed.

"Oh, to be young and have such respect for the police! Listen to me, Tetsu. You can't rely on the police. It was the same story back then. That bastard Yozo wreaked havoc all night long. If the police had arrived even a little earlier, only half the people would have been killed and injured. But do you know what happened? They arrived when it was all over and Yozo had long since fled into the mountains. That's always the way with the police: they show up just as the curtain falls. How can people like that be trusted? If you value your life, you have only yourself to rely on."

"But there's nothing to say that history will repeat itself if we let this guy go."

"Can you be so sure? Can you guarantee that it won't happen all over again? How, then, do you explain all these murders? For twenty-six years, there hasn't been a single murder in the village. And now, ever since he arrived, there's been one tragedy after another. He's been sent by the devil, that one. As soon as I clapped eyes on him on the bus, I knew it. I should have struck him dead there and then."

The sound of Kichizo grinding his teeth stabbed my nerves like an awl piercing flesh. I felt that familiar lead weight in my stomach.

"It looks like you've twice the reason to bear a grudge, then, old man," said Tetsu in a mocking voice. "Weren't you on very intimate terms with the Koicha nun?…"

"And what's wrong with that?" Kichizo retorted, even angrier now. "Why shouldn't I be on intimate terms with her? After all, don't they say that even a cracked pot can do with a broken lid? Ever since my wife was killed, I've had nobody. Just you remember, Tetsu: you can't judge a person, be it a man or a woman, by appearances. There are some things that become clear only after you spend a night with someone… She was devoted to me, and I to her. And to think that all because of that guy…"

I could hear his teeth grinding again. After a few moments, the younger man spoke.

"But is this guy really the murderer? I can't bring myself to believe it…"

The third man, who until then had been listening to the other two in silence, now intervened:

"It was him all right. I wasn't so sure of it before, but I am now because…" He leant in. "Because of her. You know, the young mistress who went to find him in Kobe. She liked him at first and she stood up for him, but now that's all changed. For one thing, she's been giving him a wide berth lately. She must have finally got the measure of him. She may be a woman, but she's nobody's fool…"

I was stunned. Although he didn't mention her by name, the "young mistress" could only have been Miyako.

"Well, does she say that he's the culprit too?"

The question came from Tetsu.

"Not in so many words… She's not like us. She's a lady of refinement and is careful about what she says. But just the other day our foreman decided to sound her out. As soon as he mentioned the guy's name, her face changed. 'Don't talk about him!' she says. 'I don't want his name spoken in my presence.' And with that, she went back indoors. That's why our foreman thinks she must have something on the guy."

Had I been abandoned by Miyako, too? But what proof could she have? None, of course. But if she'd had any suspicions, why hadn't she just asked me about them? I felt a dark sense of despair, as though I had been cast down into hell itself.

"Hmm… All the same…" Tetsu began, but just then some distant shouting carried to us.

The three men stood up.

"What was that?"

"Maybe they've caught him…"

"Right, let's go!"

The three of them set off, but suddenly the old man thought again.

"You stay here, Tetsu."

"But why me?"

"You're not afraid, are you? We won't be long. You stand guard here, just in case."

Left alone, Tetsu raised the torch over his head and looked around for a few moments. Then, unable to bear it any longer, he went running after the two others.

"Wait!… Wait for me!…"

It was now or never. I had to use this opportunity to escape my pursuers. As quickly as I could, I clambered down from the Goblin's Nose and made my way around the Echoes' Crossing, before finally arriving at the Devil's Abyss. What I feared most was finding somebody guarding the abyss, but luckily they didn't seem to have thought of that: there was nobody around.

With a sigh of relief, I turned my flashlight on, checked the area and immediately set off along the narrow path. It was black as pitch, but since I had been there once already, I wasn't as frightened as I might have been.

Soon enough, I found myself on the opposite shore. All around was dark and desolate, but at that moment in time, there was nowhere safer for me.

Feeling forsaken, as though chilled by a winter's wind, I stood there in the shadows.

A few moments later, something made my heart leap. The voice literally made me jump.

"Tatsuya! Is that you? It's me…"

The voice was Noriko's.

A VOICE IN THE DARK

"Noriko! What on earth are you doing here?"

"I've been looking for you everywhere, Tatsuya! When they told me that you'd run away into the caves, I was sure that you'd come here. I've been waiting for so long. You must have managed to escape them, but you took so long getting here that I worried they might have caught you."

"Noriko!"

I was so moved that I instinctively took her in my arms and pressed her to me.

Never before had I been in such need of compassion. The scenes that I had just witnessed had robbed me of my confidence in humanity very nearly for good. What I feared wasn't the physical risk. I truly believed that, since I lived in a country ruled by law, I couldn't possibly be the victim of this lynch mob. Sooner or later the police would turn up and make them see reason. No, what frightened me was what I had discovered about human nature.

A mob such as this could not have been formed without some instigator to fan the flames. But what I feared more than this instigator was the villagers, who were so easily manipulated. No matter how persuasive the instigator, there would never have been such an outburst, were it not for the seed of hatred contained in the villagers' hearts. Was I really so reviled by them? The very thought depressed me deeply and led me to despair.

Another thing that clouded my mind was this rumour about Miyako. I had no idea why she had suddenly begun to harbour suspicions about me. After all the encouragement that she had lavished on me and the faith that she had placed in me, this unanticipated fickleness only proved to me the inconstancy of the human heart.

After all this, the kindness shown to me by Noriko made me happy beyond compare. I was so very grateful to her. But I couldn't accept it under the circumstances.

"Thank you, Noriko. But this is no place for you. You must go back."

"But why?"

I couldn't see in the dark, but I imagined her naïve eyes widening in surprise.

"Who knows what will happen if the villagers find us! You could get dragged into all this. You might even get hurt. You have to go back. Now!"

"Don't worry. The villagers are too afraid to cross the Devil's Abyss. Legend has it that those who cross it are cursed. So long as we stay here, we'll be safe."

"I'm telling you, Noriko. You'd better go home. Your brother will be worried."

"Oh, never mind about him. Let me stay with you a little longer, Tatsuya. I'll have to go back eventually anyway."

"Why? Is there something you have to do there?"

"Of course, I'll have to bring you some food."

"Food?"

"Yes! This could go on for a long while yet. You can't be expected to survive down here without anything to eat. In a little while, I'll sneak home and come back with something for you."

"But, Noriko, what makes you think that all this will drag on?"

"It's just a feeling. Everybody's so riled up…"

"But the police won't allow this to carry on… Surely, they'll have to intervene and disperse them?"

"Tatsuya…" Noriko said mournfully. "In a mountain village like this, the police are powerless, really. If only one part of the village was causing trouble, we could get someone to talk them down, but in this instance the whole village is acting together. If the police were to intervene, they'd only make the situation worse. So all they can do is sit back and watch it play out. That's exactly what happened last summer, when there was a dispute over water for the rice paddies."

I suddenly felt forlorn.

"But Noriko, are you saying that the whole village has turned against me tonight?"

"I'm afraid so. Everyone except for evacuees like us... But you mustn't think that everybody hates you, Tatsuya. People here just lose control whenever they're reminded of what happened twenty-six years ago. For the ones over forty, that tragedy is still fresh in their minds, as if it took place only yesterday. All anybody has to do is tell them that the same thing is going to happen again, and they'll be liable to do anything. Somebody has been carefully fanning the flames..."

"But who?!"

"I don't know."

"Has it been going on for long?"

"Not that I know of. It looks like Itaru and Kichizo are the ringleaders, so it must be coming from the House of the West. I'm sure of it. "

"Who is Itaru?"

"He's the young foreman at the House of the West. They say he lost his wife and children in the massacre."

My heart began to thud when I heard this.

"The foreman at the House of the West? Noriko! Then maybe the person behind all of this is the head of the House of the West! Could it be that he's the one pulling the strings?"

"It could be... But then again, when things get this bad, nobody is powerful enough to stop it—not the head of the House of the West, nor even the village mayor."

I felt more and more forlorn.

"What should I do then, Noriko?"

"You just need to sit tight and wait it out. They'll come to their senses eventually. Right now, they're baying for blood, so there's no talking to them. The slightest provocation would only make matters worse. Sooner or later, they'll calm down and see how foolish they look brandishing their bamboo spears. For now, though, we must wait."

"They have spears?!"

"Yes! It isn't spirit they lack… But the one you really have to look out for is Kichizo. He's got an enormous wooden club. He's been telling everyone that he'll kill on the spot if he sees you. So be careful: he's capable of doing what he says."

I remembered seeing Kichizo's fierce expression in the torch-light, and a chill ran down my spine. I'd had a lucky escape.

I fell silent. There was so much weighing on my mind, but I hadn't the strength to talk. A few moments later, I felt Noriko's cold hands clasp my cheeks in the darkness.

"What are you thinking, Tatsuya? There's nothing to worry about. You just have to hide here for now. No one will dare to cross the Devil's Abyss. Not even Itaru or Kichizo. Those two brutes are even more superstitious than most. You'll be safe here. I'll bring you something to eat. I've even discovered a shortcut that nobody knows about. The tunnel is no wider than a rabbit warren. That's why I'm wearing this."

I reached out and felt that she was wearing some kind of overall, like the air defence ones worn during the war.

"It may take two or three days even, but you have to hold out. You mustn't give in. You've got to keep going till it's all over."

Never had I known such daring. The very word "despair" meant nothing to her. She was so courageous and optimistic. How was it that such a delicate body could harbour such a strong soul?

"Thank you, Noriko. I'm entirely in your hands."

"Don't worry. You can depend on me… Ah! Here they come!"

We instinctively took refuge in a nearby tunnel. At almost exactly the same time, the opposite bank of the Devil's Abyss was lit up by the flames of torches. My pursuers came running with cries and shouting. Seeming to have clocked that I had crossed the abyss, they stamped their feet furiously and hurled insults over the water.

Noriko grabbed my arm.

"Don't answer them! They still don't know for sure that you're here."

I had no intention of replying.

"Look! The one nearest us, holding the torch... That's Itaru. And Kichizo is just behind him."

Itaru was an old man with white hair. He must have been around sixty. By the light of the torch, his face looked deeply lined and red, and his eyes were bulging. As for Kichizo, he really was carrying an enormous club.

Noriko was right, though. None of them dared to cross the Devil's Abyss. They just stamped their feet, incandescent with rage. For a good hour, they carried on hurling abuse across the water. Then, after some discussion, they left, leaving only a couple of men to guard it.

"See," said Noriko. "Just as I told you."

The guards sat down, surrounded by their miners' lamps. They began singing folk songs, between which they would resume hurling insults at me. In the end, however, they settled down and fell quiet. They seemed to have fallen asleep.

Seeing this, I too must have relaxed for I was suddenly overcome by weariness and lapsed into a deep slumber, my head resting in Noriko's lap.

For how long did I sleep there? I had terrible nightmares, and I dreamt that somebody was calling out my name. I awoke with a start.

"Tatsuya-a-a-a!"

The voice I heard in my dream echoed through the darkness.

"Tatsuya-a-a-a! Help me-e-e-e!"

Was I still dreaming? I wondered. No, this was no dream. I could really hear somebody calling out my name in the darkness.

I leapt up.

"Noriko! Noriko!" I whispered.

But there was no reply. Fearfully, I turned on my flashlight. There was no sign of her anywhere. I glanced at my watch. It was 10.20. It must be morning, I thought.

Then I heard the voice again.

"Tatsuya! Tatsuya-a-a-a! Where are you? Help me! He's going to kill me-e-e-e!…"

Wide awake now, I bolted out of the cave. My guards seemed to have left already. The bank opposite was shrouded in darkness. But from that darkness, once again came the voice:

"Tatsuya-a-a-a!"

It seemed to get closer then further away again. All the hairs on my body were standing on end from the sheer terror of it.

Ah, that voice! It was Haruyo's voice.

CHAPTER 7

TERROR AT THE ECHOES' CROSSING

I hesitated for a moment. It wasn't out of cowardice. I simply had no idea what was going on. But the very next moment, I heard that plaintive cry for help again.

"Tatsuya-a-a-a!"

My decision was made. No matter what the danger, I couldn't just leave my sister calling for help. I had to go to her. Thrusting the flashlight into my pocket, I headed straight for the narrow path back to the other side of the Devil's Abyss. I was so used to crossing it now that I was oblivious to the danger.

When I reached the midpoint, I heard my sister's voice again. This time it was much clearer, but it wasn't coming from the same place. It was as though she was on the move.

Of course! Somebody was chasing her... The realization filled me with dread. It wasn't my sister's assailant that frightened me so much as her poor health. The doctor had ordered her to take as much rest as possible. The least excitement, the least exertion was bad for her heart. As if that weren't enough, the events of last night must have taken their toll on her as well...

I continued across as though in a dream.

"Haruyo! Haruyo! Where are you?" I cried out, forgetting the danger in which it might put me.

Again, that strange voice rang out, echoing eerily.

"Tatsuya-a-a-a-! Tatsuya-a-a-a-! Help me-e-e-e! Help me-e-e-e!"

Every one of my sister's cries reverberated. The noise of her frantic race through the tunnels, punctuated by the sounds of tripping and stumbling, was amplified grotesquely by the acoustics.

My sister and her attacker were at the Echoes' Crossing.

"Haruyo! I'm coming, Haruyo! Hold on! I'm on my way!"

Shouting all the while, I ran in a daze. I was no longer afraid of anyone. Ready for anyone, be it Itaru or Kichizo, I wielded my flashlight.

She must have heard me.

"Oh, Tatsuya! Come quickly!"

Her cries, which until then had been cast into the void, suddenly regained a sense of hope and life. The sound of her footsteps and her cries were becoming more and more distinct. I was running at full pelt, but still I couldn't get there fast enough.

The Echoes' Crossing was so tortuous that, despite my proximity, it was taking me an eternity to reach her. Each and every move that my sister and her assailant made was amplified, so much that they always seemed to be only a stone's throw away. It was so excruciating that I felt as though I were having my lifeblood squeezed out of me.

"Haruyo! Haruyo! Are you all right? Who's following you?"

"Oh, Tatsuya! Come quickly… It's so dark that I can't see him… But… but… he's going to kill me! Oh, Tatsuya! Tatsuya-a-a-a!"

There was silence. I stopped dead in my tracks. Then suddenly there was a scream.

After a brief scuffle came the sound of something falling, followed by footsteps rushing off. Then an unexpected, deathly silence.

A feeling of dread rooted me to the spot. I was paralysed. At last, I managed to pull myself together and broke into a run.

A few moments later, I came upon my sister's body in the dark.

"Haruyo! Haruyo!"

I tried to lift her with my arms, but there was something strange in her chest preventing me. With horror, I saw that it was a stalactite. One of the many stalactites that hung from the roof of the cave had fallen and impaled her.

"Haruyo! Haruyo!" I called out frantically.

Still alive, she managed to open her eyes, which were already clouding over. She searched for my face and, with a groan, mumbled:

"Tatsuya…"

"Yes, it's me, Haruyo. Hold on."

I held her close to me. A nearly imperceptible smile spread across her pale lips.

"It's too late for me," she said. "It isn't the wound… It's my heart…"

She winced in pain and continued:

"It's all right… I'm just happy that I was able to see you before I die…"

"You mustn't talk like that, Haruyo! But who was it? Who could have done this to you?"

Once again, a faint smile crossed her lips. She had a mysterious look on her face.

"I don't know who it was… It was too dark to see anything. But I bit the little finger on their left hand, so hard that it almost came off… You must have heard the scream."

I stared at her in surprise. At the corner of her mouth there was a trace of fresh blood. So, the scream that I heard earlier wasn't Haruyo's but her assailant's.

She winced in pain again and gasped as though she were sobbing.

"Tatsuya… Tatsuya…"

"What is it, Haruyo?"

"I don't have long left… But don't let me die alone. Please, stay with me. Hold me in your arms. I'll be happy dying in your arms…"

I stared at her in horror and astonishment. A startling suspicion crossed my mind.

"Haruyo! Haruyo…"

But she no longer heard me. Instead, she just carried on speaking as though in a delirium.

"I don't have long left, Tatsuya… There's no use hiding it any more. If only you knew how much I've loved you… how much I've adored you… how I'd die for you. I don't love you as a sister, though… because you aren't my brother… But you, Tatsuya, you've only ever seen me as your sister. It made me so terribly sad…"

So she did know! She knew that I was not her real brother. And all this time she had harboured a secret tenderness for me, intruder that I was in her family. I was struck by an indescribable sense of melancholy.

"But none of that matters now," she continued, "so long as I can die in your arms. Only, don't leave me, Tatsuya… Not until I die… Then, when I do, remember me kindly and take pity on me."

She talked and talked, until in the end she ran out of breath and her words became incoherent. Her eyes were still open, but she no longer saw anything. Her face had a childlike purity about it.

And so, just like that, lying in my arms, she breathed her last.

I closed my eyes and gently laid her body back down on the ground. I noticed that in her left hand she was carrying a *furoshiki* and a flask. I untied the cloth bundle and saw that it contained rice balls inside a bamboo wrapping. I gasped, and my tears began to stream. She had met her end attempting to bring me something to eat.

I cried for a long while, holding her lifeless body to me. And yet I knew that now was not the time for this. I had to alert the police as quickly as possible.

I tied the *furoshiki* that my sister had prepared with such love to my belt and slung the flask over my shoulder. Flashlight in hand, I stood up, but that was when I heard a voice.

"You bastard!"

That voice, so full of hatred, exploded like a bomb amid the darkness. I was in danger. Suddenly, I felt something rend the air just above my head, but instinctively I had just managed to duck in order to escape the blow.

"What are you doing?!" I cried.

I turned on my flashlight to see the face of my attacker. My whole body was seized by an electrifying fear when I saw Kichizo.

Having missed me with that first blow, he stood gnashing his teeth as he held that enormous club between his gnarled fingers.

Seeing his eyes, I realized that Noriko had not been exaggerating. The bloodlust was written in them. He had no desire to talk things over and clearly meant to kill me.

Dazzled by the light, he shielded his eyes with one hand, while with the other raising the club to take another swing.

"Now you'll get what you deserve!"

Leaping like an animal, he brought the club down, but once again he missed, as I ducked just in the nick of time. The club smashed into a boulder. Carried by the momentum, Kichizo was thrown forward and, with a terrible cry, he dropped his weapon, which went rolling off. The club's impact against the rock must have sent a shock through his hand, and, while he was recovering, I headbutted him right in the middle of his torso. He hadn't seen the attack coming, and, despite his size, went flying backwards, clasping both hands to his chest. I used the opportunity to run away as fast as I could, but my eyes had not readjusted to the darkness, and I was running blind. Suddenly, I realized that I was heading for the Devil's Abyss. I wanted to turn back but already I could hear Kichizo bellowing as he raced after me.

I could no longer turn back. Once again, I found myself cornered, chased over to the far bank of the Devil's Abyss.

AN INJURED FINGER

I was at the end of my tether. This was no time for me to be hiding in a place like this.

With Haruyo dead, the only surviving member of the Tajimi family was Kotake, who was no use now. Who would be there to make the arrangements for Haruyo's funeral, if not me? Besides, there was now another duty weighing on my shoulders. I had a clue about my sister's killer. Half his little finger had nearly been bitten off. I had to notify the police as soon as possible.

If only I could get out of this cave!

On the other bank of the Devil's Abyss, Kichizo stood guard as he tended the fire. Beside him, I could see Itaru's fearsome-looking face. These two ringleaders watched me with unwavering hatred. Judging by Kichizo's menacing air, there was little point in trying to talk to them.

My only hope now was that the police would arrive. Now that there had been a murder, the police would have to intervene—and when they did, they would need my evidence. No matter how obstinate they were, Kichizo and Itaru would have to hand me over. Such were my expectations, but I couldn't understand why the help was so slow to arrive. There was a lot of coming and going around Kichizo's fire. The men grew more and more animated—perhaps they were drinking sake. But still the police didn't come.

I felt wretched. What if they decided to cross the Devil's Abyss?... I was wracked with nerves as I hid there in the Fox's Den. I would probably have gone mad, were it not for the grim ideas that occurred to me then.

What were those ideas, you ask? Allow me to tell you... As I watched Haruyo's final moments, my first thought had been to wonder whether her death was a part of this series of murders.

With the exception of Koume and Myoren, poison had always been the preferred method right from the very start. But according to Kosuke Kindaichi, Myoren's case had been different. He suspected that even the killer hadn't planned to murder Myoren. It was certainly true that no scrap of paper had been found by her body...

What about my sister, then? I had been so distraught that I didn't have the presence of mind to check for any slip of paper. But what other name could have been written beside hers? It would have to be someone who matched my sister... The only candidate was Miyako Mori.

Haruyo's poor health had forced her to divorce. She was certainly no widow like Miyako, but in the village she passed well enough for one. In addition, they were both of them sisters of the respective heads of the families—one of the East, the other of the West. What cruel logic! If Haruyo hadn't been killed, then Miyako might have been.

And yet... Why was I not entirely convinced by this line of thought?

If all these murders had been the work of a madman, the Tajimi family had certainly paid too high a price. In Koume's and Kotake's case, they both belonged to the family, so it couldn't be helped, but what about Hisaya and Haruyo? Could it be that they had not in fact been selected from their pairs by chance? In other words, was the murderer not disguising the systematic murder of the Tajimi family among a series of seemingly random killings?

If that was right, there could surely be only one culprit... Who but Shintaro Satomura could match the killer's profile? I recalled the fearsome face that he had worn when I happened to see him on the night of the Koicha nun's murder.

Yes, it must have been Shintaro! Everything slotted into place. It had been him all along. He was the one who had secretly denounced me to the police. He was the one who had posted that accusation in front of the village hall. It had all been his doing. After having massacred the entire Tajimi family and framed me, he would finally get his hands on the great Tajimi fortune. Perhaps even he was the one who had whipped the villagers into this current frenzy. Perhaps, foreseeing that I would be arrested but released on account of a lack of evidence, he had skilfully manipulated Kichizo and Itaru, hoping that they would kill me.

Yes, there was a coherence and a logic to it all. The sheer horror of it sent a chill down my spine.

But then what role had Noriko played in all these intrigues? Was she aware of Shintaro's plan and feigning ignorance? No, it was unthinkable. How could so innocent-seeming a girl turn out to be so duplicitous? Besides, Shintaro would never have let anyone in on his dreadful scheme—not even his own sister.

That day, in the pitch dark, in the bowels of the caves, I lay down and tossed and turned like a worm. My body flushed hot and then cold, so much that I even feared I was falling ill...

There was a part of me that wondered whether I shouldn't take advantage of the situation to explore the furthest reaches of the caves in search of the treasure, but I lacked the resolve to do it. My head was teeming with these terrible, distressing ideas, and what was more, I had misgivings over the accuracy of my map.

According to the map, it was the fifth tunnel leading out of the Fox's Den that would take me to the Dragon's Jaw and then on to the Trove of Treasure. But since the map had been drawn simply with brush and ink, I felt little confidence in using it as a guide in so complex a labyrinth.

After my recent exploration of the caves with Kosuke Kindaichi, I knew only too well how tortuous the structure of the Fox's Den was, but it was shown imperfectly on the map. In the end, the only solution would be to arm myself with ropes as we had done the other day. If only I had some rope, I could have explored them on my own. In fact, help in any form would have been welcome. I thought of Noriko, but that day she didn't come back…

It was not until the following morning that Noriko returned.

"Oh, Tatsuya, you're over here!" she cried, clinging to me. "I couldn't find you over there. You can't imagine how worried I was."

"Noriko, you're back!"

"Yes… I'm sorry for leaving you yesterday without a word. But you were sleeping so peacefully that I didn't want to wake you."

"I thought as much. I'm just glad you're back. Weren't there any guards?"

"The guards are still there, but they must be worn out from all the commotion yesterday. They're fast asleep. You must be starving. I wanted to come back yesterday, but something terrible has happened…"

"It's all right. Haruyo brought me some food yesterday."

"What?!"

She practically jumped back, and looked at my face questioningly.

"You mean… you saw Haruyo yesterday?" she asked breathlessly.

"Yes… She died in my arms."

Noriko let out a cry and looked at me in terror.

"But… but, Tatsuya… It wasn't… it can't have been you! Tell me you didn't do it!"

"What are you talking about?" I said sternly. "Why would I kill my own sister? I loved my sister. I adored her. And she adored me. What possible reason could I have to kill her?"

As I said this, tears suddenly welled in my eyes. Hot, burning tears streamed down my face. Irrespective of Noriko's last words, I was so grateful to her for the kindness she had always shown me, especially when I had felt so forsaken and alone. Her warmth had touched me deeply. I felt overwhelmed by the sadness of losing her.

"Forgive me! Forgive me, Tatsuya!" Noriko cried, throwing herself around my neck. "I'm sorry I doubted you even for a moment. I've always had faith in you. It's just…" She hesitated for a moment. "There's somebody who's claiming to have seen you kill Haruyo…"

"Kichizo! He would go around saying something like that… He saw me holding her just after she died. Besides, he's always had it in for me… But tell me, Noriko, what are the police doing? Why haven't they come to rescue me?"

"They can't, Tatsuya… Haruyo's death has only added fuel to the flames, and now the villagers are out of control. They want to take matters into their own hands, so they've staged an intervention to stop the police from going any further than the Echoes' Crossing. There's no telling what they'll do if the police try to break through. The police's hands are tied. But this can't go on for ever, Tatsuya. The police won't just let this go. You have to be patient. Hang in there just a little longer!"

"If you say so, I'll do my best… Who's taking care of the arrangements for Haruyo's funeral?"

"Oh, you don't have to worry about that. My brother's taking care of it."

"Shintaro!?"

Suddenly, a chill ran down my spine. I looked at Noriko searchingly, but she just looked like her usual innocent self.

"Yes… He's a military man, after all. He's very practical in tricky situations."

"Yes, you're not wrong there…" I felt choked, as though a fish bone had lodged itself in my throat. "Is he all right, by the way? He wasn't hurt at all, was he?"

Noriko looked at me strangely.

"He's absolutely fine. Why do you ask?"

"Oh, good. I'm glad."

Although I had asked this in as offhand a manner as possible, I felt a terrible sense of unease in my chest. Why was this? Could I have been wrong in my suspicions?

Haruyo had told me that she had practically bitten off her assailant's little finger. Whatever the degree of the injury, it must have been painful. Not only that: if it was as bad as Haruyo made out, then it would be very difficult to hide it from others.

"Tell me, Noriko, have you heard anything about somebody injuring their finger? Have you seen anybody wearing a bandage over the little finger of their left hand?"

"No… Why do you ask?"

She looked as innocent as ever. I couldn't believe that she was lying. But in that case, I must have been wrong about Shintaro… I no longer understood anything.

SHINTARO AND MIYAKO

It had all made sense, my reasoning had been flawless, so much so that I now felt all the more despondent and bewildered.

"Noriko, did Eisen come from the Maroo-ji temple last night for the vigil?"

"Yes, he came. Why?"

"And his little finger wasn't...?"

But Noriko was categorical in her denial of this, too. She had been the one who served the tea last night, so she would have been sure to notice something like that. Neither of his hands had been injured.

The picture was getting less and less clear to me. Who was there besides Shintaro and Eisen? I went over all the details of the case in my head once more, but I couldn't see a likely suspect. Could Haruyo have been mistaken?

"What's the matter, Tatsuya? Do you think that this person with an injured finger has done something?"

"It's not that... It's just something that worries me a little. Next time you go out, Noriko, can you look around to see if there's somebody with a wound like this?"

"Of course. I'll come and tell you the minute I find someone."

"Thank you. And the next time you come, could you bring me some string? Strong string, like the kind they use for kites? Or even just some ordinary thread if you can't find that. The longer, the better. Maybe five or six reels?..."

"What do you need string for?"

I was reluctant to answer, but she would find out sooner or later.

"Well, I'm so bored down here that I thought I'd use the opportunity to explore the caves. I need some string to do that. I'll use it as a guide to prevent my getting lost."

While she was listening to me, a strange glint flashed in Noriko's eyes.

"Tatsuya," she whispered. "Are you going to look for the treasure?"

298

I had been caught red-handed! I blushed crimson. Initially, I couldn't get my words out, but then I managed to clear my throat.

"You know about it?..."

"Of course I do. It's an old legend. And besides..." She lowered her voice. "I know somebody else who's been looking for it, too."

"Who? Who's been looking for it?"

"My brother!"

"Shintaro!"

Her words took my breath away. I looked Noriko right in the eyes.

"Yes. He doesn't talk about it because he's ashamed, but I know now what he's been up to. Every evening, when he goes out with a pickaxe and a shovel, it's obvious that he's hunting for the treasure."

I remembered the strange garb that he had been wearing when I saw him on the night of Myoren's murder. Had he been looking for the gold, just like me?

"He'd be so hurt if anybody were to find that out. I haven't breathed a word of it to anyone... I feel so sorry for him, you know... That man has lost everything: his standing, his job, his hopes for the future... Not only that. He lost out on love as well..."

"Love...?"

"Yes. He's still in love with Miyako. But he's so proud that he'd never dare to ask for her hand in marriage—not the way things are now. Miyako's wealthy, with plenty of diamonds. My brother, on the other hand, is penniless and out of work. He could never bring himself to propose. He thinks that if only he could find the treasure... That's why he goes out every night, hunting desperately for something that may not even be there

299

in the first place. Whenever I think about it, I feel such pity for him…"

Now I was well and truly confused. Shintaro must have wanted to get his hands on the family fortune. Rather than waste his energies searching high and low for a treasure that might not exist, why not set his sights on one that was already within reach? Could he really be the murderer? Was the injury done to somebody's little finger just the hallucination of a dying woman?

"Noriko, is Shintaro certain that Miyako would marry him if he were a wealthy man?"

"Absolutely," Noriko replied without a moment's hesitation. "But the thing is, the money is neither here nor there. If he proposed to her tomorrow, she'd accept him in a heartbeat. Why else would a woman with her beauty, her wit and her wealth hole herself up in an out-of-the-way village like this? She's been waiting for him. She's pining away, just waiting for him to propose. Now that I think about it, I even feel sorry for her. All Shintaro needs to do is to put aside that pig-headed pride of his and marry her… Although, if I'm being perfectly honest, I really don't care that much for Miyako…"

Shortly afterwards, on the pretext of having to help with the funeral arrangements and needing to sneak past the guards, Noriko took her leave. I was overcome by a feeling of intense loneliness then.

Noriko's tale had come as a great shock to me. Both that and the story I had overheard yesterday at the Goblin's Nose had revealed astonishing subtleties and complexities in Miyako's character and psychology. Yet at the same time, they had stirred a feeling of immense sadness and terrible despair within me. Was I in love with Miyako?

But enough of all that… The following day, having slipped past the guards' watchful eye, Noriko returned to me once again.

She told me that the villagers' rage had yet to abate, and that thus far the police had been unable to make them see reason. Still, there was apparently a faint glimmer of hope. It was possible that Choei, the high priest from the Maroo-ji temple, would intervene. He was very old and had been bedridden for a long time, hence why he had charged Eisen with dispatching all of his duties at the temple, yet Kosuke Kindaichi had seemingly thought that a priest of such high rank could be able to influence the villagers, so he had gone to the temple to seek his help.

The mention of the priest Choei reminded me of something else as well. Before her murder, Baiko had told me that there was something concerning me that was known only to her and the high priest of the Maroo-ji temple. After her death, I had wanted to pay a visit to the temple, but the series of murders had prevented me from making good on my intention.

"That's wonderful news, Noriko! Really, I'm so fed up with being stuck in this darkness."

"I shouldn't think you've much longer to wait. Just hang on."

"Now, Noriko, about that other matter…"

"Oh yes, the string? I've brought some with me."

"Ah, thank you. But what I actually meant was whether you'd noticed anyone whose little finger had been injured."

"Ah, about that…"

Noriko looked at me furtively and coughed to clear her throat.

"I kept my eyes peeled, but I didn't see anybody who'd injured their little finger."

She seemed frightened somehow and no longer dared to meet my gaze.

"Are you certain about that, Noriko? You aren't hiding something in order to protect someone, are you?"

"Me? Lie to you?! Of course not… Anyway, I went to all the trouble of bringing you this string. Let's go and explore the caves. I've got a little bit of time today. A treasure hunt… How romantic!"

She stood up, suddenly in high spirits. Yes, she knew all right. She knew who had injured their little finger, and she was protecting them. But who was it?…

PASSION IN THE SHADOWS

That day, as Noriko had suggested, we went to explore the caves together. As Kosuke Kindaichi had taught me, I tied one end of the length of string to a stalactite and, unwinding the string as we went, we made our way through the caves.

As I have already mentioned, there were five tunnels leading away from the Devil's Abyss. I had already explored three of these with Kosuke Kindaichi. There remained, therefore, the fourth—that is, the Fox's Den—and the fifth. According to my map, however, the fourth and the fifth rejoined one another at a point further on. Faced with this choice, I consulted the map and opted for the tunnel in which we had the least chance of getting lost: the fourth.

The tunnel forked almost immediately. This whole area had already been explored by Kosuke Kindaichi, however, so I didn't have to spend a long time weighing our options. I had counted the number of turnings: if memory served, Kosuke Kindaichi had found Dr Kuno after the thirteenth turning. So at least as far as that, we could forgo an exploration of those tunnels. It wasn't long before we found the turning.

"We're here," I said. "That's where Dr Kuno's body was found. Look, do you see that marker on the stalactite over there? Kosuke Kindaichi left it so that it would be easy to find again."

"So you haven't gone any further than this before?"

"Not yet."

"Let's go, then. How exciting! I'm curious to see how you'll use the string."

"Aren't you afraid?"

"Not as long as I'm with you."

Soon enough, we found the fourteenth turning. I tied the string that I had been unwinding to a stalactite and took out another reel, one end of which I fixed to the same stalactite. We then pressed on, while I unwound this second reel.

The tunnel was long and branched out in all directions. Before we investigated these subsidiary branches, I fixed the second length of string to another stalactite and repeated the process with a third reel. The first of these smaller tunnels soon proved to be a dead end. We made our way back to the starting point, while I rewound the third string and replaced it in my pocket. We then continued down the tunnel with the second string, but this too proved to be a dead end. Rewinding the string and retracing our steps, we made our way back to the end of the first reel.

"It's not a bad method at all," said Noriko. "It's like a piece of theatre. And there's certainly no risk of getting lost."

"Exactly. You don't really need the string when it's a dead end, but the tunnels often intersect and, without knowing it, you can wind up back where you started. It's easy to lose your sense of direction. Otherwise, you might think that you're heading back, whereas in actual fact you're going deeper and deeper into the caves. That's where the string comes in handy, so you don't get lost."

I then told her how just the other day Kosuke Kindaichi had ventured into one of the tunnels and found himself back where he had started, unwittingly stumbling upon me.

"It's frightening, isn't it! Just imagine if the string were to snap…"

"Precisely. That's why you mustn't pull on it too hard."

We were delving deeper and deeper into the caves. No matter how much I said that we should turn back, Noriko was enjoying the experience so much that she insisted we keep going. We encountered one fork after another, some with multiple offshoots, and, as we explored them one by one, we were forced to unwind a third, a fourth, then even a fifth reel of string. In this way, we found ourselves unexpectedly back in the first gallery.

"How funny!" exclaimed Noriko, more and more delighted. "If it weren't for the strings, we might never have known that this was where we started."

We worked our way back and finally ventured down a long tunnel with very few offshoots. We walked on and on, but the seeming absence of any end point only made us more uneasy.

"This doesn't seem right, Noriko. This tunnel just keeps going. We should turn around and head back."

"No, just a little further. If we don't find an end soon, then we'll turn back."

But after a few more yards we stopped dead in our tracks. We both hurriedly switched off our flashlights and held our breath in the dark. Up ahead, we could hear what sounded like voices.

"Tatsuya," whispered Noriko hoarsely. "Stay here. I'll go on ahead and check it out."

"Are you sure?"

"Yes, I'll be fine."

I heard her walk off into the darkness, but clearly she didn't have far to go, for only a few moments later she returned, shining her flashlight around.

"Where are you, Tatsuya? You can turn your light on, it's all right."

I did as she asked and saw her come towards me, her eyes shining.

"Do you realize where we are?" she asked. "We're right beside the Devil's Abyss."

"The Devil's Abyss?" I asked, surprised.

"You said so yourself: if you go far enough the fourth tunnel loops back onto the fifth. Without realizing it, we must have started walking along the fifth tunnel and found ourselves back here."

I felt totally confused. But on reflection, this escapade had advanced our search considerably. The treasure had to be located somewhere near the junction of the fourth and fifth tunnels. We must have walked right past the junction without spotting it.

"The junction must be where we tied the first string," said Noriko. "That was where we took the path on the left. Tomorrow we'll take the one on the right. Let's just tie the string here—I think it'll be closer that way. This will be the string that we follow tomorrow."

She attached the second reel to a stalactite. Then she slipped past the guards and left the Devil's Abyss. That evening I slept in the fifth tunnel.

The following afternoon, Noriko paid me the third of her clandestine visits.

"I'm sorry I'm so late, Tatsuya. You must be starving. I'd planned to come earlier, but the guards were on the alert."

She proceeded to unwrap the packed lunch that she had brought for me.

"But I've got some good news for you. We might be able to get you out of here before the day is over."

"But how?" I asked, my pulse quickening.

"The high priest from the Maroo-ji temple has come to intervene. He was so ill that he hadn't heard about everything that had been going on lately, but yesterday Kosuke Kindaichi went to see him. The news came as such a shock to him. So this morning he showed up at the House of the East."

"You mean, Father Choei is at the house right now?"

"Yes, he's gathered together all the leaders of the village and is giving them a thorough scolding. Even if they won't listen to the police, they can't very well ignore him. Especially since he's gone to this trouble in spite of his ill health. So I'm sure somebody will come for you soon."

A bittersweet feeling rose up from the pit of my stomach. At last, I would be able to leave these caves! At last, I would be able to escape this darkness! My heart leapt with joy, and I trembled with excitement. Once I was out, the series of murders in Eight Graves would be over. All I had to do was find the murderer—the man with the wound on his finger.

"Are you sure, Noriko? You aren't just saying this to give me false hope?"

"Of course not, Tatsuya! You just have to hold on a little longer."

"Oh, Noriko!" I cried, suddenly taking her in my arms. "Thank you. It's all thanks to you. If it hadn't been for your daily visits to keep me informed, I'd have gone mad down here in the dark with all the fear and worry. Or before I even got that far, I'd have probably tried to flee and been clubbed to death by Kichizo and his friends. He's really got it in for me. I can't thank you enough, Noriko!"

"I'm just glad it will all be over soon," she said.

Noriko's body quivered like a little bird against my chest. Her frail arms clung to my neck and our lips met…

My memories of what happened next are a little foggy. We were suddenly swept up by a torrent of fierce passions. The darkness made us forget our inhibitions. Our bodies dripping,

306

we clung to one another, panting and groaning. A beautiful pink mist enveloped us.

Noriko eventually pulled away from my embrace and looked up at me ecstatically, as she brushed away her stray hairs. The demure flush of her cheeks was charming in the light of the torch.

"Tell me," she said after a while.

"What is it, Noriko?"

I felt as though I were dreaming, while Noriko had already landed back on terra firma.

"About that person with the injured finger. What are you thinking? That the person…"

"Noriko…" I sighed. "Did you find this person? Tell me! Tell me who it is!"

"No, I don't know for sure yet… But I don't understand. What's the significance of the injured finger?"

I hesitated for a moment, but, seeing that she wouldn't talk without some kind of explanation, I decided to reveal to her what Haruyo had told me.

"Whoever has this injury on his finger must be responsible for the murders," I said. "Or at the very least he's responsible for Haruyo's murder. So tell me, Noriko! Who is it?"

A terrible look of anguish disfigured her face. She tried to speak, but the words caught in her throat. Her face turned ashen, her lips were parched, and her gaze darkened.

"Noriko!" I said, placing both my hands on her shoulders. "What's the matter with you? Pull yourself together!"

She shook her head two or three times before pressing her face to my chest and bursting into floods of tears.

"Noriko! You know who it is, don't you? You know who killed my sister! Who is it?"

She shook her head violently against my chest.

"Don't ask me, Tatsuya! Don't ask me… I can't tell you… I'm too afraid to say it… Oh, don't ask me, Tatsuya!"

A thought suddenly crossed my mind.

"But why, Noriko? Why can't you tell me? It wouldn't be Shintaro by any chance, would it?"

"What?!" she cried, jumping back.

It was then that it happened. That voice like a cracked bell assaulted our ears.

"There he is, the bastard!"

Startled, we both turned to where the voice had come from, but already there was no shadow of a doubt in my mind: it was Kichizo. He was carrying a torch in one hand and his club in the other. One heavy step at a time, he was making his way towards us from the entrance of the tunnel. The soot from the flame left a thick, oily trace along the ceiling, and the pine bark crackled, sending sparks flying. In the torchlight he looked more terrifying than a demon from hell.

CHAPTER 8

MORTAL DANGER

"Run, Tatsuya!" Noriko cried out, suddenly jumping up.

Her voice snatched me from my daze. I leapt to my feet and made a dash for it into the tunnel, following in her tracks.

"Tatsuya! Take this!" she shouted, throwing me a flashlight.

I caught it, and we ran on frantically. Then I thought of something:

"Noriko, you'd better go back. Surely Kichizo wouldn't dare lay a finger on you?"

"Never, Tatsuya!" she said, panting. "Didn't you see his eyes? You may be the one he wants to kill, but he'd never leave me alive with the knowledge of his guilt!"

"I don't know what to say, Noriko. I'm sorry for dragging you into all this and putting you in such danger."

"It doesn't matter. But for now, we need to keep running. He's coming this way!"

Even though we had explored the tunnels only once, we still had an advantage over Kichizo. Our steps were surer, whereas Kichizo would stagger and stumble from time to time. Little by little, we increased the distance between us. On the other hand, we were at a disadvantage in being unable to turn off the flashlight. Without the light, it would have been too dangerous, and we wouldn't have been able to run. But it was our light that Kichizo followed.

Exasperated by the widening gap, Kichizo kept hurling abuse at us from behind. Each time he did, I jumped as though feeling the lash of a whip. We had no choice but to flee. The two of us were running desperately, relying on the string that we had left there the previous day. That was how we reached the spot where we tied the first reel of string.

"We're saved, Tatsuya!" Noriko cried, pulling the string off the stalactite. "We'll remove each string as we go. That way, Kichizo will get lost. The tunnels are so complex that he'll end up losing his way at one of the turnings. Meanwhile, we can escape across the Devil's Abyss."

Her plan was sound, but it was still too early to breathe a sigh of relief. We hadn't gone fifty yards, when I was caught right in a beam of light that pinned me to the spot.

"Ah-ha-ha! So there you are! I heard your voice, so I knew all I had to do was wait... But who's that with you?"

The light moved from me across to Noriko.

"Well, well, what have we here? If it isn't Satomura's sister!... And what have you two been getting up to down in these caves?..."

The light returned to my face.

"You seem to enjoy company... I can certainly give you a companion on the journey to hell if that's what you want."

It was Itaru. He was wearing a headband over his white hair and was carrying a pickaxe in one hand and a lantern in the other. He had the sinister glint of a murderer in his eyes.

Itaru took one step closer. I couldn't move. He took another step. Still, I couldn't move a muscle. But that's when it happened. All of a sudden, Noriko cried out and pulled back her right hand. The next moment, an object hit Itaru's face, raising a cloud of dust that spread all around. He dropped his pickaxe and clutched his hands to his face.

"Now! Tatsuya!"

Noriko grabbed my arm, and I finally came to my senses. Holding hands, we ran back into the tunnels.

It was only afterwards that I learnt how Noriko had managed to blind him.

"I was worried about getting caught when I came to see you," she told me, "so I always carried two or three eggshells filled with ash, just in case. For a beast like that, though, I should have added chilli pepper…"

In any case, we found ourselves at the junction of the fourth and fifth tunnels, but there was no question of venturing down the fifth tunnel, for that was where Kichizo awaited us.

"This way, Tatsuya! It's our only option…"

"But, Noriko, we don't know what's down there. We've never gone that way before."

"It's better than waiting here to be killed!"

I could see the flame of a torch approaching us from the fifth tunnel, and from the fourth we could hear Itaru's furious roar. We ran instinctively, setting off down the unexplored tunnel.

Oh, what darkness!

Stretching out before us was an endless void. What did it conceal? Demons? Snakes? Even if it did, now was not the time to worry about that. There was a very real danger behind us, threatening us and driving us on into the dark recesses of the caves.

Like the other one, this passage, too, branched off into innumerable smaller tunnels. However, pursued by these two homicidal maniacs, we had no time to think, let alone to tie any strings or make out landmarks. We fled in anguish, running from one tunnel to the next, each time getting more and more lost. Even if we managed to escape Kichizo and Itaru, there was nothing to ensure that we would ever find our way out of that labyrinth.

"Tatsuya!" Noriko said, suddenly stopping and grabbing hold of my arm. "What was that sound?"

"What sound?"

"Listen… There it is again! It sounds like the wind."

She was right. I could hear what sounded like the moaning of the wind somewhere off in the distance. The wind stopped immediately, but Noriko's eyes glittered.

"It is the wind! I'm sure of it. There must be a way out nearby. Let's go, Tatsuya!"

The sound returned intermittently, but still we couldn't find any way out. Eventually, the moment came where we abandoned hope. At almost exactly the same time, we both stopped in our tracks and sighed. We cast a desperate glance at the cold wall that loomed in front of us. We had reached a dead end.

"Tatsuya, switch off your light."

We quickly turned our lamps off, but it was already too late. The lantern that Itaru was carrying had already found our silhouettes. Beside him stood Kichizo. Realizing that they had finally cornered us, they stopped dead. Bathing us in the light of the lantern, they looked us up and down.

Itaru laughed malevolently.

"It's the end of the line…"

He exchanged glances with Kichizo and they both burst into terrifying, blood-chilling laughter.

They stood about twenty paces from us. Slowly, they each took a step towards us, Kichizo with his club and Itaru with his pickaxe.

Noriko and I stood motionless, our backs against the wall. Clasping our hands tightly, we watched them advance towards us. Nobody spoke. I felt as though I were drunk: it was as if I had witnessed this scene several times already.

They took another step forward.

That was the last time we saw them alive. I didn't realize what was happening at the time, but that rumbling that we had taken for the wind suddenly picked up again and increased in intensity. I was knocked to the ground, as though hit by the blast of an explosion. The noise repeated two or three times, and the air all around trembled violently. Hard objects suddenly struck my head, and that is the point at which my memories fade. I lost consciousness.

A RAIN OF GOLD

How long had we been passed out? Come to think of it, it cannot have been for long.

When I regained consciousness, I could still hear that same noise, although it was much fainter now. Darkness reigned in the tunnel. I pricked up my ears. What had happened to Kichizo and Itaru? And what about Noriko?

"Noriko! Noriko!" I whispered, feeling around me.

My hand immediately encountered soft flesh. I took her body in my arms.

"Noriko! Noriko!"

I shook her as I called out her name. Then I heard her draw a heavy breath as if she were sobbing.

"Tatsuya?" she asked, sitting up. "What just happened? What's happened to Itaru and Kichizo?"

"I don't know… Where's your flashlight?"

"My flashlight?… Oh, it's here."

Noriko had passed out still holding it in her hand. I shone it on the area around me and immediately recovered my own. As I leant over to pick it up, I was petrified. Granted, I had been on the receiving end of some terrible shocks lately, but never had I experienced anything like this. Scattered around the flashlight, there were two or three coins, just like the ones that I had found in the sarcophagus.

"What is it, Tatsuya?"

Her voice brought me back to reality. With a trembling hand, I picked up one of the coins and silently showed it to Noriko. I tried to speak but couldn't. The words wouldn't come out. There was a look of complete astonishment in Noriko's eyes. She leant over and picked up two more coins. As we looked around with our flashlights, we found another six of them, bringing the total to nine.

We stared at each other in silence.

"It's so strange, Tatsuya... Why are they scattered around like this?"

We didn't have to wait long for an answer. The wind picked up once again and shook the cave from top to bottom. Noriko and I immediately clung to each other as we felt more of these coins rain down on our shoulders. We instinctively looked up, and Noriko let out a hysterical cry.

"Look, Tatsuya! Up there! They're falling from up there!"

The vault of the ceiling was extremely high, almost three storeys above our heads. The walls were lined with great pillars of stalagmites towering up and intertwining like snakes. Curiously, however, they all stopped about six feet below the top of the vault itself, and it was from there that the coins were raining down as they slipped over the edge. Some more fell right before our eyes as we gazed up. We looked at one another.

"Tatsuya! It's where the treasure is hidden!"

I nodded silently.

The initial excitement began to leave us, and we regained our sense of composure.

Why had those coins been hidden all the way up there? I supposed that when the samurai had hidden the treasure, the ceiling could not have been so high. Probably the floor level had been only six or seven feet below the vault, but over the centuries erosion had lowered the floor, resulting in the new configuration of the cave with an enormously high vault. Who could say whether the samurai had known that this would happen, but the shelf on which they had hidden the gold was made of harder rock and had thus avoided the ravages of time. Abandoned on that shelf, the treasure must have escaped the view of so many adventurers over the years.

What irony! How many had risked life and limb searching for it over the centuries, only for the treasure to remain diabolically invisible? And now we, who had strayed here by pure chance, had it rain down on our heads...

But Fate had not finished toying with us. If it had offered us this gold without demanding any effort, it had also blocked our way out.

Once we had been jolted from daydreaming about the gold, we remembered Itaru and Kichizo and began to search for them with our flashlights. It was then that we came face to face with our cruel reality. The path by which we had come here was completely blocked by rocks and soil.

The tunnel had collapsed. The cave-in had buried Itaru and Kichizo and imprisoned us in this chamber. We rushed over to the wall of debris and began frantically clawing at it with our hands, but soon enough we realized that it was futile.

We clung to each other desperately.

"Noriko! We're done for! There's no way out. We'll end up starving to death here..."

A nervous laugh escaped me.

"Fate has given us the gold but blocked our way out," I said. "We'll die of starvation while we cradle the gold, just like King Midas."

I laughed again. But while the desperation of our situation made me shed buckets of tears, Noriko showed far greater self-restraint.

"Stay calm, Tatsuya! We aren't going to die like this. They'll come and save us. Even now, they'll be coming to our rescue."

"Do you really think so?… But who, Noriko? Nobody knows that we're trapped down here!"

"That isn't true. Everybody in the village knows that you're on this side of the Devil's Abyss. And if Itaru and Kichizo crossed the abyss in spite of their superstitions, then it's because the high priest from the Maroo-ji temple must have succeeded in convincing the villagers to come and rescue you. Incensed by this, Itaru and Kichizo would have rushed here to try and kill you before the others could reach you."

I found out afterwards that Noriko had been quite right about this. Angered by the fact that the villagers were relenting, Itaru and Kichizo had crossed the forbidden abyss, only to meet their tragic end there.

She continued:

"They'll definitely come to find us. Who knows, they may even be looking for us right this minute. Even if the villagers refuse to cross the Devil's Abyss, that won't stop the police… Of course! Kosuke Kindaichi will be there as well. When he finds the strings linking the fourth and fifth tunnels, he'll understand immediately. If he just follows the string, he'll be able to reach the crossing point without any problem, and from there it isn't far. Since Kindaichi knows how to use the string, he'll go through each of the tunnels with a fine-toothed comb. That means we'll have to listen carefully for any sounds. They'll surely be calling your name. As soon as we hear anything, we'll shout back, so that they know we're here."

Noriko got to her feet and picked up the coins that were lying on the ground. She then dug a hole and buried them. Surprised by this, I asked her what she was doing. She laughed.

"Finders keepers… These are yours, Tatsuya. Let's hope we'll be conscious by the time that help arrives, but if they find us passed out, they're liable to steal them. That's why we have to hide them. We can come back and get them after we've been rescued. There's sure to be an awful lot more up there on that ledge."

What a curious creature woman is! Though we did not know yet that anybody would come to find us, she had already divined the future. What's more, her diligence did indeed prove to be of great benefit to me. Everything she said came to pass. We were saved in exactly the way that she had envisaged. Only, it took three whole days...

After she had finished burying the gold, she came over to me and stared at me with a serious look in her eyes.

"Now that that's been taken care of," she said, "all that's left is to discuss the matter of the murderer. There's something I'd like to ask you..."

She adopted a very serious tone and looked at me sternly.

"You said something odd before... You asked me whether the person who'd been bitten on the finger was my brother. It follows then that you must suspect him. But why would you think that? Why do you think that he'd commit this series of senseless murders? Do you really believe that he's capable of murdering people in cold blood, people who have absolutely nothing to do with him?"

This was no longer the Noriko I knew. She was resolute. She loved her brother just as fiercely as she loved me, and so she couldn't let any slander against him go unchallenged, regardless of where it originated.

Overwhelmed by this fighting spirit of hers, I didn't know what to say. She had boxed me into a corner, so I had no choice but to answer and unveil my deductions to her. I explained to her that I believed this series of murders to have been committed in order to cover up another objective: namely, the murder of

317

the entire Tajimi family. Noriko suddenly shuddered and turned pale as she heard me out. She reflected on this for a long while with her eyes lowered, but eventually she turned to me with tears in her eyes.

She gently took my hand in hers and whispered to me with trembling lips.

"I see it all now. You're absolutely right. It's the only explanation for this series of terrible murders. But I assure you, Tatsuya: my brother isn't the murderer. If only you knew him, the very suspicion would never have crossed your mind. Shintaro is an honest and decent man. He would rather starve than lay a finger on the fortune of another. But in any case, he isn't the one whose little finger was injured…"

"Who, then, Noriko? Tell me who it was!"

"It was Miyako… Miyako Mori!"

I felt as though I had been knocked over the head with a blunt instrument. The shock paralysed me with horror. For a moment I was speechless.

"Miyako… Mori…" I repeated, short of breath.

I thought I was going to suffocate.

"Yes… She tried to treat the wound in secret, but it didn't work. The wound got infected, and sepsis spread throughout her entire body. Her flesh swelled up and she turned purple. She was in a very serious condition. Dr Arai rushed to treat her, but it was only then that he found out about the wound. That was this morning. But nobody outside knows what caused the wound."

"Miyako… Of all people… But why her?…"

"It must be as you imagined. She must have wanted my brother to take over as head of the Tajimi family. She must have told herself that, with all that vast fortune, Shintaro would finally ask her to marry him. Terrible, cruel Miyako! Poor, pitiful Miyako…"

She pressed her face to my chest and burst into floods of tears.

THE AFTERMATH

Part 1

My story has almost reached its end. The treasure has been discovered, and so has the criminal. But there are still many questions left to be answered…

Before attending to these, however, I must explain how we managed to get out of that cave. Everything happened just as Noriko predicted. I never imagined that they would find us so quickly. And it was all down to Kichizo's torch. Owing to the poor ventilation in the caves, odours lingered for some time. His torch had produced a huge amount of smoke, and so our rescuers had been guided in part by the smell.

What they didn't know, however, was that Kichizo and Itaru had ventured well beyond the Devil's Abyss in their hunt for me. As soon as Choei had calmed the villagers, the rescue team, which consisted of Kosuke Kindaichi, Inspector Isokawa and a handful of officers, headed straight for the Devil's Abyss, where they started calling out my name. Concerned by the lack of response, they made their way across the abyss.

Having discovered the reel of string that stretched between the fourth and fifth tunnels, Kosuke Kindaichi immediately realized what I had been up to. So far, so good. However, when they found in the fifth tunnel a packed lunch that had been trampled along with a strong smell of smoke, Kosuke Kindaichi began to fear the worst: he rightly doubted that I or whoever was helping me (for he knew that somebody must have been helping me) would have been carrying a burning torch.

That was when their nerves began to get the better of them, but still they decided to follow the string and venture deeper into the tunnel. They arrived at the point where the two tunnels converged. The string stopped there, but the smell of camphor continued on. Careful as he was, Kosuke Kindaichi unwound his rope before proceeding. That was how they reached the spot where the cave-in had occurred. Fortunately, we realized the collapse had not been too severe, for we could hear their voices and their footsteps from the other side. We banged frantically on the walls and on the floor, shouting ourselves hoarse.

This is how they realized that there were survivors on the other side of the collapsed tunnel. They quickly formed a rescue team for this difficult and dangerous task. The tunnel was deep, narrow and cramped, and what was more, they feared that there could be another collapse at any minute. Despite everything, they worked tirelessly day and night, helped by labourers who were brought in especially from the town of N——.

On the other side, Noriko and I, though immensely grateful for the efforts of our rescuers, were exasperated by their slowness and wracked with anguish. The whole operation lasted three days and three nights, for the duration of which we were stuck in a state of extreme stress, mingled with hope and worry.

On the morning of the fourth day, we were saved at last. They managed to dig a hole all the way through the debris. Embarrassing though it is to say, but I very nearly fainted when at long last I saw somebody come through that hole. He was soon followed by the others, including Kosuke Kindaichi, Inspector Isokawa and Shintaro. I even spotted, through eyes blurred with fatigue, Eisen from the Maroo-ji temple, who, to my surprise, appeared to be crying. Last of all came a familiar face, but one that I couldn't quite put a name to.

"Tatsuya-san," he said. "Tatsuya-san, it's me… Your lawyer from Kobe? You haven't forgotten old Suwa, have you? You've had quite a time of it, it seems."

When I saw him burst into tears, I wondered why he had come all this way. But already I felt as though I was hallucinating.

From that point on, for a whole week, I roamed between dream and reality, in the grip of a high fever. The terror, the excitement and the unnatural strain of having been trapped in that cave for three whole days had taken their toll on me. Noriko even told me afterwards that Dr Arai had expressed grave fears for my health on several occasions. As for Noriko, she fared better than I did. She rested in bed for two or three days, after which she stayed by my side, nursing me.

After a week, I was over the worst of it. But as soon as I was out of danger, Miyako began to preoccupy my mind. I lacked the courage to raise the subject with the people around me, and they in turn seemed to avoid mentioning her name. My recovery progressed quickly, however, and I was told that I would be back on my feet in no time at all.

One day, Kosuke Kindaichi came to see me.

"Ah, you're back on top form, I see!" he said, entering the room. "You look quite, quite well… Now then, I've come to bring you a message."

His manner was offhand, as usual.

"Oh?"

"It's from the high priest at the Maroo-ji temple. He'd like to speak with you at the temple once you're fully recovered. He has something to tell you. And since he was instrumental in saving your life, I think you ought to go and thank him."

"Ah, I'd been planning to do that anyway. I'll go there right away."

"Shall we go together," Kosuke Kindaichi suggested. "I'm on my way back to the House of the West right now, as it happens."

He had offered to accompany me, anticipating the unpleasantness that might arise if I were to run into any of the villagers along the way. I accepted, thanking him for his kindness.

"You're still staying at the House of the West?" I enquired.

"Yes," he replied. "But I'll be heading home before long."

"And the inspector?…"

"He's had to return to Okayama, but he'll be back in two or three days' time. Apropos of which, there was something I wanted to ask you. Once the inspector is back, I'd like to get everyone together to go over these recent events. I thought it would be a good idea if we were to do it in the annexe."

Seeing no reason to object, I readily agreed. Leaving the conversation at that, the detective then saw me all the way to the outskirts of Bankachi.

"Well, this is where I must leave you," Kosuke Kindaichi said. "Do give my regards to Father Choei. Try not to be too surprised by what he has to tell you…"

With these cryptic words, he smiled and trotted off. I was left with a strange feeling. Was there anything that could surprise me yet? After all these terrible experiences, I would have believed myself immune to surprise…

How wrong I was, though. A great surprise did now await me at the very end of my adventures.

For all his venerable years and ailing health, Choei had retained a hale and hearty complexion. His movements had been limited ever since his most recent attack, but his speech was still normal. He received my words of thanks, reclining in bed.

"No, no," he protested. "I'm just glad that you're safe and that you came to no harm. Forgive me for taking so long to

322

intervene, but I hadn't the least inkling of what was going on. I heard you were having difficulties, but… Anyway, thank you for coming all this way to see me."

"I was told that you had something to tell me…"

"That is correct… Eisen! What are you looking so nervous for? It's unbecoming of a priest. Please, get a grip on yourself."

It was obvious that Eisen was very attached to the old priest, of whom he took the greatest care. Yet he seemed oddly agitated and refused to look me in the eye.

"Tatsuya," the priest began, "what I have to say to you actually concerns Eisen. I have learnt that the two of you have not been on the best terms ever since a certain misunderstanding occurred. I would ask that you let bygones be bygones and forget about all that. You see, you and Eisen share a very deep bond."

"Reverend Father!" Eisen interjected.

"It's all right. Calm down. The time has come to reveal everything. You see, Tatsuya, Eisen had some very difficult experiences in Manchuria, experiences that have completely changed the man. Nobody, except Baiko, has ever realized this, but Eisen was once a teacher at the village school. His name back then was Yoichi Kamei. Your mother was very dear to him."

How could I not have been surprised by all this? So Eisen was my father! Twenty-eight years after I was born, and I had at last met my real father. My whole body began to tremble, and I felt as though I was burning. It was a strange and unfamiliar feeling that in its sheer intensity far surpassed simple longing or resentment. Unable to speak, I stared at my father's face. He was crying too much to look me in the eye. It was hardly surprising that nobody in the village had recognized him. He had changed so much since then. Nothing remained of that handsome man whose portrait I had discovered in the folding screen. Just as wind and snow will strip a beautiful mountain landscape bare, so these last twenty-eight years had completely transformed my father's fine features.

"Tatsuya, you seem to recognize the name Yoichi Kamei."

Choei watched my reaction carefully. I nodded. I told myself that this was no time to hide things and that it would be best to explain everything.

"Only recently I found, hidden away inside a folding screen, a number of letters between my mother and this man. I also happened to find with them a portrait of the young man, which my mother seems to have treasured."

Choei and Eisen exchanged a look of astonishment.

"The photo of this Yoichi Kamei was taken when he was twenty-seven," I continued. "His face... well, it was the spitting image of me. So I believe I already know what our connection is."

Eisen brought his hands to his eyes and burst into tears.

"Kindly control yourself!" Choei reprimanded Eisen smartly. "That's quite enough of that. Tatsuya, you appear to know most of the story already, but I'll permit myself to add one thing that you may not know yet and that is important here. Twenty-six years ago, when the tragedy took place, Eisen—or should I say, Yoichi Kamei—spent the night here. That is how he was able to escape the massacre. He sincerely believed that he was the cause of those terrible events, so he took the decision to leave the village and become a priest. He took his vows and decided to impose on himself the strictest form of asceticism: that is why he ventured as far as the depths of Manchuria. However, because of the war, he was forced to return to Japan, and it was then that he came to see me. He regrets having abandoned you, but it was by force of circumstances that he did so. I hope that you'll forgive him."

Eisen was still crying. I nodded as I felt the tears welling in my eyes.

"Very well," Choei continued. "Turning to more recent matters... When Eisen learnt that the twins, Koume and Kotake, were searching for you as their heir, the news came as a great shock to him. Ever since you were born, there had been rumours—rumours about which the twins and Hisaya cannot have been ignorant. Why, all of a sudden, when they had been so completely indifferent to your fate for all these years, had they suddenly taken it upon themselves to find you? Eisen was so worried that he took advantage of a trip to Kobe to make some enquiries about you. In other words, he himself didn't know whose child you were." Choei smiled wryly. "As it turns out, however, a single look is enough to establish that..."

"That's all clear enough," I said, before turning to Eisen, "but what I don't understand is why you accused me of being the murderer when Brother Kozen was killed."

My question seemed to cut Eisen to the quick. He in turn looked to Choei for help.

"Ah, yes," said Choei, leaning towards me. "Eisen told me about that. Ever since you arrived in the village, Eisen's conviction that you were his son had increased with each passing day. It frightened him. It was as if you were a living reminder of the sins of his past. It also tormented him that he didn't know what was going on in your mind. He wondered whether you knew the secret of your birth. It seemed incredible to him that you could have been unaware of the rumours, and so he reasoned that you must have known that you were not in fact Yozo's son. Yet, in the brazen knowledge of that, to try to take on the inheritance of the Tajimi family... Eisen found all that a terrifying prospect. The very notion that his own son could be a monster, ready to kill his grandfather and brother just to get his hands on the Tajimi family's fortune! He even wondered whether it wasn't divine retribution for the sin that he had committed. Then, at the height of his torments, he witnessed Kozen's murder with his own eyes. He was convinced that you had meant to kill him instead, knowing that he was your real father and fearing that he might reveal the secret of your true identity to prevent you from inheriting the fortune. But it is important to say that he did not know you then, and he was going through a terrible crisis of conscience. So you must forgive him."

In other words, it was not me that my father had been accusing then, but a feeling of guilt regarding his own past. Once I understood this, I found it very easy to forgive him.

"If I had known that I wasn't a member of the Tajimi family, I would never have come here," I said. "But there's something else I'd like to ask. It's you, isn't it, Brother Eisen? You're the one who's been sneaking into the annexe via the secret underground passage. My sister found a map of the tunnels that you must have dropped accidentally. Why have you been doing that?"

Once again, Choei offered an explanation.

"My dear Tatsuya… asceticism can go only so far in relieving man from his worldly torments. Eisen believed that he had put the past behind him, and that is why he had the courage to return to the village. But over time, the memory of your mother came back to him. The letters that she had pasted to the screen were the only remnant of their shared secret. When Eisen learnt that this screen was still in the annexe, a team of wild horses couldn't have held him back. He would regularly take the secret passage to go and see it, but ever since your arrival, he was tormented by feelings of regret and took to wandering around the underground tunnels. Ah, yes… You, Haruyo and Noriko spotted him down there, by the Goblin's Nose, didn't you? As ever, he had been wandering about the caves, longing to see you, but it was then that he heard a terrible cry that frightened him off. You saw him as he was fleeing, desperate to get away.

326

But his presence there sprang from a desire to see you. I hope this will allay your suspicions."

I nodded silently. My eyes misted over as I remembered that night in the annexe when I had sensed somebody else's presence and felt hot tears on my cheeks.

"So that's it," I said. "And there I was, thinking you'd been hunting for the treasure."

"Oh, no," Eisen protested, speaking for the first time. "I was passionate about treasure-hunting when I was young. I even found scrolls with strange maps and poems in this very temple. The Reverend Father allowed me to copy them… Yes, there was once a time when I would spend my hours prowling around those caves, hunting for the treasure, but no more—that was a dream, a dream for which I am now much too old."

"It's no dream," Choei insisted, "for the treasure does indeed exist."

As if suddenly having remembered something, Choei then turned to me.

"In fact, I wouldn't be at all surprised if the place where you and Noriko were stuck turned out to be the very spot where it is hidden… According to the men who unearthed the bodies of Itaru and Kichizo, there had already been a cave-in once before. They found an old skeleton there, and with it, the crystal beads of a rosary, which made them think that it was a monk. All this put me in mind of the lines preserved here in the temple: *'Whosoever ventures upon the Trove of the Buddha's Treasure Shall know the dread of the Dragon's Jaw.'* I wonder whether the cave-in didn't occur precisely at this Dragon's Jaw… In which case, you may well have been trapped in the Trove of Treasure itself!"

I'm sorry to say that on that occasion I merely bowed my head without uttering a word.

THE AFTERMATH

Part 2

On the evening of the thirty-fifth day after Haruyo's death, we gathered together in the House of the East to put an end to this woeful affair. In attendance were Kosuke Kindaichi, Inspector Isokawa, Dr Arai, Shokichi Nomura, Eisen, Shintaro, Noriko and Mr Suwa, who had come all the way from Kobe again. Including me, there were nine of us in total.

The guests were served a real feast. Though it was a solemn occasion, this was the first time that I had been present at such a relaxed and informal dinner since arriving in Eight Graves.

Like me, Kosuke Kindaichi was not a big drinker. After a single glass of beer, he looked flushed and began scratching at his messy hair. It was then that, at the inspector's invitation, he commenced his stammering speech.

"As Inspector Isokawa knows only too well, I've often had occasion to investigate cases for the Okayama police force. Never before have I encountered a case riddled with so many difficulties. Without any false modesty, I am forced to admit that all too often this case got the better of me. At any rate, the criminal would have been exposed even in my absence. Worse still, I knew who the criminal was from the very outset. From the moment that Tatsuya's grandfather, Ikawa-san, was murdered, my suspicions fell on Miyako. This may sound presumptuous to you, but that is far from the case. For, you see, I was not the only one to suspect her. There was in fact another person who knew: namely, Shokichi Nomura, the culprit's brother-in-law and the head of the House of the West."

Stunned by this news, we all turned to Shokichi Nomura. He, however, wore an impassive expression, his lips pressed tightly shut.

"If I tell you the circumstances that brought me to the village, to Nomura-san's house," Kosuke Kindaichi continued, "you will understand why. Nomura-san told me that he harboured some serious doubts regarding the death of his brother Tatsuo—that is, Miyako's late husband. He died during the course of the war, and the cause of death was officially recorded as a cerebral haemorrhage, but Nomura-san was not convinced. He believed that it was a case of murder. More specifically, he strongly suspected that Tatsuo had been poisoned by his wife Miyako..."

Dumbstruck by this revelation, we all stared at the head of the House of the West. Shintaro in particular looked deeply surprised and anguished, but Shokichi Nomura's face remained inscrutable, just like a Noh mask.

"Nomura-san was devoted to his brother," Kosuke Kindaichi continued, "and he couldn't bear to keep these suspicions to himself. He wanted to uncover the truth and to avenge his brother. That is why he called on my services when I was in the area, investigating another case. Thus, I arrived in the village of Eight Graves, charged with investigating Miyako..."

Clearly, this was the first time that Inspector Isokawa had heard of this. He glared at the detective with a look that seemed to say, if only you had told me sooner, the case would have been solved that much quicker. However, Kosuke Kindaichi seemed to ignore this look of reproach and merely continued with his story.

"As soon as I arrived in Eight Graves, I learnt quite a few things from Nomura-san. In particular, he outlined to me his reasons for suspecting Miyako. But these suspicions lacked substance. Even if they were well founded, it would have been impossible to prove. I was therefore on the verge of declining the case, when news arrived of Ikawa-san's murder in Kobe. What was more, it was Miyako herself who had volunteered to go to the city in the first instance. If you will allow me to add one further detail, Nomura-san informed me that Ikawa-san's death very closely resembled that of his own late brother, and insisted in any case that I observe the developments for a little longer. All this led me to revise my position. I decided to extend my stay. Shortly thereafter, Hisaya was murdered. There could no longer be any question of my taking the case on."

Everybody was listening to him with rapt attention. We didn't even dare to cough. Only Mr Suwa carried on sipping his beer.

"It is perhaps a little undiplomatic of me to say so in front of the man concerned, but Nomura-san was burning with the desire for revenge. His loathing of Miyako was such that when Ikawa-san and Hisaya were murdered, he immediately suspected her. He informed me that their deaths were identical in every way to that of his brother. That may well have been so. And indeed, Miyako did have the opportunity. Before leaving for Kobe, Ikawa-san had asked her to write him a letter of introduction to Suwa-san. So she would certainly have had the chance to swap his pills. Moreover, the poisoned medicine that killed Hisaya, as everybody knows, was prepared at Dr Kuno's pharmacy: Miyako, who often visited the doctor, would have had ample opportunity to intervene. But therein lay the problem. You cannot accuse someone of murder simply because they have the opportunity. Nobody commits murder just because they can. No, you must also have a motive. So what possible motive could Miyako have? The murder of her husband aside, what could she possibly have to gain from murdering Ikawa-san and Hisaya? We know now,

330

of course, that Hisaya's murder was essential to her plan, but at the time that was still unclear. His death muddied the waters. Or rather, no: if Hisaya alone had been murdered, it would have been easier to deduce the murderer's plan. But Ikawa-san had already been killed by then, so it was logical that we needed to find a motive that explained both of these murders. We were stumped. To make matters worse, we had to find something that linked both of these crimes to the murder of Nomura-san's brother. Tatsuo, Ikawa-san and Hisaya… If these three men were all victims of the same killer, we could only conclude that it was the work of a madman. However, as you all know, our heroine Miyako was possessed of a brilliant intellect. One could hardly believe that she had committed these murders under the influence of some mental illness. The motive was even harder to find after the murders of Brother Kozen and Mother Baiko. In short, it wasn't until the very last moment, when the final victim met her end, that the motive could be established conclusively. In a way, the criminal was protected by this lack of clarity over the motive. In fact, she could have concealed her motive perfectly, had she not left the scrap of paper by the mother abbess's body. That was her first mistake, and for two reasons…"

The lawyer replenished Kosuke Kindaichi's glass. The detective paused and, after quenching his thirst, resumed his monologue.

"Until we had managed to establish the motive, we were at a total loss. What possible motive could connect the four murders that began with Ikawa-san and ended with Mother Baiko? They almost seemed to have been completely random killings. But now, with this scrap of paper, the murderer revealed the semblance of a motive for the very first time. We were supposed to believe that somebody, having been diabolically inspired by the destruction of the Kotake cedar, was making a series of sacrifices to the shrine of the eight graves. In order to do this, the murderer was eliminating one member of every analogous pair in the village. Credible though this may have been, it was also wholly unrealistic. Crimes committed by fanatics of this kind are usually violent affairs and rarely so devious and subtle. But still, the scrap of paper was interesting, insomuch as it revealed what purported to be a motive. Perhaps the criminal wanted to exhibit this apparent motive only to camouflage another one—the real one... This was the mark of a top-class criminal mind. From that moment on, we knew that we were dealing with a formidable adversary and not some maniac. When criminals manage to conceal their motive, they have already achieved more than half of their goal. To be perfectly honest with you, I had very nearly given up, but it was this sudden realization of the murderer's ploy that helped me to regain my fighting spirit. In other words, the criminal had showed her hand a little too soon."

Kosuke Kindaichi took a deep breath before carrying on.

"Yes, that was yet another mistake. The criminal chose the wrong time to reveal this scrap of paper. Mother Baiko died while eating the meal that had been delivered to her from the House of the East. The circumstances left no doubt that the dish must have been poisoned in the Tajimi kitchen. Hence, the murderer had no reason to go to the hermitage in person. So what, then, was that scrap of paper doing there? Had the murderer gone to the trouble of taking it there afterwards? That was the only explanation. But when? Our intelligent murderer knew that it was too risky to go to a house where a body was waiting to be discovered in the dead of night and plant that piece of paper. So the best time to do it would have been when Tatsuya and Miyako went to the hermitage together and discovered the body of the mother abbess. It couldn't have materialized at any other time. At that point, one of the two must have dropped the piece of paper clandestinely, hoping that the other would find it later. The killer believed that this would be the best time to do it, and so the plan was put into action. However, there was, as it happened, no worse time to do it, for just before Tatsuya and Miyako's arrival, Myoren, the Koicha nun, had sneaked in and searched high and low around the body. The murderer committed a serious blunder in ignoring this fact. Myoren could have testified that there was no piece of paper left beside the mother abbess's body. It would have been a disaster, and so that very evening the killer went and strangled Myoren to death."

At this point, someone in the audience let out a high-pitched moan. Startled by this, we all looked around. It was Shintaro.

I turned to him calmly.

"That evening, when the Koicha nun was murdered, I saw you coming down from the hill from the hermitage. You looked so terrifying that I was sure it must have been you who killed her. But since that isn't the case, my guess is that you must have spotted Miyako in the vicinity of the hermitage. Am I right?"

Now everybody in the room turned towards me. Inspector Isokawa snorted in disapproval, while Shintaro nodded grimly.

"Yes, I did see Miyako. But I couldn't have said for certain that it was her. She was disguised as a man and I only caught a glimpse of her. She didn't know that I'd spotted her, of course. But I thought it was strange to see somebody who looked something like Miyako coming out of the hermitage. I went to take a look and that was when I found the body. I told myself that Miyako had no reason to kill Myoren, so I thought it best to keep quiet. That's why I never told anyone about it. But you saw me…"

Shintaro mopped his brow. The inspector snorted again and gave us both a look of reproach, but, as though to smooth things over, Kosuke Kindaichi intervened.

"That neither of you informed us of this is deplorable, but it's too late for that now. Anyhow, whichever way you look at it, the fact of Myoren's murder was our oversight. Never did I imagine that the killer could be so industrious! What's more, I had my own doubts about the value of Myoren's testimony. Besides, that scrap of paper was so small that, even if she did claim not to have seen it, we could never have been entirely sure that it hadn't actually been there. None of that factored into the killer's reasoning, however. Our killer preferred to take the lead and silence a dangerous witness. It was a daring move, but also, come to think of it, the surest. It was this that suddenly put me in mind of Miyako Mori. Until that point, she had been only the object of a vague suspicion held by Nomura-san, but now, for the very first time, I had uncovered some support for this theory in her actions. The trouble, however, was that at precisely the same time, Dr Kuno appeared on the scene as a suspect, too. In fact, the doctor was an even likelier suspect than Miyako…"

"But what on earth could Dr Kuno have to do with these murders?" Dr Arai interjected, speaking for the first time. "What was his part in all this? Was he really the author of those scribbled notes?"

Kosuke Kindaichi had a very curious glint in his eye as he stared at Dr Arai. His was the smile of a mischievous child.

"Indeed, he was."

"But why?"

"Because, Dr Arai, the architect of this whole series of murders was none other than Dr Kuno. And why had he devised such an elaborate plan? All because of you, Dr Arai. All because of you…"

THE AFTERMATH

Part 3

"What?!" Dr Arai called out in a shrill voice.

His cry was an expression of surprise and outrage. The usually mild-mannered doctor was white with fury and his lips were trembling. The rest of us were stunned and kept looking from Dr Arai to Kosuke Kindaichi and back again.

"Forgive me for surprising you, Doctor, but what I have just said is neither a lie nor the product of a fanciful imagination. That Dr Kuno came up with such a bizarre plan was undoubtedly down to you. That isn't to say, of course, that you are in any way to blame for it. Naturally, the fault lies with Dr Kuno. He is, so to speak, a voice from beyond… At any rate, his loathing of you ran deep, for you had stolen practically every one of his patients. Not only could he not let go of this grudge, but no doubt he would have liked to see you hanged, drawn and quartered. That being impractical, however, he devised a plan to murder you."

"To murder me?…"

Dr Arai's face grew paler and paler. Embarrassed to see the entire company staring at him, he picked up his sake cup, his hand trembling violently.

"Oh, yes," Kosuke Kindaichi continued. "Dr Kuno certainly wanted to see you dead. But he knew very well that if you were murdered, suspicion would immediately fall on him. After all, the entire village knew of the hatred that you inspired in him because of all those patients that you had stolen from him. And so he racked his brains to think of a plan that wouldn't bring suspicion on him. What he devised was, essentially, the series of murders that took place in the village. The Koicha nun's prophecy that the twin cedar tree had been struck down because the shrine required human sacrifices came at exactly the right time, so the doctor concocted a plan whereby one of every pair in the village would be eliminated in a series of superstitious killings."

"But…" Dr Arai interjected, still astonished, "but you mean to say that Dr Kuno was prepared to kill all these innocent people just to kill me?"

"Precisely. He was ready to kill as many people as necessary, for the simple reason that he never had the least intention of carrying out his plan."

"I don't quite follow you," said Dr Arai, staring at the detective in amazement. "What do you mean? You've lost me, I'm afraid."

With an ingenuous smile on his lips, Kosuke Kindaichi looked at the doctor.

"You'll forgive me for asking, Doctor, but you seem to me to be a mild-mannered and peaceable sort. Have you ever hated anybody? Have you ever loathed someone enough, say, to wish them ill or even dead?"

The doctor looked at Kosuke Kindaichi and, without a word, nodded feebly.

"I would be lying to you if I said I had never experienced anything of the kind. But, of course, I never dreamt of acting upon that desire…"

"Quite so, quite so." With a look of satisfaction, Kosuke Kindaichi scratched his shaggy head. "We ordinary members of the public commit murder in our minds on a daily basis. If only you knew how many times the inspector here has dreamt of killing me!… Joking aside, however, Dr Kuno's desire for murder was nothing more than that: a dream. He never intended to put his plan into action, and so he allowed himself to imagine the most grandiose scheme possible. So long as people delight in these kinds of plans, they will never commit the deed itself. And if Dr Kuno had been content to keep these thoughts to himself, this tragedy might never have occurred. But the doctor had the misfortune to set these thoughts down in writing. That was the true source of this tragedy."

"Do we know how Miyako happened to get her hands on the diary?" asked Shokichi Nomura, speaking now for the first time.

"Indeed, we do," Kosuke Kindaichi replied. "The Koicha nun served as an unwitting intermediary for this. Dr Kuno went about foolishly carrying that book of secrets in his doctor's bag. After the light-fingered nun stole his doctor's bag, she must have thrown the diary out, having no use for it. Unfortunately for Dr Kuno, it was Miyako who found it."

The entire company gasped. Kosuke Kindaichi's gaze darkened.

"You never know where the origin of a crime lies. It's perfectly possible that even if Miyako had never found Dr Kuno's diary, she would still have committed some set of similar crimes. And yet it cannot be denied that this diary served as the stimulus for the ones that were committed. How astonished Miyako must have been to discover inside those pages that curious plan for a series of murders—and not only that, but also to find her own name listed beside Haruyo's. She was smart enough to realize that Dr Kuno had no intention of carrying out these plans, but at the same time, she must also have realized that the plan perfectly suited her long-held wish to eliminate the House of the East. For every member of the House of the East was listed among the names of the victims. Thus, their fate was sealed. Unlike Dr Kuno, Miyako had the will to put the plan into action and, one victim at a time, she carried it out."

337

An oppressive, gloomy silence fell over the guests. Kosuke Kindaichi cleared his throat as though to break the sombre mood.

"Dr Kuno reaped what he sowed," Kosuke Kindaichi continued. "But his fate was truly pitiable. How horrified must he have been to see that the victims were falling according to the plan that he himself had devised, although in his own scheme, of course, with the exception of Dr Arai, he hadn't decided which of each couple to kill. He didn't dare to confide what was happening to anyone, and instead he was forced to look on in horror as each murder took place. All he knew was that his own plan was being implemented, a fact that drove the poor man to despair. At first, he pretended to be none the wiser, but when the scraps of paper began to appear, he realized that sooner or later his handwriting would be recognized. How could he absolve himself then, having concocted that absurd, extraordinary plan? Could he admit that even in his advanced years, his jealousy towards Dr Arai had led him to dream up this murderous scheme? He opted instead to flee. He had no option but to hide, but he had the misfortune of letting himself be tricked by the murderer and led into the cave, where he was poisoned. Who knows what was said to deceive him? Possibly the murderer suggested that he hide until the rumours had blown over. Then a solution would present itself. And since it was a woman , he let his guard down and trusted her."

"So, Miyako was familiar with the layout of the caves?" I asked.

"I believe so," Kosuke Kindaichi replied. "For a woman as intelligent as she, it would have been impossible not to be intrigued by the legend of the gold. I imagine she must have spent a long time exploring those caves. There is, as it happens, physical evidence that she must have frequented the caves. Inspector, if you would be so kind..."

My eyes widened when I saw what Inspector Isokawa extracted from his satchel: three gold coins.

"According to the testimony of Brother Eisen here," the inspector began, "these three coins were until recently hidden in the sarcophagus under the wax corpse at the Monkey's Seat. He had known their location for a long time but chose not to remove them, lest he disturb the repose of the deceased. It is said, after all, that monks are free from the sin of avarice. Nevertheless, I must salute his honesty. At today's rates, these coins represent a small fortune. Moreover, their discovery would tend to suggest that the legend of the gold may not be such a fanciful story after all. This certainly warrants further investigation…"

Noriko and I exchanged a clandestine smile, but we immediately averted our eyes and kept our peace.

"Where exactly did you find these coins?" Noriko asked innocently.

"Ah, yes, how careless of me not to mention it. We found them at the back of Miyako's bureau. At the very least, it proves that she had been in the caves very recently. It's possible that she found them on the night of Koume's murder. Perhaps she had been examining the sarcophagus when the twins arrived. Who can say whether they came across her by chance or whether she had been waiting for them purposely, but in any case, as soon as they appeared, she pounced on them and strangled Koume. It didn't matter for her plan which one she killed, but it seems that she had intended to kill Kotake, since that was the cedar tree that had been struck down. It would also explain why she had mistakenly crossed out Kotake's name on the piece of paper."

"Actually," I whispered, "she could never tell them apart."

"Is that so?" said Kosuke Kindaichi. "That was another of her mistakes, then. Until that point, none of her victims had

339

anything in common. After that murder in the cave, there were two who did: both Koume and Hisaya belonged to the Tajimi family. Imagine my surprise when I realized that, with the exception of Tatsuya, who was a relative newcomer, the only member of the immediate family now left was Haruyo. And she had all the qualities necessary to be added to the murderer's list of victims. In other words, she could find her name alongside that of Miyako herself, as the two unmarried women in the village. It was at that point that the motive for the murders finally became clear to me: the criminal was trying to do away with the House of the East entirely. The other killings that had been committed before then were mere camouflage to hide this fact. When I realized this, I was stunned... By then, I had known for a long time that Miyako was behind these murders, but I had yet to find the motive. What could she possibly have to gain by the murder of the House of the East? The answer was: nothing directly. But if we inserted Shintaro into the picture, it all took on a much more serious aspect. Nomura-san had already informed me that, after the death of her first husband, Miyako had considered marrying Shintaro. I deduced that these crimes must have been the joint work of the couple, but I was mistaken in this. What I failed to appreciate was the conflict of complex psychologies, the clash of their different senses of pride."

Shintaro nodded, his eyes dark. If he had just set his pride aside and married Miyako, none of these murders would have taken place. Then again, if he had done that, it would have meant marrying a widow with the death of a husband on her conscience.

"Now that I had more or less established the motive and the identity, what could I do?" Kosuke Kindaichi continued. "There was no conclusive evidence. I had no grounds on which to accuse Miyako and Shintaro—for at that point, I still believed it was both of them. I had little choice but to wait. I reasoned that Haruyo would be their next victim, so all I had to do was catch them in the act... At least, that's what I thought. In the event, however, the killer was smarter than that. I doubt that Miyako expected the body of Dr Kuno to be found anywhere near as soon as it was. It is my opinion that she was planning to attribute all the killings to him. That was the version of events that she wanted us to buy: that the doctor had killed all these people and simply disappeared. Perhaps the body would be discovered eventually—after six months or a year—but by then it would be nothing but a skeleton, and we wouldn't be able to tell who had died first: the doctor or Koume. Worse yet, if Miyako had killed Haruyo immediately after Koume, we might never have been any the wiser. We would have believed that the doctor had lived for a while down in the caves, during which time he could have murdered Koume and Haruyo. After that, we would have concluded that he had fled into the depths of the caves, where he had then put an end to his life, leaving his calling card on his chest. However, after Koume's murder I insisted that we undertake a manhunt in the caves, because from the moment that Dr Kuno's hat was found in the vicinity of her body, I suspected that he was already dead. It was because of this hunt that the killer suddenly had to change tack. You see, if we discovered Dr Kuno's body, we would immediately realize that he had been killed before Koume, and it would no longer be possible to attribute Haruyo's death to him either. That was when she selected you, Tatsuya, to be her new scapegoat."

I had been vaguely aware of this before, but now that Kosuke Kindaichi pointed it out, a chill of retrospective horror ran down my spine.

"Please don't misunderstand me," the detective said with a dark look in his eyes. "Even if Dr Kuno's body hadn't been discovered early, Miyako would still have set her sights on you sooner or later. Most likely she'd known, from the moment she picked you up in Kobe, that she would have to kill you at some vague point in the future. Oh, yes… Miyako even told me that when she killed Haruyo, she had intended to poison the meal that Haruyo was taking to you. That way, everyone would have concluded that you were the culprit and that, having carried out your massacre, you had been driven to commit suicide by poisoning yourself in despair. But you arrived on the scene too quickly to allow her to execute this plan."

Once again, I shuddered. It was a miracle that I was still alive.

"And yet," Kosuke Kindaichi continued, "even before she cornered you, she had managed to devise a truly terrifying stratagem, which she pulled off with great aplomb. She was the one who sent that letter to the police. She was the one who put up that poster in front of the village hall… Yes, it was all her doing. She was even the one who sent you that strange letter back in Kobe, the one warning you not to return to the village. It was she who had come to look for you in person, so it was only natural that you wouldn't suspect her of sending it. How extraordinarily she manipulated every one of us! What's more, she was careful never to accuse you of being the murderer in so many words. She was able, by means of far more effective gestures, to persuade Itaru and Kichizo that you were the culprit. That is how the mob was fired up."

Kosuke Kindaichi sighed.

"When I said earlier that the killer was smarter than me, the mob is what I was referring to in particular. Who could have ever imagined such a thing? It shames me to think how I could have let it get to that. And during the confusion, Haruyo was murdered… That is what makes me say that this case got the better of me."

Disappointed in himself, Kosuke Kindaichi fell silent. After a few moments, he whispered under his breath:

"What a formidable woman! What a heinous woman! By day, she seduced men with her beauty and wit, and by night, arrayed in darkness, she metamorphosed into a murderous demon who stalked the recesses of those caves… She was a gifted poisoner and a murderer of genius!"

Nobody spoke. An oppressive stillness hung over the entire company. Breaking the silence, I suddenly asked:

"But what exactly has become of Miyako? Nobody's told me. What happened to her afterwards?"

The guests looked at each other in stunned silence. Kosuke Kindaichi cleared his throat and said simply:

"Miyako-san is dead."

"Dead? You mean… she killed herself?"

"No, she didn't kill herself. But her death was a terrible affair. You see, Tatsuya, it was a real battle between her and your sister. She eventually died from the injury inflicted on her by Haruyo. The way she met her end was truly awful… She, who was once so beautiful, actually turned puce! She breathed her last, swollen and in agony…"

I wondered then whether Haruyo hadn't been aware of everything. Naturally, she couldn't have foreseen Miyako's terrible end, but perhaps, just before she died, she had realized the identity of the person who was about to kill her. Although Haruyo had found herself in total darkness, and although her assailant didn't say a word, she must have realized that it was a woman when Miyako put her hand over her mouth, and deduced who it must be. Yes, Haruyo had known, all right. That explained the mysterious smile that she had given me when I asked her who it was. She wouldn't say the name, but she knew that in having bitten Miyako's little finger she had already exacted her revenge. I wondered whether Miyako's excruciating end hadn't been exactly what Haruyo had hoped for, and I shuddered.

With a faraway look in his eyes, Kosuke Kindaichi continued his story.

"Her final moments were dreadful. It was a terrible moment of suspense. Not for her, but for me. When she died, all her secrets would die with her. No matter what it took, I just had to extract a confession from her before she died. You see, I had no conclusive evidence: only a series of hypotheses. At first, she thought she would have the last laugh. It was a real battle between us, though it wasn't a game of wits so much as a test of endurance. But the moment I mentioned Shintaro's name, she lost. I took advantage of her weakness. 'If you take your secrets to the grave,' I told her, 'Shintaro will be the one who pays.' She relented there and then. Sobbing convulsively, she confessed. 'Shintaro didn't know about anything. I was the one who did it, all on my own. If he ever finds out, he'll despise me. I only wanted him to inherit the Tajimi fortune without knowing anything…' Terrible woman though she was, I couldn't help feeling a pang of pity when I thought of her despair."

After she confessed everything, Miyako had asked Kosuke Kindaichi to send a telegram to Kobe, summoning Mr Suwa. The lawyer had arrived the very next morning. She barely had enough time to put her affairs in order before she expired. That was the day after my rescue from the cave. In spite of everything, she had, I was told, enquired after me right up to the moment of her death.

"It would appear that my story has reached an end," Kosuke Kindaichi said.

Each of the guests was lost in thought. Suddenly, a cheerful cry issued from the corner of the room. It was Mr Suwa.

"Well, now that's over, we should drink a toast! After a gloomy tale like that, what we need is a bit of good cheer!"

Tears were glistening in his eyes, for he himself had loved Miyako.

Understanding his state of mind, I stepped up to lighten the mood.

"Well, if you don't mind, there is something I would like to say. Kindaichi-san?"

"Yes?" he replied.

"You told me the other day not to be too surprised. It's true that I've had more than my fair share of surprises since arriving in this village, and now it's my turn to surprise you."

The other guests stared at me in bewilderment. Noriko and I exchanged a mischievous look. My heart felt ready to burst and I couldn't control my voice, but I managed to steel my nerves with a sip of beer. Not without a note of solemnity, I began:

"Kindaichi-san, you said earlier that the legend of the hidden gold might be more than just a legend after all. Well, it just so happens that you are correct once again: I found where the gold was hidden."

The guests suddenly grew animated. They all looked at each other as though I had lost my mind. Noriko and I gazed at each other and smiled again.

"Please, don't be alarmed. I haven't taken leave of my senses, and I haven't dreamt it up either. If I requested the presence of Suwa-san among us this evening, it is because I have a question to ask him. Well… If somebody finds a hidden treasure, who is the rightful owner? I really don't know a thing about the necessary legal formalities… And as it happens, there is also another announcement that I should like to make—and that is that Noriko and I are to be married… Go on, Noriko, show them the gold."

Noriko stood up and took countless gold coins from the dresser beside the alcove. I doubt there is any need to describe the storm of applause and cheering that this elicited from the audience.

EPILOGUE

I could finish my story here, but for those readers of a more exacting disposition I shall add the following few superfluous lines.

We found 267 gold coins. Together with the additional 3 that Miyako had kept in her bureau, that made a total of 270. Not quite 3,000 *tael* of gold, but perhaps the companions of the monk whose skeleton was found at the Dragon's Jaw had managed to escape with a number of *oban*. At any rate, those 270 coins in today's terms already made a tidy sum.

The day eventually came when I informed Shintaro that I intended to refuse the Tajimi inheritance. When giving him a reason, I cited the uncertain matter of my birth. Staring at me in silence, Shintaro shook his head.

"I cannot accept that, Tatsuya. What man, after all, can say with any certainty whose child he is? What man in the world could point to another and say without a shadow of a doubt, 'That man is my father'? Only the mother knows this for sure, and there are cases where even she could not swear to it."

I showed him the photograph of Yoichi Kamei that I had found in the lining of the folding screen.

"Just look at this, Shintaro. Do you really think that I could have the nerve to insist on my rights to the Tajimi fortune after seeing this?"

He compared my face to the one in the photograph in silence. Suddenly, he took my hands. He was a formidable man, but now I saw tears glisten in his eyes.

These days Shintaro is busy with the construction of a lime factory in Eight Graves. The region is rich in lime, and experts predict a prosperous future for the company.

"As soon as there's new activity in the village," Shintaro told me, "modern engineers and technicians will come flooding in. Maybe they'll even change the locals' way of thinking. Frankly, I don't see any other way to reform their superstitious ways in this loathsome village. That's why I really have to make a success of it."

On a separate occasion, he also told me:

"I've decided never to marry, Tatsuya. It isn't so much the memory of Miyako, but a man of my experience naturally finds it hard to trust again... That's why I hope that you and Noriko will have many children. With your blessing, I'd like to name your second son as my heir. Look on it as a small compensation for the hardships that your mother faced. And besides, it's what Hisaya would have wanted."

In the end, I decided to wait for the hundred-day anniversary of my sister's death before returning to Kobe. Mr Suwa had found a house for us in a western suburb of the city. Strange are the ways of the world: as soon as the newspapers broke the story of the gold's discovery, many turned to me, asking to borrow money; yet, at the same time, many others in fact offered me loans. As the saying goes: nobody lends to those in need, while everybody lends to those who have.

I asked my newfound father to come and live with us in Kobe, but he declined the offer.

"I have a duty to take care of Father Choei," he told me. "And a young couple doesn't want an old man getting in the way. Perhaps one day, when my legs give up, I'll come and be a burden to you, but until then I'd like to live out my days, praying for the souls of all those unfortunate victims."

Out of respect for Haruyo, I abstained from all intimacy with Noriko under the roof of the House of the East. She understood my reasons perfectly, but a few days before we left, she whispered something in my ear that stunned me.

I had no doubts. I knew that it was in that cave that my own life had formed in my mother's womb. Now it had happened again: once had not been enough. The implacable laws of biology have their own histories that keep repeating themselves.

I took Noriko in my arms and held her to me, swearing that our unborn child would never know the pain and suffering that I had endured.